House of Lies

House of Lies

Mary Turner

Acknowledgements

Special thanks to my son-in-law Paul for his help and for putting up with my constant requests and threats.

Also thanks to Anne who keeps me right even though I constantly nip her brain, not forgetting Janey who went through the final proofing.

I would also like to tell my family how much I love them as I continually drive them all crazy.

Part One

Chapter One – 1956

The biting wind fiercely blew the leaves off the trees forcing them to swirl aimlessly around the deserted playground of the bleak Victorian school populated by the children of Prestonpans. Inside, the pupils were kept warm by the huge green radiators that were constantly manned by the elderly janitor.

Sally Baxter, a skinny waif like child, sat back in her seat and listened to the programme being relayed to the class through the huge wooden radio that was attached to the wall. For her, this was the highlight of the week. 'Around Scotland' was the programme, which today was being broadcasted from the border country, and if she closed her eyes and listened really hard, she could visualise wonderful exciting places. At that very moment, she was in the farmyard enjoying the sounds and smells of the animals she had conjured up in her mind. Lambs leapt and danced pirouettes like prima ballerinas, while their mothers chewed contentedly at the lush green grass, paying no heed to the hungry siblings suckling hurriedly at their teats, their tails wagging at lightning speed.

It was spring and new life was bursting out all around.

The storyteller had transported his young listener to a different world, far away from her troubles and the foul weather outside.

'Sally – Sally Baxter.'

The teacher's voice gave her quite a start. She was so engrossed in the programme; she hadn't seen the boy entering the room carrying a note from the headmaster.

'You have to report to Mr McKay at once child,' she said harshly, annoyed at the interruption during radio hour.

She wasn't the only one. Sally was not pleased either, as she had a fair idea why she was being sent for yet again, especially during her favourite period of the week. This time she was going to tell her dad.

As she walked along the long corridor she could hear the radios blaring as she passed by the other classrooms.

'Why me?' she said between her teeth. 'Why me? It's not fair. It's not fizzin' fair.'

Approaching the door to the headmaster's room she began to tremble, even though she knew she had done nothing wrong. She had only to deliver a note from her teacher and it terrified her.

Bending down she pulled at her ankle socks the heels having slid down into her ill-fitting shoes, then tugging at her cardigan sleeves and catching the cuffs in the palms of her hand, she tried stretching the well-worn garment to make it fit. Her small thin legs shook slightly and she felt an overwhelming urge to use the toilet. Dancing up and down and tightening her stomach muscles, she breathed deeply. She waited a few minutes until she regained her courage, and with a deep intake of breath, she knocked anxiously on the door.

'Enter,' the voice roared from within.

Slowly she opened the door and walked in.

The inside of the headmaster's room frightened almost every child in the school. Despite having a fairly large window, the old blackout blind that was always half drawn forbade the daylight from entering the room and etched dark shadows on the wall.

Sally was particularly alarmed by the contents of a glass case hanging on the wall directly behind the headmaster. Two stuffed owls with piercing eyes stared down at her, their wings spread ready to swoop on any unsuspecting prey. Beside the owls was another stuffed animal with a plaque informing the young reader that it was an otter. On the shelf under the case sat a large chiming clock ticking loudly, two small silver cups and a potted plant. The walls of the room were painted chocolate brown, and to add to the gloom, bottle-green velvet draped each side of the window. A photo of a very old man (who's face more menacing than the headmaster's) filled a large dusty looking frame.

Constantly covered in all kinds of papers, Mr McKay's solid oak desk with its double row of deep drawers dominated the room. A double glass inkwell lay in the centre of his desk, a black bakelite telephone on his right side and a globe of the world to his left. The room was lined with shelves of leather bound books, a few wooden cupboards, a large grey metal filing cabinet, coat stand and a few wooden chairs were all that furnished the room. What was even more fearsome was the fact that it was Mr McKay's room. The room was a haven of authority.

Walking timidly towards the giant of a man, she stammered.

'Sa... Sally Ba...Baxter sir, you se...'

'I know. I know girl,' he barked agitatedly, not allowing the child to finish her sentence.

She looked into the unsmiling twitching face of the headmaster and goose pimples appeared on her skinny arms and legs.

'Your brother and sister have decided not to join us today again Sally.' Glowering, he looked at her while shaking his head. 'Not good enough, not good enough at all.' He stared hard at Sally for a few seconds before saying impatiently, '*well*... go and look for them!'

Gratefully she left the office and went into the cloakroom to fetch her coat. She wandered along the polished wooden floor between the rows of outdoor clothes until she found it. Grabbing it with both hands, she jumped high in the air, flicking the collar up clear away from the hook. Pulling on the shabby green garment, the sleeves fell down past her fingertips. Fastening the coat with what buttons remained, Sally looked along the rows of smart comfortable coats and wondered if she would ever have one of her own instead of the constant 'hand me downs' her mother seemed to acquire. Still, the coat was warm and covered the rest of her worn out clothes.

Sally, due to her studious nature never missed school, but being constantly sent to look for her younger brother and sister, who played truant two or three times a week, was now affecting her studies. Seeing them into their classrooms became pointless as they would run off again at playtime and it was useless speaking to her mother as she refused to do anything positive regarding it. This was to lead to severe consequences shaping Sally's life forever.

Nellie Baxter, for reasons of her own, resented her eldest daughter. Although only eight years of age, Sally was expected to have the evening meal ready for her parents returning from work as well as taking care of her siblings. She tried hard to keep the house clean and tidy although she was fighting a losing battle as Hugh and Bess seemed to enjoy nothing more than messing it up. All this responsibility had made Sally older than her years but still her selfish mother resented her efforts.

Nellie worked outdoors in the market gardens, pulling sprouts and leeks, shawing turnips, cutting cabbages, planting and gathering potatoes depending on the time of year and the vegetables that were in season. Although it was hard work she preferred it to dreaded housework and looking after bairns.

Her husband Tom, who was employed by the local brick works, situated next to Prestongrange coalmine, was aware Nellie passed too much responsibility onto Sally. He hated seeing her treat his girl with contempt, but he was also not fully aware as to the extent of Nellie's cruelty. His wife ruled the house and as she was the stronger of the two parents he kept quiet for the sake of peace. As long as he could escape to the 'Black Bull' he was a contented man.

Nellie also enjoyed her drinking sessions and that's when the fights between them usually began.

She was as hard as nails was Nellie Baxter, and had a tongue that could cut through steel.

'Dad, have you been listening to me?' Sally asked her father. 'It's our Hugh and Bess. Dad, please go and see Mr McKay,' she pleaded.

Tom opened his eyes and looked into his eldest daughter's face, her soft brown eyes imploring him to listen. He had been trying to take a nap but it was impossible as Sally was determined to get his attention.

'You know I cannae go, it's up tae yer mam,' Tom sighed. 'A cannae dae anything aboot them two, yer mam sees tae aw that.'

'But dad, she disnae.' Sally was nearly in tears. 'She gets letters all the time from Mr McKay and she puts them in the fire. I'm getting into a lot of trouble because I'm missing my lessons dad. I get a cross against my name when I'm not there to answer the register checks as I'm away hunting for them. They dinnae even ask Sam to go and look for them because Miss Main said a boy's education is more important than a girl's. It's me that gets belted if I don't know what the teacher is talking about. The bairns in the class are now calling me 'The Whipper in'(truant officer) because I'm always looking for them two.'

'*All right* I'll have a word when she gets back from the doctor's.'

She went over and sat on the arm of her father's chair.

'You'll speak to her, really speak to her?' she persisted.

'Aye!' Tom said with a hint of annoyance.

'What's up with her anyway?' Sally asked curiously.

'She jist feels a bit off,' Tom replied. 'She's never really been the same since she lost the last bairn. You see hen, when wee Jimmy died, she just clung awe the mare tae Bess, her bein' the youngest an' all. That's how Bess gets away wi' so much. She'll get better, you'll see. It'll pass.'

'He's got to be joking,' Sally thought. 'Jimmy died at birth and that had been over two years.

Nellie Baxter sat in the waiting room of the doctor's surgery knowing full well what was wrong with her. She hadn't said anything to her husband as she had been trying mustard baths, Epsom salts and gin, all the remedies she had heard of. Nothing had happened, but maybe if she asked the doctor for something he might help if he knew she didn't want it. Another bairn was the last thing she needed. She would have to stay in every day. Then there was Tom's job, with the rumours that the works were closing in the next year or so. Another bairn? Definitely not!

'What's she looking at?' Nellie thought as she caught the receptionist peering over her glasses. 'What're you lookin' at?' she said aloud.

The shocked receptionist averted her eyes and went hurriedly about her business.

'Mrs Baxter you're next,' the patient leaving the doctor's room called out when she passed through the waiting room.

Nellie rose and entered the consulting room.

Mrs Irvine, a small woman with nice tidy grey hair looked over at the receptionist.

'Cheeky bugger her. You should 'ave answered her back Annie. My, she's in mare need tae be lookin' efter that family o' hers. My daughter works at the school an' she says there's goin' tae be trouble there. Oor Isobel, you ken, she's the Headmaster's secretary,' the woman's chest swelled with pride at her daughter's achievements, 'well, she telt me the social workers are tae be brocht in.'

Mrs Irvine pulled a handkerchief from her pocket and wiped her left eye, which was constantly running. With 'tutting' sounds and a shake of the head she continued, 'Four bairns at school an' three o' them never there. Her oot aw day an' the bairns draggin' themselves up... an' that hoose!'

She never got to finish as the door to the doctor's room was thrown open and Nellie stormed out. Murder was in her dark eyes as her facial expression warned anyone who got in her way to stand aside. Her blonde shoulder length hair flew behind her and as her coat flapped open, her once shapely figure, now grossly over-weight, was revealed.

Tom was having his usual nap on the chair while Sally washed dishes in the kitchen when Nellie burst in.

'Where is everybody?' she yelled.

Tom jumped to his feet still half asleep. 'What's up?' he asked sounding groggy.

Sally ran through from the kitchen. 'I'm here ma and our Hugh and Bess are round the back. What's happened?'

'Nothin's bloody well happened, except I'm pregnant again, Tom bloody Baxter!' She venomously spat out his name.

Sally made a quick exit, as she knew only too well what was to follow.

'That's aw your bloody well good at, makin' bloody bairns. How are we goin' tae manage noo? Who's goin' tae wash, cook an' clean wi another mooth tae feed?' She made to punch the astounded man but he caught her fist in mid air forcing her arms to her sides and holding them there.

'Nellie, a warn ye. Hit me an' a'll hit ye back. A've taken aboot aw a can take fae you, an' besides, it's wee Sally that does everythin' aroond here. The place is stinkin' because *you* never clean. Sally has her work cut oot lookin' efter Hugh an' Bess.' As his wife struggled to free her arms he shouted, 'calm doon wumman for God's sake.'

'Oh a'm lazy noo am a?' screamed Nellie. 'Dae ye think workin' oot in the fields is a bloody picnic?'

'No,' Tom replied, 'but ither weemen work an' bring their faimlies up withoot this carry oan. Stay at hame an' be a proper mither.'

'An' what wid we live oan? Your pittance! Dinnae make me laugh.'

Sally was in her room perched on the end of her bed with her hands over her ears.

'Oh God, not tonight. He was going to speak to her about them two skipping school.' Feeling hot tears sting her eyes she let herself fall backwards onto the bed. 'Not now he won't.' It was then she thought about running away. 'Where too? Auntie Mary's? No. She only has time for our Sam. That's where he'll be now,' she mused. As she lay sobbing, the smell of dried urine filled her nostrils as Bess constantly wet the bed. The cunning child would wake up and rise from the sodden side, roll Sally over, then slip into the dry area causing Nellie to accuse Sally of the dirty habit. Sally's denial only resulted in further punishment.

While the two girls shared a single bed, Hugh slept on a mattress on the floor.

A cupboard in the wall and a small chest of drawers was where all their belongings were kept. Sam had the 'hole in the wall' in the back kitchen. It had once been a coal cellar but it now contained Sam's bed. The door had been replaced with a curtain, which Sam drew for privacy. Once enclosed in his bed area, his only light was a torch Auntie Mary had given him.

Chapter Two

Nellie sat in the waiting room with her two children, one at each side. It was a long shaped room with chairs running along both walls which were completely bare, no pictures or posters to be seen anywhere. Two small tables sat evenly placed in the centre of the room each holding a large ashtray.

'Mam,' Hugh whined, tugging at Nellie's sleeve.

'What now?' Nellie asked clearly annoyed.

'I'm needing Mam,' Hugh moaned looking at his mother, his face distorted with discomfort.

'We canny go onywhere in case we're called on,' said his mother sharply.

Just then the door at the far end of the room opened and a man and woman with a boy in his early teens came out. The boy's head hung so low his face was barely visible. The woman had obviously been crying, while the man's face looked as if he was about to burst a blood vessel. The veins in his neck stood out like blue rivers on an atlas while his mouth was taut. They walked smartly passed the three figures that sat waiting then disappeared through the exit door.

'Has he been skipping the school an awe Mam?' Sally asked concerned.

'What a stupid question, how dae a ken what the lad's been up tae?'

'Maybe it's his da' that's been sent fer,' Hugh said in a know-it-all manner.

'Hugh, big people don't get sent tae children's panels,' Sally informed him.

'Wheesht,' their mother said as she noticed the door open again.

A small woman in her late forties dressed in a brown tweed suit called out. 'Mrs Baxter?'

Nellie nodded in response.

The woman spoke with a Glasgow accent. 'Will you come this way?' She walked towards the door leaving Nellie and the children to follow on.

Once inside, the woman pointed to the three chairs in front of a large table, before taking her place beside a row of sombre looking people.

Three men and two women formed the panel.

The men reminded Sally of the undertakers that came when old Mrs Walker next door died.

There was silence for what seemed ages. The man in the middle kept his head bowed as he studied the pile of papers in front of him. He was short, bald, and wore what the kids would have called Milk Bottle Glasses.

Although feeling terrified, Sally had the awful urge to giggle, but thought better of it.

The two men on either side of the one who reminded her of the undertaker, sat weighing the children up. They looked as if they had reached their decision already. At both ends of the table sat the women. At the right side there was the one who had brought them in and at the other side a huge fat woman who could have easily taken up two chairs. Sally looked at the fat lady and could not believe her eyes as she had a wee goatee beard that danced up and down with the constant movement of her jaw.

'Now then,' the voice of the small man interrupted her thoughts, 'you'll be Mrs Baxter and, let me see.' He looked down again at the papers. 'Hugh and Sally.' He gave a half-hearted smile in the direction of the children.

'Now, Mrs Baxter-r-r,' he rolled his r's.

'Aye?' Nellie answered, sitting up straight in the chair, cocking her head in an over confident manner.

'Your children have been brought before this panel today to find out the reason for their persistent truancy. We have to establish the cause, and take any steps we feel necessary.'

Sally listened but could not believe what she was hearing. It wasn't her that was in question here.. It was Bess! She only had to give her account of the situation.

Bess was in bed with measles... He's making a big mistake. As her mind went into over drive, she felt the fear in her stomach turn to panic.

'First of all Mrs Baxter, why did you ignore the letters the Headmaster Mister, Mister...' He once again looked through his notes.

The thin man on his left whispered quietly in his ear. 'Mr McKay.'

'Oh yes, Mr McKay sent you.' His chin almost rested on the table as he looked towards Nellie.

'I never got any letters,' Nellie said indignantly.

'You never received them?' the man asked in disbelief.

'No,' Nellie answered. 'The first I knew about it was when I got this letter telling us to come here,' she lied brazenly.

'Well, I have all the dates here,' he said abruptly. 'You were sent ten letters from the school. Eight given to the child and two sent by post. There have also been visits to your home by the school board who could never find anyone at home.'

'Well you'd hardly expect a bairn that wisnae goin' tae school tae give me letters aboot hersel' noo would ye? She would maist likely tear them up.' Nellie looked down at Sally giving her a scowl.

'No. No Mam. You're not going to blame me,' thought Sally shaking her head in disbelief.

'Can I ask you why your husband hasn't come along today?' the fat lady at the end of the table asked.

'He can't spare the time off work,' Nellie barked. She could stand men asking questions but women she regarded as being nosey cows.

Then, the sound of water hitting the floor turned the place upside down. Hugh jumped up from his seat. The pool of urine lay at his feet as a small river ran down his leg.

'A said a while ago a wis needin' Mam! Am sorry, honest am sorry.' Biting his bottom lip he tried hard not to cry.

Nellie was on her feet as was the panel that were now looking over the table at the mess on the floor. The woman in the tweed suit scurried off to find a bucket and mop while the others demonstrated their disgust by tutting and muttering to each other.

Nellie was having a go at Hugh who was now crying his head off.

Back came the small woman and handed Nellie the pail and mop as if she didn't know what to do with them.

Nellie was going to hand it to Sally, but she thought better of it.

After the floor was clean, Nellie was asked if she would like to take Hugh to the toilet downstairs at the entrance, but on hearing they were going to ask Sally a few questions she declined. She sent Hugh off on his own, thinking it's a bit like shutting the door after the horse had bolted.

The man in the middle, who by now had established himself as the spokesman, cleared his throat and said, 'Let us proceed. Now then young, eh, eh...' down his eyes went to the papers again. 'Sally, tell me do you like school?' he asked with that half smile on his face.

'Yes sir,' she replied almost in a whisper.

'Speak up child,' said the fat woman, irritation now evident on her face.

Sally knew what her father would have said if he was here, 'she hasnae laughed since she had the hives'. The thought of her dad somehow gave her added courage.

'Yes sir,' she answered much louder. Sally noticed the two men that flanked the spokesman did all the writing. They seemed to write every time a question was asked.

'What do you like most of all about school Sally?'

'Sir,' Sally replied, 'I like the wireless.'

'The wireless?' the wee man asked with interest. He turned to the man on his left and said something that Sally couldn't hear.

'Sally is that why you don't go to school? Do you stay at home and listen to the wireless?'

'No sir. We get to listen to the wireless on Thursdays, see?'

'Oh yes, yes and is it only Thursdays you like? Is that why you are never at school?'

Sally couldn't believe this. Grown up men and they couldn't understand what she was saying. Indignantly she replied, 'I always go to school sir, except when I've to go looking for Hugh an' our Bess. It's them two that skips, not me.' Although she felt her mother's fist dig into her ribs she had her say.

'I sometimes miss the register because of them.' She felt a mixture of frustration and fear as she told her side of the story. The fear was of her mother and not of the row of people facing her. They would sort things out she was sure.

The door opened and Hugh's face peeped into the room.

'Come in boy,' the man said.

As Hugh sat down his discomfort was obvious.

They didn't ask Sally any more questions as Hugh's entrance had interrupted the flow of conversation.

The man then turned and asked Hugh some questions. Hugh told them he hated the school and stayed off to go to the brewery where he watched the men working. He liked the horses and the draymen could swear like troopers.

Mixed expressions appeared on the panel's faces at the mention of the draymen; disgust formed on the women's faces while the men bowed their head as if stifling a smile, in fact one quickly covered his mouth with the back of his hand.

Clearing his throat while composing himself, the man addressed Nellie.

'Your daughter referred to her sister Bess. She implied that it is she who stays off school and yet we have no mention of such a child. Could this be an error?'

'No,' said Nellie. 'Oor Bess is a good wee soul and never causes a day's bother. It's this yin that causes me grief.' She stared down at Sally. 'She's lazy and cheeks back aw the time; of course, a blame her da.' He takes her side aw the time. Nae discipline you see. Nae discipline at aw.'

'He hasn't this time Mrs Baxter, or he would have been here to speak for her.' As the fat woman spoke, Nellie's face turned crimson with rage.

She hissed through her teeth, 'I've telt you before. *He has tae work*! He's the only breadwinner in oor family. I don't work as I've four bairns tae look efter.'

Sally sat motionless and listened to the lies that tripped off her mother's tongue. She would never forgive her for this. She knew her mother couldn't say she worked because it was 'on the side', whatever that meant, but the rest, no she couldn't and wouldn't ever forgive her mother.

The meeting was called to an end and Nellie and the children had to sit out in the long room until they were recalled. Another family also sat waiting their fate; whatever they had been up to.

They waited about ten minutes and were called back in but this time they weren't asked to sit down. Sally just caught the words '...a year's probation and if it persists it would lead to the children being sent into care. Do you understand?' The man asked looking towards Sally and Hugh. They nodded their heads in unison.

He then had a stern warning for Nellie and bid them all good day and turned his interest once again to the papers on his desk.

'Hitler should be his bloody name,' Nellie snorted as she led the children out of the building.

'I thought he was deid,' Hugh added.

'Aye,' agreed Sally, 'and the undertaker that buried him was along side him.' Nellie and Hugh laughed and for a moment Sally forgot the anger she felt for her mother a few moments earlier.

The next few months that followed the day of the hearing were uneventful. Sally saw a change in her mother and she wondered if her life of misery was over. She had less chores to do as Nellie had given up work. The money coming in was less, so Tom and Nellie couldn't go out much. Sally thought her mother was feeling guilty for the ordeal she had put her through. Bess and Hugh were both attending school although they had to be taken and collected by Nellie.

The knock on the door that night changed the calm that prevailed for so short a time.

'I'll get it Ma,' Sam called, as he was on his way out himself.

In the back kitchen, Sally was trying to wash Bess's neck in the basin that sat on a low table. The youngster squealed and wriggled, as Sally's fingers felt rough and bony on her flesh. She was convinced her elder sister was trying to drown her.

Hearing the familiar voice calling her mother's name. Sally stopped struggling with Bess to hear what was about to be said. Bess, rising from the basin, was about to shout abuse at Sally.

'Shush!' Sally demanded.

They both stood still. Sally peeped through the door and Bess watched Sally's face with interest.

'I'm short Nellie. I ken you like workin' at the tatties, an' if you could get a couple o' bairns tae help, you could manage. You could dae with the money surely with another on the wey.'

Mrs Begbie was the woman who organised the potato pickers, known as the tattie squads. She always had plenty willing workers but she needed experienced workers to keep the young ones in hand.

'OK Flo, I'll talk tae Tom when he comes in. He's as sick as I am withoot his bevy. He still gets oot mind, dinnae think he doesnae, but no' as much.'

'You'll talk to Tom then?' her friend mimicked. 'Well, I'm flabbergasted, I never thocht you needed permission tae dae onything. Am I looking at a changed wuman here?' laughed Flo Begbie.

'No you daft goat, a'm keepin'a low key till the heat dies doon.' With a flick of her hand, she asked, 'you want a cuppa tea Flo?'

'Tea now is it?' With raised brows Flo laughed. 'The quicker you're back wi' us the better. Tea ye're offerin' *me!*' She prodded her chest in mock amazement.

'Dae you fancy a wee nip then?'

'Naw, yer awe right. I've got tae go an' round up everybody for Monday.' You could have two stents ye ken, the bairns could work along side ye. Double money. Think of it girl!' Holding up one side of her skirt Flo playfully did a twirl as she made for the door.

Nellie shouted, 'See you on Monday then, you daft bugger.' The door shut behind her and Nellie, still laughing shook her head gently from side to side.

Tom and Nellie talked it over and decided she should give it a go. Their plan was to give Sam notes telling the school the children were ill. It was less than a month till the school holidays, so what the hell, they wouldn't bother now surely.

Tom changed his way of thinking quickly because he didn't like cutting back on his nights out, besides the town had opened a new Social Club and he was itching to try it.

Monday came. Sally, Hugh and Nellie stood at the corner of the street waiting on the van to pick them up. Sally hadn't spoken very much over the weekend. She felt like a clockwork doll only moving when she had to and speaking when necessary. She was furious and disgusted at her mother's change in attitude, knowing that Nellie's actions would only lead to more trouble. As she found it impossible to reason with her parents she became terribly subdued.

The van appeared and stopped in front of them. The door opened and they were told to hurry in. Sally couldn't believe her eyes, there were more children than adults. She had been to the tatties before, but always during the school holidays. 'God,' she thought to herself, 'if the other squaddies are like this there cannae be anyone left at school.' This thought comforted her somehow, until she looked over at Hugh. He was sleeping on his feet. She felt a wave of pity for him as his face looked almost angelic. For all his tough acting, he was still a small boy. She never stopped to think that there was only eighteen months between them.

The whole business had affected Sam too as he had to look after Bess. He had to take her to school and also collect her at the end of the day before taking her home. His chores weren't finished there as he had to clean the ashes from the fire before setting it and getting it going before everyone came in from work. It made no difference if the weather was hot, since the fire was needed to provide hot water. If that wasn't enough, he also had the shopping. Although Sam complained, a few slaps from Nellie made him toe the line. She tried sweetening him up by giving him half-a-crown on Fridays, but it did nothing to relieve the resentment he felt towards his mother.

At night when the children came home from working with their mother, they were often too worn-out to eat a meal. All they wanted was to sleep. Some of the children had fun, but not them, they were kept hard at it, Sally more so than Hugh, as she had to help him keep up. The injustice was; they never saw one penny for their day's toil as Nellie claimed both wages.

Chapter Three

Peggy Samuel was a very smart woman who kept a tidy house, in actual fact; she could have been accused of being house-proud. As she had no children of her own she looked after Sam when he was born for almost a year as Nellie suffered from depression. When it was time to give Sam back to Nellie, Peggy was heart broken. Peggy's husband Peter, who was the manager at the coalmine, adored his wife and saw that she wanted for nothing. It pained him greatly that his wife never managed to conceive, as she would have made a wonderful mother.

Although Peggy was Tom's only sister, they had not spoken for over six years. It wasn't due to *them* having words, it was Nellie and her. Peggy told Tom he had let himself go marrying Nellie, as she was a greedy, dirty woman, furthermore she had watched Sam become seriously neglected as he started smelling of stale milk and sick.

When this reached Nellie's ears, she sought out and attacked her sister-in-law leaving her with a broken tooth and a black eye. Peggy vowed to get even. Her very words were, 'It may take years, but I'm a patient woman.'

As Peggy hadn't seen Sam for a week and four days, she began to worry. She put on her hat and coat and went down to meet him coming from school. She hadn't done that since he was a small boy, as back then it was the only way she could get to see him, but as he grew older he visited his aunt by himself. Although she loved that boy like a son, she could not take to the others. She was nice enough to them on the odd occasion they called at her house, but there was only room in her heart for Sam.

It was Bess who first saw Peggy at the gates, and as she tugged at Sam's jacket she announced, 'There's Mutton Peggy, Sam.'

Seeing his aunt smile over at them he swiftly looked down at his sister.

'Don't let me hear you say that again,' he hissed as he pulled violently at her arm.

'Ma calls her that,' she whined looking up into his face.

'She would, wouldn't she,' he spoke quietly from the side of his mouth like a ventriloquist.

'What's up auntie Peggy?' asked Sam as he approached, his face now expressing concern.

'You tell me Sam,' she replied gently.

'Ah!' he said casting his eyes down at Bess. 'She's only gone and took Hugh and Sally tattie howkin' and left me to look after everything at home, including this yin.'

'She never has, after getting into trouble an all.' A sly grin appeared at the side of Peggy's mouth unseen by Sam.

'Got ya Nellie Baxter,' she said to herself. 'Working on the side and using the children. The Social will be delighted when they hear that.' Warm satisfaction flowed through her veins, as this was the kind of information she had been waiting on.

'Never mind Sam, you come over this weekend and we'll have a nice tea. Scones? I'll bake scones and fairy cakes and I'll get some boiled ham from the store and make sandwiches.'

'Can a come tae?' pleaded Bess.

'Most definitely not!' Mary snapped, 'and tell your mother it's years since she ate meat so she wouldn't know mutton if it jumped up and bit her on the bum!'

The three figures jumped from out the van. Nellie was about to swing a small sack of potatoes onto her shoulders when the two men dressed in black suits stood in front of them.

'Mrs Baxter, we would like a word with you.'

Nellie looked at them inquiringly. 'And who are *you* then?' she asked impudently.

'I'm Mr Graham from Social Services and this gentleman is from the benefit office. I'm here to have a word about the children Mrs Baxter.'

When Tom arrived home Nellie told him about the men and soon after an argument started. They blamed each other for the situation. Tom felt he had to get out of the house so he put his jacket back on and, still unwashed, he left, slamming the door behind him. He would think this out over a few pints.

The houses were old and consisted of a living room, bedroom, back kitchen and a very small toilet. The toilets in the houses were at one time large cupboards or 'presses' as they were known. They had been turned into toilets around the time the gas mantles had been removed and electricity installed. The houses were damp and had a smell of their own. That added to the smell of Nellie's house made it unbearable to the unsuspecting visitor.

Sally sat on top of an old orange box that had been discarded and left at the back of the house. As she had moved it from it's original spot the earth where it once stood crawled with slugs and woodlice. With elbows resting on her knees she supported her chin in the palm of her hands and watched as they scurried out of the light looking for a dark corner where they could seek refuge, then looking up she surveyed the land before her; it was the drying green belonging to her mother where the grass almost reached Sally's waist. Her mother seldom used her drying green preferring to hang the laundry around the fire and draping cloths on the pulley that stretched the full length of the living room. Although the coal fire blazed in the room the constant steam from the clothes made the air damp. Her neighbours jokingly remarked, 'she was hopeless washing clothes as they appeared dirtier after she was finished.' At the bottom of the garden stood the dilapidated 'outhouse' or 'outside lavatory.' Although the pan was long gone the bricks still stank to high heavens, its wooden door, now well rotten, hung dangerously by one rusty hinge.

'What a dump,' Sally thought wearily. 'I wish I wasn't here. I wish I was another person.'

The neighbours on either side had nicely cut drying greens and one of them had turned the old lavatory into a garden shed. Potted plants hung on the walls and neat little window boxes were placed on the back window ledges.

One of the neighbours, an elderly couple, often treated Sally to tea and allowed her to watch 'Children's Hour' on television, which was really special as not many families had television at that time, but she hadn't seen them for weeks now, as she never had the time.

'What's going to happen now?' wondered Sally, the man's words tormenting her thoughts.

'Court for you now,' he had threatened Nellie.

'Oh God, things can't get much worse,' she sighed. 'At least we won't be dragged off to the tatties any more!'

Once again Sally and Hugh found themselves sitting facing a much larger table. This time though, her dad was there too. They weren't on their own; another four families sat in the seats with their backs to the wall facing the very long table.

There was no one as yet sitting at the table, but they were told to stand when the court officials entered the room.

Nellie turned to Tom and asked if the rest of them – nodding in the direction of the other families, heard each other's cases. Tom said that it wouldn't matter anyway as they were all here for the same reason.

'Court stand,' someone ordered.

As everyone stood up the chairs scraped on the floor. There was a blue carpet on the floor but it ran along in front of them as if it was the forbidden line. The table directly in front was raised slightly as it stood on a small plinth. The door in the far corner opened and a group of people walked in, one after the other in silence.

'Who are all them?' Hugh whispered to Sally.

'Don't know Hugh but it'll be all right. Our dad's here.'

Their case was heard first, much to Nellie's annoyance, as apart from the humiliation of others hearing her business, she wanted to listen to their downfalls.

Sally and Hugh were not asked to speak this time. It was mostly the people in the centre of the table who did the talking. The man in the middle of the table did smile down at the children when he made reference to them. The woman at the end took notes between blowing into her handkerchief. Sally was disappointed with her father as he said very little. She was sure he knew how to save the day.

'This is Miss Thomson children,' said the sheriff turning towards the woman at the other end of the table, 'she will take you out. Go with her as I would like to talk some more to your parents.' They followed Miss Thomson towards a small adjoining room and, as they looked back at their parents, Hugh almost fell over as his foot caught the inside of Sally's shoe.

When the children were gone, the sheriff turned and addressed Nellie and Tom. 'In view of the situation I think we must take strict measures to protect these children and to ensure they get the most out of our education system. Mrs Baxter, you broke the law when you deprived Hugh and Sally of their schooling and to force them to hard toil is quite out of order.

Mr Baxter, you too were aware of what was going on and you took no steps to stop it. I have no alternative but to place the children, Hugh and Sally Baxter into a Children's Home for no less than three years. In the meantime, you will both be watched closely by the Social Services to ensure similar events do not occur with the remainder of your children. Have you anything to add?' The sheriff looked over his half moon glasses at the two very shocked faces.

Nellie shook her head while Tom said in a very humble voice, 'No sir.'

'Miss Aldridge will explain to the children,' the sheriff continued after allowing a few seconds for his words to sink in.

'They will be taken to a fine home on the outskirts of Kirkcaldy where they will be properly cared for with the best of education and religious instruction. You may go with Miss Aldridge and say your goodbyes.'

They both followed Miss Aldridge in the same way the children had followed Miss Thomson a few minutes earlier.

The children sat and waited patiently in the small room. They wanted to go home. Their dad said they would go for chips and lemonade before they caught the bus.

Miss Thomson was nice and she spoke to them in a quiet voice. She gave them both a caramel. The large sweet filled Hugh's mouth completely causing sticky slavers to seep out from the corners of his lips. He made a sucking sound as he retracted the sweet juices back into his mouth.

When the door opened they both jumped to their feet. Sally never thought she would be so pleased to see her mother, but she couldn't understand the look on Nellie's face. She looked sad and her mouth quivered as she walked slowly over to them. The next action shocked Sally to the core as Nellie took them both into her arms and hugged them. Apart from taking hands and the slaps they got from her, Nellie never had any bodily contact with them. Sally couldn't recall a single time her mother cuddled or kissed her. The only one who was given the odd hug was Bess. The times Sally yearned for her mother's affection was numerous. Now Nellie's hug made her feel frightened.

Tom followed after his wife and put his hands on both their heads while his mouth too quivered slightly.

'It's happened,' Sally shouted in panic. 'It's happened. We are going away. We're going...' she didn't know who to look at. Her eyes looked at her mother then darted towards the two women standing in the doorway.

'No! No!' She tore at her father's jacket as she pleaded.

'Tell me it's not true Dad,' she sobbed wrapping her arms around his waist. Tom pulled wearily towards the door his eyes filled with tears as Sally was dragged along the floor holding tightly to his trouser legs.

'Now stop this,' Miss Thomson said sharply as she prised Sally's fingers from Tom's trouser legs.

Almost choking, Hugh spat out his toffee. He just stood rigid and yelled.

'Da' oh da'!' Sally screamed as both he and Nellie left the scene.

Tom and Nellie left the children in the care of the two women after leaving as quickly as they could. Tom was ashen faced and shaken while Nellie had quickly regained her composure. For a short time back there, she almost acted like a real mother.

'A wish a kent who reported us 'cause a widnae be responsible for ma actions.' Tom said between his teeth.

'Aye yer right.' Nellie looked at him from the corner of her eye. 'Come oan, let's go an' get a bloody drink.' With that, the two of them hurried away from the court building.

Miss Thomson drove the car and Miss Aldridge sat in the back with the children.

Hugh continued crying aloud, while Sally sobbed quietly her chest heaving with every breath.

'Please children, please. You will make yourselves very ill.' Miss Aldridge was truly concerned. 'It's not as bad as it seems. You'll like it there. Here...' she pulled a bag of sweets from her pocket and offered them to the children. Sally shuffled closer towards her brother putting her small arm round his neck and forcing his head onto her shoulder. They took no notice of the sweets but their sobs lessened as Miss Aldridge began telling them what kind of things they were about to see.

This was the first time either of them had ridden in a motorcar. If it weren't for the situation, they both would have been beside themselves with excitement but under the circumstances they took no pleasure in the journey however Miss Aldridge was informing them they would be going over the water in the ferry. This caught their attention and the sobbing was beginning to subside.

Miss Aldridge had a way that made children trust and feel safe with her as she was used to dealing with this kind of situation.

They started taking an interest in their new surroundings and of things that whizzed passed the windows of the car. Sheep, cows, tractors and once a fire engine managed to catch their attention.

The excitement crossing by ferry also helped take their minds off their dilemma. The sea was calm and the weather was warm so they were able to go on deck. Hugh was gaping up at the Forth Bridge and wishing he could have crossed by train as Miss Aldridge had told them that the people who crossed by train often threw pennies over into the sea for good luck.

Hugh said that his mind was made up; he was going to be a deep-sea diver when he grew up and get rich by collecting all the money from the bottom of the seabed. As the escorts laughed heartily, Sally only managed a faint smile.

The journey took them into Fife and Miss Thomson pointed across the water and informed them, 'that's Edinburgh over there. That's where we have just come from.'

They still had a good few miles to go and as the day had been a very dramatic one for them both they soon were fast asleep.

'Come on Sally wake up pet. Hugh! Wakey wakey! We're here.' Miss Aldridge gently shook them both.

As the children slowly opened their eyes, they pushed themselves back up the seat as they had slid half way down. Hugh yawned and scratched while Sally, realising she hadn't been dreaming, jumped up as she became aware once more of their situation.

Miss Aldridge put her hand on Sally's arm hoping to reassure her. 'It's ok Sally, you'll like the Matron. She is a nice lady.'

'Are you staying with us?' She asked pleadingly.

'Well! Only a little while as Miss Thomson and I have to get back, but we come out here very often.'

Sally, beginning to trust her, thought she smelled nice. She thought Miss Thomson was nice too but a bit mousy and she sniffed a lot.

As the car was driven through large iron gates, the sound of gravel beneath the wheels cracked and crunched as it wound its way around a circular drive way.

The children looked up in amazement at the size of the house that confronted them. They had never seen such a house, certainly not in the area they came from. Climbing from the car they approached the front door that was encased inside a small glass porch, cautiously.

Miss Thomson rang the bell.

The sound of children laughing and shouting came from the other side of a high wall that joined on to the house.

The door opened and a rather large lady stood before them.

'Hello Susan,' the Matron addressed Miss Aldridge warmly. She then nodded towards Miss Thomson and said stiffly, 'Annie,' before looking down at the two frightened faces. Bending down, her face now level with the children's, she smiled. 'Well then, another two wee lambs come to me for shelter. Come away in the four of you. It's a long way you've come and you're starving I'm sure. Come into the sitting room and I'll ring down and let cook know you have arrived.'

They were led into a room that was bright and cheerful. Two large green leather sofas flanked the fireplace while a low pine table ran lengthways down the centre. As there was no fire in the grate, a massive highly polished brass fan stood in front of the fireplace. Sally had seen nothing like it before and stood looking round the room taking everything in.

The Matron's desk was by the window while a few wooden chairs lined the walls. A china cabinet stood in the other corner full of cups, saucers and nick knacks, but what caught the children's eyes were the rows of piggy banks that sat on the cabinet and the mantle shelf. There were even some on window ledges.

Catching them staring at the banks, Matron laughed. 'They belong to the children. They all put something in them each week. See...' she took a bright red one down and held it towards the bemused children. 'They all have different names on them and you both will have one as well. Now then,' she motioned towards the settee with her hand and they all sat down. 'I am Matron, and you must be Hugh and Sally. I know you are going to be happy here. I just know it.' She smiled towards the two ladies who brought the children all the way in the car.

'You are looking well both of you, your holiday must have done you good?'

'Yes Matron, we were glad of the rest,' Miss Aldridge answered. Miss Thomson just nodded.

The door opened and a small round woman came in carrying a tray holding a teapot, milk and sugar. A young teenage girl bounced after her carrying a similar tray of sandwiches and scones.

Lifting the fancy nylon cover from the long coffee table, the matron revealed china cups and saucers like an amateur magician.

'Children,' she said while turning the cups up into the saucers, 'this is Cook and she gets called 'Cook' by us all.'

The small woman looked at the mystified children.

'I think we have a lot of fattening up to do eh Matron?'

Sally and Hugh remained quiet as if they had forgotten how to speak.

'This is Cathy children.' She now looked towards the

girl who was placing the sandwiches and scones on the table.

'Sally and Hugh have come to stay with us Cathy. You'll be able to have a chat later when they have had some tea and I get them settled in.'

'Right Matron,' Cathy smiled and left with Cook.

Although Sally felt hungry she hardly ate a thing. The bite she had taken from the small rectangle sandwich felt like a foreign body stuck in her throat. No such thoughts entered Hugh's mind as he tucked in as if there was no tomorrow.

Matron chatted to the two ladies making light of the situation as she was trying to make the children feel at ease.

After tea Miss Thomson and Miss Aldridge took their leave. Matron was left alone with Sally and Hugh who were both showing signs of apprehension.

'I think you're going to like it here as we are all one big family but like most families, there are rules to be adhered to children,' Matron informed them, the smile still on her face. 'And like all families, when you break the rules, you are punished.'

Sally and Hugh's faces visibly change colour. As they quickly looked at one and other, a mask of horror shaped their small faces.

Seeing their fear she quickly assured them.

'Don't worry. Don't worry, we don't hit or hurt in any-way, we run on a point system. You get points for being good and you lose them if you are bad. The more points you collect, the bigger your reward. For instance, we have a fair in the town near here, and so many points earn you the right to a visit. Supervised, of course. You are given a special pass that allows you on the rides as many times as you like without charge.'

She stopped speaking for a moment and stroked her skirt as if brushing off some imaginary crumb. Looking back into their faces she continued. 'The ladies who help here we call aunties. I will introduce you later. In the meantime I think I will show you both to your rooms and get you bathed and into some better clothing.'

Now Sally's eyes lit up. 'Better clothing, well that sounds good,' she thought. She knew she looked awful and was aware that her coat was grubby and a size or two larger than she needed. She had a pair of shoes on her feet that were just about through at the toes and would disintegrate at the sight of polish. Her socks had disappeared down the back of her shoes showing red flesh about to blister. Hugh's appearance was no better as the behind of his trousers shone like a cracked mirror, the cracks being small tears in the thin material and the back pockets were completely torn off. He wore sandals, like Sally's shoes, they were far too small but being open toed helped, although the lack of socks allowed his toes to droop over the rims.

They were taken from the matron's private sitting room and briefly shown the room next door that was used by the children. The room itself was spacious and colourful as children's paintings were dotted around the walls. There was an old battered piano sitting to the side of the bay window with a scattering of music sheets on top. An oak bookcase filled with children's books and board games centred the wall to the left while an oversized dolls' house took pride of place upon a low table to the right. Various shelves housed numerous toys from trains to spinning tops, rag dolls to lorries. Adjacent doors lead to the quiet room where children could read or draw in peace.

Outside in the hall a very wide staircase, its carpet faded with age, led up to the bedrooms. Under the staircase the door there led to stairs going down into the kitchen and laundry rooms. The dining room was also down stairs. There was a smaller room at the end of a dark passageway that was used to store various pieces of equipment. It also led to the back door that opened onto a beautifully manicured lawn and down to their very own orchard. At the back of the orchard there was a gate that let to old unused stables. The cobbled ground was now over grown with weeds furthermore the doors to the stables were barely holding together as the rusty old hinges had seen better days.

There was a gardener who tended the grounds along with the children who helped when they could.

The Matron took Hugh and Sally by the hand and led them up stairs. On reaching the first landing, she opened the first door they came to.

'This is your room Sally. You will be sharing with Rita. You will meet her later because she has been taken out today. She's gone for new shoes.'

'Its... it's lovely,' Sally said faintly.

The room was like the rooms downstairs, very clean

and bright. Two single beds with top covers that matched the curtains were neatly made. Both girls had their very own set of drawers and at the bottom of each bed sat a wicker stool holding a neatly folded towel. Sally liked what she saw and smiled broadly as Matron pointed to her bed.

'What about me?' Hugh tugged on Sally's coat.

'You'll be along the landing Hugh. Don't worry wee man, you will be sharing with George. Come and I'll show you.' Matron turned to Sally, 'do you want to come too?'

'Yes,' she answered quietly.

Hugh's room was exactly like Sally's except it was at the other end of the landing.

The door next to Sally's room housed three more girls while a smaller room on the same landing was kept for the night staff. There were more rooms on the floor above, the largest being matrons private sitting room with a small adjoining room for her bed and dresser. Cook slept in one of the attic rooms where she too had a very small sitting room.

The Home usually housed anything from twelve to fourteen children at any one time as well as Matron, three members of staff, who took turns sleeping over, as well as cook and two ladies who helped clean the house.

Chapter Four

The children had been in the 'home' for a few months and had by this time settled in. Hugh still had to be watched as he had taken a couple of tantrums and threatened to run off. He was gaining in confidence and some days he was difficult to handle.

Sally, on the other hand enjoyed being there as she was overjoyed at having her very own bed as she had no memories of ever sleeping by herself... and wearing a *nightgown*! She was so used to climbing into bed in her knickers. Decent clothes (although plain and basic) were provided along with two pair of footwear! Black laces-ups for school and a pair of brown leather sandals for every day wear. Slippers too, she had slippers! Hugh had been supplied with grey trousers and jumpers as well as two pair of shoes. As far as he was concerned, *two* pair was far too many to clean.

Most of the other children were friendly except for one older girl who slept on the top landing. She constantly scowled at Sally, sending daggers as a warning that she had to be avoided at all costs. Rita, who shared the room with Sally, was quiet and withdrawn but as the days went by, she started talking more. Although both girls were the same age, Rita looked much older. Being very tall and often clumsy had made her extremely self-conscious and insecure.

Another change in Sally's life took place at the end of each week. Sunday school. She loved it. Dressed up in their best clothes, they all followed each other into church. Illness was the only way to escape this weekly sojourn, and you had to be really ill at that.

Hugh disliked Sunday school and couldn't understand why anyone went to school on a Sunday anyway. Normal school was bad enough but he hated the Sunday classes. He thought it was stupid talking with your eyes shut to people that were invisible.

The primary school was only ten minutes walk from the house and all but four of the children, who were older, attended. Rita and Sally became good friends very quickly and went everywhere hand in hand together. At first Hugh tagged along but as he got to know the other boys, he followed less.

Both girls were down at the orchard playing when they heard the house bell ring. Matron or one of the 'aunties' rang it when they wanted everyone in.

'What's up now?' Sally stopped swinging on the branches and adjusted her skirt.

Her friend shrugged her shoulders. 'How do I know? We had better go and see. Come on Sal, I'll race you.'

Running on ahead, Rita reached the back door first as her long legs took one stride to Sally's two.

'I won. I won,' she cried as Sally fell on her friend.

Barging into the kitchen they nearly knocked Cook over.

'Careful you two,' she called after them. 'And remember Sally, it's your turn to help tonight.'

Between quick short breaths she called back.

'I know. I won't forget Cook.'

As they approached the childrens' sitting room, their ears were filled by the noise of chatter and giggles. Seldom were they all gathered together in the one place as downstairs held the ping-pong table and was equipped with books and paraphernalia to suit the older residents.

Auntie Helen was on duty with auntie Margaret and as they both sat in the middle of the room, one of the younger children had Helen in a strangle hold and she was trying to make him stop.

Matron walked into the room behind the straggling girls, her facial expression looking unusually severe.

'If you will all be quiet, I have something to say.' She clapped her hands demanding silence, 'Please children,' she commanded sharply.

The noise abated slowly as everyone stopped what they were doing. Matron stood patiently, hands clasped in front of her. With eyes half closed, she waited until there was complete silence.

'That's better.' Looking around at the vacant faces she took a slow intake of breath and continued. 'Mr Jones the gardener left his jacket in the shed yesterday and when he returned, the shed door was open. His jacket was on the ground and the contents of his pockets scattered all over the place, but his wallet containing six pounds has gone missing. If any of you know about it or think you can help in anyway, please come and see me in my sitting room.' She looked slowly at all the faces as if she could read minds. Perhaps she was looking for some tell tale signs, some body language that would give her a clue.

Sally, although innocent felt very guilty. She could not understand this feeling. She had been accused many times in the past of doing things of which she was completely blameless, although she never felt so awful as she did now.

'What if we are blamed and get taken from this place.' Her mind now racing made her cheeks blush.

'I couldn't bear it. What if Hugh's up to his old tricks? Heavens...' her heart was beating very hard inside her small chest. She wanted to shout and tell them all that it wasn't her but she remained silent.

Matron left the room and the chatter started once more, only this time it was low and there was no laughter.

A week had passed and the Matron had got no further with the investigation. She had spoke to them all individually and Sally was no exception.

It was a dreadful experience for most of the children except for a few who didn't care one way or another. Among them was the horrible Sandra. She didn't bother Sally much except for the odd remarks and a few dirty looks but Rita was terrified of her and became quiet and withdrawn when she was about. It was some time before Sally became aware of this, as her roommate was quiet when in the company of most of the others. On one or two occasions Sally noticed bruising on Rita's face and when questioning her, she would say she had fallen or knocked her face on something or other. The Matron had also questioned Rita about the frequent bruising on her body but had been told similar stories so she had a word with Sally. During that particular interview Matron had marvelled at Sally getting Rita to talk and take an interest in events outside the house. Seemingly Rita had never taken to anyone before, as it was hard for her to trust. Sally was unaware her young friend had experienced a far worse life than her own and had been abused by members of her own family. Rita only told that information to Sally in later years.

Matron presumed Rita's nightmares had also stopped since Sally befriended her, although this was something she was reluctant to ask but Sally could have told Matron that they had not gone away. When Rita was having a bad night, Sally would hug and comfort her until she fell asleep again.

The truth about Rita's bruising came to light when Sally, who was supposed to be on laundry duty, went back up stairs to fetch a skirt she wanted to press. She was about to push open the door of her room when she heard Sandra's voice. The door was slightly open so she stopped and listened.

Sandra had Rita's head against the wall and her hand was around her throat. 'I told you I wanted two shillings a week, so get me the rest.'

'I had to put the rest in my bank. Please stop it, you're choking me,' gasped the frightened girl.

'You better get it back then,' taunted Sandra, 'or the Matron will know who stole the gardener's money.' She turned Rita around quickly and pushed her back onto the bed, causing the terrified girl to jerk with pain.

'I never stole anything,' sobbed Rita.

'I can easily get a witness to say you did. Wilma will back me up,' snorted Sandra. She was referring to one of the other girls who shared her room on the second landing. There were three in the room and Sandra who was thirteen was the youngest. The other two were both fourteen.

'You leave her alone.' They both looked towards the door where Sally stood.

'Oh, so we have a hero,' smirked Sandra. 'I was going to see you anyway as I want your money too. Don't get any ideas shortie or you'll get what your pal's just got,' snarled Sandra.

'Think so,' Sally said confidently, the nerves in her stomach going like a steam engine.

Moving quickly towards the door, Sandra threw a punch at Sally and as Sally very smartly ducked to one side, Sandra hit her fist on the frame of the door. Bending her body like a knife she tucked her painful hand into her waist and groaned.

Sally took advantage of the situation and jumped on to Sandra's stooped back knocking her to the floor. Once on the ground she set about the bully. Driven by fear and adrenaline, Sally punched and slapped at the screaming, curled up figure beneath her, knowing full well if Sandra was allowed up, *she* would be the one on the floor. She was unaware of the Matron and one of the staff rushing into the room. They pulled Sally off the screaming girl and helped her up onto her feet.

Shocked at the scene before her, Matron gasped in disbelief, 'Sally Baxter, what's come over you? Go down stairs at once and sit outside my room till I come down,' Matron demanded.

The sobbing Sandra was taken into the bathroom where her bleeding lip was attended. She was then taken to her room and told to stay there till the Matron sent for her.

During the grilling from Matron, Sally explained what she had heard also that she pounced on the other girl in self-defence. Rita had to admit that her life was being made miserable by Sandra's bullying. Sandra and her roommate had taunted her about her height and skinniness since she came to the home, also she had begun to demand money and her personal effects. Thanks to Sally, that never happened again, but it cost Sally ten valuable points as the Matron had to punish her for fighting.

Although Sandra remained there, she never bothered anyone again as no one took her seriously. She became a laughing stock amongst the older girls as the respect she had been shown by her followers was born out of fear, however the mystery of the gardener's money was never solved but everyone had a fair idea where it went.

How Sally wished that Hugh could have settled in but he just couldn't. He longed for home and missed Bess dreadfully. She felt that she had been here all her life instead of only eighteen months. She enjoyed every single day. School was sending good reports and was amazed at her capabilities; furthermore she had started to learn the piano. What fun they had on winter nights, singing songs and playing games in the large sitting room. Life was good, safe and clean.

Cook baked a cake for Sally's tenth birthday and they had a party in the dining room. Her eyes filled with tears when Matron gave her a manicure set encased in a beige leather case as a birthday present. She had never been given anything like it before. A zip went around the heart shaped case that contained scissors, nail file, a nail buffer and a few things that were strange but interesting. The 'aunties' gave presents of socks, books and a pen and pencil set, but her most treasured gift was the brooch she was given by Rita. It was only a small bunch of plastic flowers, but she pinned it on to her jumper and wore it with pride. It had been given with so much love.

The children were often taken to visit different places. A small bus took them to places like the zoo, museums, theatres and the circus. The point system worked well. If you were under a certain level, you were left behind. The next exciting outing was three weeks away where the ice rink was to be the venue.

One thing Sally and Hugh were not allowed was home visits. Hugh cried for his mother often but Sally's thoughts were of her father. She did miss him a lot but what hurt most was the total rejection that engulfed her during the hours of darkness. Not once had he written or attempted to get in touch. Her silent sobs and hot tears were saved for the wee small hours when sleep was not forthcoming.

Very few of the children had visitors calling but the majority received the occasional letter. On one occasion, the children had a visit from Sam. He was driven over by auntie Mary and uncle Pete who were out for their usual Sunday run, showing off their new car. That was the first contact they had with home. They had learned from Sam that they had a new baby sister and he had left home and was staying with auntie Mary and uncle Pete.

Hugh had been more interested in the news than Sally as she saw anything or anybody (with the exception of her father) from 'over the water' as being a threat.

After the visit, Hugh grew more and more difficult to handle, as tantrums became a regular thing with him. He kicked and roared when things didn't go his way and became a frequent pain in the neck.

It was a Friday night; Sally and Rita were lying on their beds rolling with laughter. Sally was telling Rita things that had happened to her. Silly things. Things that were not particularly funny at the time, but Sally saw the humour now.

'Here's another,' giggles Sally.

'Aw, no, stop it Sally, I'm sore,' Rita howled.

'No,' Sally insisted. ' Listen! The teacher told my Mam that I needed glasses. My Mam took me to the optician, listen Rita, stop laughing,' Sally said giggling herself. 'My Mam took me to the optician and there I was looking at the chart...A...B...C...D..., the optician was angry. I didn't need glasses at all. I didn't know my alphabet. He told my Mam to bring me back when I could read. Ha! Ha!' With tears streaming down their faces they both rolled about laughing.

'What did your Ma say?' spluttered Rita.

'She called me a stupid bugger and belted me across the head,' choked Sally.

The door opened and Patsy, the girl who was in the next room popped her head in.

'Sally, Matron wants a word with you.'

'Thanks Patsy,' Sally answered drying her eyes on the back of her hand.

'It's the optician that wants to see you,' squealed Rita.

'Aye, maybe he's heard that I can read now.' Laughing, Sally got off her bed and made a face at her friend.

Reaching Matron's room, Sally knocked on the door and entered.

'Sit down dear,' Matron swept her hand towards the sofa. Sally sat down and looked questioningly at the Matron.

'Sally, Hugh and George have run off again. This time they have taken sixteen pounds from my handbag. They also broke into their own banks. Now I have to let you know but I don't want you to worry Sally. They will be found and brought back, that is the main thing.'

'When did this happen Matron?' Sally asked with a note of regret in her voice.

'It happened shortly after dinner and the police are now looking for them.'

Leaving the Matron's room, the daftness and fun she had felt minutes ago was now replaced with anger. 'Hugh,' she thought, 'I'll kill you for this.'

Chapter Five

Hugh and George spent the night in a scrap yard. They lay in waiting until the scrappy left for home. Then, climbing the wall, they broke into the scrappie's old caravan. Looking around, they were intrigued by the amount of old rubbish that filled the van. There was hardly any room to swing a cat as old cardboard boxes of every shape and size took up every space on the floor. They were filled with all kinds of junk. As the two rogues rummaged inside the boxes, they became more intrigued. There were boxes of old plugs and wiring, assorted nails, parts of cars, old biscuit tin boxes, gas masks, rusted cutlery, all kinds of bric- a- brac and old gas mantles. They moved a pile of dinner plates and old books from the long greasy looking seat and sat down. They planned to enjoy themselves, as they were now free.

They had bought bags of buns, bottles of juice, sweets and comics. Hunger was not a problem this time as they had money. They had learned not to run off without money as they had done in the past.

It was fun playing cops and robbers especially now that the game was for real. The next morning they made their way to Kirkcaldy.

The beach took up most of their morning, throwing stones at tin cans that bobbed up and down in the water. George came up with the idea of fishing, so they decided to go for some food and buy a couple of fishing rods.

The town was at its busiest on Saturday mornings so they mingled among the crowd, thinking no one would notice them. After all, they were a good few miles away from Olive Bank.

They were in Woolworths buying the fishing rods when George saw a boy from his class at school. The boy caught his mother's attention and pointed towards the two runaways.

George took hold of Hugh's arm and forced him down under the counter. 'Run. A think we've been spotted.' They raced towards the door knocking down a floor display of umbrellas sending the bright coloured articles flying in all directions. Running only helped draw attention to the young absconders as they bumped and bashed their way out into the street.

The police were quickly alerted and they were both soon tracked down. They were found in the public park, sitting along side the goldfish pond dangling their fishing rods in the water.

They were brought back to the House in the police car. That alone was a great adventure, as they wanted the driver to put on the sirens and flashing lights.

As well as a loss in privileges, their pocket money was suspended till Matron's money had been paid back. Twelve pounds had already been returned, as they hadn't had time to spend it all.

During the summer, the children were often boarded out to couples that were willing to welcome them into their homes for a few weeks holiday. Because families could not be split up, no one ever took Hugh and Sally, as they came as a package. That was until their second year.

The couple meant well and agreed to take them both. Sally didn't really want to go as she was becoming more insecure when leaving her safe haven but they were soon taken off by car to Scone in Perthshire, but their stay with the McFarlane's was miserable.

'Don't touch this and don't touch that,' was all Mrs McFarlane could say. Bed was so early that Sally said to Hugh, 'It's hardly worthwhile putting your clothes on in the morning as it will soon be time to take them off.' Did he not go and repeat it to Mrs McFarlane.

The couple had fifteen-year-old twins who resented their houseguests from the start, referring to them as 'Home brats.' They broke crockery, stole fruit from the dish and various other tricks, blaming everything on Hugh or Sally. They broke a pane of glass in the neighbour's greenhouse and the 'home brat's' were held responsible. They hated being at the McFarlane's but they had to resign themselves, no matter how reluctantly, to the fact they were there for a full month.

The only exciting aspect about the place was the dense woodland that skirted the back of the house; there they often escaped out of their hosts' way. They loved to imagine they were Hansel and Gretel as they wandered deep into the heart of the woodland. One day they came upon a small thatched cottage surrounded by white picket fencing tucked away in a small clearance. Terracotta gnomes coated in moss with faces worn away with age and stone birdbaths filled with clear fresh water were scattered around the garden between tall flowers and shrubs. Smoke billowed into the sky from the chimneypot that sat tall and straight like the mad hatters hat. As they stood staring in wonder, an elderly lady opened the door of the cottage. Her face seemed to light up with joy at seeing the youngsters. Giving them a very pleasant smile, she beckoned them to come closer. They walked over cautiously towards the gate where the woman stood. She sat them down at the garden table before disappearing into the house. She appeared quickly carrying a wicker tray of biscuits and lemonade. After she sat down beside them she learned all about their holiday at the McFarlane's.

She began telling them about her cottage and how she had lived there for years with her husband who had died a good few years back. He worked for the people at the big house and as he was the woodsman it was only fitting they lived in the woodsman's cottage. Those days were long gone as servants and the like were no longer employed there but she was allowed to remain in the woods. The gnomes were said to be the guardians of the cottage and fairies allegedly dwelled there too, but you could only see them if you believed. The children listened in awe, their eyes growing larger at every word the old woman spoke. Thanking her for the lemonade, they promised to visit another day before making their way back to that awful family.

'Did you believe her back there?' asked Hugh.

'Of course not, silly. She was only a nice lady telling us a story.'

Both of them jumped the low fence and went into the house by the back door where they just about fell over the case that stood in the small porch. Looking at each other enquiringly Sally frowned and shrugged her shoulders.

'*There* you are!' Mrs McFarlane stood at the sitting room doorway with her hands on her hips, her piercing eyes like lasers penetrating their faces. 'I can't stand thieves,' she yelled. 'If you wanted chocolate... you have your own money. You just had to *ask* me and I would have *given* you some of your money.' She resembled a raving mad woman.

'Just a minute Mrs McFarlane,' Sally interrupted. 'We took nothing and we don't know what you are on about.'

'My Bourneville chocolate! That's what I'm on about. It's gone. It was in the drawer.' Grabbing them both by the arm she pushed them towards the kitchen door then pointing furiously at the cupboard drawer she screamed,' That bloody drawer. It was in there!'

'Ask your own two, as it wasn't us,' Hugh added cheekily. 'I don't even like Bourneville chocolate,' he informed her. 'It's like taking laxatives. Makes you shi...'

'Hugh!' Sally stopped him by quickly putting her hand over his mouth.

'*Well! I've never heard the like!*' the irate woman declared venomously. '*You come into my home and... and...you ungrateful toe rags!*'

'And you never gave us money and it's not yours, it was for us,' Hugh piped in.

'Well we'll call it quits then shall we. Know what I mean?' She spoke haughtily before growling, ' *It will pay for damages*!'

Five days was all they lasted. Back at the home, Matron heard the McFarlane's accusations and drew her own conclusions. She interviewed both children and although Hugh's track record was nothing to go by, she knew Sally was telling the truth but that was the last time they were out on holiday.

The whole incident cost them a few points but Sally was not bothered, she was back home.

Funny thing was, Hugh never attempted to run away again also his behaviour vastly improved.

The McFarlane's were taken off the fostering list and they were never allowed to have children from the home again.

Chapter Six

Christmas of that year was fast approaching. The children were helping to decorate the large Christmas tree that stood in the playroom. All of the decorations were hand made. Bright coloured lights were placed loosely around the tree and the branches were dotted here and there with cotton wool. The usual gold star took pride of place at the very top.

Matron was on her knees repairing a long paper chain that had been accidentally broken. Sally sat beside her on the floor making balls out of silver paper. All year silver paper was saved for that very purpose.

'Well Sally,' Matron began, 'you are into your last year. Another eight months or so and you'll be leaving us.'

Sally felt panic in her stomach but looking up into Matron's kind face, she managed to force a smile.

She had been thinking the same thing a few weeks before but managed to bury the thought at the back of her mind. She really didn't want to dwell on the fact. She knew it was going to be a terrible wrench as this was the only place she thought of as home.

Since coming to Olive Bank, Sally had become a different person. Schooling had improved her enormously and her habits were completely transformed. Before she came to the 'home', she thought nothing of eating with her fingers. Now she would never dream of doing such a thing. Her mother use to say, 'fingers were made before forks and knives,' and many a time a pot of potatoes with gravy mixed through was put onto the kitchen table where they all delved in.

Prayers were always said before each meal. 'Please and thank you were said at all times. Sally had changed beyond recognition. Her body as well had changed from the small skinny lass she had once been, into one that could have been described as being slightly on the plump side. It was little wonder, as she was made to eat everything before leaving the table.

The meals were good and very nourishing and only once did Sally create a fuss. It happened away back in the early days of Sally's arrival. She was given milk jelly and after one taste, she refused to eat it. It made her feel sick. Given that the rules were you did not leave till you ate everything, she was forced to finish it. She threw up all night and was never forced to eat milk jelly again.

Auntie Helen popped her head round the door and beckoned to Matron. She handed the decoration to Rita who had joined them on the floor.

'Excuse me girls,' Matron left to see what was wrong. She was gone only a few minutes and when she returned, her face beamed with delight. 'Where is Hugh?' she asked looking around the room. He was in the small adjoining room, and when called, came out with a 'what's up' look on his face.

'Sally and Hugh, come through to the sitting room. There's someone here to see you.'

They both looked vacantly at one another before looking back at Matron

'Come on then,' she said eagerly, 'you won't find out who it is standing here.'

Apprehensively Sally followed on behind with Hugh anxiously tugging at her skirt.

Matron held the sitting room door open for them, allowing them to enter.

Standing awkwardly they looked along the room at the man whose back was to them as he gazed out into the garden.

Closing the door gently behind her the matron left the room. Sally's heart raced when she heard the gentle click of the door behind her. Her mouth seemed parched as a surge of fear shot through her as she thought they were in big trouble. Hugh now clinging to Sally's arm, also trembled slightly.

Turning around slowly and facing the children, the man now waited for a reaction, but no one moved or said a word. Sally's mouth fell open and her eyes almost popped out of their sockets when she realised who was standing at the window.

'What kind of welcome is this then?' the man spoke.

Sally and Hugh ran forward and practically knocking him over, threw themselves into his embrace. 'Da, Da, Oh da!' they both called simultaneously. They embraced tightly for a few moments before Sally broke away. 'Why have you taken so long in coming to see us Dad?' her voice pleading for an answer. 'You could have come through to see us ages ago. You could have even written!'

Ignoring his daughter's remarks, he now held her at arms length, looking her over in disbelief. 'My, my. How you've baith filled oot. And how ye baith have grown.' Glancing at Hugh and giving the top of his head a brisk rub, he remarked, 'you look sae grown up. A can hardly believe you ur the same wee laddie.'

'Have you been treated well?' He asked Sally.

'Of course we have dad but it would have been nice to see you now and again.' Her voice had softened as her eyes welled with tears.

Feeling dreadful and overcome with guilt, Tom did his best to explain. 'Yer mother has nae been well at awe since she had the bairn, so a could never git away hen.'

'My mother,' thought Sally, 'I hate her.'

'Never mind, a'm here noo and what's mare, a have the Matron's permission tae take you baith oot for the day.'

Excitement flowed through their veins as they set out with their father.

They spent time in town looking around the busy shops. Christmas trees were everywhere. Fairy lights and decorations brightened up shop windows where great arrays of toys were displayed in every department store. Carol singers well wrapped up against the crisp cold day stood in groups belting out Christmas cheers loud and meaningful while the Salvation Army band kept them in tune. The hustle and bustle of last minute shoppers added to the great excitement of Christmas.

Tom Baxter held onto his children's hands and felt glad he had faced up to his wife and made the effort to see his children. Nellie made a fuss every time the subject was brought up. If it wasn't the money for the fare she was objecting to, it was the illness she always developed whenever Tom made to leave.

Sally said he could have written, but how could he explain to her that he could not write. He never learned how.

'Da, I'm glad you came,' Sally said tugging at the bottom of his jacket and looking up into his face lovingly.

'So am I Da,' Hugh piped up.

'A widnae have missed it fur onything.' Feeling a huge surge of emotion swelling in his heart, he quickly added,

'Aw come oan, a cannae buy you much but we'll find something.' Squeezing their hands, he practically skipped along the pavement with them.

They went into a well-stocked toyshop and had a good look at everything before Hugh picked out one of the Dinky toys that were displayed expertly on the shelves while Sally chose Emily Bronte's Wuthering Heights. As it was the first time Tom had ever bought them anything, he felt good.

After they had window-shopped and visited places that mattered to them, Tom took them into a restaurant where he wanted to treat them to a decent meal. It had been some time since he had eaten, and he too was starving.

The decor in the dining room was very homely and Sally was amazed at the plates hanging around the walls.

A dozen small round tables, each covered with white linen cloths, filled the room. Small glass dishes, each holding a small sprig of holly with its glossy prickly leaves and bright red berries centred each table. Like most places at this time of year a large Christmas tree took pride of place in the corner near the window.

The restaurant was so busy they were about to turn around and head for the door, when a table became vacant. They were quickly ushered towards it by a pretty waitress who gave Tom a cheeky wink. She was dressed all in black except for her white lace collar and matching tea apron that was typical of waitresses in most establishments.

With the pretence of studying the menu, Tom ordered fish teas for the three of them. Still gazing around the walls, Sally gasped, 'Da, look at the plates on the walls.' She had seen nothing like it before.

'There's mair plates oan them walls than what's in yer mother's scullery,' Tom remarked.

Hugh now looked around the room and asked, 'Why do they keep them on the walls? Have they no cupboards?'

Tom and Sally exchanged looks and laughed.

The food that was placed in front of them was piping hot and looked as well as smelt delicious. Hugh picked up his knife and fork and delved into to the white steaming flesh of the fish. His fork was almost at his open mouth, when Sally's reprimanding voice stopped him from biting into the awaiting delicacy.

'Oh not here Sal,' Hugh pleaded.

'Yes,' Sally said sharply, staring at him in disgust.

Hugh reluctantly put his fork down, and Tom watched

in amazement as the two of them thanked God for what they were about to receive. He was astonished at the scene before him.

'Now can I eat?' Hugh asked cheekily.

'Yes, when you take your gloves off,' Sally said in a motherly fashion.

He was not having any more of Sally's bossiness, so he looked her straight in the eyes, and said adamantly 'No!'

'Hugh take your gloves off,' she spoke between her teeth, glancing over at the nearest table, hoping the couple seated there would take no notice.

'No,' he snapped, determination sparking from his cheeky eyes.

Tom felt strange. He knew he should take command of the situation, but he felt he had no right to interfere. He felt divorced from the situation. He did not know his children any more, but he gave it a try. 'Just leave him,' he said humouring Sally, hoping to defuse the situation.

'No Da, he knows better', she was adamant.

'I'm not taking them off. My hands are cold,' his stubbornness was rearing its head.

'I'll tell Matron,' she threatened. 'Everyone's looking at us Hugh.' Sally glanced embarrassingly at the tables on both sides of them and all eyes were on them.

'Well, *so*. It's *you*. Eat your fish and leave me alone,' Hugh replied.

'Will you give ower you two,' Tom pleaded.

'See you Hugh, you embarrass me no matter where we go. I hope you're happy, you've spoilt my day.'

'Sally, please eat your fish and forget about Hugh's gloves.' Tom gave her arm a gentle squeeze.

Sally said no more and watched while her brother ate and drank with his gloves on.

It should have been a joy going to the tearoom but it turned out to be awful for Sally. Her father said she took everything too seriously. That was funny for him to say when she was given the weight of the world to carry on her very young shoulders.

When they returned to Olive Bank, Matron showed Mr Baxter around the home. She also had a cup of tea with him before she took Hugh and Sally to the station to say their goodbyes.

It was awful; Sally cuddled into her father for the very first time in her life, feeling a great outpouring of love for him. Hugh said cheerio easily, but Sally's heart was broken. She did not want to leave the home but wished her dad could have stayed with her.

Her father's visit put her back a bit as she became withdrawn and remote. It was evident that she was suffering from homesickness and as Matron was worried about her health, she advised against further visits.

With help from Rita, Matron gradually restored Sally back to her usual happy self.

Chapter Seven

This was to be Sally and Hugh's last summer at Olive Bank. If all went well, they would be going home at the end of August.

Matron knew that it was not going to be easy for Sally as she had become used to life at Olive Bank and soon she was to return to the life she had so despised. She could only hope that the education and love she had received would help her through the labyrinth of life. Hugh was different, he was his own person and nobody could ever change him.

Sally had grown taller and was not the frail slip of a girl she had been when she first came to Olive Bank. There was now meat on her once scrawny bones and her fuller cheeks looked glowing with health. The dramatic change in the girl had altered her facial appearance greatly and it was evident that she was turning into a beautiful, intelligent young lady.

Matron was aware of the void Sally's leaving would create as she was loved by the staff and most of the children but her concern was for Rita who would be totally lost once Sally left. There was a younger girl in the room along the corridor from Sally and Rita who's name was Susan. She had come in from a broken home where neither of her parents was able to take care of her. She was a pretty child with dark curly hair and a chubby little face, but her pale blue eyes were filled with sadness. She reminded Matron of Rita when she first came to her, quiet, frightened and very disillusioned.

Matron encouraged the girls to befriend Susan, and very slowly they managed to gain the frightened girls trust. Her plan had started to take shape. She hoped when Sally left, Rita would feel responsible for Susan just as Sally had done with her. Thanks to Sally, Rita now knew what real friendship meant, and was capable of extending that friendship to others without fear of being exploited. Rita would be at Olive Bank until the age of sixteen but Matron hoped she would stay on, as she had began to look on her as her own.

The three girls sat by the edge of the slow flowing stream dangling their feet in the cool water. Rita threw a pebble into the stream making a gentle plop, followed by continued rings.

'Five weeks, Oh Sally what are we going to do without you?' Rita was asking with slight panic in her voice.

'Do you have to go?' asked Susan.

'Yes,' Sally answered her. 'I'm afraid so. I'll never forget you all though and I'll come back and see you.'

'Promise?' Susan said.

'I promise. Do you really think I would just go and forget you all? I could never do that. You are my family. I don't know what will happen when I go home. Matron has been told my mother has a new address.'

'Maybe you'll like your new house,' Rita added.

'Rita, it'll not make any difference where my family live, it won't be like here,' Sally answered sadly.

'If you robbed a bank you would be sent back,' Susan said, quite pleased that she had come up with an idea.

'Silly,' Rita scolded her, 'she would be put in jail for that.'

Maybe that would be better than living with that lot,' Sally answered dejectedly.

She looked at both girls and they laughed. They lay back looking up at the bright blue sky. Not a cloud was in sight. Birds were chirping happily in the trees and the smell of clean country air filled the girls' nostrils. The sun warmed their skins and the crystal clear water from the stream cooled their feet.

Sally would miss this all right, and leaving Rita was going to be a terrible wrench.

'Come on you two,' Sally said jumping up suddenly, 'Cook's taking us into town shortly so we had better get moving.' Drying her feet on a piece of old towel they had been given for that purpose, she looked over at the younger girl. 'Hurry up Susan, where's your socks?'

'She's lying on them,' answered Rita pushing Susan over on her side and pulling her socks free.

'Give them here,' Sally said as she grabbed the socks and helped Susan pull them on her small damp feet. Quickly she pulled on her plimsolls and when they were ready they went arm and arm towards the house.

Somehow Matron arranged that Susan and Rita were not taken out for the annual two weeks holiday. Visits to

Glasgow Zoo and Edinburgh Castle were arranged for the children who remained at the house. A few picnics and a trip to the seaside were also included. It had been a grand summer, one that the girls would remember forever.

When the time came to leave, Sally reluctantly packed her small case. Rita sat on the side of her bed watching quietly. She had no laughter in her heart moreover her eyes were red from crying.

Going over to the small hand basin in the corner of the room, Sally took down her tumbler and removed her toothbrush. She then carefully folded her face cloth and put them both into her sponge bag.

Few words were spoken. They said hardly a word to each other all morning.

One of the Aunties came into the room and looking at them both, knew the pain they felt. Standing for a moment or two, she gave a sigh and walked towards the case on the bed.

'Everything in pet?' she asked Sally.

'Nearly.' Her answer was low and quiet.

'Oh come on now, you're not going to the end of the earth you know. You can always write to each other.'

'It's not fair,' Rita ran to the bemused woman and put her arms around her waist. 'It's not right that Sally has to go.' Rita's face creased with pain as the hot tears flowed freely from her red swollen eyes once more.

Sally fell onto the bed and she too started to cry. Auntie led Rita over to the bed and sat down with one child in each arm. Her own heart swelled with sadness as she fought back her own tears. She could not let the children see she too felt sad. 'All right, all right, that's enough now. Stop this nonsense. Come on Sally, and you too Rita, you're both too big to cry.' she said.

Doing as they were told, they washed their faces, regained some composure then threw their arms around each other in a warm embrace, their bodies still heaving heavily in unison.

Auntie lifted the small brown cardboard case and the children followed her out reluctantly, dragging their feet. Looking back into their bedroom for one last time, Sally felt a terrible sense of loss.

Hugh was already in the sitting room waiting. He was repeatedly dropping and sharply pulling on his yoyo looking not the least bit upset at leaving Olive Bank. Sally never could understand Hugh. Here he was cleaner, healthier and older and yet he remained unperturbed.

'Ready sis,' he snorted, quickly pulling the yo- yo up and depositing it into his pocket.

'Yes,' she replied wearily, sitting down heavily on a near by stool.

Matron came into the room and walked over to where Sally now sat. Looking down at the forlorn child she said gently. 'Sally, you are taking away more than you came with and I don't mean personal things, I mean in here,' she pointed to her head. 'You know what I mean?'

Sally nodded.

'Never forget what you have been taught. Sally, you are a wise and thoughtful girl and we are going to miss you. You'll never know what you have done for Rita. Don't let anyone or anything change you. Use the education you have gained and add to it in your next school. Try and keep at your piano lessons'

Sally looked at her from the corner of her eyes.

'Yes I know that's going to be difficult,' she knew what Sally's look meant.

' The new school you'll be going to may teach music Sally. Ask. Now your father is in the small sitting room waiting for you both and the taxi is waiting at the door. We have to go now.'

She bent down to Hugh who was sitting on his case. 'Well young man, no more running away all right? You get stuck in at school and make something of your life.' She knew within herself she was wasting her breath. 'You will be going over the Forth Bridge by train Hugh, you'll like that.'

'Aye,' Hugh replied nonchalantly, 'so I will.'

Matron held out her hand and Hugh shook it. She turned once more to Sally and gave her a short tight hug.

'Go now, say goodbye to the rest quickly as your father will be becoming impatient.'

The taxi drove away from Olive Bank. Sally and Hugh watched the small group at the door from the back window of the cab. Hugh waved vigorously while Sally just watched until they were out of sight. Her heart ached but she would not let Hugh or her father see her cry.

Although Tom laughed and joked with Sally he could not get her to cheer up. He tried telling her about their new house, but she was not the least bit interested. She felt she would never be happy again.

The bus stopped and Tom Baxter stepped onto the pavement carrying a suitcase in each hand. Sally and Hugh followed on each carrying a small brown paper parcel. As the bus moved off, Sally stood on the pavement looking around at her new surroundings. She was in a different part of town and although the area had once been familiar to her, it now looked strange. The last time she was here the houses were old, now she was looking at a row of new buildings. They consisted of three blocks, all of which had four houses, two upstairs and two down. Access to each house was gained by entering the passageway in the middle of each building. That passage led through and out to the drying greens at the back of the houses.

Tom Baxter looked down at the children and indicated to the house directly in front. 'There's the new house. What do you think then eh?'

Clutching her parcel tightly into her chest, she felt none of her father's enthusiasm. She felt lonely and forlorn but there was no turning back.

Hugh began to tug excitedly at her arm.

Getting no reply Tom continued, 'Wait till you see it. Take his hand Sally. It's the bottom house.'

They entered the gate and went up the path and into the close.

Nellie was sitting in the armchair beside the well banked up fire with her contented baby on the rug at her feet. She had been doing the crossword that appeared in the Daily Record. Bess was up at the table reading a comic that was spread out in front of her when the three travellers walked in.

Looking up Nellie smiled weakly as she folded her paper. She sat back in the chair dispassionately, showing no sign of excitement as if they had been away for a few hours instead of three years.

'There you are then.' She looked them over as they stood in the doorway. 'Well now, you have put on some weight girl,' she said to Sally, 'and you've fairly grown, and you an' aw Hugh. Well, well!' Looking now at Tom she said abruptly, 'S'pose you'll want fed.'

Disappointment surged through Sally's heart as she felt like an unwelcome visitor. She had hoped for a warmer welcome, as her mother had not seen her for years. 'Don't bother with lunch for me,' Sally looked directly into her mothers cold eyes, 'I'm not hungry.'

'Lunch now is it, lunch? Did you hear that Bess, Sally doesn't want lunch?' Bess had her elbows on the table with her hands supporting her head grinning at her mother.

'And what about you Hugh? Do you want lunch?' her voice mocked Sally's.

'Yes ma, I'll take something to eat.' Hugh on impulse, hurried towards his mother throwing his arms around her neck almost choking the bewildered woman. 'I'm glad to be back home.'

Nellie's back stiffened as she half-heartedly patted her son's back before drawing him from her as if he had just burned her neck. 'Well that's fine,' she said awkwardly adjusting her buttoned up cardigan. She had never been the kind of parent to express her feelings physically or verbally as she had none towards her children as her selfishness never allowed them into her heart.

Tom bent down to Sally and whispered, 'Come, I'll help ye through wi' yer case.' He led Sally through to the end of the hall and opening the door he ushered her in. 'You'll be sharin' wi' Bess,' he said, his expression was one of silent apology as he looked into Sally's anxious eyes. Then his tone changed to one of false enthusiasm, 'It's quite a wee room but a suppose ye've been used tae sharin'. The bathroom's next-door. Yer mother his emptied the top two drawers o' the tallboy for ye. She gave Bess the bottom yins, as she's the wee-est.'

Silently Sally looked around, disappointment etched on her face.

'I'll leave yi tae take yer coat off and come through when you're ready.' He made to go but hesitated. 'It will be awe right Sally... gie it time.'

As he left Sally on her own he was gripped with terrible weariness. He felt so inadequate and ashamed seeing his daughter so terribly unhappy. He was to blame for everything that had happened and he could not put it right.

As she looked around the room, the awful sinking feeling in her chest began to drag her down. She had been here before as the once familiar smells filled her nostrils. 'She hasn't changed one bit,' Sally thought. Looking at the double bed she knew she was back at square one. 'At least it's a double,' she thought. The last time she shared with Bess it was only a single mattress on the floor, forcing them to sleep close to one and other; now at least she could distance herself by keeping to her own side of the bed.

The walls of the room were painted yellow reminding Sally of thick lumpy custard. At the window dark miserable looking curtains floated like magic as the wind blew in the open window. Bare floorboards were covered in part with small threadbare rugs and in the corner of the room a pile of dirty clothes lay. Wrapping paper from devoured chocolate biscuits, dirty cups and chewing gum wrappers were strewn across the floor but it was not the bareness of the room or the untidy mess that Bess had created that sickened her; it was the old familiar smell. Bess still wet the bed.

Sally emptied her case and put her clothes away tidily in the drawers she was given. Her two pairs of shoes were put with her slippers under the dresser. Personal things were left in her suitcase and stored under the bed. She straightened her back and took a deep breath, the way they did in the home when they had to face Matron.

The kitchen, like the old house led through from the living room but both areas were much bigger.

Sally once more stood awkwardly at the living room door.

'Come on in,' Tom said. ' Sit doon Sally. What's up wi' ye lass? Ye're hame.'

Sitting down on the sofa, she rubbed her hand along the edge of the cushion feeling the thick woolly edging. It was a vast difference to the previous sofa that was so badly torn items such as old vinyl records; newspapers and various bits and pieces were stored in the arms. Bess suddenly threw herself heavily down beside her.

'See,' said Bess pointing to the corner. 'We've got a T.V. Bet you didn't have one at that place you were at.'

'We did so!' the voice said from the kitchen. Hugh came darting into the living room and faced Bess. 'We had a T.V. a long time before you,' he chanted.

'No you never,' Bess hissed at him.

'Right, get it stopped right now!' demanded Nellie popping her head into the living room her thin lips drawn tight. 'And what are you laughing at Tom Baxter?' she questioned.

'Nothing,' Tom replied trying to still his laughter. 'I was just thinking it's starting again. Welcome home Hugh.' Tom laughed nodding at his young son.

Sally was the only one who failed to see the funny side as she hated being home and right now she hated them all.

Three weeks she had been home but it felt like a lifetime since she left Olive Bank. It did not take Nellie long to get her eldest daughter back into shape as the regular baby sitter, cook and dishwasher. The washing of the clothes was made easier now, as they had acquired a second hand washing machine. It had to be filled from a hose that attached to the tap and it was emptied the same way. The machine was filled with hot water and to get it to boiling point an element attached to the end of a cable was dropped into the machine the other end plugged into the electric socket. It was a dangerous combination-water and electricity- but that was the way it was done.

Although Bess was now eight (the same age as Sally had been when she was sent to Olive Bank) she was no help at all as she was as lazy as ever, and Nellie still let her off with things. Hugh was never in. He had become involved with a wild crowd. When he did happen to be at home, he and Bess argued non-stop.

Sally was given more and more to do with Lucy and she resented her mother for this, but never once did she resent the baby. She was now two and a half years old and was a bonny looking child with a very sweet nature.

'Now Sally, remember what I said. Put the bairn doon about eight o'clock. If she greets, change her an' gie her a drink. Hugh an' Bess can stay up till ten. We will be hame around eleven. Try an' get the dishes done an' dinnae answer the door.'

Leaving Sally with those instructions, Nellie and Tom made their way to the local Social Club where they were both members. Once inside, they went their different ways as Nellie had her own female friends who preferred sitting in the main hall where the dancing and entertainment took place.

Tom however, spent his evenings in the public bar beside his mates from the factory where he now worked. As he worked from two until ten each night, drinking during the week was now out of the question, but he made up for it on weekends. Both he and Nellie were habitual drinkers and valued members of the club.

Nellie however split her evenings between the club and the Gothenburg Tavern where she sat among the men drinking drink for drink. It was at that time considered a 'mans' pub where bad language and rude talk was the norm. Her nights out were now made easy, as Sally was there to take care of the children. She never once stopped to think how her daughter felt about the responsibility put on her young shoulders.

Nellie had become more cautious around her husband, especially when he had been drinking heavily as he had become more assertive. His new found courage had led him into assaulting her on a couple of occasions, something he had never done before. He seemed to have developed a split personality, but the aggression only appeared when he had been drinking heavily, a stark contrast from his easygoing nature when sober.

The first assault on Nellie happened a few months after the children were taken into care. He became riddled with guilt and blamed himself for his inadequacy. Finding solace in the bottle he begun drinking heavily, aggression quickly substituting his placid temperament. It was then Nellie had taunted him about being useless and gutless and had laid the blame on him for the children's misfortune. Tom struck out slapping her once across her sneering mouth drawing blood from her bottom lip. Nellie stood with her hand over her bleeding mouth almost in awe of the worm that had finally turned.

The second assault happened the day after his visit to Olive Bank. He had been haunted all night by his guilty conscious drowning his sorrows until he became inebriated, now the simplest way of coping. Both times had filled him with enough courage to hit out at Nellie. She was now very careful how she spoke to Sally when Tom was around.

At the club, Nellie's arms were wrapped tightly around the neck of a stocky red headed man as they danced around the floor to the slow dreamy music that came from the resident band. Although the man was a stranger to the club they were laughing and joking together as if they knew each other well. As the music stopped they remained absorbed in conversation, the stranger still gripping Nellie firmly round her waist. His grip eventually slackened allowing Nellie to straighten her skirt before walking away. Haughtily she pulled back her shoulders, stuck out her chest, her breasts almost bursting out from her low cut top and grinned all the way back to her table.

Flo Begbie had watched her pal cross the floor looking pleased with her conquest. As she came nearer to Flo she winked, a look of self-satisfaction spread across her face as she laughed.

'Well! Well! Come on, who is he?' Flo asked impatiently.

'How should a ken?' Nellie tossed her head to the side while sniffing indignantly.

'Come oan Nellie, you tell me or I'll, I'll oh, come oan.' Flo leaned against Nellie giving her a prod on the arm.

Nellie checked for eavesdroppers by scanning the nearby tables before whispering to her friend. 'His name is Jack Brown an' he bides in a caravan. He's workin' at the power station.'

'He's bidin' at Bruces Camps?' Flo asked curiously.

'A never asked him were his van wis.'

'It's no' like you.'

'A'll tell you nae mare you cheekie bugger.'

'Go on,' said Flo eagerly, giving her friend a nudge.

'Well, dinnae say oanythin' but he's asked tae see me,' Nellie grinned.

'He's asked yi oot?'

Nellie nodded while grinning from ear to ear.

'And are you gaun?' asked Flo, her jaw dropping in amazement.

Looking down at the table, Nellie pointed to the glass of vodka that sat in front of her. 'Is that mine?' she asked.

'Aye. A got them in,' Flo answered impatience apparent in her tone.

Lifting the glass Nellie took a few sips and settled back in her seat aware of Flo's impatience.

'Well! Are you gaun. God this is like drawin' bloody teeth.'

Still holding her glass she looked seriously into Flo's eyes. 'Now dinnae you say onythin' Flo for if it gets back tae 'you know who,' there'll be hell tae pay.'

'Of course I'll no clype. For fizz sake Nell you ken me better than that,' Flo said quite indignantly.

'I'm seeing him oan Friday. He's coming roond.'

'That's risky is it no?' Flo asked, her eyes nearly popping from their sockets.

'Naw, Tom works till ten oan Fridays. The kids can get a treat, pictures or somethin'. As long as a watch the time.'

Nellie had it all neatly planned. Who was to know? Flo? Nellie knew enough about her to keep her quiet.

They left for home at ten thirty. Tom hadn't had too much to drink and Nellie was in high spirits. It had been a grand night and the both of them were in a good mood.

The house was in darkness when they reached home as Sally had the children bedded and fast asleep. Although she too lay in bed, sleep was hard to achieve, as her mind could not be still. As she lay among the shadows in the room, her mind was filled with thoughts and plans. She hated this house and she hated her mother. She listened as the door opened and heard her mother and father fall against the wall laughing and whispering loudly before finding the light switch on the lobby wall. Closing her eyes tightly she tried hard to fall over, as it would be nothing for Nellie to haul her out of bed to make them some supper.

The school Sally went to was about a mile from her home so when it was fair weather she walked to school as her mother would not give her the money for the bus. She liked school very much and in no time at all, she had found a new friend. She was called Anna and was the same age as herself. Occasionally Sally would go home with Anna at lunchtime instead of going to the dinner hall. Her mother was a lovely sweet woman who was always interested in what the girls had to say. She treated Sally with kindness and approved of her friendship with her daughter.

Anna's mother knew all about Sally being in a children's home and it puzzled her as to why such a well mannered child should have been sent there. She did not know the full story and did not want to pry but she knew whatever the reason, Sally was not to blame. She was also aware of the work Sally had to do at home because Anna had told her. Sally had been invited round many times for tea but had to refuse as she had the chores to do when she arrived home and weekends were impossible as she had to help her mother with the children.

Sally's schoolwork however was satisfactory and she never missed a lesson. There was nothing to disrupt her studies now as she was at High School and well away from Hugh and Bess. She felt free and safe at school.

She also took the Matron's advice and approached the music teacher. He was delighted that Sally could play the piano so well and said it would be a pleasure tutoring her.

Anna's mother gave her the use of their piano when she managed to go around at lunch times. Her own parents knew nothing of her musical ability and she had no intention of telling them, knowing that her mother would once again use this to taunt and tease her before putting a stop to 'this nonsense'.

Arriving home from school, her mother handed her a vanilla envelope and stood back and watched with folded arms as Sally studied the handwriting. The excitement engulfed her as she recognised Matron's stationery. Smiling broadly she turned the envelope round intending to tear it open, but noticing it had already been opened she felt an inward rage. She looked coldly into her mother's smug face and would gladly have slapped her. Her private mail was always opened by Nellie.

She took out the letter and sat down at the table and read it. Matron relayed the news from Olive Bank and let her know that everyone was well. She hoped Sally was happy and settled. She had enclosed a postal order for the sum of twenty-six pounds that had been the remainder of her savings. Advising her to spend the money wisely or perhaps start a bank account, she closed with good wishes.

Sally read the letter, folded it neatly and put it back into the envelope.

Looking over at her mother, who was now attending to the baby, Sally asked sharply, 'Where is it? Where is my money?'

Anger shrouded Nellie's face as she peered at her daughter through narrow slits making her face look extremely ugly. '*Your* money! *You*r money! Let me tell you, it's *mine*. A hiv tae feed an' cleid yi.'

Looking directly into her mother's eyes, she retaliated by yelling, 'Clothe me, my clothes came from the home. Nothing I have came from you.'

Nellie rose sharply, placed the bemused child on its feet then flew at Sally. Swinging her fist at Sally's head, the single blow knocked her off the chair and on to the floor. She got onto her feet instantly and ran out the door towards the bathroom where she locked herself in.

Running along the lobby after her distraught daughter, the door was slammed on her face. Nellie screamed at her through the bathroom door. 'Come oot o' there my lass, right now! Come oot, ye little upstart that ye are. Claes? That's anither thing, you're a selfish wee brat. Bess could be daein' wi' half that stuff, an' by God you'll share in future. You come oot noo Sally or you take what you get when ye dae. I'll bloody well swing fir you.'

Sally did pay for it as Nellie beat her relentlessly, taking care not to leave traces on the parts of the body that could be easily seen. She swung her against the wall and punched her repeatedly.

Friday morning arrived and Sally dragged her bruised and battered body out of bed. Her head ached and her eyes felt hot and gritty. She had suppressed her sobs all night, as Bess would have taken great joy from her unhappiness but her body had heaved heavily under the covers until she had finally found sleep.

Entering the living room, her dad was helping Hugh put on his shoes as his mother was never up in the mornings. She always stayed in bed until the children had gone to school. Lucy was usually washed and dressed by Tom before his wife rose from her bed.

Seeing his daughter's forlorn expression, Tom asked, 'Whit's wrong wi' you this mornin', you look half slept?'

'Nothing Dad. Bess has been kicking all night and has hurt my back,' she lied.

'We'll hae tae try an get-single beds.' Tom said sympathetically.

On impulse Sally put her hand into her skirt pocket, drawing out the letter from Matron. She held it out towards her father.

'What's this?' he asked smiling.

'A letter from Matron,' she said, pushing it forward into his hand.

Reluctantly Tom took the letter and looked it over as if studying the contents. 'Oh very nice,' he said, handing it back to Sally. 'Very nice.'

Sally watched in amazement. 'He never mentioned the money. Why?' she thought.

This puzzled her all day. 'Why had he made no commented, unless her mother had warned him not to. No, she wouldn't have said anything to him. She was almost sure of that. He would never have let her mother keep all that money!'

She discussed her father's attitude towards the letter with Anna, who, after some deep thinking, came up with her conclusion. 'Sally, I've got it, maybe your father can't read. Maybe he was pretending to read it.'

'Oh no Anna,' she was horrified at the very idea.

Seeing her friend recoil, Anna quickly apologised. 'I was trying to figure it out Sal, sorry I didn't mean anything by that.'

Giving a slow sigh Sally faced that possibility. 'That's ok. I'm sorry too. Maybe you're right Anna. Maybe he can't read. When I come to think of it, he never buys newspapers. If there's any bought, it's her that buys them and reads them.' They both had their heads together trying to solve the mystery.

'Does he fill out forms or write letters?' asked Anna.

'No, he never wrote to me when I was in the home.' Pondering for a moment she added, ' Come to think of it, when Matron gave him things to sign, he asked to speak to her in private.'

'That's it then, your Dad can not read,' Anna said sympathetically.

Realising her friend was right; she said sadly, 'I'll never tell him I know as I think he would be terribly embarrassed.'

Sally dreaded going home that afternoon as she feared a repetition from her mother, and as usual, her father would not be around to prevent it.

When she entered the house, the strong fragrance of lilac filled her nostrils. Furniture polish was very seldom used, as there was very little furniture to polish, but what they did have was polished to perfection. The fireplace was gleaming and a lovely fire burned brightly in the grate. Mesmerized, she stood gaping, as there wasn't a thing out of place.

Nellie came through from the kitchen singing. On seeing her daughter she greeted her cheerfully. 'Oh, it's you Sally hen. I've made a nice tea tonight an' you're all havin' it early, because...' she started putting the plates down on the table, 'because you're goin' tae the pictures tae night. My treat. There's a good yin at the Regal. It's a comedy an' Jerry Lewis is in it. You like him, don't yi? Nellie smiled, her eyes twinkling as they creased at each end.

As she looked into Nellie's face, she momentarily saw her mother look younger. She was almost beautiful when she smiled and she noticed her hair was expertly waved.

'I don't really want to go out ma. I'm not feeling well. Besides, *you* go out tonight.' Sally was trying to figure her mother out. She was up to something; but what?

Noticing her look of apprehension, Nellie gently laid a hand on her daughter's head. 'Look Sal, I'm sorry. Me an' my temper,' she spoke softly as she stroked Sally's hair. This unusual act made Sally feel uneasy. Her young body tensed as a sickly feeling gripped the pit of her stomach. Her mother's show of tenderness just did not feel right. She had always longed to be touched with affection by her mother but that was now in the past. She had realised a long time ago that Nellie was incapable of loving her.

'I was way, way out o' order,' she continued, her head cocked to one side studying her daughter's face. 'I'll give ye a bit extra fer yoursel', but dinnae let oan tae the others. OK?' Her expression now looked longingly at Sally as if they were partners in crime.

'Come oan, sit doon at the table an'a'll gie the ither two a shout. They're in the room playin' wi' Lego oot o' Lucy's way, as she puts every mortal thing in that mooth o' hers. I'm staying in the nicht wi Lucy tae let you oot fer a change. Besides, Flo will be roond, so get a move oan, eat yer meal an' get ready.'

Nellie stood at the window and watched her three children cross the road, then she hurriedly took the dishes into the kitchen and started to wash up. She still had the baby to get ready as Flo was picking the child up and minding her for a few hours. If she was in her night things she could be put straight to bed when she was brought back.

Flo arrived shortly and collected Lucy as arranged. 'How will a ken he's gone?' she asked.

'I'll put the corner o' the dish towel oot the front windae when he goes.' She giggled like an excited teenager on her first date.

'Oh Nellie! A tell ye, ye're takin' a big chance.' Biting her bottom lip, Flo was now regretting her part in Nellie's scheme, as she knew there would be hell to pay if Tom Baxter found out.

'Life is yin big chance Flo an' am takin' my chances when a get them. This is really excitin' a tell ye.' Nellie clicked her tongue on the roof of her mouth and winked.

With the house to herself, Nellie hurriedly slipped into the new dress she bought with Sally's money. She had it hidden away in case Tom or Sally saw it.

Sitting on the sofa, make-up on, hair done, she waited. Thinking he wasn't going to show, she began to feel foolish and greatly disappointed. At that moment the faint knock upon the door caused her to jump, her heart rate increasing as a great surge of adrenaline rushed through her veins like steam from a boiling kettle. Going swiftly to the mirror that hung above the fireplace, she stared briefly at her reflection patting her hair gently. Her lips shaped into a perfect o as she inspected the red lipstick that was plastered on her mouth. Only then did she feel a slight panic in her breast. What if she was caught? Tom Baxter would kill her for sure. 'What the hell,' she whispered inwardly. As she opened the door he nodded as if to say, 'Is it all right to come in?'

Nellie stood back and ushered him in before her neighbours came out into the stairway.

Sitting down, Nellie offered him a whisky.

'I didn't think you'd come,' she said.

Looking around his surroundings and not directly at Nellie, he answered abruptly, 'I said I would.'

'Well, so you have,' she said sarcastically eyeing him

from head to toe. He looked as if no effort had been made to tidy him-self up. As he had taken the glass from her she noticed his hands and nails were anything but clean

They chatted for some time and had a few more drinks.

He asked if she usually stayed in most Fridays and she told him she normally went to the club with Flo.

Then he asked about her family and if Tom worked till ten every Friday.

'What's all this, twenty questions?' Nellie asked.

He said he was just taking an interest. There followed an awkward silence then, suddenly, he grabbed her and started kissing her hard, so hard that Nellie's mouth hurt. Pushing on his chest she managed to break her mouth from his but she was unable to break his hold. With no time to protest he grabbed at her hair pulling her head backwards before kissing her forcefully once more. As her teeth burst through her lips, she felt hot pain as the sweet sticky taste of blood pushed into her mouth. She struggled in vain against his lustful embrace. His deep irregular breathing unhinged Nellie as her fist thrashed about wildly trying desperately to land a punch at her molester, but his free hand managed to hold her down firmly. Pushing her flat onto her back, he quickly pressed his hand over her mouth to stifle any squeals or protests. Forcing his self on her gave him greater sexual pleasure as the more Nellie struggled, the more his excitement increased. The ripping sound as he tore at her dress alerted her of her imminent fate. As he lay heavily down on top of her, she managed to sink her teeth into the side of his hand. As he felt his flesh puncture he cursed aloud while giving her such a punch she thought her teeth had been knocked out as her head jerked backwards. Terrified that she was about to be murdered she lay still hardly daring to sob. He molested her in such a violent way she wished she could pass out.

After he had finished with her, he calmly drained his glass of whiskey as if nothing had happened.

Nellie rose up slowly from the sofa and in a half sitting position, she spoke through bruised and swollen lips. 'Get out, get out you dirty bastard. Get out before I call the cops.'

He looked down at the pathetic woman and smirked. 'Really Mrs Baxter, and what would Mr Baxter say about that? His wife the whore!' He laughed loudly and left, closing the door gently behind him.

As Sally had felt awful sick she left the others in the cinema enjoying the film. She just had to get home. Her head throbbed so much her vision became impaired. Nausea and the feeling of weakness overcame her.

Arriving home, she was about to go through the gate when a strange man came out from the close. Looking at Sally he smiled and said 'good evening.' Without answering, she carried on up the path and into the house.

As Nellie was already in the toilet vomiting she did not hear Sally come in. Expecting her mother to be in the sitting room with her friend Flo, Sally was surprised when seeing the room empty. ' Ma! Ma! Where are you?'

she called. Getting no answer she called again. Making her way along the corridor to the baby's room, she heard her mother retching.

Standing at the toilet door she called, 'Are you all right ma?' The long silence that followed made her feel concerned, so she hammered on the door and called yet again.

'I'm all right,' Nellie finally replied. 'Go and put the kettle on, I'll be through shortly,' she spoke urgently.

When Nellie was sure her daughter had gone, she hurriedly opened the door and sneaked into her own room. Brushing passed the wardrobe; she caught a glimpse of her own reflection in the mirror. She stopped and stared at her image. Gasping in horror, she touched the side of her face with caution. It looked like it felt, swollen and bruised. Her lips had already turned purple, the skin taut over the bruised blood. The front of her dress had been completely torn apart. Moving away from the mirror, she very quickly changed in to the clothes she had worn earlier, and, bundling up the torn dress, she hid it under blankets that lay folded at the bottom of the cupboard. Tidying up her hair, she went into the kitchen to face her daughter.

'What are you doing home so early?' She spoke with difficulty.

Sally turned around, and seeing her mother's injuries, stared open mouthed. Walking slowly towards Nellie, she raised her hand intending to touch her mother's face, but Nellie drew back quickly. 'Ma what's up? Did Dad do that?'

'No he's still at work. A fell an' hit ma face oan the...
the table. Ye, a tripped over the threadbare patch oan the
carpet and hit ma face. A had...had that silly wee light oan.'
She flicked the back of her hand towards the small table
lamp that sat in the alcove beside the fireplace. 'What
are you daein' here onyway?' Nellie turned the questions
away from her to Sally.

Without taking her eyes from her mother's injured
face she answered. 'I wasn't feeling well so I came home.
Bess and Hugh are coming straight home after the film
ends.' Sally questioned her mother once more. 'Where's
the bairn?'

She took a minute to think before answering. 'Flo was
here when a fell so she took the bairn hame for a while
till a recovered.' Turning away from Sally she took her
coat down from the hook on the door before stammering,
'Eh! I'll get some fresh air noo. A feel the need o' fresh
air.' She had to get out and meet Flo as her story had to
be corroborated. If Flo came in now she would give the
game away for sure. One look at Nellie's face and Flo's
expression would speak volumes.

'But I made tea. I thought you wanted tea?' Sally asked
still bemused.

'I'll get a cup when I get back. You have some Sally; it'll
do you good. You look as white as a sheet right enough.'

Sally was left standing in the middle of the living room, the
fire still glowing casting long shadows flickering on to the
wall like a projectionist's broken film. She looked down
at the worn carpet and then at the table. Shrugging her
shoulders, she turned and walked back into the kitchen.

When Tom arrived home from work, Flo verified Nellie's story although she was annoyed at herself for becoming involved. Both women saw the funny side of the situation when Tom suggested she bought herself a new carpet.

The following Friday Nellie left for the club, leaving Sally in charge of Bess, Hugh and Lucy as usual. Sally had protested as she wanted to go to her friend's, but Nellie put her foot down.

'You'll dae as you're telt young lady. You were oot last Friday an' what did you dae? Came hame early. I have to go; your Da'll be in after ten. Watch the T.V. with Bess and don't go out. If Flo comes, tell her I'll meet her over at the club. All right?'

Flo did call just after her mother left.

'She's just gone Flo,' Sally informed her.

'A didnae think she would hiv gone oot wi' her face lookin' like a well skelped erse,' Flo remarked.

'You know what she's like. She doesn't care about anything or anybody as long as she gets out. It's not fair. I never see my friends for watching the bairns. I hate her sometimes. I really hate her.'

Flo was astonished at Sally's outburst. She had never spoken out like that before, at least not to her. She was really rather shocked at Sally's anger.

Later that evening when Bess and Hugh were watching T.V. Sally took the baby through to give her a bath. She was down on her knees leaning over Lucy who splashed happily in the water, when she felt the hot tears flowing down her cheeks. She began to sob uncontrollably, and, burying her head into her folded arms, she leaned on the edge of the bath. Her whole body shook in uncontrollable spasms. The baby tried to lift Sally's head up and when she couldn't, she threw her wet chubby arms round Sally's head.

'No cry Sassie. No cry Sassie,' the baby said worriedly.

Sally looked into the infant's enquiring face and watched as her tiny lips began to quiver. Aware that she was upsetting the child, Sally smiled through her tear stained face, and still quietly sobbing, she lifted the baby out of the water and hugged her wet body into hers.

Tom Baxter came home from work that night, and as usual, Sally had supper ready for him. The other children had been fed and the baby was now asleep in her cot. Hugh and Bess were ordered to go to bed, and Bess, as usual, defied Sally. Tom gave a roar sending them both scurrying off.

Sally was sitting on the chair trying to let the hem of her skirt down while Tom had gone into the kitchen to wash the supper dishes. He often did this to help Sally when the others were out of sight.

The door of the living room flew open and Nellie stormed in. She made a direct line towards her daughter and immediately began to slap her hard about the head and face. The skirt Sally had been sewing was thrown across the room as she tried to protect her head from her mother's blows.

On hearing Sally's screams Tom ran through from the kitchen then witnessing his wife's violent behaviour he immediately sprang to his daughters defence. Pulling at his wife, he too joined in the fracas.

'You spout your mouth off to Flo would you? You ungrateful little weed,' Nellie yelled, her breath reeking of alcohol as she had been drinking heavily.

Again Sally covered her head and face with her arms as her mother started to hit out once more.

Tom grabbed his wife by the collar and pulled her once more away from Sally. He threw Nellie across the floor and she landed on all fours. He then picked her up and slapped her hard across the face. Shaking her violently, he spat out his words. 'If a ever catch you liftin' yer hands tae that lassie again Nellie Baxter, so help me God, a'll kill ye. You hiv a great need tae try it wi' oor Bess, as she's a liar an' a bloody thief, but dinnae you touch her again.' He pointed over to where Sally was sobbing for the second time that evening. 'A hope a hiv made ma sel' clear?' He snorted as he growled. '*Do you understand?*'

Nellie jumped before cringing. 'Aye right. *Right!* A jist lost the heid.'

'Well that's an *end* tae it. A should hiv prevented this long since, but it stoaps here noo! You'll no' lift an ither hand tae her again as long as a live. This worm has turned.'

That night, sleep was a long time coming to Sally as her aching bones and blinding headache ravished her young body. Turning left then right or lying flat, she found no ease. Her mind was too active to switch off, as the horror of that nights occurrence repeated in her mind like a record that had become stuck in a groove. She could take no more. Life was so unfair. She had to get away. She didn't know how or where to go, but she knew she would have to distance herself from her violent mother.

Bess lay asleep in the bed next to Sally, and although she was now in a bed by herself, she could still smell her sister's dirty wet mattress, also, as Bess seldom washed properly, the foul smell of body odour added to the stench in the room. Yes, she had to think about escaping. 'Oh, if only her Dad would leave and take her with him. Oh and the baby too.' She had grown to love the baby.

Flo called in as she usually did on Saturday afternoon, and was astounded when Nellie told her what Tom had done. She was flabbergasted, as she knew he was not a man given to violence, but the proof was staring her in the face. She felt she was to blame, not only for her friends injuries, but for Sally's beating as well. She meant no harm to the lass; in fact, she was rather fond of her and couldn't understand Nellie's resentment towards her. She only mentioned Sally's temper tantrum because she was so surprised.

As Nellie did not want to go out that evening, Flo's attempt at persuading her failed, as she was adamant about staying in doors. She said she was feeling poorly, but the truth was, she did not want any one to know Tom Baxter had finally retaliated. He had done so before but this time was different. He had become the strong-minded man she once longed for instead of the easygoing coward that she perceived him to be: besides, people would not believe she had fallen yet again.

As a result of this, Sally was able to visit her friend. She had tea with Anna and her parents, and Anna's aunt Ruby and uncle Jimmy joined them. Having no children of their own Ruby and Jimmy simply adored their young niece.

Being a musical family, they often spent pleasant evenings around the piano singing solo or in unison. This reminded Sally of the happy times she spent at Olive Bank. The secure feeling she had felt there, had become a vague memory, but somehow in the presence of these loving people, it had come rushing back, filling her very being with a longing to be loved.

When it was time to go home, Anna's mother walked to the bus stop with Sally and made sure she boarded the right bus. This amused Sally, as she was so used to travelling on her own. She enjoyed being looked after, and being fussed over made her feel good.

Each night Tom came home from work, he nodded his head towards his eldest daughter, silently asking if everything was all right? Sally knew his meaning and nodded back. If she was in bed when he arrived home, he never failed to ask her in the morning. The threat Tom had made to her mother that Friday night only added to Sally's worries, as she now knew she could never tell her father if Nellie attacked her again. He just might keep to his word and carry out his threat and kill her mother sending him to prison for the rest of his life.

A month had passed since that awful evening and things had gradually improved. Nellie's treatment towards her had changed for the better, although she gave her the occasional slap, sometimes it was well deserved. Tom had also made sure she was allowed to go out a few evenings in the week, and although money was tight, she was to have a little pocket money at weekends. She was beginning to settle down and put the past behind her. She also noticed that her parents seemed to be tolerating each other better but would it last?

Nellie still frequented the club with Flo, and as it was Friday, she was getting ready to leave. Lucy was already asleep in bed and Hugh was staying with his friends, and although Sally thought it unfair, she came to the conclusion that he was better out of the way, as he and Bess argued constantly.

Nellie left after giving the usual instruction to the girls, ' Don't open the door unless you ken whay it is.'

Sally washed the dishes while Bess, grumbling under her breath, dried them. She hated doing any kind of work but recently, to her horror; Nellie had made sure she did her fair share of the work.

Everything done, Sally settled down in the arm chair and opened her book. She very seldom watched the television, as she much preferred to read. Although the television was on, the volume was turned down.

She hadn't been taking much notice of what Bess was up to, but when she looked down she caught her slipping something into the old handbag she was playing with. Sally rose from her chair and grabbed at the bag as she had recognised the manicure set Matron had given her a few years ago.

'I thought that's what you had,' she scolded Bess. 'You can't have that, I've told you before not to touch my things.'

'You don't use it,' Bess shouted, her brows creasing as her bottom lip pouted in temper.

'It doesn't matter if I use it or not it's mine so just don't touch it Bess, everything you get you either lose or break.'

Bess started screaming with rage causing Sally to wallop her arm but Bess screamed even louder. 'Shut up Bess, you'll waken Lucy and I'll give you another.'

'I'm telling Ma,' Bess yelled. 'She'll belt you sare for hittin' me an' bein'shelfish!'

'Shelfish?' Sally laughed. 'Selfish Bess. Say s-e-l-fish.'

'Awe urn't you a smart ar ...' The loud rattle on the window caused Bess to stop almost at once.

They both turned quickly towards the window and froze with terror as a man's face stared back at them. Grabbing at Sally's arm Bess screamed.

Slightly shaking Sally shouted towards the face at the window. 'What do you want?' Her skinny legs knocked together in fear.

The man grinned and made a gesture with his index finger bidding them to come towards him.

Bravely she yelled again. 'Who are you and what do you want?'

The man beckoned them over again. 'Dinnae be frightened. Yer Mother sent me to watch you till yer

Faither gets hame,' he answered. 'Look!' He held up a brown paper bag. 'A went an' bought sweeties for you all.' Peering down into the bag he spoke enthusiastically. 'It's a mixture. Toffees, chocolate buttons, jellies; come oan, open the door.'

'Go away,' Sally called. ' Go on, git!'

'It's ok Sally,' Bess said jumping up and down. 'He kens Ma an' he's got sweeties.'

'Shut up Bess,' she pushed her sister to the side. 'He's not getting in here.'

As the man moved away from the window, Sally plucked up the courage to go and look through the side of the curtain.

'Shush!' she held her finger to her lips to quieten Bess.

They heard the stair door slam, the hollow sound echoing through out the close. There was a few seconds silence before the doorknocker rattled.

'Shush!' Sally again silenced Bess.

'Do you think he's goin' tae murder us Sal?' Bess whispered.

'Shush up!' Sally motioned to Bess again.

Sally, although scared to move, tip toed once more towards the window and closed the curtains. They now stood in semi darkness. Her young heart pounded furiously against her rib cage. She could almost hear it beating as it rapidly pumped her life's blood through her veins.

'If he goes away Sal, knock oan Mrs McKenzie's door,' Bess suggested.

Mrs McKenzie lived in the house opposite them in the stairway.

'We can't take the chance,' Sally whispered to Bess.

'Maybe Ma did send him,' the younger girl said.

'Bess, she didn't. I have seen him somewhere before but I can't think where.'

They heard the passage door close with a bang.

'He's gone this time,' whispered Bess.

'Maybe,' answered Sally. 'I'll peep out of the curtains and see if he goes by. If anybody passes I'll knock on the window for help.'

Sally was looking out from the side of the curtain, when Bess stepped out of the living room into the hall. Sally caught sight of her as she disappeared from the living-room and ran towards the door, but it was too late, Bess had opened the door and was almost thrown down the hall with the force of the door being pushed wide open.

The man loomed up before them his anxious eyes peering from a good few weeks' facial hair, his filthy brown raincoat was open and flew wildly behind him. He was like the devil himself as his carrot red hair hung below his collar.

All of a sudden, Sally remembered where she had seen him. He was the man who came out of the building and said 'good evening' the night her mother fell over the carpet. Although he was much cleaner then, she was sure it was the same man.

'Get up,' he growled at Bess.

Bess began to cry and looked pleadingly at Sally.

'What do you want with us?' Sally stammered. 'My

Dad will be here any time now,' she informed him. 'He's finishing early tonight.'

The man grinned, 'I doubt that.'

The baby, wakened by all the noise, whimpered.

'Go in there,' he pointed to the living room and both girls did as they were told, Sally walking backwards and Bess being pushed by the man.

'You sit there,' he pointed to the chair at the side of the fire and pushed Bess roughly towards it. The baby was now crying much louder.

'Let her go to the baby,' pleaded Sally.

He smirked. 'Do you think I'm daft?' he spoke mockingly. 'She'll be out that door like a shot. Baby my foot.'

By now Bess was crying quietly and by the way she fidgeted she was about to wet herself.

'Here,' the man said tossing her the bag of sweets. She stopped crying immediately, opened the bag and looked in.

Sally's eyes never left the man who stood at the opposite end of the table.

'Come here,' he demanded.

Not daring to move, she cautiously waited to see which way he was going to come at her. He moved along the left side of the table and Sally moved up the other. Stopping he laughed and moved in the opposite direction. Sally did the same.

The quick movement developed into a chase with Sally now screaming at the top of her voice.

Bess had stopped crying and was taking in the scene

before her, eating the sweets at the same time. She sensed the man was after Sally and not her.

Lucy's demanding cries grew louder.

'You want me to harm the screaming brat through there?' he tossed his head towards the hall. The chase had slowed down a bit.

Sally, whose voice was now full of urgency, pleaded, 'No! Oh no, please! Please! Don't touch the baby.'

'Well stop this *right now!*' he demanded.

Standing still, her body tense, as she watched the man lunge towards her, then grabbing her violently by the arm, he turned swiftly towards Bess pointing his finger threateningly, 'move and I'll cut her throat.'

Bess's eyes grew wide with fear. Her jaw dropped open revealing the sticky half chewed sweet. Nodding obediently she coiled her self into the chair.

Pulling the terrified twelve years old into the kitchen, he then pushed her non-to gently against the kitchen wall, causing her head to crack against the facing of the cupboard door. She grimaced but did not cry. Panic stricken, every nerve in her small body quivered as if over come with severe cold.

Pressing his full body weight against her slight frame caused Sally to gasp for breath. She felt his hot breath on her neck and the stubble from his unshaven face burned and tore at her tender skin, reducing her to tears. Cold sweat ran down her back, causing her thin blouse to stick to her body like a second skin. Closing her eyes, she struggled for air. This was not happening. She tried to pretend she was back in Olive Bank, safe and happy, but it was useless; she could not divorce what was happening from her mind. Like a wild animal he groped and clawed, his stinking breath coming in short uncontrollable pants.

The tears flowed from the whimpering child's eyes, as she prayed with great urgency. 'God please help. Please help.'

'Stop that gibbering girl and listen to me. Do as I say and take....'

Suddenly, the loud continuous banging on the front door stopped him in mid sentence. Hesitating momentarily, his darting eyes cased the kitchen for means of escape, and, as the door still clattered, the baby's ear-splitting screams filled the house. Voices called through the open letter box.

Letting go of Sally, the panicking man leapt onto the sink, forced open the window and made his escape into the night.

Jumping up from the armchair, Bess ran to the front door, where Mrs. McKenzie from across the hall, stood with a thunderous look on her face. 'What's going on here?' she demanded. Pushing Bess to one side, she stomped into the living room. 'Wee Lucy's screaming her head off. We can hear her across the landing. Between screaming and gr...' Looking towards the kitchen door, she caught sight of Sally who lay unconscious on the kitchen floor.

'Bess go in quickly and get George,' she gave her a gentle push. 'Hurry lass hurry.'

Mrs McKenzie ran up the hall into the room and lifting

the sobbing child before returning to the kitchen where Sally lay.

George McKenzie came running in and without hesitation lifted Sally through onto the couch.

Mrs McKenzie spoke softly, 'Bess, get Lucy some milk. Good girl.' Although the baby had quietened down considerably, her tiny body still heaved uncontrollably as she knew something was not right.

Slowly Sally came round but still in shock she remained silent staring into space.

Bess kept babbling on about a man chasing them and taking Sally into the back kitchen. It was then Sally's cries became quite inconsolable.

The neighbour stayed with the girls while her husband went to the telephone box to call Nellie at the club.

They knew all about Nellie Baxter and how she carried on, and they were well aware that they would get no thanks for interfering, in fact, quite the opposite.

Nellie appeared shortly with Flo tagging on behind, and the McKenzie's relayed what had taken place. They could not get much out of Sally as she was obviously suffering from shock, but Bess managed to give her version of the night's events.

'OK Mrs McKenzie, I'll deal wi' it noo,' Nellie said. Half smiling she ushered them into the hall and out into the lobby.

'You need tae send for the police and the doctor,' Mrs McKenzie added while being shown the door.

'We deal wi' oor ain thank you,' Nellie said impudently. 'I'll hear what Sally has tae say, then I'll decide what tae dae. Oor Sally is very dramatic an' Bess exaggerates you ken.' Shutting the door behind her neighbours she muttered 'Silly cow.'

Flo was bending over Sally trying to get her to take a drink of tea. 'Come on lass, take it. There's nothing like a gid cuppa tae get things goin','

As Nellie knelt down beside Sally she touched her hand gently, but Sally drew it away quickly as if she had been burned.

Nellie looked up at Flo with concern in her eyes.

'Sally, who was the man?' Flo asked for the fourth time. 'Dae you ken him? Does he live aroond here? Sally, you've got tae tell us,' she sighed.

Nellie then asked the question that weighed heavy on her mind. 'Sally hen, did he touch ye? What happened?' Getting no response, she pleaded,' We're only tryin' tae help.'

'A think you really should git the doctor,' Flo advised Nellie.

Springing to life, Sally called out frantically, 'No! No! No doctor!'

' Awe right, awe right! There will be nae doctor sent fer...but tell me who wis he? Who wis the man Sally? Did ye ken him?' Nellie asked gently.

'The man who came out the stair the day you tripped on the carpet Ma.' She blurted out.

Feeling the blood drain from her face, Nellie looked up at Flo. 'Good God!'

Flo closed her eyes tight and shook her head from side to side pulling Nelly to her feet. They walked out of hearing distance from Sally. Bess was sitting on the chair with Lucy on her knee out of earshot.

'This could become mucky Flo,' Nellie said to her friend ringing her hands nervously.

'You're telling me!' Flo said. 'You canny hush this up Nellie. He could come back. Fer goodness sake, what's Tom goin' tae say when he finds oot you kept this from him. A think you should tell him, but ye better tell Sally no' tae mention who the man wis. Tell her tae keep that bit quiet in case her Da gets hurt. Yea, that's it; say somethin' like that.' Looking anxiously into Nellie's face she bit her lip while her eyes moved quickly scanning Nellie's worried expression.

'We've got tae find oot what happened Flo,' Nellie's voice trembled. 'We'll have tae tell him something.' Jumping into action she sent Bess into the room with the baby but before going, Bess had to have her say.

'It wis Sally who opened the door ma, no me.'

'Oh shut up Bess,' her mother said impatiently. 'Go on, get through the room an' keep the bairn amused fer ten minutes.'

The women sat down on the sofa beside Sally, and slowly, between sobs and the occasional nose blowing, they managed to coax the story from her. Nellie looked visibly sickened, as she knew only too well what she herself had to endure at the hands of that evil man, the difference being, she had encouraged him, Sally had not.

If Tom Baxter ever found who Sally's assailant was, he would surly find out that he had visited the house on a previous occasion. Both Flo and Nellie tried convincing

Sally that it would be better for her father's safety, to deny ever seeing her attacker before. They put it into her head that Tom would be 'done for murder' if he found out who did this, and 'anyhow, he hadn't really done any bodily harm. Not proper harm, like,' said Nellie. ' Not worth taking chances.'

As they all expected, Tom Baxter was beside himself with rage. He punched his clenched fist into the palm of his own hand while pacing up and down in front of Sally. He spoke venomously through clenched teeth, 'If a git the bugger who did this, I'll bloody well kill him and a'm no' jokin'. A'll bloody swing fer him.' Turning to Sally once more, he spoke almost accusingly. 'Are you tellin' me the truth, you hiv nae idea whay the bugger wis?'

Red eyed and exhausted, Sally gulped and quivered. ' No Dad, I told you. A've never seen him afore.'

Her father's threatening statement was all she needed to confirm her mother's assumption. The frightened child really believed her mother was trying to protect her father and felt momentarily drawn towards her. She gave her mother an expressionless glance, and Nellie acknowledged with a very slight nod.

She was sticking to the story. She couldn't even give an accurate description of the man, or so she led her father to believe. Nellie felt a tremendous weight lift from her shoulders. She had no doubt that the child's loyalty to her father would cause her to lie, but she was unsure of Tom's capability of getting to the truth. Her fears were uncalled for, as her husband's handling of the situation made Sally aware of his intentions. If he had handled her with tenderness, maybe she would have told him the whole truth. His rage had only made her more fearful.

Tom calmed down eventually, and Nellie, in her manipulating way, managed to persuade her man not to involve the police or doctors, since Sally had not been physically hurt; and it would just make things worse for her, especially at school, people would make more out of it.

Tom asked Sally what she wanted to do, and she said all she wanted was to forget about the whole incident.

For fear of repetition, Tom abandoned his usual weekend plans and contented himself at home. Nellie too, although grudgingly, stayed in-doors beside her family. Her reasons were somewhat different from her husband's. She was not giving Tom the opportunity to question his daughter further.

The half bottle of rum and the few bottles of light ale she had purchased earlier from the Railway Tavern's jug bar – the small room attached to the local pub—made her night by the television pleasurable. The jug bar was so called, giving that the children would be sent there with the ale jug for their parents' nightly tipple. Access to the tiny room led in from the street and the publican was the only one who could see who came in. There had recently been placed two chairs and a small circular table in there, making it difficult for the casual customer, for there was little room left once two seated customers filled the chairs.

Sally watched as her mother slowly emptied the last of the rum into her glass. Although Nellie said little all night, Sally became aware of her mother's change of mood and quickly made herself scarce. It wasn't long before she heard the familiar raised voices of her parents, and pulling the bed covers over her head, she clamped her hands over her ears and quietly singing, tried hard to suppress the verbal abuse that was filling her young head. Any change of heart Nellie had shown recently, had been thrown in to obscurity, as once she became intoxicated; her old nasty vicious self reared its ugly head.

When Monday arrived, Sally still did not feel like leaving the house as she had became visibly terrified. The fear of that man stalking her at school haunted her, so Nellie wrote a letter to her teacher, informing her that her daughter had a bad bout of flu. As it happened, Nellie was feeling pretty awful herself as she had a terrible job keeping down her food and suspected she had an ulcer so she was glad of Sally's help around the house.

Tom, quite unsympathetically, regarded his wife's condition as being self-inflicted. He recognised a hangover when he saw one, as he too had been in the same position on numerous occasions.

The following Friday, Nellie assured Sally she would not leave her alone with the children as she too was unsure of Jack Brown's intentions. She couldn't risk the police becoming involved as everything would come out.

Sally was aware her mother would soon tire playing the martyr and she would be left at risk once more. It was time to figure out her plan of escape.

Chapter Eight

The sticks sparked and crackled, radiating their heat upwards, the flames playing menacingly against the small pieces of shining coal that balanced awkwardly on top.

It was a cold February morning and the room felt very chilly. Bess, half dressed, huddled into the armchair and stared down into the fire as if hypnotised by the imps and hobgoblins she visualised dancing up from the flames.

Nellie, still in bed, waited for her cup of tea.

Tom and Sally darted around trying to get breakfast on the table as well as organising the children.

Hugh was dressed and busily stuffed his pockets with elastic bands and marbles he had retrieved from the kitchen drawer.

Tom's attention focused on Bess and an angry yell from him, snapped her out of her trance like state.

'Get a move oan. You're goin' tae be late as usual.'

'I'm cauld da.' she whined as she hugged.

'Get your bloomin' claes oan then,' he snapped.

'But I canna find ma socks.'

Sally intervened. 'They're on top o' the dresser. I told you that already.'

She spread herself out lazily and called to Hugh, 'Give me ower me socks will ya?'

He tossed his head towards the dresser and said cheekily, 'Get them yersel', you lazy dumplin'.'

Exasperated, Sally crossed the floor and grabbed the socks from the dresser and threw them at Bess. 'If it'll hurry you on, there's your blooming socks. Now move!' she commanded.

Sally wanted them out the house quickly. If her plans were to succeed she would have to get the children well out of the way. It wouldn't do to have them leave the house at the same time as she did.

Finally dressed, Bess stood at the table finishing off a piece of toast. Sally gave her back a sharp prod and growled, 'Hurry up you. Hugh is waiting. Move Bess!'

'Ok, Ok oor Sal, you're surely feelin' better this mornin',' she said impudently.

Before she could reply, Tom's voice called from the back kitchen, 'You're goin' tae be late yersel' Sally.'

'I'm o.k. Dad, the late bus gets me there in time. No time to spare though, but I'll make it.' She glanced through at her father and smiled. 'That's if them two get a move on.'

Studying his daughter with affection, he found it hard to believe Nellie had no love in her dark heart for this child. Why? He could not understand. She was her own flesh and blood. Could it be that the lass looked so much like his own mother? As well as resembling her, she had also inherited the same fine qualities that she had. Sally was gentle natured and could be very funny and witty when she was in the company of friends. She didn't lose her temper often, but when she did, it upset her afterwards. No trace of Nellie could he find in his daughter; but Bess, she was totally different. She was Nellie's clone, lazy, spiteful and wretched.

'You share ye're able tae go tae schuil the day Sally?' Tom asked.

'I'll be all right dad. Don't worry,' she assured him.

Going into her bedroom, Sally pulled her case from under the bed. Opening it up, she pulled out a thick jumper. It was a bit short but she thought it would help keep her warm, so she pulled it on top of the one she was already wearing.

Slipping her fingers into the small pouch that was attached to the lining of the suitcase, she retrieved two and sixpence she had managed to save from her weekly shilling. Quickly checking it was all there, she dropped it into a small cloth purse and placed it into her coat pocket.

Lifting her old battered school bag and her coat, she walked back into the living room where her father sat relaxing alongside the now blazing fire. Holding a mug of steaming hot tea against his chest, his mouth curled up almost in a smile, gave him the look of contentment.

She was very tempted to run to him, throw her arms around his neck and pour out her fears, but, young though she was, she knew that was not the answer.

Quickly she recovered from her compulsion, and pulled on her coat, and, putting her arms through the straps of her bag, she turned and left the room calling, 'cheerio' to her parents. It troubled her that she was deceiving them, but there was no other option; she had to go.

Once outside, her stomach reeled with nervous excitement. Filling her lungs with the cold morning air, she composed herself, then walking briskly, she crossed over to the other side of the road, taking care that none of her school friends were about. The bus she was about to catch went in the opposite direction to the one she would normally have taken to school, and, as that would be passing soon, she hid in the alley until it had gone by.

She then decided to walk towards the next stop, just in case she was seen boarding the bus by her neighbours. The stop that she eventually waited at was one where few passengers stood. When she eventually boarded the bus, she cast her head down in case anyone recognised her, but as there were few people on the bus, the chance of any recognition was slim. On her right hand side, two men were engrossed in their newspapers, while an elderly lady rummaged through her shopping bag desperately looking for her purse. The others were too busy talking to give Sally a second look.

She sat at the very back of the bus and could hardly be seen, as the seat in front of her was high backed. The bus conductor came to the back of the bus and collected Sally's fare. 'A single to Edinburgh,' she said. Although travelling by bus was nothing new for Sally, she had never ventured into Edinburgh by herself. The city was ten miles from her hometown and it took the bus a full hour to reach there. As she had been on the bus now for fifteen minutes she was well away from her neighbourhood so the people who now boarded were complete strangers. She began to breathe more easily now relaxing onto the back of her seat, the fear she had felt turned yet again to nervous excitement. Feeling the adrenalin flow through her veins, she began to understand why Hugh had run off so often in the past. The adventure and mystery of it all felt like fun. She realised it wasn't going to be easy reaching her destination as she had very little money. The bus she was on would take her as far as the city terminus; the rest of the journey would depend on her cunning.

The bus stopped once more to allow a stream of passengers to board. That uneasy feeling returned once more as a middle-aged woman carrying a boy sat down heavily beside Sally squeezing her small frame against the side of the bus. Sitting the small boy on her knee she gave Sally a sideward glance. She ignored them both by gazing out of the window. The child's feet shot sideways accidentally kicking Sally on her kneecap causing her to flinch, but she still ignored them. The woman straightened the child's legs and scolded him gently.

Now turning to Sally, she apologised on behalf of her restless infant, 'I'm sorry lass'.

'Oh no,' thought Sally to herself. Then smiling weakly she said almost in a whisper, 'It's all right.'

'Where are you off to?' the woman asked. 'Do you go to school in Edinburgh?' She was looking at the school bag on Sally's back.

This is what Sally had dreaded. She knew she would have to lie. It was against her nature to do so, but this was a desperate situation. She knew this wouldn't be the last lie she'd have to tell on her journey.

'Yes,' she answered.

'You'll be late this morning then,' the woman informed her.

'I know,' replied Sally. 'I've been staying with my granny and she wasn't well this morning.'

'Oh! Where does she stay?' she enquired.

'Who?' Sally asked stupidly.

'Your gran.'

'Oh. Oh! Eh! Just on the outskirts of town.' She wished the woman would just shut up. She was contemplating getting off at the next stop, when to her relief, the woman rose up lifting the child into her arms.

'Well, I get off here. I hope you don't get into trouble,' she smiled kindly.

'Trouble?' Sally asked panicking.

'Yes, you know, you're late for school.' She looked at Sally and frowned.

'Oh yes,' she answered. She watched the woman struggle down the aisle with the child and felt relieved. The bus stopped and the woman and child got off.

'Thank God,' she sighed burying her back into the upholstery.

Walking through the bus station, she suddenly became aware of the hustle and bustle created by commuters as they passed by in all directions hurrying to allsorts of important places mixed with eager shoppers hoping to clinch that special bargain in the sales.

Just before Sally turned into Princes Street, she stopped outside the familiar Milk Bar café where Nellie usually treated them all when visiting the city. She wanted to loose the school bag so she decided to go in, have a drink and leave her bag in the toilets as she was leaving.

The chatter and laughter from women sitting in little groups brightened the downstairs room while in the far corner three sailors watched and whispered to one another. A young couple sat at the bottom of the stairs the woman nursing an infant while her partner studied a till receipt.

Sally walked to the counter and ordered a strawberry milk shake. The young girl behind the counter studied Sally momentarily.

Feeling she had to explain her presence Sally informed her somewhat guiltily, 'I've to meet my Auntie outside'. The young girl chewed on gum, tossed her head backwards, her poker -straight hair falling away from her shoulders.

'Nine pence,' she said, snapping her gum between her teeth. Pushing the glass towards Sally, she then stretched over, plucked a straw from a box on the counter and stuck it in Sally's drink.

Paying the girl, she then found a seat away from the other customers, sat down and drank her milk shake.

Before she left the bar, Sally found the toilets, washed her hands and left her schoolbag tucked down the side of a bin.

As Sally walked along Princes Street she decided that since she was so close, she'd have a walk round Woolworths as that was her favourite store. It was always so very busy with customers stretching over the counters trying to catch the shop girls' attention waving their goods before them and getting annoyed if someone was served out of turn. It amazed her how many pencils and pens were lined along the stationery counter. She loved that part of the shop best of all. She browsed through the books and comics and stood for a while watching the man engraving names on bracelets and plaques. She thought he was ever so clever.

Upstairs, she walked through the paint and hardware department her thoughts returning to the time Nellie sent her here by herself to buy a tin of magnolia paint, as she hadn't enough to finish the room. She had been scared travelling to town by herself and ran all the way from the bus station to the shop and then all the way back to the bus without stopping. She could almost feel the pain in her fingers as she grasped the heavy paint tin.

Continuing down the aisle she arrived at the toys. Having had few of her own she paused to admire the dressing up dolls. She often yearned to own one but was never that lucky. Her friend Anna had one, which had many different outfits.

Anna, oh Anna, she had forgotten about Anna. She suddenly felt very deflated. If she were to miss anyone, it would be Anna.

She didn't feel like staying in the shop any more. She had to get out and head for the station. She was only delaying her journey by looking around the shop.

As she stepped out into the street, she noticed two policemen standing by the kerb. They seemed to be watching the people at the opposite side of the road. Her imagination started to run wild. She thought they were maybe looking for her. They were definitely watching the steps that led down to the station. She darted back into Woolworth's and spent another hour walking up and down inside the store.

Looking out into the street for the fifth time, she was relieved to find the policemen had moved on. Slipping out of the shop, she mingled among a crowd of pedestrians who waited for the traffic to clear. Another policeman stood in the middle of the road, but he was busy directing traffic. Keeping well in the centre of the crowd, she crossed the busy road, and reaching the steps that led down to the station descended them two at a time. As she neared the bottom, the familiar smell of soot clad walls filled her lungs. It was a special smell, a smell that she wished she could bottle. It was the smell of exciting journeys and far away places or to some it would remind them of fond fare wells or home sweet home.

Trains pulled into their prospective platforms and doors flew open, spewing out people from all walks of life.

Back pack travellers, men in long over-coats and split pea hats, soldiers home on leave and mothers with children, bombarded the weary looking ticket inspector who stood by the barrier checking the authenticity of their tickets.

Trains slowly puffed their way in and out. Doors banged, whistles blew and the continual sound from the tannoy announced the times of the arrivals and departures of the great steam trains.

Mesmerised by the activity around her, Sally was suddenly aware that she had no idea what train she would have to catch. There were so many. Not having a ticket was also a problem, but she was here now and she had no intention of turning back.

She decided that this was where she had to become as cute and fly as her sister Bess.

The first thing she had to do was to find out from where the train to Kirkcaldy left. She tried to read the board but couldn't understand it. If she asked someone they might become suspicious and ask questions. What was she to do?

She sat down on a near by bench to think the problem through. A man and woman stood in front of her and she could not help but over-hear their conversation. She couldn't believe her ears. He was actually telling his companion that the train going to Kirkcaldy left in twenty minutes from platform five. Sally just knew she was doing the right thing. Wasn't God leading her? Everything was going to be all right.

Then the voice from the tannoy began announcing the stops the train would make before reaching Kirkcaldy. Sally listened very carefully.

Making her way towards the platform, she noticed a very plump eccentric looking lady with six small children, heading in the same direction. Sally trailed behind the children and when the woman reached the ticket inspector, she had such a carry-on finding her tickets and keeping the youngsters in check, the poor man gladly ushered the motley group through the barrier. The woman bounced along the platform and Sally followed on as if she were part of the family.

The six carriages attached to the engine were half empty, but as the train continued on its journey, they would soon fill up.

Sally walked on through the corridors, looking into every compartment. She had to find the right one, preferably near one of the toilets, as she would have to have somewhere to hide when the other ticket collector came round. She had only been on a train once, but she had watched everything that had taken place. She and Hugh had come home by train from Olive Bank with her father. She remembered her father telling her that the ticket collector came round after the train drew away from each station. She reckoned if she sat in a carriage with other children and adults, she wouldn't be so conspicuous.

She found the perfect compartment occupied by a man, his wife and their three children. Two other ladies, one elderly and the other in her late teens, sat opposite the family and Sally sat down next to them. The children were aged from about six to ten years and they had just started to quarrel over who sat at the window. The mother was trying to sort it all out and asked the ladies opposite if they would mind letting one of her girls sit at their window.

'I don't know' the elderly woman said 'maybe this child would like to sit there.' She was referring to Sally.

'No, it's all right' Sally assured her. The last thing she needed was attention.

The mother thanked them and pushed one of her girls over towards the window seat. She looked over at Sally and said 'If you want to look out when we cross the Forth Bridge just come over here beside the girls.'

'Thank you,' Sally said to her, 'I will.' The train pulled away and Sally sat back in her seat. She loved the sound of the chugging, as the engine gathered speed. It went quite slow through a long tunnel and stopped when coming to the other end to allow more passengers to alight. She over heard the man tell his eldest daughter that they were now in Haymarket station. He laughed when his daughter asked if they were 'nearly there' as they had been on the train for barely five minutes.

The train started to move once more and as it gathered speed Sally moved into the corridor and headed towards the toilet. Closing the door she stood with her back against it. She hadn't been there long before she heard the collector call out for the tickets. When she was completely sure he had passed, she slipped back into the compartment and sat down.

The children were looking out of the window whilst their father read a paper. Both women sitting along side Sally were also reading. The girls' mother closed her eyes and rested her head against the back of her seat looking thankful for the rest. Feeling relatively safe, Sally also rested her back against the seat and relaxed her eyes wandering around the compartment wall admiring the framed pictures that hung above the passengers' heads. They were mostly pictures of sheep grazing peacefully in green pastures. Her attention now turned to the seating, and as she ran her hands over the edge of her seat, it gave her the feeling of peacefulness. She loved the feel of the material. 'Fancy blue velvet on train seats,' she thought.

The rack above was stuffed with brown parcels and shopping bags belonging to the family. The three girls had taken off their coats, which were also squeezed into the rack. Although it was warm in the compartment, Sally kept her coat on, in case she had to make a quick exit.

Nearing South Queensferry the children in the compartment jumped for joy as they were about to cross over the Forth Bridge. She smiled as she remembered her brother Hugh's excitement when he crossed over on his way home from Olive Bank.

'Come over here pet.' The girls' mother beckoned Sally. 'Come on. We're on the bridge now.' Sally went over and stood beside the window and as the train slowed down, the father of the children rose from his seat and gave his three daughters one penny each. He opened the window of the train and the girls threw their money out into the water. 'Make a wish now,' their father said.

'Haven't you got a penny?' one of the little girls asked Sally.

'Yes I have,' answering almost in a whisper, 'but I need it for something else.'

'You could have thrown it out and wished for more pennies,' the smallest child said. 'Then you would have a lot of money.'

'You're silly Margaret,' the oldest girl chided. Focusing once more on Sally, she asked, 'why are you by yourself? Where's your mummy?'

Taken off guard Sally found yet another lie tripping off her tongue, 'I have no parents.'

Looking up wide-eyed at Sally, the youngest spoke again. 'Who makes your dinner then?'

Red faced with embarrassment at her young sisters frankness, the eldest girl looked apologetically at Sally. 'Don't mind her. She opens her mouth and nonsense falls out.'

Sally smiled, 'I stay with my auntie and I'm on my way to stay with another auntie for a few days. You see, she's ill and I'm going to take care of her.' Beginning to believe her own story she began to feel immensely important.

'We're going to our granny's to stay for a week.' The girl took Sally by the wrist and pulled her down onto the seat beside her. In no time at all the girls were chatting as if they had known each other forever. They asked their mother's permission to stand out in the corridor and she let the two eldest go, as long as they stayed at the door of the compartment where she could see them. This suited Sally as she was nearer the toilet door.

Finally reaching Kirkcaldy, Sally said her goodbyes to her newfound friends before disappearing into the crowd.

It was now well into the afternoon and she was beginning to feel cold and extremely hungry. She wandered aimlessly around town looking through the shops until they began to close up for the day. A fruit machine arcade was open so she sheltered there for a while watching mothers amusing their children by giving them pennies to slip into the machines. She watched a few boys as they rolled coins down small wooden shoots trying to land in squares without touching the lines allowing them to double or triple their money. She could not risk going to Olive Bank just yet, in case Matron sent her packing.

The hunger she was feeling began to pain her stomach as a sick headache now gnawed in her skull. She had held on to her last shilling for as long as she could, but she could no longer ward off the desperate need for food, so she made her way to the chip shop. Inside the shop, she watched as the man lifted a pail of chipped potatoes and, as he threw them into the large pan, the fat crackled and sizzled as the cold wet chips came into contact with the hot smoking fat. Pulling the lid over the chip pan, he turned round and gave Sally a huge grin.

Being the first customer of the day she had to wait a bit longer until the chips were ready. A bag of chips and a small bottle of orange juice was her order. The man very kindly allowed her to sit at one of the tables. He spoke to her as he worked, and very soon he had her laughing. If he wasn't speaking, he was singing. A door behind the counter opened and a woman appeared wearing a white apron and looked as jolly as the man she had joined.

They started to speak to each other in Italian, making Sally feel uneasy. Thinking that she was the topic of discussion, she left in a hurry leaving her orange juice but taking her few remaining chips.

The streets were now almost empty. Papers that had been carelessly discarded now blew across the street as the wind started to rise. Now and again a gap appeared in the swift moving clouds giving a quick glimpse of the full moon that lay behind. The town no longer felt safe and Sally shivered, as fear crept into her already frozen body.

It was time to make her way to the house. Drained of confidence, she walked towards the bus stop. Having no money left, she decided to throw herself on the mercy of the bus conductor. She was sick of lying, and the terror of the night made her fear the wrath of God, for hadn't she lied all day, and to her horror, she realised she had enjoyed it. She kept telling herself God would understand and she would have a long talk with him before she went to sleep.

As she stood waiting for the bus, a hand gripped her firmly on the shoulder. She felt her legs almost give way as she staggered backwards in fright. 'Sally? I thought it was you. Oh I'm sorry I didn't mean to frighten you. Where are you going?'

Recognising the woman she sighed in relief. She was the gardener's daughter who lived near Olive Bank.

Her hand spread over her heart, making sure it was still beating, Sally answered. 'I'm going back to Olive Bank.'

'Does Matron know you're coming?'

'No. No she doesn't,' and in the same breath she asked, 'Mrs Knox, can you pay my fare. I'll give you it back later?' In spite of the fright the woman had given her she was extremely glad she had turned up.

Although only a fifteen-minute journey, she felt it took hours as she longed to be back in the safety and cleanness of the home as well as the love and kindness

Matron gave to her children. She longed for the happy times with Rita, sitting in the kitchen joking with cook or lying in bed giggling at silly things that they had done or said. Yes, she longed for all those things and more. Her heart raced with anticipation. She was almost there. Her journey was almost over.

When the bus stopped at the foot of the hill they both got off. Thanking Mrs Knox once more she watched as the woman hurried along the street looking back twice and giving a small wave. She now stood alone by the iron gates that lead to Olive Bank and seeing the house lights in the distance filled her with joyful anticipation. She slipped in through the gates and made for the safety of the house. Walking along the long driveway towards the house, Sally began to feel uneasy as the trees swaying in the wind cast dark shadows across her path. The moon slipped quietly behind a darkened sky like a thief in hiding. In the darkness of the small copse to Sally's right, an owl hooted. Bushes rustled as birds fluttered within, annoyed at the disturbance. Sally now ran as if the devil himself was after her, constantly looking over her shoulder, until she reached the gravel path. Slowing down she began to march briskly. The sound of crunching beneath her feet reminded her of the first time she and the two social workers drove up this path. She was scared of the unknown then. Little did she know she had been sentenced to three years of happiness?

Reaching the lawn, she ran the few yards towards the front porch. Reaching the door she banged on it with all her might. The lights went on almost immediately, although to Sally it felt like ages. Scurrying feet clipped clopped across the tiled floor of the porch before the dark silhouette appeared behind the net screening on the door window.

Momentarily speechless, Matron stood before the trembling child. 'Sally! Oh my God.' She crossed her hands onto her breast while gasping for air. 'What in the name of Mercy are you doing here? Come in, come in.'

Keeping her eyes on Matron, Sally almost stumbled into the porch. Matron grabbed her arm quickly before leading her towards the familiar sitting room, where once inside, she hugged the weeping child for quite some time.

In between sobs, Sally tried telling Matron about the man who attacked her and the misery she had endured since going home. She then gave a step-by-step account of her adventurous journey. The matron was dumbfounded. Travelling so far by herself with so little money.

'Sally we will have to let your parents know you're safe. They'll be worried.'

'No Matron, my da' will be worried, but my mother won't be.'

'Sally, no matter what your mother feels towards you, she'll be worried because you've disappeared. I still have to phone the police. Do you understand? You can stay here till we see what's to happen but, although I'm glad to see you, you were quite wrong to run away. Anything could have happened to you child. Don't you realise that?'

Sally's head hung down low as she started to cry once more. Her eyes stung with burning hot tears while her face felt swollen and bloated. She had never cried so much. She wished she were dead. She wished her mother dead, and she wished the red haired horrible man was dead too. All her pent-up emotions from the last six months spilled out leaving her shattered, torn and totally exhausted.

Sally was taken up to Matron's own private quarters where she was put to bed in the small adjoining room that led from her own.

When Cook was informed of Sally's arrival, she took a glass of warm milk and a digestive biscuit spread with butter and jam to the bedroom and sat with Sally till Matron made the phone call to the police station. She had been right. A search had been formed, as Sally hadn't been seen all day.

The following morning the sound of children laughing and shouting wakened Sally from her sleep. She thought the events from the previous day had all been a dream, and being quite disorientated it took her a good few seconds before realising where she was. In spite of having a good sleep, she still had little energy. Very slowly, she dragged herself up into a sitting position. Swinging her legs over the bed, she was about to rise when Cook came into the room.

'And where do you think you're going young Sally?' she asked in her usual brisk manner. 'You can get your legs back into that bed right now or you'll be fed your favourite milk jelly for the rest of the week.' Cook laughed, remembering how Sally hated the pudding and was very sick when made to eat it.

'You remembered?' said Sally. 'Cook is Rita still here?'

'Yes love she is. Didn't you know? Matron is trying to adopt her.'

'Really, that's great.' She was thrilled at the news although a touch of jealousy stabbed at her heart.

'She'll be up to see you when she gets out of school. Matron wants you to have complete rest so that means bed! Pull your covers up now and let me sit this tray down in front of you. Now, eat every bit of that. It's a nice fresh egg from Susie the hen. She was going to lay one with your name on it but she didn't have enough notice.' She gave a hearty laugh. 'I've cut your toast into soldiers and your tea is nice and hot, so eat!'

Sally thanked Cook and ate her breakfast as ordered. With her pillows propped against the brass headboard, she observed her surroundings. Being a very small room, there was only space for the single bed Sally lay in, along with the tall five-drawer dresser that stood at the foot of her bed. A lovely mother of pearl vase sat on top of the dresser holding a bunch of silk carnations. The only flowers Sally had ever seen, apart from the real ones, were made from plastic. Two photos also sat upon the dresser, one at each side of the vase. An elderly couple (whose stiff severe countenance gave them a look of grandeur) filled one of the frames while a handsome smiling sailor adorned the other. Sally rose up onto her knees and took the photo of the sailor in her hands. Across the bottom it read '*To my Molly Love Sam.*' Sally looked closely. It was obvious he was thinking of his sweetheart at the moment the photo was taken as love shone from his earnest eyes. She guessed his eyes were blue, as he looked fair. It was hard to tell with a black and white photo but one thing was sure; he was real handsome.

Matron tiptoed into the bedroom, suspecting Sally to be asleep. She stood for a few seconds and watched as Sally admired the photo.

'He was killed in the war,' she explained while stepping towards her.

'He was very handsome Matron, just like a film star. Was he your brother?'

Giving a rather loud sigh she took the frame gently from Sally's hands, and placed it back on the dresser. Turning, she took both of Sally's hands in hers, giving a weak smile. 'We were to be married after the war, but he never came back. His ship was sunk.'

As if in deep thought, she stared into space for a few seconds, then, as if someone kick started her, she jumped, lifted Sally up and put her back into bed.

Tucking her firmly in, she said, 'Now, that's our little secret. Don't tell the others and don't let them know my name, otherwise we'll have some calling me Molly instead of Matron and that would never do. All right?'

'OK Matron, I'm sorry about....' she nodded towards the photo. 'And I'll never tell,' she said pulling an imaginary zip across her mouth.

'And just to make sure you don't keep yourself awake wondering, the other photo is of my parents,' Matron said with a mocking tone. Sally laughed and Matron joined her. She then sat down on the bed and took Sally's hand in hers.

'Are you feeling better?'

'Yes Matron, I feel a lot better except for a bit of weakness.'

'That will pass with rest. Sally, I have to tell you that a policewoman will be calling in. She will be here around eleven to have a chat with you. I would like you to tell her about the man who attacked you.' Seeing agitation in the child's face, she tried to reassure her. 'Now Sally, no one is going to harm you. This must be reported. Your parents were wrong to let the matter rest. What if he attacks some other little girl and does serious damage?'

As Matron studied Sally's troubled face she was overcome with sorrow. She wished she could keep her at Olive Bank. This girl trusted her so much she had risked her life to come to her. If she was ever to be rewarded for her dedication, this was surely it.

'If you say it's all right Matron, then I'll tell her everything, but promise you'll be with me?'

'Of course I'll be with you.' Matron rose, and with a few swift flicks of her hand, straightened out the patchwork quilt she had been sitting on. 'Now have a rest, and no more photo studying.' She left the room and Sally lay back against the pillow thinking.

She had no choice now. She would have to tell the policewoman everything. Everything except the man's description, and the fact she had seen him before. She had promised her mother, besides, she had to protect her father. Hadn't Matron just said that the man could cause someone serious damage? That someone could be her father. As she lay mulling over her story, she was suddenly aware that she would not be telling a fib at all.

At least, not a very big fib because she really had forgotten what the man looked like. She remembered that he was dirty, smelly and unshaven, but that could apply to lots of people. Bess was asked right after the event, and all she could say was, ' he had sweeties', so it would not be too unusual for Sally to give a vague description.

Matron returned at eleven o'clock with the policewoman and both of them sat at Sally's bedside. She liked the look of the policewoman who had the skill to put her at ease. They spoke about all sorts of things at first, Sally's piano playing, school, and her friends Anna and Rita. Slowly the policewoman approached the subject that Sally had dreaded; the reason for running away.

Lying back on her pillow she told of the incident that happened that awful night. She found herself speaking without crying. It was becoming easier. She told her about the man grabbing at her body and tearing at her clothes. Shivering she stopped. They sat in silence waiting for Sally to continue, but she said no more.

The policewoman had listened sympathetically to the child. It was she who broke the silence. ' Sally. Did he do anything else?'

Sally just stared blankly back.

The woman now asked, 'did he show you anything?'

'Yes,' she answered.

'Oh my God,' the policewoman muttered very low.

Sally screwed up her eyes and looked enquiring at the woman. 'He showed Bess and me a bag of sweeties.'

Both women sighed with relief. She was then asked if there was any other reason for running away.

Courageously she told of her mother's violence towards her, and although things had become slightly better of late, she was still very frightened of her mother's temper.

Writing the details in a notebook, the officer asked her once more if she could describe the man who attacked her but Sally said she couldn't remember.

'What will happen to me now?' Sally asked the policewoman.

Magical words filled Sally's ears. 'You will stay here until this has been sorted out. You may well have to attend a hearing, as you did run away causing a lot of anxiety for your parents as well as the local police. Still, I wouldn't worry too much. Just let things happen, you're safe and that's the main thing.' Smiling she rose. Patting Sally gently on the head, she turned and left. Matron accompanied the policewoman to the door and while they were in the stairway she said sadly, 'she's had a bad time of it.'

'Looks like it. It's a good job there are places like this for kids to turn to. Mind you, this is an exceptional place Matron. Your kids really love being here.'

'Well most of them do. I try to make them feel as if we are all one family. It works most of the time, but family sadly is alien to lots of them. Trust is important as well although that does take time. Sometimes it's hard to get their trust at all as life has let them down so often. Still, we can't give up.

Rita took the stairs two at a time. She ran up them as if the devil himself was after her. Dashing into the bedroom she yelled at the top of her voice, 'Sally Sally.'

Rita threw herself onto the bed and both girls hugged each other swaying back and forth.

'Oh, it's good to see you Sally. Oh, it really is, this is great, I've missed you.' Rita was overexcited.

'Rita, hold on, you're squeezing the life out of me. I've missed you too. You'll never know how much.'

'How did you get here by yourself?' Rita knew there was something going on as matron and cook were talking in whispers and scurrying around late last night.

'Why are you in bed Sal, and why have you to rest? Have you been ill?'

'No not really, but I'll tell you all about it later.'

'I couldn't believe it when cook told me you were here. She wouldn't let me up to see you until you'd rested. All day I've wished school was over. Oh, it's magic.' She talked excitedly not stopping to take a breath. 'No one told me you were coming back.'

'Rita, I ran away from home.' She stopped her friend babbling on.

'You've what? You've run away!' The look on her face was one of scepticism.

Sally nodded her head.

'That's why Matron didn't tell you. She didn't know I would be coming back. I just ran away.' Sally explained.

'Will you get to stay then?'

'I really don't know, but I'll be here until something is sorted out. I'm not going back home.' Sally informed Rita.

'Was it that awful?' Rita's eyes widened.

'Yes it was Rita, but I'm here now,' Sally replied.

The two girls talked for ten minutes before one of the staff (or aunties) chased Rita down to do her chores.

Sally remained in bed for a few days before she was allowed down stairs. The two girls caught up with all the news, but Sally for some reason told Rita nothing about the man who broke in and caused her distress.

Sally was to remain in the same bedroom until things were sorted out.

Matron knew there would be an enquiry as Sally's parole had been broken. It wasn't certain that she would remain at Olive Bank either so Matron thought it best to leave her where she was for the time being.

A week passed before Matron received word concerning the hearing. Sally would be collected by a social worker and taken by car to Edinburgh. The journey would take her back across the water to where she lived. Matron had to prepare a report and send it on to the court.

In ten days time Sally would know her punishment, if any. The worse punishment they could possibly give, would be for her to be sent back home. Sally prayed every night that would not happen.

Everything during the days ahead led to uncertainty for Sally. The fact that she wasn't moved into a dormitory, or that she hadn't been enrolled in the local school, made her worry. She had been given tuition by Matron herself and spent a lot of time at the piano. The days felt long when the children were at school. Helping the housekeeper and cook passed some of the time.

At the weekend Sally, Rita, and four other children were taken into town and as a special treat, they were taken to the cinema to see 'The Ten Commandments.' They spoke about the film all the way home and wondered how they managed to part the Red Sea. Wasn't it only Jesus who could do that? Then how come the man in the film did it?

The day arrived when Sally had to face the music, she was up and ready to leave very early. Rita had just come down for breakfast when Sally was about to go. The social worker, Miss Aldridge, was having a word with matron, so it gave the girls a few minutes to hug and say their good byes. Matron also hugged Sally and told her to be strong and not to run away again as it wasn't the answer. They all stood waving as Sally's car disappeared out of sight.

Cook turned and shook her head at matron. 'Poor wee lass, God be with her,' she said almost in tears.

'Yes cook, I'm sure He will be. After all, wasn't it He who brought her to us in safety.' She answered with a slight smile. ' The Lord moves in mysterious ways, his wonders to perform.'

'I hope you're right matron,' Cook said as she led Rita back into the house. 'Come on, everyone will be wanting fed and here I am standing on the doorstep,' she said trying to be jovial. Rita normally would have answered back, but this time she walked in silence. She went about all day in silence, only speaking when answering questions. She never made conversation at school and when she came home at four thirty, she went straight to her room.

Sally's journey was also in silence. She was now worried as to what was going to happen to her. Having to face her parents was a terrifying thought. She didn't want to be left alone with her mother. Her mind was in turmoil. She also thought her dad would be so angry he would let her mother beat her up. Cold sweat started to form on the palms of her hands. She would have to tell them not to let her mother near her. What if they sent her to another home? She knew there were others that weren't nearly half as nice as Olive Bank. She had heard people comment on them.

She remembered sitting on the lawn with Rita and one of the other children who had come to stay for a short while because the place he came from had closed down. She remembered he had told them that the matron there put you into a cold bath if you misbehaved.

His hair had been practically shaved off it was so short. The girls there had their hair cut in the same way. The Matron at that awful home said it was to discourage nits. Rita used to refer to some places as 'jaggy jersey homes'. That made Sally laugh but she wasn't laughing now, as she didn't find it funny any more.

The morning was cold, wet and windy. Crossing over on the ferry was exceptionally rough and Sally was sick. When they drove off onto the jetty, Miss Aldridge suggested a cup of hot tea would help to settle both their stomachs, as she was feeling quite sick herself. Finding a cafe, they stopped the car and went in.

Sally felt a lot better after her hot cup of tea and round of buttered toast.

They continued on their way and reached their destination around eleven. The shops around the Sheriff's

Building were busy with housewives doing their daily shopping. Traffic was also building up. The wind had dropped and the rain had stopped but the sky was still very heavy.

The Court buildings were now familiar to Sally. They both walked through the corridor and ascended the stairs to the waiting room adjacent to where the hearing was to take place.

Sally wriggled and squirmed in her seat. She just could not sit still. Rising up, she crossed the floor and peered out of the dirty looking window. Eyes searching the street below, she nervously bit her fingernail to the quick. It bled. She peeled the rugged nail from her finger and gasped as she did so.

'What's wrong?' Miss Aldridge looked at her small charge. 'Come back here and sit down.' Walking back over to her seat, she did as she was told. Every time footsteps passed the door she jumped up.

'Sally, stop that, nobody's going to harm you,' Miss Aldridge insisted.

'My mother will go for me,' she said turning white with fear.

'She won't Sally. She's in a different room. You go through there with me and your parents sit a bit away from us. Sally, your mother will not harm you. I promise,' she reassured her.

'What if I get sent home?' Sally enquired.

'I don't know if you will or not, but I'll tell you this much, I'll be keeping an eye on you if you do. Your father wants you home Sally. He will see you're all right.'

Sally wasn't too sure about that. Her father didn't know half of what went on because of his shifts. She knew he had dared Nellie to harm her, but it still went on.

In the courtroom, Sally sat beside Miss Aldridge and watched every move the magistrate made. He looked through the papers that lay in front of him, glancing up every now and again. Sally couldn't take her eyes off his glasses. She had never seen anyone wear glasses that were in half before. She looked for her parents, but couldn't see them.

She thought ' if I can't see them, they can't see me.'

At last someone spoke. It was a man who sat in front of the magistrate's table. He was talking to the magistrate. They were referring to Sally's breach of parole. The magistrate asked for the Matron's report and read it in silence. He then asked Sally to come forward a little to enable him to see and hear her better.

Sally looked up into Miss Aldridge's face and waited for her instructions.

'You can step forward with her, I can see she's unsure,' the magistrate said to Miss Aldridge. He now addressed Sally. 'Don't be frightened Sally, I just want to find out a few things, and you are the only one who can help me.'

Sally and Miss Aldridge stepped into the centre of the floor.

Looking to the side, Sally's heart almost stopped with terror. She could now see her mother. She looked away quickly to avoid their eyes meeting.

Trembling, she fought very hard to keep tears from her eyes. Aware of the magistrate's gaze, she focused her attention on his kind face.

'Sally, you had quite a journey I see. Weren't you afraid?' he asked.

'No,' Sally said barely audible.

'Well, I think I would have been,' he said, trying to put her at ease. 'What made you take this amazing journey?' he continued.

Shuffling from foot to foot, she answered. 'I wanted to go back and see my friends at Olive Bank,' she answered avoiding the real reason.

'Don't you think you should have discussed this with your parents?' the magistrate asked.

'No,' she whispered again.

'Don't you care about causing them worry?' he asked.

'No,' Sally said again, then as an after thought she added, 'well I do care about my da'.'

'And why not your mother?' the magistrate asked, leaning over the desk.

'I don't like being skelped and punched for nothing.' Her voice was now adamant and fearless.

'Your mother beats you?' the magistrate asked.

'Yes and I hate it. I watch the bairn, do the shopping, and make the tea, clean the house and she still hits me. I don't know what to do. I feel safe at Olive Bank. I hate living with my mother.' The warm tears escaped from her stinging eyes, and seeing her cry, Miss Aldridge stooped down and wiped the distraught child's face.

The magistrate waited until she had gained some sort of composure before carrying on.

'What about your father Sally, does he... er hit you?'

'No Sir, but he works at night time, and... and he's not there when it happens.' She answered sniffing after every second word.

'Is that why you ran away then Sally? Is that the only reason?' The magistrate was trying to be as gentle as he could with her.

'No Sir,' she looked up at Miss Aldridge who nodded as if to say, 'it's all right.'

'My mother leaves us alone at the weekends while she goes to the club. It was one of the Friday nights and a man broke into the house and frightened us. I don't want him to come back,' she continued.

Nodding, the magistrate held his hand up, palms outward; signalling her to stop He then turned and spoke to another man who sat by his side. 'We need not subject the child to any further distress, as we have the statements she made earlier to the police along with the matron's report.' He then turned his attention to Sally's minder, 'Miss Aldridge, could you take Sally into the small room and I will have you called when I want her to return?' As Sally was led out, she could feel her mother's black eyes burn into her back. She then heard the words, 'We will discuss this with you both...' The door shut behind her and she heard no more.

Time dragged on and Sally thought they were never coming to fetch them. On the table lay a few newspapers and a magazine. She lifted the magazine. Screwing up her nose, she looked at the uninteresting cover and put it down again. The door eventually opened, and they were called back into the room.

'Miss Aldridge,' the magistrate spoke. 'Can you bring the child over here.' He pointed to the floor in front of his desk. Clasping his huge hands together, he held them tightly against his chest. Clearing his throat, he proceeded to talk in an earnest manner. 'Sally, we can't have you running around the country now, can we? So we have to punish you for breaking your parole. We also have to make sure you are safe, so we have decided to send you back to Olive Bank for one year.'

She could have jumped up and down with joy as she found it hard to contain her excitement. The magistrate was still speaking but she heard nothing else. His last words were all she wanted to hear.

'..during that year you will spend the occasional weekend back home to enable you to get to know your mother better as she has promised to change. You will not be left alone during those visits. I can assure you of that. Now, go with Miss Aldridge and have some lunch before you return to Olive Bank.'

Outside the courtroom, Sally grabbed the young woman's coat and tugged at her squealing with glee. Miss Aldridge laughed as she ruffled Sally's hair.

'Sally, I have never heard anything like this before; your punishment is just what you wanted. You're being sent back to Olive Bank for running away to Olive Bank,' she laughed heartily and Sally joined her.

Their journey back was in total contrast to the one earlier in the day. Instead of being one of solemnity, it was full of joy and chatter. She was now like a completely different person.

The weather hadn't changed, it was still dull and drab, but the atmosphere in the car was bright and sunny. The terrible wind that had made the ferry crossing so hazardous that morning had died down considerably, making the crossing back over a lot smoother.

As the car approached the house, Sally bounced up and down with delight. She could hardly believe her eyes. It looked as if the whole household was standing on the path awaiting her arrival. Matron had been notified by telephone that they were on their way back, so needless to say, Rita stood guard all afternoon at the front window. One signal from her, and they were all out to greet Sally. They hugged and cried, cried and hugged until they felt quite worn out.

Being back at the children's home felt absolutely great. Soon the happenings of the last year were just like a bad dream. She moved back into her old room, as Rita's roommate had gone to live with her grandmother, who had been granted legal custody of her.

Matron went through the usual ritual purchasing new shoes and clothes for Sally. The ones she had were too short and her shoes were on the small side. She was again enrolled in school and attended church every Sunday. Soon everything was back to normal and Sally's mind shut out the dreadful past.

She had been back almost two months when she had a visit from her father. She was delighted to see him and spent the whole day with him. It was the beginning of May and the weather was lovely, so they made their way towards the park. It had a boating lake, play area, fishpond, putting green, tennis courts and crazy golf. The flowerbeds were in bloom with pansies of all colours and shades.

Sally and her father made for the little tea hut. He bought a small bottle of lemonade for Sally, and tea for himself. They served the tea in a paper cup that Sally thought was a novel idea. They made for a bench and sat outside enjoying the sunshine and their refreshments.

Tom Baxter was glad of the seat, as he wanted to talk to Sally about the situation at home. He started talking about how Lucy was growing, and how she was missing her. He spoke about getting a change in hours so that he could be home at nights. Then, with a great deal of dithering, he told her there was another bairn on the way. Nellie was pregnant again. Jumping to her feet, she now faced her father. Her day was spoiled once more. The mention of her mother was bad enough, but she was having another baby. 'Oh aye, she'll be wanting me back now Da, won't she. She'll need someone to fetch and carry. Well, she's had it. I'm not coming home to run after her again.' Tears flowed in anger.

'Your hame visits start in two weeks Sally, an' you hiv tae come hame. She winna start onythin again. You'll see a difference. Honest hen.' He was begging her to listen. 'She wis hurt at what you said in court you ken. The magistrate has her oan probation as weel.' Looking into his daughter's eyes, he saw a lot of hate and bitterness.

'I didn't say anything I didn't mean. She wasn't hurt either da. Mad maybe, but not hurt. No one could ever hurt my ma,' her voice quivered in anger as she clenched her teeth.

'You're wrong Sally. She is truly sorry.' Her father was trying hard to convince her of his wife's anguish, but Sally wasn't having it.

'I know I have to come home da, and I know I have to face her, but don't tell me lies. She'll never change. She speaks to you like dirt at times and you let her.' She watched her father's head drop and his eyes stared at the ground. She wished she hadn't said that, but it couldn't be retracted. Getting to her feet, she stood in front of him. She longed to throw her arms around his neck and comfort him, but she couldn't bring herself to do that. Seeing his daughter's concern, he took her by the arm and pulled her back down beside him.

'Da. What about the other thing, you know, the man?' she looked awkward

'Sally dae you hiv any idea whay he wis?' he asked. 'Was that the very first time you ever saw him?' he continued questioning.

'No da. I saw him coming out of the close the....' she answered without thinking

Tom sat up straight as if he had been given a jolt. 'Come on Sally, when did you see him?'

'I don't know what I'm saying da, you've got me all mixed up with all that talk about ma. No I hadn't seen him before, I told you.' She sounded annoyed.

'He winna be back tae frighten you again onyway. There'll be some boady in every nicht,' Tom assured her.

He was disturbed, as he knew deep down Sally wasn't telling him everything. He let the matter drop but he knew there was something not quite right. She showed annoyance but it was to go on the defence and he knew it.

Things at home were also puzzling him at the moment. Since his wife found out she was pregnant, she had become quiet subdued. Her attitude towards him was different too. She spoke to him with respect, sometimes adding the occasional endearment. A stark contrast to the time she fell with Lucy. He would never understand the woman, but this was totally out of character for Nellie. Her friend Flo hardly ever came round since Sally went away. That too was a mystery, as they had been as thick as thieves for years. Yes, there was an answer to all of this somewhere but he would just have to wait until it all pieced itself together. He had the feeling that Sally was the key to the mystery.

'Come on da, you promised me a game of crazy golf.' Sally stood up and pulled at her father's arm. She wanted to get him away before he started asking more questions.

As they passed the fishpond, Sally began to laugh as she told her father the story of Hugh, and how he was caught fishing in the pond the day he ran away. They both laughed as they visualised Hugh sitting at the side of the pond with his fishing rod dangling in the water.

'Oh da, it's not funny really,' she said hiccupping as she laughed.

'A ken lass,' her father answered. As they looked at each other, they began to laugh hysterically once more.

Linking arms with her father, they made their way to the crazy golf.

The journey back and forth from Olive Bank to Sally's house was now becoming familiar to her. Her first weekend visit was two weeks after her father's visit, and three months since she last saw her mother. The social worker drove her home on the Saturday morning and arranged to pick her up late on Sunday afternoon.

Her father met her at the gate and escorted her into the house. Going into the house felt strange, although she had only been away for a few months. The rooms seemed, somehow, much smaller. The smell from the kitchen wafted out to greet her. She couldn't believe it. If someone had told her, her mother could bake a cake, she would have fallen about laughing. Nellie came through from the kitchen and welcomed her daughter with open arms.

'Sally, oh hen.' She hugged her daughter, then, holding her at arms length, she looked her up and down shaking her head slowly as if she couldn't believe what she was seeing.

'Will you look at you,' she went on, 'you've put weight oan already.' She smiled. 'Come away and sit doon and I'll fetch you a drink o' orange. My! It's hot in here the day.' She spoke aloud as she walked back into the kitchen to fetch the orange.

Sally shot a bewildering glance at her father.

'A telt ye,' he whispered. 'She's a changed wuman. Gie her a go lass.'

Sally wasn't going to give her mother an inch! She had seen her play-acting many times before but never as much as this. No, she was not impressed, but she nodded to her father and mouthed, 'all right da.'

Nellie came back into the living room carrying a metal tray with McEwan's beer logo covering the centre. The tray held a glass of fizzy orange and a slice of sponge cake that had been slightly over baked. In her other hand was a small three-legged stool. 'Now eat this and you'll get a proper meal later.' She laid the small stool in front of Sally. When her mother was free of the tray, Sally noticed her swollen stomach for the first time. She wondered when the baby was due. She hadn't given her father much opportunity to tell her, as she had cut him short whenever he approached the subject. Now that it stared her in the face, she was full of curiosity.

Her mother became aware of her gaze and Sally flushed with embarrassment. Giving a small grunt as if clearing her throat, Sally asked, 'Where's Lucy?'

'She's with Bess. I've sent her along to the co-op for a message or two and she took the bairn in the push chair.' Nellie was now sitting opposite Sally with a cup of tea in her hand.

'Hugh's along the shore with his pals. He's never in that laddie.' Nellie sat forward in her seat, and without warning she added further to Sally's embarrassment by grabbing her hands in hers. In a rather pathetic plea, she said, 'Sally, I am trying, I really am. I really don't know what makes me the way I am, but I'm trying to be better.'

'Oh here goes the act again' thought Sally 'you're going to have to try a lot harder than that,' she said into herself. Drawing her hands away from Nellie, she lifted the glass that lay on her tray. She really did not want more orange, she just had to break the physical contact with her mother. 'Oh, I know ma.' Sally hoped she sounded as convincing as her mother. 'We'll all try harder.' she added.

Nellie seemed satisfied with Sally's statement. 'That's my girl,' she said showing relief.

'*Her* bloomin' girl,' Sally thought. 'I'll never be her girl, I'll never forgive her as long as I live.'

'What are ye goin' tae be daein' efter?' Tom asked Sally.

'I would like to go and see Anna, and maybe call and see our Sam,' she watched for a reaction.

'Oh, Sam hardly ever comes round. And a hear he's goin' tae be stayin' oan at school. That pairs tryin' tae make him intae somethin' he's no'.' She detected a slight flicker of the old Nellie in the reply.

'If there's onythin' in Sam's heid, he'll get the chance tae bring it oot,' added Tom quickly.

'Well, we'll see.' Nellie wasn't going to argue.

Sally found it all quite amusing but she knew that through time it would be back to normal. Nellie couldn't sit on a time bomb forever; she'd have to erupt.

The front door opened and a commotion was heard in the hall. The wee body came flying through the door and into the living room. Catching sight of Sally, the child screamed in delight. 'Sassie, Sassie.' She ran and threw her arms around Sally's legs.

'Come on up and give me a kiss.' Sally hadn't realised how much she had missed Lucy. 'Oh, you're getting a big girl Lucy!' she exclaimed.

'I is four now,' Lucy said with pride, thumping her chest with her chubby finger.

'I know, did you get my card?' she looked towards Nellie as she spoke.

'Yes Sally, she got it,' Nellie answered for Lucy.

'Four, oh my, you're almost as old as me,' Sally joked.

'So you're back now?' The voice came from Bess who stood at the door and sneered.

'I'll not be going the messages now that your home,' she said.

'Don't be cheeky you,' Tom swung round and confronted Bess. 'You'll be daein' a lot mare from noo on lady, and Sally bein' hame will make not a ha'pennies worth o' difference'.

Sally did visit Anna and as the day was so beautiful the two friends sat out in the garden most of the afternoon. Anna's mother provided them with a picnic and left them alone to catch up on past events. Sally told Anna a bit of her story but left out the parts she wanted to keep to herself. When she left Anna's she went straight home, as she had stayed longer than planned. She didn't visit Sam.

The weekend went quickly and without incident, just as her father said it would. Weekend visits were planned for once a month to enable Sally to come to terms with her family and surroundings once more.

Nellie was visited regularly by the Social Worker and some improvement was made regarding the house. It was being kept a lot cleaner and as the weekend drinking had stopped, more food was being bought. Bess was the only one who made no effort. She was just as dirty as ever. Washing wasn't commonplace with her, as she had to be forced under the water. Sometimes she even had to be held over the sink. Although her bed-wetting had stopped, the room was just as smelly. She always left it to the last minute when needing to visit the toilet, so she consistently dribbled her pants. Her underwear always stank and as she left it lying around the room, it added to the already offensive smell. As Sally was away, Lucy slept in her single bed, sharing the room with Bess. Hugh had a room to himself now, and although the boy was bodily clean, he was very untidy.

Chapter Nine

The summer was now long gone. Nellie had the fire roaring in the grate as the winter had come with a vengeance. A carpet of hard frost covered the ground. It was nearing the end of October and her baby was due any time.

This was the only pregnancy she had that was sickness free. It was the mental agony she had to contend with. She knew within herself that it wasn't Tom's child. She had confided her fears to Flo, who didn't want to become involved any more so their long friendship had cooled considerably.

Nellie's attention was all now directed towards her husband, as she had no one else to turn to. Her bad temper had turned everyone against her. Flo had been the only friend she had, and now she was alone. Her confidence diminished, she began to cling to Tom more and more each day. He naturally was delighted at his wife's transformation and saw it as an attempt to salvage any affection that he still had for her.

Tom had gone to work, Bess and Hugh had left for school and Nellie sat in the living room drinking a strong cup of tea. She watched the flames from the fire leap fiercely up the chimney and gave a slight shiver. Pulling her cardigan around herself, she lay back and closed her eyes momentarily. Lucy had been dressed, fed, and was now playing happily under the table with her dolls. She did this often, as she imagined she was in a house of her own. The area under the table was her private world. The house felt very peaceful, but the silence was soon broken by the child's scream.

Nellie jumped up and saw terror in the child's eyes as she pointed to the mat in front of the fire. A huge spark had jumped out of the fire and a large hole was now appearing in the middle of the fireside rug. Nellie dropped on to her knees, grabbed the small chrome shovel that hung on the companion set and began to beat furiously at the smouldering rug.

It was then a sharp pain gripped her side, shot across her stomach and made her gasp for breath. Clutching her side, she took a few short pants, all the while making sure the mat had stopped burning. Gritting her teeth, she sucked at the air while struggling to put the blackened mesh guard in front of the fire. Once more she was over come by pain. She gave another few small pants and waited till the pain subsided.

She sat still for a few moments until she was sure the pain had gone. Rising again, she went into the kitchen, washed the breakfast dishes, leaving them on the sink top to dry. Going into the hall she made for the bedroom intending to make up her bed. Pain returned once more, and the severity of it forced her to her knees in agony. She couldn't move, she felt the child pushing itself downward.

She had to get help quickly.

'Lucy. Lucy,' she cried out for her daughter.

Lucy came running through to her mother.

'Go across and knock on Mrs McKenzie's door. Tell her to come quick. Oh, Oh, hurry, hurry,' she heaved and lay down on the floor.

To enable her to reach the door handle Lucy ran through the kitchen and fetched a small stool. With great difficulty the child turned the chub lock, held it until she had pushed down the small button, making sure that the door would not lock behind her. She flew across the hall and banged on the door of the neighbouring house, as if the devil himself was after her.

'Oh my God. Oh! Oh!' Nellie looked between her legs, and, as she pushed, the baby's head appeared. Taking some more deep breaths she gave another push and the baby slithered onto the floor.

Mrs McKenzie reached Nellie, and seeing what had happened, she sprang into action. Wrapping the baby in a large towel, she then put a blanket round Nellie. 'I'll only be a second Nellie. I'm going upstairs to ask the Andersons to phone for the doctor. Now you come with me Lucy and Mr McKenzie will look after you for half an hour while I get mummy seen to.'

Nellie was very grateful for her neighbour's help as she herself felt so weak and helpless. She hadn't had a proper look at the baby yet, as there was still a great deal of panic. Nellie's afterbirth was still to come and the child was still attached to the cord. Waiting the arrival of the doctor seemed to Nellie like hours but it was really no time at all until he was attending mother and child.

'Oh aye Nellie, a fine healthy boy with a mop of ginger hair. He'll be impatient all his life I'm afraid,' the doctor teased Nellie. 'He came into the world in *his* time. He couldn't wait a minute. Aye, I'm afraid you've got a demanding boy on your hands.' The doctor laughed while washing his hands in the basin of water Mrs McKenzie brought through for him.

Mrs McKenzie had helped wash the baby and dressed him in the gown and shawl Nellie had at hand. The floor in the lobby had been thoroughly scrubbed and tea brought through to Nellie, who was by now propped up in bed. Mrs. McKenzie had lit the fire in the bedroom and made up the cot, which had previously been used by Lucy until she had been given Sally's bed. She shared the bed with Sally during her home visits, as Sally did not mind. She loved her little sister, and besides, Lucy didn't wet the bed, unlike Bess, who had started wetting again. It happened shortly after finding out her mother was to have another bairn. She had been seen by the hospital doctors who came to the conclusion that she was either too lazy to get up, or she was suffering from jealousy.

The doctor was leaving now and Mrs McKenzie had volunteered to stay on until the nurse arrived. Tom had also been sent for.

When the doctor had gone, Lucy was taken in to see her new baby brother. She wanted to pick him up and play with him. Mrs McKenzie was laughing and explained to her why she couldn't.

'Mrs McKenzie,' Nellie said softly. The elderly lady turned round and Nellie continued, 'I can't thank you enough. I know I'm not the best of neighbours, but I really do appreciate what you've done this morning. I...'

'Oh go on with you – women stick together at times like this. You can do the same for me some day.' Nellie smiled, and Mrs McKenzie laughed at her own joke as she was well past the age of child bearing.

Tom Baxter walked into the bedroom two hours after the birth of the child. He stood by the cot looking down at the newborn infant. 'He's big Nellie. Yes, he's lying there like a bairn a couple of months old. And where did he get his ginger hair from?' he looked questioningly at Nellie.

Avoiding eye contact, she plucked at the bedclothes, removing imaginary threads.

'Sometimes babies take colouring from past generations Tom, didn't you know that?' Nellie now looked up at him and gave a weak smile. 'His hair will fall out in a month or so, and his true colour will appear,' she added.

'It's funny looking at him lying there when all the rest had right black hair.' He was still puzzled.

She felt like yelling and telling him to shut up about his hair, but she managed to keep her cool

'He's going to be tall,' she said, ignoring his remarks. 'Come here now and give your wife a kiss for going through such an ordeal. Did you know he was born in the lobby?' The subject was changed and Tom never mentioned the baby's hair colour for some time.

Sally came home a few weeks after the baby was born and stayed for a full week. She helped look after Lucy and enjoyed doing so as she wasn't forced into it. She was beginning to get along better with her mother, and sometimes she even felt a great sympathy towards her. She was always having bairns! She thought her father should be ashamed of himself at his age, after all, he was in his middle thirties and far too old for all this.

Sally had no inclination to hold the baby, for the funny thing was, she couldn't take to her new brother at all. There was something about him that she couldn't explain. She wished she knew why she felt like this. It wasn't jealousy, she was sure of that. She just felt nothing for him. She didn't even think he was cute, even though she had at one time stated that all babies were cute. He cried a lot and what the doctor had said in a joke was absolutely true. He was very demanding. She knew she could never hurt him, but there wasn't any love felt for the infant.

Lucy was different. Sally could love her to bits. It was because of Lucy that Sally's trips home became something to look forward to. The house was also a lot cleaner and the bedclothes were being washed more frequently. Bess was being made to smarten up as well. This was her father's doing as he was determined not to let Sally down again.

A month before Sally was due home for good, Tom bought bunk beds for the girls' room. Lucy slept on the bottom and Sally on the top. Bess was still in her single bed and created a fuss because she wasn't allowed to sleep on the new mattresses.

Anna and Sally had laughed hysterically about this, as they imagined Sally on the bottom bunk and Bess wetting on the top bunk. Sally said it would be dangerous to sleep on your back with your mouth open.

Anna was excited at the thought of her friend coming

home and her mother had said she was welcome to stay over any weekend, if it was all right with Nellie and Tom. She also told Sally to bring Lucy round so that they could meet her. She had told them such a lot about her.

Things seemed to be looking up again for Sally, but she had thought that before and her world had collapsed around her.

Sally had gone round to visit Sam a few times when she was on home visits. She thought her older brother was turning out to be really handsome. His thick raven hair was swept back and tapered at the neck in the latest style. His square handsome jaw always had traces of black shadow, no matter how much he shaved. Dark black eyes shone from beneath his thick bushy eyebrows. He was only sixteen, three years older than Sally, but he could easily have passed for eighteen.

Her Auntie Mary always made her welcome, except Sally didn't like all the questions she asked. She was a very nosy woman although very likeable.

It was during one of those visits something was said that made Sally think. It was the week she came home after the baby was born and she went to visit Sam. They were sitting round the fire having tea, Auntie Mary had the small coffee table laden with scones, cakes and biscuits and she was asking Sally all about the baby.

'Has he got a name yet Sally?' she asked.

'Yes, he's to be called Robert.'

'Does he sleep all night?' she questioned.

'No, he's not as good as Lucy was.' Sally remarked.

'I hear she had him by herself.'

'Yes.' Sally was only half listening, as she had grown tired of her aunt's constant questions.

'And I hear the baby has red hair,' Mary continued.

Sally looked into her Auntie's face and tried to figure out all the interest. She was never interested in any of the others.

'Yes he has,' she answered.

'Funny that when all the rest of you are so dark,' her Auntie's mouth puckered as if ready for a kiss, an expression she used when feeling vindicated.

Sam was too busy feeding his face and speaking to his Uncle to be listening to women's chitchat. He wasn't very interested in the baby either as he had called in to see him only once. To be honest, he had gone to see his mother, the baby was lying in her arms and could not be very easily ignored.

Sally eventually excused herself and said her goodbyes. It was dark very quickly at nights now and Sally didn't like to be out alone.

All the way back home the question about the baby's hair disturbed her. Was that why she didn't bond with him? If so, why? This question made her feel uneasy, after all, she knew people with red hair and she liked them, why then did it make a difference now? She just didn't know.

It had snowed heavily through the night and when the children looked out the window in the morning they leaped up and down with excitement. It was the first snow of the year and it was really deep. Sally had completed her year at Olive Bank and although she felt sad at leaving, it had been easier this time. She had celebrated her thirteenth birthday the week before she left. She had been home for three weeks and apart from baby Robert's constant crying, things hadn't been so bad.

'Come oan you lot,' called Tom. 'The snaw'll be melted by the time you lot get up an' oot. It's a guid joab it's Seturday, you'll be able tae play aw day long.'

Hugh was first dressed and at the table. Tom filled a bowl of porridge for him and he ate it as if he were starving.

'Take yer time eatin,'' Tom scowled.

The rest of the children sat down at the table as Hugh left.

'He didn't wash,' Sally informed Tom. 'He threw his clothes on this morning. I bet his neck has a thick tide-mark.'

'Maybe he washed last night,' Bess said haughtily.

'He'll no' be oot there long,' Tom laughed. 'It's a nirl (bitter cold). He'll be in shortly, his hand nippin' like blazes an' his nose dreepin' like a runnin' tap.'

Jumping from her chair, Bess exclaimed, 'I'm going round the back to make a snowman!'

'Eat yer breakfast first, or you'll no be goin' onywhere.' Tom filled the remaining bowls with porridge and left Sally and Bess at the table while he walked over towards the fire to help Lucy finish dressing. Lucy was slow in moving as she was forever stopping to gaze into the fire.

Bess and Lucy played round the back of the house while Sally watched them from the kitchen window.

They started rolling a snowball around the perimeter of the garden until it was big enough for the body of their snowman. Then they did the same thing over again, but this time the ball was smaller. Lifting it between them, they stuck it down firmly onto the waiting body. Lucy squealed with delight!

Sally helped her father wash the breakfast dishes and made a pot of tea for her mother. Nellie had been awake most of the night with Robert who had started turning his nights into days.

Later in the day, when Sally had finished her chores and Bess had done her bit, they took Lucy out on the old wooden sledge Tom had made years ago out of an old fish crate. He had nailed runners onto the bottom to make it slide along smoothly.

They had great fun playing on the waste ground at the end of the street. The old houses that once stood there had been flattened by mechanical diggers preparing the land for building, and the unwanted earth had been piled to one side, making an ideal mountain for the sledge to glide down.

They had been playing for some time and were starting to feel their toes and fingers nip with cold. Having had enough, they decided that the next slide down the hill would be their last. Lucy was last to reach the bottom, and as Sally helped lift her from the sledge, she felt an almighty thud as something hit her ear. It was thrown with such force she struggled to keep her balance. She had been unaware of the two lads watching her until the snowball hit the side of her head. They were aged about sixteen, and laughed as they stooped to pick up more snow. They let fly once more hitting Sally on the neck, and young Lucy on the back. Lucy began to cry. Bess took to her heels and ran along the road towards the house.

Tom sat toasting his hands at the fire while sitting opposite him Nellie busily changed the baby. The door burst open and Bess flew in. Breathlessly, she pulled at Tom's arm and blurted out her story.

Tom followed on quickly behind Bess. They found the two girls huddled together; Sally of course, trying to protect her young sister, was taking the worst of the battering, as the two lads pelted the girls relentlessly. They had worked themselves into frenzy, taking great delight at the girls' distress. The girls were entirely covered in thick snow and stood shivering with cold and fear. The snow had lost its softness and pieces of hard ice stuck to the girls' hair. Part of the ball containing bits of soft muck had also found its target, smudging Sally's face.

'I'll kick yer bloody backsides,' Tom yelled. 'Pickin' oan wee lassies. Ye're young men an' should ken better.' He was furious. He grabbed at them both but one of the lads broke free and ran off. Tom, holding tightly on to the other lad, stooped down, grabbed a rather large handful of snow and coarsely rubbed the boy's face with it. He repeated this action four times as the lad struggled to get free. He spluttered and coughed as the snow found its way into his open mouth.

'See if you like it, ye bloody great bully.' Then swinging the lad round, he lifted his huge foot, kicking the protesting bully on the behind, causing him to fly head first into the snow. Picking himself up quickly, the lad ran off. When he was a good few yards away, he stopped and shouted back at Tom. 'I'll tell my father on you. He will have you for this. Don't you know who we are?' The boy yelled.

'Aye, a ken aw richt,' Tom shouted as he waved his fist in the air. 'Dae ye think yer da's money allows ye tae dae whit ye like? Ye're nothin' but bloody yobbos. You an' yer posh schoolin' an' aw. Get goin' or a'll catch ye up an' gie ye an ither o' the like.' Tom lifted Lucy up in his arms and led Sally away with his other hand. Bess followed on pulling the sledge.

'Who were they Da?' Sally asked, brushing the snow from her coat.

'Their faither owns the sawmill at the end o' Kirk Street, an' has property or somethin' up in Edinburgh. They bocht (bought) ower the auld manse. They're the twins, the Watson twins. Bloody young upstarts. You watch oot fer them Sally. For aw their money, they're thievin' little buggers an' all.'

This had put an end to their fun. By evening it had started to thaw causing the snow to turn to slush.

When Hugh was told the tale of the Watson twins, he bit into his lip and looked worriedly at Sally 'They're terrible Sally, they knocked Ian Thomson's front teeth oot because he wid na give them his bike, *and* they slashed seats oan the bus last week.'

Tom scowled. 'Enough o' that Hugh, we've heard enough aboot the Watsons.'

Yes, Sally had certainly heard enough.

Sally was back at school now and once more had taken

up with her friend Anna. As Nellie had become a lot cleaner and the house started to look like a home, Anna was invited over by Sally. She had asked her mother's permission first and was astounded when Nellie agreed to her bringing her friend around.

This was the very first time Sally had brought a friend into her home, and she felt a bit apprehensive at first. However, everything went well. Even Bess was on her best behaviour. As a matter of fact, Bess just sat and stared at Anna as if she was from another planet.

Nellie too had taken an interest. She had gone out of her way to make Sally's friend feel welcome, and even, sometimes to Sally's annoyance, had butted in on their conversation. The only thing was, Sally could not take her friend into her bedroom as was normally done with friends. There was no games or things, in fact the few toys that they had in the house belonged to the babies. There was nothing of interest to a couple of thirteen year olds except for a few comics.

The room itself was badly in need of painting, as the walls still had the awful green emulsion that was on when they moved in, the only difference was, it was now filthy and crayon scribbles added to the dirt. No expensive wall-to-wall carpeting graced *their* bedroom floor as it did in Anna's. Theirs was covered with the cheapest of linoleum Nellie could get. She bought it in an Edinburgh warehouse along with the living room carpet and a shilling a week man collected payment every Saturday morning. Any improvements made to the house were aimed at the living room and kitchen, but it didn't matter to Sally, as she was just thrilled at being able to bring her friend home now and again.

The change didn't stop there; Sally started to attend Sunday school as she was in the habit of going when at Olive Bank. She took Lucy with her and put her into the infant class. She made a lot of new friends there and was asked to play the piano on a few occasions. She thanked God for the wonderful changes in her life and decided it was time to forgive her mother.

Six months had passed and all the changes in Sally's life had been good ones, except for the occasional fights with Bess and a few cross words with Nellie, but she knew that was all part of family life. Tom and Sally had long talks about almost everything, but she still could never talk to Nellie. She just didn't know how to approach her. There were things she would have liked to ask her mother, but she felt too embarrassed and awkward, so, she relied on the snippets of information she heard at school.

She needed to talk to someone about the way she had been feeling lately. She felt agitated and weepy at times as well as short tempered. Why? She couldn't explain to anyone. Her body was changing as well and that frightened her. She just didn't understand. Sally thought about visiting Flo but she knew her mother would be annoyed, as Flo had turned her back on Nellie. That was another strange turn of events.

The summer holidays had been disappointing as the weather had been mainly wet. What good days there had been were spent on the shore. The weekends were the best as Tom and Nellie had taken them all to Gullane beach a few times. They took a picnic with them and spent the whole day playing on the sand dunes.

Sally enjoyed the bus journey and had fun with the children, especially when her parents along with another family from Glasgow who were holidaying at a near by campsite, joined in and had a great game of rounders. She couldn't remember the last time she saw her mother and father cling together in laughter, in fact, it was the very first time she had seen such a sight and she liked what she saw. She had tremendous fun, but she wasn't over keen on the sand as it got into everything, even the sandwiches.

As she had gone to Gullane beach on Saturday, Nellie was trying to catch up with the washing and ironing on Sunday, but Robert, as usual, was crying his head off. Sally had cleaned the bedrooms and was about to start on the hall. Lucy was having a sleep, as she had been up very early and Bess had gone to the corner shop for a few messages. Hugh, as usual, was out.

Nellie came through into the hall looking strained and very tense. 'Sally, be a guid lass an' take Robert oot a while. If you dinnae, I'll wring his bloody neck. That constant yellin' is beginnin' tae get me doon.'

His constant crying for attention was beginning to drive them all mad.

'Right ma.' This was a good opportunity to get out into the sunshine, so she really didn't mind. She helped Nellie get his pram ready while Robert grew red in the face with temper.

'There's nothin' wrong wi' him except tiredness an' bad temper,' Nellie said, as she laid him down. 'He'll sleep yinst the pram gets movin'. Dinnae hurry back as he's been fed an' watered. If ye meet the gypsies trade him fer a dozen claes pegs,' Nellie joked without a smile.

'A dozen? I'll settle fer six,' she said as an afterthought.

The baby stopped crying after the pram had been on the move for ten minutes. She took the pram off the main road and headed for the back streets where there was less traffic.

The houses where she now walked all had beautiful kept gardens, which were now in full bloom. Splashes of colour edged neatly manicured lawns each looking like they were in competition with their neighbours'. Couples worked together mowing grass and pulling at weeds that dared show their heads.

She stopped the pram and looked in at Robert who was now sound asleep. She decided to walk to the end of the street as it took her to the path that lead towards a quiet country lane where she would find peace and tranquillity. She had walked for fifteen minutes enjoying the birds singing in the hedgerows. A few white butterflies fluttered by while busy bees buzzed loudly flitting from one wild flower to another gathering their precious pollen. The smell of the clean air filled her lungs while the sun kissed her gently on the face.

A young courting couple, accompanied by a small scruffy looking dog, passed by giving Sally a warm smile while looking longingly at the pram. Their dog stopped and sniffed at the grass before lifting its leg and spraying over an existing scent. Sally half smiled and went on her journey. Shortly after, a cyclist passed dressed in working clothes with his haversack slung over his shoulder. She decided to stroll on till she reached the small bridge where she would turn and head for home as once over the bridge the path grew narrower causing hedge rows to protrude further, making it difficult to push the pram. As it was, the surface of the path had changed becoming stony and uneven making the pram shake violently tossing the baby from side to side. When she got to the bridge she heard voices. They seemed to come from underneath. A small stream ran below and it was possible someone was playing in the water. She turned the pram with difficulty, as the path was so narrow, it caused it to brush against the hedge. She began to feel uncomfortable as perspiration began leaking from her pores, partly from the heat of the sun, but mostly due to the struggle she had turning the pram.

She was about to start her return journey when she froze with fear. She recognised the voices from beneath her, and they were now calling her name. Sally hurried on without looking back. Her name was called once more, except it wasn't Sally they were calling, it was 'Baxter bitch.'

She knew someone was running behind her as she heard the shrubbery being disturbed, and then the hand on her shoulder turned her sharply round.

He continued to hold her by the shoulder causing her to wince with pain as his nails dug deeply into her flesh.

'Let me go, you hear!' she demanded. Her voice, although stern, quivered. The palms of her hands soaked in sweat, a different sweat that already clung to her body, the sweat of terror. She was looking into the face of one of the Watson boys while his twin was walking up behind his brother. A third boy, who looked about eight years of age, appeared through the bushes. The first Watson boy took hold of Sally's hair and as Sally began to wriggle, he started to mimic her voice.

'Let me go, you hear,' he laughed as he repeated her words several times. The other brother joined in, but the youngest stood a bit away and looked almost as frightened as Sally.

'What shall we do with her Jake?' The twin behind asked his brother.

'Well, there's no snow now Neil, so we'll have to think of something else eh!'

Sally spoke, but this time in a pleading voice. 'Please leave me; I've done nothing to you. You're hurting me--- ouch!' She dropped her shoulder in an effort to break free but Jake was now twisting her arm up her back.

Tears formed in her eyes while her breath escaped in small jerks. She didn't want to cry but she was terrified.

Jake pushed her violently across to his brother who in turn pushed her back to Jake. They did this several times and laughed loudly as Sally grew more and more distressed.

Jake turned to the smaller lad and told him to take the pram further up the path and stay with the baby.

'Go on, get moving and stay up there till I call you,' Jake shouted.

'You can't take the baby away,' she screamed frantically.

'Leave us alone, you've had your fun.'

'Not yet we haven't.' Jake grinned at his twin.

'Push her on the ground Jake,' Neil yelled with excitement.

He did just that and she landed heavily on the ground, her arm twisted underneath her. She felt as if her arm had broken and as the pain gripped her she started to moan.

It was Neil who now took over.

'Come on man, don't let her up,' Jake jumped with excitement as he egged his brother on.

Sally was trying to push herself up with her free hand, when she felt the weight of Neil Watson's body knock her back down.

'Get off me,' she screamed at the top of her voice. Her legs kicked and thrashed wildly.

With his weight bearing down on her chest, he roared at his brother.

'Help me for Christ's sake.' He cupped his hand tightly over Sally's mouth and waited till his brother put his weight on the terrified young girl's legs.

'Come on man before someone comes.' Jake was now becoming agitated.

Neil managed to straddle across Sally while Jake lifted her skirt and pulled at her pants.

Sally's head was rocking back and forth as her mouth had been stuffed with a handkerchief from Neil's pocket. She was choking and found breathing difficult.

'Go on now Neil, hurry I want one too,' Jake ordered his voice full of excitement.

'Pin her arms down Jake. She can't move her legs now.' Neil's voice was urgent.

Jake went to Sally's head and leaning over, pinned her arms by her side.

Neil tried to enter Sally as he clumsily pushed down hard. He couldn't enter properly so he pushed again. The handkerchief in her mouth stifled her screams as sweat poured out of her lifeless body.

She felt the fires of hell sear through her body as her flesh was ripped and torn.

'Like that Bitch?' Jake looked at her from an upside down position. 'We'll teach you a lesson or two.'

'Oh shit,' Neil said as he sat up.

Sally felt something wet and sticky on her leg as Neil swore before swinging his body over and standing up.

'You stupid bugger, come on and hold her arms.' Jake was hurrying his brother along.

Sally started to kick out once more as Jake took up the same position his brother had vacated. She wished she could die. The pain from her arm was nothing compared to what she was going through now.

'Watch wee brother and see how the big boys do it.' Jake mocked his twin.

'Right slut, what do you think of this?' He taunted Sally as he forced his way into her slight body.

She could take no more. She felt herself slip down a tunnel of darkness. Flashing white lights lit up the tunnel and the sound of buzzing echoed in her ears. The pain still persisted as Jake tore away at her inside.

When the two lads had finished with Sally they

whistled on the younger boy who had gone up the path out of sight.

'Come on titch,' Neil called. 'Leave the bloody pram there.'

The younger boy ran up to where the twins were standing then looking down at Sally's motionless body asked what was the matter with her.

Jake and Neil both laughed and walking away pulled the youngster along with them.

'She's sleeping, lazy slag,' Jake said.

Sally lay where she was until she was sure they had gone. Slowly she rose and looked around for the pram. She saw it in the distance and although she worried about Robert, she just couldn't run to him. Feeling light-headed she tried steadying herself as the pain between her legs burned. Putting her hand over her crotch she felt her skirt damp against her bare legs. She was horrified when she saw the huge patch of blood seeping through the flimsy material. Looking around she found her crumpled knickers and slowly slipped them on. Putting one foot slowly in front of the other she headed in the direction of the pram although every step she took tore her apart she had to keep walking or she knew she would collapse. She forced every step and when she reached the pram, the baby was still sound asleep. Leaning on the pram handle, she managed to walk home using it as a walking aid. She felt degraded and dirty and didn't know what to tell her mother. Maybe she would be blamed; they'd say she should not have gone along that quiet road by herself anyway.

Why did those things happen when her life was beginning to take on some meaning?

Opening the door she pushed Robert's pram into the hall. At the same time Nellie appeared at the living room door.

'Sleepin' is he?' she enquired.

'Yes.' She averted her eyes from her mother, as all she wanted was to get into the bathroom before Nellie spotted her skirt.

'Has he slept long?' she asked coming over and looking into the pram.

'Nearly all the time,' Sally replied lifelessly.

'You should hav' left him outside. Come oan, I'll take the pram oot the back and leave him in the fresh air'.

Sally stepped aside to allow Nellie room to turn the pram and as she did she scurried to the side.

Looking at Sally's face she realised her daughter was acting strangely.

'What's wrong, ye're real jumpy are ye no'?'

Sally shying away caused Nellie to look closely.

'What's that oan yer skirt?'

Stepping back, Sally began to cry.

'My goodness,' Nellie exclaimed, 'A've been waitin' oan this for ages. Dinnae be feared Sally. Go an' sit doon till a get him ootside.'

Sally had no idea what her mother meant. She thought Nellie knew what had happened and had expected it. She was confused.

Nellie took the pram round the back of the house and placed it under the kitchen window. Lucy was playing there with Bess so Nellie told them to stay out for a bit and mind Robert. She then went back into the house and sat down beside Sally who was still sobbing.

'It wasn't my fault ma', she sobbed.

'A ken lass, it's somethin' that happens tae aw lassies your age.'

Sally stared at her mother in amazement. 'It does?' she questioned somewhat foolishly.

'Aye, it's you changin' fae a lassie intae a young wuman. Ye'll bleed like this fer four or five days every month. Now listen tae me Sally, you bide away fae laddies noo. You hear?' Nellie's face looked very serious.

'Yes ma,' Sally replied wearily. She realised that her mother was trying to tell her about her body changes, and although she wanted to tell her what really had happened and how she felt, she thought it best to go along with this and keep the matter to herself. After all, it was a filthy dirty thing and she would only be humiliated more. Everyone would say she deserved it; anyway, it would be her word against theirs. People would believe them, as their family had lots of money, hadn't her father said they get off with murder.

'A mind when a took mine. A was sittin' oan the beach and a thought a had sat doon oan glass.' Nellie laughed as she reminisced.

'Come away an' a'll show you what you wear. Come through the room wi' me.'

Nellie took Sally through into the bedroom and sitting on the edge of the bed, demonstrated how to keep clean.

Sally scrubbed her skin until the bristles of the brush left white scratch marks against her red raw flesh. She had to get every part of her body clean. She ached all over but it didn't matter, the sorer she felt the cleaner she felt.

It took a week before the pain inside Sally's body eased but the mental scarring would possibly stay with her for the rest of her life. It also brought home to her what the man was trying to do the night he forced his way into her home. Was it to be like this forever, or was it only she that was fated?

Chapter Ten

Weeks after the attack on Sally she was taken to the doctor by her mother. Her periods had started from that awful day but they were not normal. She suffered tremendous abdominal pain and had fainted several times. Her appetite was poor at the best of times but now it had gone completely. She looked ghastly.

The doctor said there was nothing to worry about as it was only her age, however, she was to go back and see him after her next period, and he would decide what to do. When they returned home, her mother sent her to bed and made her stay there for a few days.

Nellie had indeed changed towards Sally; in fact, she had changed in lots of ways. It seemed to all happen after Robert was born. He still woke through the night but not as often. He was now one year old and had started to walk.

The following morning they woke to the sound of Robert crying. He was standing up rattling the side of his cot. Nellie was exhausted with him, as it had been one of his bad nights. He was teething and she had walked the floor with him. Tom had gone to work early, so Nellie called on Bess to lift Robert. She wanted her to take the baby from his cot and amuse him for a while so that she could rest.

Bess, still very sleepy, rubbed her eyes and yawning looked over at Sally who was turning round in her bed. 'You do it Sally,' Bess pleaded.

'No Bess, you were told.'

The two girls were busy arguing and didn't notice Lucy rise from her bed and leave the room.

Slipping quietly into her mother's room, she crept over towards the cot. As Nellie lay facing the wall, she was unaware of Lucy's presence. She was so tired it was a struggle to open her eyes. All she wanted to do was slip back into the world of dreams.

Seeing Lucy, Robert stopped crying immediately. Bouncing up and down, his face now beaming, he threw his arms over the top of the cot.

Lucy wasn't very big for a five year old, but she managed to reach the clips that let the sides down. Robert threw his chubby hands around her neck as Lucy attempted to lift him out. As he was being lifted forward, his foot knocked on the side of the cot causing him to topple over on top of Lucy. Losing her balance, she stumbled backwards letting the baby fall. Lucy's cries aroused her mother. She turned round and looked towards the cot. Through hazy sleep filled eyes, she saw Lucy lying on her back, with baby Robert across her stomach.

Sally had jumped down from the top bunk having decided to give in and go for Robert herself. When she heard the thud, she ran along the hall reaching the door of her mother's room just as Nellie grasped the situation.

'Oh my God,' she gasped as she jumped from her bed. She ran over to where Robert lay and picked him up. His small body went limp in her arms and Nellie lifted her eyes up to where Sally stood.

'Run and bang on the McKenzie's door. Get an ambulance quickly Sally'.

Sally was rooted to the spot while Lucy, still screaming, was grabbing at her legs.

'Go Sally!!' Nellie screamed.

Springing to life, she broke free of her terrified sister's grasp and ran out of the door. Bess came along the lobby slowly. Knowing something had happened, she was frightened to look into her mother's room. As she passed Hugh's room, he opened his door. Scratching his head, he asked sleepily, 'What's up?'

Bess stood at the room door and watched with Hugh. Her lips were quivering as she took in the scene around her. Nellie was sitting on the floor with Robert in her arms. She rocked him back and forth. As tears streamed down her cheeks, she repeated over and over, 'Oh no God, no. No God no. Please God not this.'

Sally appeared with Mrs McKenzie, who instructed the children to go into their rooms and get dressed. Shivering with fear, Lucy was led away by Sally. Mrs McKenzie closed the room door and sat down on the floor beside Nellie.

The police arrived shortly after the doctor and ambulance. They couldn't get much sense from Nellie as she was in deep shock. Lucy didn't understand what had happened, except that Robert was sleeping and wouldn't wake up. Tom had been brought home in a police car. One of the officers had gone to his work and broken the news to him there.

Sally was terrified that Lucy would be taken away from them. One minute she felt responsible for the death of the baby then she would lay the blame on Bess. These thoughts fluctuated back and forth until she didn't know any more. Poor Robert. Poor, poor Robert. Why couldn't she have loved that child, the child with the red hair? Why was her heart so heavy with guilt? Was it her fault? Was she condemned to a life of misery?

Nellie stayed in her room until the day of the funeral. Tom didn't want her to go but she insisted. Flo had come round to see if she could do anything to help so Tom asked her to take the younger children as he didn't want them there. Sam and Sally attended, as they were the eldest.

Sally stood along side her mother and for the first time in her young life she felt close to her. Nellie sensed this too, and she slipped her arm round her daughter's waist and pulled her near. As they stood side by side, they watched Tom and Sam help lower the small white coffin into the ground.

The police and the doctor met with the coroner, and it was decided that as it could affect Lucy emotionally in later years, the cause of death would not be made public. It had been a terrible tragic accident, and no blame should fall on Lucy, therefore the verdict was simply Accidental Death.

Sally was not well before the baby's death, now she was ten times worse. She didn't want to complain, as her mother was not all that well either, so she went back to school and tried to make the best of things.

Anna was worried about her friend's health too, as she seemed to be losing interest in everything. She couldn't make her laugh, no matter how hard she tried. They had been friends for a long time now and never a cross word had passed between them. That was until now. She became annoyed at the least little thing and their quarrels often resulted in Sally being reduced to tears. If left alone she became extremely despondent.

The house was quiet during the day, as Lucy had started school. Nellie had done a bit of work round the house and was about to go shopping. As she stood by the window buttoning up her coat, she noticed Sally being helped out of a car that had stopped at the gate. Going to the front door, she opened it just as her daughter was let into the close.

'Mrs Baxter?' Sally's escort asked.

'Aye.' Nellie answered taking Sally by the arm. She could see that she was unwell. Her dark hair framed her very pale face resembling a porcelain doll.

'I've brought Sally home as she had another fainting turn today.' She smiled down at Sally before returning her gaze to Nellie. 'I'm Miss Munro, Sally's English teacher'.

'Oh, thank you for bringing her hame. She hasn't been well for some time noo but it's gone oan long enough'. Looking down at Sally she said, 'Go an' take your coat oaf an' lie doon in the living room.' Directing her attention back to the teacher, Nellie informed her. 'I'll take her along tae the doctor an' I'll let you ken what he says. Thanks yince again'. She paused for a moment before adding, 'you were lucky tae catch me in, another minute an' a'd have been oot shoppin'.'

Guiding Mrs Munro towards the close door, she held it open allowing the teacher to pass through. 'Thank's yince mare,' she called after her.

Back in the living room Sally had done exactly what her mother had told her to do. She was lying stretched out on the sofa, her eyes half closed. She lay motionless. Her mother leaned over her frail body and covered her with a blanket.

'You ken Sally,' she said gently, 'ye've put this visit tae the doctor's off long enough, noo you're goin' wi' me the nicht.' She knelt in front of her and looked into her eyes. Eyes that used to be bright and shiny were now dull and sunken. Black shadows lay under her eyes and her skin looked dirty. She was ill, but all the medicines in the world could not cure Sally's inner feelings.

'Ma?' She blinked tired lids. 'What will the doctor do?'

'He'll have tae examine ye a suppose. Why? You're no' lettin' that bother ye a hope'. Nellie sat down on the edge of the sofa beside her frightened daughter.

'I just... I just... don't want him to.'

Nellie could not understand why she was so scared of the doctor. She hadn't been before.

'A dinnae understand you some times Sally. Ye want tae feel better don't ye?'

Sally nodded slowly.

'Well,' continued Nellie, 'you need the doctor's help an' you winna get it if he disnae ken what's wrong. He has tae examine ye tae find oot.' She went on after a few moments silence. 'He examines young lassies every day o' his life.' She stood up and looked down on her daughter for a few seconds. 'A'll make us a cuppa an' we'll have a corn beef sandwich, right?'

'I don't want anything ma,' she said.

'That's half yer trouble Sally, ye dinnae eat enough.' She clicked her tongue in annoyance. 'Right, ye're havin' a drink o' tea whether ye like it or no' cause a'm having yin.'

Later that afternoon they both went to see the doctor. They did some shopping on the way, as Nellie hadn't had the chance earlier because it would have meant leaving Sally alone in the house.

The doctor who saw Sally was one of the senior partners in the practice. He was a huge man with ruddy cheeks. He looked more like a farmer than a doctor. Sally sat beside her mother and listened as Nellie explained her daughter's symptoms.

'So lass,' the doctor addressed the frightened girl. 'You're fainting all over the place are you?' He smiled showing brown stained teeth. His grin was like the Cheshire cat she had seen in the Alice in Wonderland book. 'Well, we can't have that.' He moved from his side of the desk and made his way around to where Sally sat twirling her handkerchief around her finger that had turned purple with pressure.

Placing one of his massive fingers under Sally's chin, he tilted her head right back.

'We'll have a look into those bonny eyes and see what's going on.' He took a long silver pencil shaped torch out of his top pocket and shone the beam into her eyes.

As Sally looked up into his face she found herself looking up his nostrils. She bit hard on her lip as she felt an impulse to laugh.

Straightening up, he returned the torch back into his pocket. 'Hum.' He then lifted her hands up and seeing the handkerchief still wrapped around her finger, removed it. 'You'll strangle that finger if you don't watch out. Now let me see.' He turned her hands palms downwards and looked at Sally's nails. 'Hum,' he said once more. 'I can tell you this, you're a very anaemic girl, you know what that means? Bloodless! I'm sorry but I'm going to take a little more away from you as I'd like to send it for testing.' He walked over to the side of the room where instruments and small boxes lay on a table.

Looking up at Nellie, Sally's eyes darted wildly under her lids. Her mouth opened and closed, but no sound came out. Her throat felt so dry.

'You're awright silly,' Nellie reassured her. 'You don't feel much. It's nothing.'

Carrying a rubber armband, and with laughter in his voice, the doctor teased, 'your not frightened. A great big lass like you?' He rolled her sleeve up and placed the band firmly on her arm just above her elbow. Bending her arm, he gave a tiny area a quick wipe with wet cotton wool. He was about to insert the needle to take the sample of blood, when Sally slid down out of her seat onto the floor. Everything had gone dark, and then from a distance, she heard someone calling her name.

She came round sitting on the floor with her head bent so far forward her brow was almost on the ground. Nellie helped the doctor lift her back on to the seat. Feeling foolish, Sally apologised for fainting. 'Don't worry. Are you all right now?' he asked sympathetically.

Nodding, Sally suddenly remembered the blood sample that was yet to be taken. Seeing the anxiety reappear in his young patient's face, the doctor smiled. 'Don't worry, I took the sample when you were out.' He had sealed the precious blood in a small glass tube and was now writing on the label. 'I would also like you to be examined by a gynaecologist as I think by what your mother's saying, you're having too much trouble with your menstrual cycle.'

Not only did Sally's face flush, as if the blood in her veins had caught fire, her whole body seemed to be soaked in perspiration. She was sure the doctor would notice her distress etched face so bending her head she stared at the floor.

'What dae you think is wrong doctor?' asked Nellie.

'I don't think there's much to worry about. Some girls have no trouble and others are not so lucky. I think Sally's one of the latter. Still, I would like her checked over; meanwhile, I'll give you a prescription for iron Mrs Baxter and be sure she takes it. Liver, give her plenty of liver.' He looked down once more at his desk, and writing the prescription spoke to Nellie without raising his head.

'And how's yourself Mrs Baxter, keeping better?'

'Aye, oh aye.' Nellie answered as she helped Sally on with her coat.

'Good. Good.' He handed her the prescription and bid them both good day.

Back home Nellie prepared the evening meal helped by Bess who moaned from start to finish as she was working while Sally did nothing.

'Oh fer Pete's sake Bess, if you dinnae stop snivelling, a'll skelp yer bloody ears. A've telt you twice... Sally's got tae rest.' Nellie's frustration grew as Bess banged and clattered the dishes onto the table. 'If you break onything Bess, a'll break yer back.... Now a mean it!'

Tom came home shortly before they sat down to eat and Nellie told him of the day's events. 'So she's tae go tae hospital,' Tom said.

'Aye but jist for tests,' Nellie answered.

'I don't want to go da,' Sally pleaded.

'Haud oan noo,' Tom looked at his daughter while speaking rather rougher than usual. 'You'll be there supposin' a have tae take the day oaf work an' haul ye there masel'.'

'That's an idea Tom,' Nellie said. 'Take that day oaf an' spend the day in toun wi' us. We can take Lucy wi' us in case the school comes oot before we get back. The other two are auld enough tae fend for themselves so we can leave the key oan a string behind the door.'

'Woe up! Haud oan Nellie. We'll wait an' see,' Tom said.

'I don't want you to come da. I'll go with ma'.

'What's wrong Sally? We would wait ootside. What's awe the panic?' Tom was now looking hard at his daughter. He couldn't figure her out these past months. If you agreed with her you were wrong, if you disagreed with her you were wrong. There was no pleasing her.

'No guid making plans yet onyway as it could be long enough afore we get a date,' Nellie remarked hiding her annoyance with Tom.

It hadn't been a long wait at all. A card arrived within the month and Sally's appointment was at 10a.m. the following Tuesday. Tom decided he would go into town with them that day, as he would keep an eye on Lucy, besides, he was due a few days off, and as work was a bit slack, he knew it would be all right to take the time off. Anyway, as he needed new shoes, he saw this as the ideal opportunity to visit the warehouse where Nellie 'took on' the carpet, and as it had been paid as regular as clockwork, he could not see any problem in adding shoes to the account.

Bess kicked up a terrible fuss because she was made to go to school. She stamped her feet and threw her school bag to the floor. Ending up with smacked legs from Nellie, she set off red eyed and shaking with temper. 'I hate our Sally,' she growled through clenched teeth. Hugh walked on in front of Bess, hoping she would not catch him up. He could not stand snivelling girls, or any girls come to think of it. Breaking into a run, he distanced himself from his distraught sister.

Arriving at the hospital a full ten minutes late, Tom sat down in the waiting area with Lucy, while Nellie went forward to the nurse behind the desk. Sally dragged on behind as if her feet were twice as heavy as her body.

Handing the card to the nurse, Nellie gave an apologetic smile. Fortunately, things were running a bit late, so the receptionist asked them to sit in the waiting area until they were called. Young Lucy sat beside Sally, and in her own childish way, tried to read one of the magazines that she had lifted from a small table.

A very slim, blonde nurse took Sally to the far corner of the room and helped the apprehensive child onto the huge scales. They watched as the silver arrow stopped exactly on seven stones. She helped the nurse fill in a form by giving her personal details, then was brought back and sat down once more beside her family. Seconds later, a male voice called out her name. The large white-coated consultant stood in the frame of his door waiting to be acknowledged. Sally jumped to her feet, and turning to Nellie (who was also ready to go) asked if she could do this on her own. She wanted no one with her except the nurse. Dropping back down into the chair, Nellie looked up at Tom in amazement, 'She wants tae go in oan her ain!' she said in disbelief.

'A ken, a saw her. Mebbe (maybe) it's better that way.'

Lucy started to cry. She wanted to know where Sally had gone, so, to pacify her, Tom took her along the hospital corridor and showed her the pictures that hung on the walls.

Nellie began to feel impatient, as Sally had been gone for over an hour. She watched the door, expecting it to open any time now, but she became alarmed when another white-coated lady doctor walked into the room, closing the door behind her.

Another fifteen minutes passed before Sally eventually walked out of the room. The lady doctor also came out, but walked off down the corridor.

Sally's eyes were red and swollen, and her white face looked drawn and strained. She had obviously been crying. Nellie rose as her daughter approached. 'What have they been daein' tae you in there? What's wrong?'

'I've to stay here.' She looked so pale and her eyes had a sad far away look.

'What did they dae? Why have you been greetin? A should have bloody gone in there wi' ye!' Anger rose in Nellie's breast. 'Why didn't ye want me tae go wi' ye?'

'I wanted to do it myself ma. I'm fifteen now and I'm able to answer questions.'

'Is that awe ye were daein in there, answerin' questions? They could 'ave amputated a couple o' legs the time you were in there.'

'Leave it oot Nellie.' Tom looked at his wife and shook his head. 'Let her dae things her way.'

'I was examined ma, that's all' Sally wasn't telling Nellie everything. She was totally embarrassed by it all. The questions had been awful as well. Sally was glad she had gone in by herself.

The nurse came forward once more and asked Sally to go with her to the day room, as an other consultant wanted to have a word with her. Nellie stood up, determined to go with her this time, but the young nurse informed her that the doctor, who had already seen Sally, now wanted a word with her and Tom.

They looked at each other with puzzled expressions. A second nurse led them into the small room that adjoined the one Sally had been in a few minutes earlier, then, taking Lucy by the hand, the nurse led her out of the room promising to take care of her until her parents were ready to leave.

The doctor sat at his desk and without speaking, motioned with outstretched hand towards the two wooden seats in front of his desk.

As the door closed behind them, they sat down and waited for the doctor to speak. He studied Sally's parents through narrow slits and saw they felt very uncomfortable.

Nellie moved about in her seat and waited to be told exactly what was wrong with their daughter.

'I'm Doctor Beckett and I take it that you are Sally's parents'.

'Yes we are.' Tom looked at him with enquiring eyes.

'Well Mr and Mrs Baxter, I have examined Sally and I've found no reason to suspect there is anything unduly wrong. Except,' he looked at them both for a good few seconds without finishing his sentence. 'Mrs Baxter,' he looked directly at Nellie. Do you know your daughter has been abused?'

Once again Nellie and Tom stared at each other.

'What are you sayin' doctor?' Tom looked vacant as his jaw gaped open.

'I'm saying Mr Baxter, Sally has been sexually abused.

The doctor studied the parents' reaction and saw the anguish in both their faces. Tom punched into his own palm, as his face contorted with anger.

The doctor spoke once more, ' She has been very badly traumatised and refuses to talk about it. Do you know anything about this?' He directed this question at Tom.

'Didn't you ask her?' Tom barked.

'Of course I didn't. I'm a doctor Mr. Baxter, not a policeman, but who ever did this to her has left her in a bit of a mess. Are you quite sure you don't know anything?' He looked accusingly at Tom.

Reading the doctor's mind, the vessels around Tom's neck filled to near bursting with the hot blood that raged in his veins. His jaw muscles tightened and his eyes stared with a look of disbelief at his accuser. 'Oh wait a minute... Oh no you dinnae! You think it was me, don't ye? You dirty bastard. A'm her da fer Christ sake!' A look of horror masked his face. 'A've had it!.. A've bloody had it in here.' His chair toppled over as he jumped to his feet. ' She's ma bloody daughter, ma ain flesh an' blood an' you think...' He stopped, finding it hard to say.

Shaking his head in anguish, he looked down at the doctor who sat back in his chair, hands poised under his chin as if in prayer.

'A didnae dae onything, but a'll tell you something doctor,' he stood thumbing furiously at the doctor, 'she'll bloody well tell me whay did, an' when a dae find oot, a'll bloody well swing fer the bastard; so you can write me oaf as yer number one suspect!'

Nellie had been on her feet during Tom's outburst, tugging at his arm and yelling at him, but he paid no heed.

At one point, he had thrown her aside, almost toppling her to the floor as he had the chair.

'Tom, Tom, sit doon! Please sit doon! He's got tae ask you. Can't you see?' She tugged with urgency at his sleeve. 'Of course it's ridiculous Tom, we awe ken it wisnae you, so will you sit doon.'

Breathing deeply and still shaking with temper, Tom righted the chair and reluctantly sat down, panting as if he had just run the race of his life. He still stared hard into the doctor's eyes, convincing him that he was not the type to do such a terrible thing.

The doctor sat forward in his chair and the stern accusing look slid from his face.

'I had to see your reaction Mr. Baxter, and I'm sorry for offending you, but I just had to know. I am satisfied now. You see, I already have asked Sally about you and she was just as horrified at the suggestion, but what I can't understand is why she is protecting the perpetrator. However, what I am concerned with is the girl's state of mind. If you take the heavy-handed approach, you will only cause more harm than good.. No! What she needs now is loving care, and through time the mental scarring will heal. It's best you leave her to tell you in her own time what has happened.'

Tom, holding his head in his hands cried openly, ashamed of him self for failing his daughter. His beloved Sally. 'Where was a?' he was thinking to himself. 'Where was a when this happened? A should hav' been watchin' her. A've failed her once again.' All these thoughts mulled inside his head.

The doctor's voice came to him in short bursts as if he was speaking through a narrow tunnel. This anguish was too hard to bear.

'Sally should go in to a convalescent home for a short while and be given some help.'

Interrupted by a sharp knock their attention fell on the pretty face that smiled from the partly opened door.

'Oh come on in nurse,' he beckoned. 'Would you be so kind as to pull that chair over for Sally?'

She led Sally towards her distressed mother and placed a chair at her side. She sat down gingerly. Her thin legs trembled beneath her despite there being very little weight to withstand. Hanging her head low, she was aware of the thunderous beating of her heart as its vibration could be felt throbbing relentlessly against her ribs. She couldn't look at her father, as she was unsure of his reactions, she only knew the dreadful feelings of guilt and shame.

'Sally, I have had a talk with your parents and we think you should have rest. I am going to refer you to a hospital where you will get just that.'

'I don't want to go into hospital,' she pleaded. If she could have found strength, she would have jumped to her feet, but as she was feeling so tired and drained of all human dignity, she sat looking sad and dejected. What she would have given at this moment for her mother's embrace. She felt so empty and alone. She could hear her mother's sympathetic voice, but she couldn't feel the warm comfort of her mother's arms.

'It won't be for long. It's just to get some strength back into your body. We have to get you well lass'.

'There's nothing wrong with me. I won't go, I don't need to go.' She sobbed and looked into each face with pleading eyes. She even found the courage to look her father in the face.

Tom bit hard into his bottom lip to stop it from quivering. 'Does she have tae go? We could look efter her oorselves. She can get awe the rest she needs at hame. The wife will see tae that, besides, it's no' goin' tae dae her ony good if she frets.' Although he had regained some composure he wasn't going to let the matter slip. He intended to get to the bottom of this and he wouldn't be able to, if Sally went away.

Sighing with empathy the doctor spoke directly to Tom.

'Look, it will take a few weeks anyway before we can get her a bed...'

Again Sally interrupted, this time almost screaming, 'I don't want to go. I didn't even want to come here'.

The doctor struggled to be heard above her protests, while Nellie and Tom were on their feet trying to calm her down.

'Listen, listen,' the doctor's voice was now raised as he tried getting Sally's attention. 'If by the time we get you a place you still feel the same way about going, fine. We won't force you, but you think it over and perhaps discuss it with your parents. It's not like a hospital you know. You don't stay in bed you....'

'I don't care! I don't care!' she cried again.

'Awe right Sally,' her mother said, 'We'll leave it fer noo an' we'll see'.

Nellie had a few words with the doctor before leaving with Sally. Holding her firmly by the arm, she led her out towards the reception area. Tom lagged behind still in deep shock.

Lucy had had a wonderful time as the nurse had brought her a box of toys and she played happily at the reception desk.

'Look Sally!' She spotted her sister approaching. ' Them's stickle bricks. Look! I've made a man.' She proudly held up the toy and waited for an encouraging word from Sally, but none came.

'Come on Lucy.' Sally took the child by the hand and pulled her none too gently over to where her coat lay.

As they made their way towards the bus stop, Nellie and Tom hardly said two words to each other. Sally walked on behind holding on tightly to Lucy's hand.

'But why aren't you goin' for shoes da?' Lucy had asked a few times but receiving no answer, she persistently went on asking. She wanted to know why they were going straight home. 'It's not fair. We were to go to Woolworth's an all. It's not fair'.

Sally gave her a dark look and jerked her small arm as if to say 'enough!'

Tom stopped in his tracks and turned round sharply. 'If you dinnae stop that whinin', I'll gie you a skelp roon the ears'. He looked at Sally as if he was about to say something to her. He thought better of it and walked on.

The bus journey home was the same. Lucy had had a sniffle, as she wasn't used to Tom reprimanding her. She was used to hearing him at Bess, but very seldom did he get angry with her or Sally. Hugh had been hit often, but never her, oh no, never her. Whatever was wrong? Lucy was beginning to sense something was not quite right.

They arrived home before two o'clock and much to Lucy's dismay, she was sent to her room. She protested loudly, but seeing the look in her father's eyes, she scurried away without another word. He had something to sort out and he knew it had to be done there and then.

Feeling very scared, Nellie said very little. She had a feeling something dreadful was about to happen. The worry she was now feeling was for herself knowing that the truth would now surely come out. She stood over by the window nervously wringing her hands together.

Sally sat on the sofa staring into the fireplace. The ashes from the previous day were still in the grate. She shivered and hugged herself but it wasn't with cold.

Without speaking, Tom paced the floor, every few minutes disappearing into the back kitchen. Now standing in front of his wife, he pointed towards the sofa, and Nellie, like a frightened dog obeying it's master, sat down. She looked up at this man who was once so easygoing and easy to manipulate, and couldn't help feeling that she had changed him completely by her bad temper and spiteful behaviour. The worm had certainly turned. His sister had once used that phrase and it had come to pass.

'The worm will turn some day Nellie Baxter.' Mary had said, and she was right, he certainly had.

Mother and daughter sat together. Their eyes followed Tom as he paced back and forward, as if he was waiting on his cue. He was trying to keep calm, and finding the right words was proving difficult, so, stopping in front of Sally he looked down at her bent head. All the things he was about to say left him, and he simply asked, 'who the hell wis it Sally?'

Her stomach churned and she still averted her eyes from her father. 'I don't know da.' She gave a slight moan as she answered.

'Christ Sally, you must ken somethin'. Look, you're almost leaving schuil, you only hiv a few mare months, so you're no' daft. It's no' as if you're a bairn.'

'I don't know what you're on about da?' She murmured, her voice faltering.

Tom now turned his attention on Nellie who was clutching at the hem of her dress, looking irritable.

'An you're no' sayin' very much aboot it are ye? Ony ither mother would be oot o' their mind, but you! Oh no, you just sit there sayin' nought. Maybe you ken somethin' a dinnae.' A long strand of hair fell down over his brow. He stood with one hand on his hip while running his other hand through his hair; catching the loose strand and brushing it back into place. 'An' what did you say back there, eh? Calm doon Tom! The bloody doctor says she's been torn tae bits an' you say calm doon!' He started to pace once more before stopping yet again in front of Nellie.

'It's no' that long ago you treated her like... like bloody Cinderella, except there wisnae ony bloody Prince Charmin' for her! Oh no! A bloody rapist fer oor daughter.... Tell me Nellie, somethin' puzzles me. Why the sudden change towards Sally? Why all oaf a sudden dae you change tae the carin' mother? Tell me? Dae you have somethin' tae hide or am a missin' somethin?'

Nellie jumped up as if a spring had tossed her off the sofa.

'That's enough now! Do you hear? That's a bloody 'nough. I've listened tae awe I'm goin' tae. It's no my fault what happened here. I'm jist as shocked as you, but a dinnae go makin' a damn fool o masel.'

'Oh no,' he retorted, pushing her with both hands back down onto the sofa.

Sally was sobbing loudly but neither of them heard. They were too engrossed in their own private battle.

'Stop it. Stop it you two!' she screamed between her sobs. 'Stop it.' Red blotches covered her face as hot stinging tears streamed down her cheeks.

They both stopped and looked at the sorrowful figure. Sally's cries suddenly made them aware of what they were doing to her.

Tom collapsed into the armchair nearest to his daughter, and with elbows resting on his knees he rocked his head back and forward in his hands.

Sometime later, he looked towards Sally, and in a voice much softer, he asked her once more

'Dae you ken the man's name Sally?'

Again, she answered, 'No!'

'When did it happen then?'

There was silence.

'You must ken when it happened.' His sad eyes were pleading, but still no answer came from Sally.

'Sally, a'm talkin' tae you!' Realising he had yet again raised his voice, he cleared his throat and reverted back to the quieter tone.

'We ken it wisna your fault Sally. Whoever did this could be waitin, fer some ither young lass. Take oor Lucy for instance'.

Sally looked up quickly at her father.

'Aye lass, you hadnae thought o that had ye?' he smiled faintly.

The thought of the Watsons putting Lucy through the same torment almost made her sick, but she still remained silent. Even if people believed her story, as she knew her father would, they had money, and money gave people power. Her father had said that once and she had never forgotten it. She would be made out to be bad and her father would go after them, just like her mother said, so she had to be silent.

Unable to bear the tension, Nellie had to get out of the living room. She made to rise from the sofa, 'A'll make a cup of tea,' she stammered.

Tom looked across at her. 'You'll dae nothing oaf the kind. A dinnae believe this, we're talkin' aboot somethin' important here, an' awe you can think o' is bloody tea! Tell me Nellie, are you fer bloody real?' He was half laughing but in a sarcastic manner.

'Dae you care aboot ony o' this?' he asked her.

'Of course a dae. A care aboot them awe.'

'I'm no' talkin' aboot the lot o' them Nellie,' he pointed violently towards Sally. 'A'm talkin' aboot her. You never cared very much when you used tae leave her wi' everythin' tae dae. Remember, when you ran wi' Flo. Dae you think fer yin minute a didnae ken the score?' He stopped to give Nellie a chance to answer, but she only hung her head.

'You didnae care two bloody hoots then.' Pointing again at Sally he ranted, 'she even ran oaf tae a bloody children's hame. Imagine. Running oaf tae a hame before she wid bide here wi you!'

'That's awe in the past Tom. A ken a wasnae a guid mother, but I changed. A ken a wis jealous o' Sally. You gave her awe the attention, didn't ye? A regret the past, but you winnae let me forget will ye?'

Covering her ears Sally tried blocking out their voices, but it was impossible. She was almost at the point of calling out her tormentors' names when something was said that changed her mind.

'No a winnae let ye forget. If it wasn't for you, she wouldn't have been attacked by...' Tom stopped suddenly, his mouth widened as he drew in air. He looked as if he had solved a great mystery. 'Of course! Oh for Christ's sake, how could a hiv been sae blind. That's it.'

His attention now focused on Sally.

'Sally,' he said going down on his knees beside her. 'Was it yon time? Remember, the man who broke in? He watched closely for a reaction.

Sally saw the chance to put and end to the interrogation; after all, it had been a long time since, almost two and a half years. He would be long gone now. Her father was safe; he couldn't do him any harm.

Nodding her head convincingly she agreed. 'Aye da, it was him' she said.

'Oh my God! Nellie gasped. She sat with her hand covering her mouth.

Exhausted Tom rose slowly. With his head cocked to one side he looked at Nellie curiously.

'Nellie, dae ye ken whay he wis?'

Moving her hand swiftly from her mouth she hissed at Tom. 'Of course no. Well, how the hell wid a ken who he was?' she cried indignantly.

'A thought for a minute you kent somethin', but a'll tell you this, an' make nae mistake, a'll find oot. You stopped me then wi' yer "*It'll harm Sally*,"' he mimicked his wife. 'But you'll no' stop me noo.' Tom turned and walked into the lobby.

'Where are you going da? Sally shouted after him.

'A'm goin' oot lass, a've got a lot o' thinking tae dae.' He put on the jacket that hung on a hook near the door. Then the door slammed shut.

Nellie and Sally sat a good while in complete silence. The living room door creaked open and Lucy's timid voice was heard. 'Can I come through noo ma?'

Tom had walked with burning fury raging deep with-in. His tormented mind churned over the day's events almost driving him to the point of insanity.

He didn't know where to start, but he had to find Sally's attacker. Stopping at the baker's he was lucky enough to purchase the last two pies. He went along by the harbour wall and ate them as he was feeling the want of a meal. He couldn't go back to the house yet. He didn't know what more to do but he wasn't going to let this lie, he just couldn't so he decided to go for a beer. That was three hours ago.

The noise in the Public Bar was awful. Tom sat and watched the men in the corner as they enjoyed a game of darts. A good few of the tables were occupied by groups of old men playing dominoes. There were shouts and swearing as the excitement of the game overcame some of them. Two very drunk men in working overalls stood at the end of the bar. They sounded like scalded cats as they sang out of tune, making up their own words to the parts of the song they did not know. It was a pub that could be termed 'A Man's Pub'. Saw-dust was scattered sparely over the floor and in the corner there stood a pile of broken chairs; chairs that had come to grief in the regular Saturday night's brawl, no doubt over some unsuspecting drunkard's head. The huge cloudy mirror behind the bar was dotted and streaked with brown rust marks. It had miraculously escaped the many missiles that had frequently been thrown during the weekend fracas.

The air hung thick with cigarette smoke, the nicotine stained walls oak coloured with years of neglect.

Tom rose and walking over to the bar, ordered himself another half pint and a nip of whisky. He couldn't put up with the noise any longer, so he took his drink into the small Snug Lounge next door. The small round shape of the room resembled an old castle turret. There was no decor at all. The walls were bare except for a couple of electric bars that fitted onto the wall. One round table and four chairs filled the little room. No one was in the snug so Tom welcomed the quietness. When you required a drink, attention was gained by knocking on the hatch door. The locals referred to the room affectionately as the 'Moose's Hole.'

Tom, sitting on his own had downed a good few whiskies when the door opened. Looking towards the intruder, he screwed his eyes to enable him to focus better.

'Hi Tom, what are you daein' here? You dinnae usually drink here.' It was Flo. Being on her own she sat down beside him.

'Flo. Flo. How are yyyou? Aye, sit yersel' doon.' He stretched over and took her hand. 'Flo, what're you wantin' eh? A nip?' He fumbled in his pocket before pulling out a pound note.

'Thanks Tom, a whiskey will dae just fine. You've still no' telt me what's brought you along this end.'

Stretching over to the hatch door, Tom rapped demandingly. Looking thoughtfully at Flo, he grinned.

'A've been walkin' Flo. Walkin' an' thinking.'

The hatch door flew open and the barman appeared in the frame. The burly looking man smiled a toothless smile at Tom, and seeing Flo, he winked at her knowingly. Tom bought her a whisky and pushed the drink towards her.

The hatch door slammed back down, leaving the two of them in peace.

Tom watched her lift the glass and sip the golden liquid.

Becoming aware of Tom's gaze, Flo shifted in her seat. She felt suddenly uncomfortable.

He stared at her in silence, his body swaying slightly.

'Right Flo, you… you were there that nicht. You ken whay he was.'

'What are you oan aboot Tom?' She asked frowning.

'A've kent you a long long time Flo, haven't a?'

Flo nodded her reply still wondering what he was getting at.

'You were a guid freend tae Nellie. Tell me, what happened?'

'I've never been ony different wi' Nellie Tom. A'm still here if am needed. You ken that. It's just that we grew apart. You ken how it is.' She was really uneasy. She didn't like his questions, and the way he studied her was quite disturbing.

Without taking his eyes from her he threw back his whisky and slammed the glass back onto the table before stretching his body over and peering into her face. He bared his nicotine stained teeth and growled low and clear.

'You baith put me oaf that night. Why?' His eyes glazed over and his head swayed.

'Tom, what are you oan aboot? She felt the palms of her hands sweat as she tried acting cool. She stared back into his eyes all the while quaking inside.

'The night Sally was *raped*.' His voice quivered with emotion.

'*RAPED*!' Flo's face drained of colour. '*Raped*? Tom *what*? Sally was never…Tom what are you sayin'?' She clutched the collar of her coat aware of Tom's quest.

'*RAPED* Flo. Dae ye ken what rape is? *Raped Flo*, bloody *raped*.' His face had turned beetroot as he tightened his hands around the half pint-tumbler.

'Who, who telt you that Tom?'

'Flo, we were telt by a doctor at the hospital. He said she had been badly torn. The bastard tore ma bairn.' He was shaking, his shoulders visibly moving up and down while his eyes filled with tears. He put his glass down and grabbed Flo's hands.

'Flo, you've got tae help me,' he begged.

'A canna help you Tom. A dinnae ken who he was. Tom, go hame, it's doin' you nay guid drinkin' like you're daein.'

'A'm no' goin' back until a ken who he is. A ken you ken. A ken Nellie kens.'

'What's makin' you say that?' Flo felt her face flush with guilt.

'A just ken. Why didn't ye baith make a to-do that nicht? A'll tell ye! You wanted it hushed up. Didn't ye?'

'Noo you jist listen tae me Tom,' she leaned forward until her face almost touched his. She could smell the whiskey on his breath.

'A have nothin' tae dae wi' this. You want answers? You ask Sally. She's the only yin that kens.'

'She disnae ken him. She can hardly describe him. Flo, she was only *thirteen*. What kind o' person would dae that eh?' Tom sobbed as his fists banged on the tabletop causing Flo to jump.

She felt sorry for him and wanted to tell all she knew. She felt sickened that Sally had gone through such an ordeal but she never suspected rape. Her aching head felt as if it was about to split open as nausea gripped her stomach at the thought of that evil man violating a child.

A sudden and violent feeling of extreme loathing for the man she knew to be the culprit spilled from her.

'There's this guy at the old caravan site who ...who.... Noo a'm only tellin' you what a've heard,' she said nervously.

'Go oan then,' he urged.

'Well, he's been hauled in for indecent exposure; ye ken what a mean?'

Tom nodded.

'And he's supposed tae have interfered wi' Peggy Tully's lassie.'

'But that lass isnay right in the heid,' Tom sat open mouthed.

Terrible, isn't it?' Flo took another sip at her drink. 'No witnesses.'

'What?' asked Tom.

'Nae witnesses...she had nae witnesses. The fact that she is-err- no' the full shillin' went against her, that an' her age see? She's the age o' consent. Nae witnesses. The poor lass had nae case.'

'Who *is* this bastard Flo?' His heart pounded against his rib cage.

'He used tae go tae the club years ago. The Irish chap, red haired, ruddy faced bloke.'

'You mean yon Irish bloke that use tae dance wi Nellie?' He screwed up his face.

'A dinnae ken aboot that.' She was amazed at Tom's remark. Neither Nellie nor herself thought for one minute Tom had noticed anything.

Slowly Tom shook his head before taking a handkerchief from his pocket to wipe his eyes.

'Flo. Did you think a didnae ken? *A* saw them but a left her alane tae enjoy herself,' If a hadnae seen her, it would 'ave got back tae me onyhow. Half ma mates go doon the club. Dinnae lie Flo. This isnae somethin' tae sweep under the carpet.'

'You want another?' This time it was Flo who offered to buy the drinks.

'Naw, I have tae go. A've had enough onyway.'

'Tom, a dinnae want involved, but am really awful' sorry for young Sally.'

'Aye,' replied Tom. '*Young* Sally she is an awe.'

Tom rose, staggered slightly but regained his balance quickly. He left Flo and walked towards the railway line. The caravan site Flo had mentioned, lay at the other side of the track. The clock from the far away church tower struck nine. Looking at his cheap wristwatch he found it to be five minutes fast.

The night was crisp with a slight wind. Clouds scurrying past revealed the large bright moon at regular intervals.

Tom knew where he was going. He knew this man although he had never spoken to him. When he had seen him around, he always gave Tom the impression that he was grinning at him.

Climbing the embankment, he listened and looked along the railway line before crossing. As the steam train had just recently been replaced by the new and much quieter diesel engine, greater care had to be taken when crossing the line. At the other side of the track, he slid all the way down the steep embankment landing in one of Mr. Bathgate's fields. Cursing under his breath, he struggled to his feet swaying slightly. Jack Brown's caravan was situated at the far end of that field. The site once housed several vans, but they had all moved to a new location at the other end of town where toilets and showers were provided.

He tread carefully through the field. As it had rained continuously at the beginning of the week, the ground was soft and mucky. He reached the dilapidated farm shed that stood alongside the old battered caravan, which wasn't made for permanent residence as it was a bit on the small side, but it was big enough for someone on his own.

Closed curtains prevented Tom from seeing in. He stood inside the doorway of the shed and listened. He heard a woman laugh, so decided to wait hoping that whoever was in there would go away soon. A pile of bricks lay inside the doorway at Tom's right. Sitting down upon them, he leaned wearily against the wall. He saw a piece of old sacking lying on the ground, so he used it to cover his legs.

Back home, Sally had gone to bed, but there was little chance of sleep. She tossed and turned as she listened for the key in the door. Nellie too could find no rest. Instead of going to bed, she curled up on the sofa, and like Sally, she listened for Tom's footsteps. Unable to stand the uneasy, restless feeling, she decided to go and look for him. She crept into the girls' bedroom to tell Sally of her intentions. Sally heard her come in, and sprang upright. What's wrong?' she whispered to her mother.

'Nothing, except he's no' in yet. A've decided tae go an' look for him. Listen oot for Lucy will ye.' Nellie crept back out. Bess stirred and turned over unaware of the situation.

As the dimly lit street was empty, Nellie could hear the echo of her own footfall as she walked along the uneven pavement. Her long shadow sprawled before her on the badly cracked slabs. The night sounds filled her ears although there was nothing to be seen. A barking dog, rustling of leaves and as she passed the old tenement building a baby's cry could be heard.

She walked towards the Black Swan, the pub that Tom usually frequented. It was in darkness except for a light at the back of the building. She walked to the back door and knocked lightly. She waited for a few minutes and knocked again. The door opened very slightly.

A stocky figure, shirtsleeves rolled back, revealing dark blue tattoos asked gruffly, 'What is it?'

'It's me Jock,' Nellie informed the bar man. 'It's Nellie, Nellie Baxter.'

The man opened the door wider and looked her up and down. His tone of voice became more courteous. 'It's you Nellie lass, what dae you want?'

'Has Tom been around this evenin' Jock?' She nodded unconsciously willing him to answer yes.

'No, A've no' seen Tom fer ages. Why? Is there somethin' up?' He opened the door a bit further, hoping for some gossip.

'No. Nothin' tae worry aboot. I'm ... I'm just lookin' for him.' Disappointment was evident in her voice.

'He's no' done a runner has he?' Jock laughed.

Nellie thought the man a bit ignorant at the best of

times, and chose to ignore his remark. Without another word, she turned and walked away, leaving the inquisitive barman none the wiser.

She walked on to the club but it was in darkness. It was never busy during the week and most likely had closed on time. She didn't know where else to look, except, maybe the chip shop. 'Maybe he was hungry an' decided tae go for a carry oot,' she thought to herself.

There were a few people in the shop but there was no sign of Tom. The man behind the counter spotted Nellie, and as he knew her well, he called to her.

'Hi Nellie, how you doin?'

'Fine,' she called back half-heartedly, and went to walk away.

'How's Tom?'

She turned and stopped for a second before answering. 'He's fine too Albert.'

That told her one thing, Tom hadn't been near there either or else Albert would have said so.

She walked slowly back home looking at every one who passed. There wasn't anywhere else she could think of. Tom wasn't in the habit of going to anyone's house, so that was out as well.

There was nothing left for her to do except go home. She did think of going to the police station, but thought better of it. He would be home soon and things would blow over in time.

Closing the door of the house she walked into the living room and threw her coat over the settee. Hearing her come in, Sally rose out of bed and went through beside her. Nellie had gone through into the kitchen and was about to fill the kettle when Sally appeared at the door.

'No luck Sally, a couldnae find him.' She continued filling the kettle. 'Want a cuppa?'

'No thanks,' Sally replied, then hesitating, she changed her mind. 'Or maybe I should mam, my head's sore.'

'A ken how you feel, mine is splitting as well. Take an aspirin wi' yer tea an' get back tae bed.

'I can't sleep ma I'm worried. I wish my da would come in.'

'He's just walkin' off his anger Sally. He'll come back when he's ready.'

'But he's been away all day and it's now past twelve o'clock.'

Nellie sighed, 'A ken Sally, God only knows where men get tae when they go oot.'

Sally knew that was not true of her father. He never went out without saying where he was going and he always told what time to expect him back. She knew her mother was very worried and was trying to make light of the matter.

They sat down and drank their tea. Sally went back to bed while Nellie lay down on the settee, once more pulling her coat over her body to keep warm.

Tom shivered and drew the old sacking over his shoulders. He gave a slight moan as he tried to move. Not only had his legs stiffened up, both feet had taken cramp, still he was determined to quiz this man. He wasn't going to go until he did.

Suddenly the door of the caravan was thrown open, and the tall frame of a woman stepped down onto the ground. The frame of the ginger headed man appeared at the door as the woman turned and hurled abuse at him

'You're just a bloody pervert,' she shouted.

'Take's one to know one,' he answered back.

'I'm no pervert. I would never dream of that. I thought you were a bit odd, but two women at once, you're a bloody pervert all right'.

'Here,' he called, 'you forgot this.' He threw something at her and she stopped to pick it up.

'Ten bob, that's all that was worth,' he shouted as he closed the door.

The woman went around the side of the caravan and headed along the narrow lane cursing as she went.

Tom waited a few minutes until he was sure she had gone. He then went over to the caravan and listened at the door, in case there was anyone else with him. There was silence. He knocked on the door and waited.

The door flew open. Jack Brown stood in the doorway, shirt open all the way down, his braces dangling at each side of his trousers. His feet were bare and his ginger coloured hair was tousled. He held on to the frame of the door to steady his swaying body. He was about to continue his abuse but stopped when he saw that it was not his previous visitor returning.

He had obviously been drinking heavily. He blew a few times as if extinguishing an invisible flame. Trying to recognise his caller, he screwed his eyes in an effort to focus.

'Who are you?' he asked unpleasantly.

'A would like a word wi' you.' The tone in Tom's voice was just as nasty.

'Bugger off,' he growled.

Tom stepped up onto the iron step that was placed against the bottom of the door. Jack Brown tried to pull the door closed, but Tom caught the edge and forced it back open. Jack was almost pulled out, but Tom gave him such a shove, he fell backwards and landed heavily on the floor.

'Get up you dirty bugger!' Taking hold of the man's shirt, he dragged him to his feet. They stood face to face, their noses almost touching. Tom could smell his foul breath, a mixture of drink and tobacco. The pathetic drunk he was looking at was easy to handle.

'You fond o' wee lassies eh?' Tom shook him violently staring into his eyes, his face distorted with hate.

'You're mad. You're mad,' the man shouted.

'You think sae? Ye've seen nothin' yet man.' Tom yelled placing his strong hands around the terrified man's throat and applying pressure.

'You've got it all wrong. I don't even know you.' Choking his now husky voice pleaded with Tom to stop. 'Leave off' the man spluttered.

Releasing one hand but still holding him by the throat, Tom threw a punch hitting him on the side of the face. He repeated the blow a few more times, and as the blood ran from his nose, Tom pushed him back onto the floor. He landed between the seats that ran down both sides of the caravan.

'Oh man, what? What?'

Tom stood over him an' watched as he struggled to his feet.

'Yeh, get up you bastard. Get up so a can knock ye back doon. You bloody child molester.'

Grabbing the man again, he threw him down onto the seat of the caravan, pinning him down by placing his knee on his stomach.

'You've got the wrong person. I never touched anybody.' He pleaded with Tom once more. 'I don't even know you,' he cried his mouth spewing blood. He raised his hand and drew it over his mouth spitting what look like a tooth from the corner of his mouth.

'Aye ye bloody dae. Take a look. Take a bloody guid look!' Tom pulled him up again and stared into his face once more. 'You know me all right. I am Tom Baxter! Aye, you ken me awe richt; Nellie Baxter's man? Ring a bell?' He spat venomously.

Realising whom his assailant was and why he had come Jack groaned. 'Look,' he stammered. 'That was a long while ago. I didn't even want your wife. She threw herself at me,' he whined spinelessly. 'She threw herself at me *honest*. Look, if she didn't want it she wouldn't have let me,' he now had Tom's attention.

'Go oan,' Tom, still holding him by the neck was listening to something he was not prepared for.

'She asked me to the house. She wanted me to call. She wanted to play rough.' He had started talking and couldn't stop.

Tom was in shock. 'He's had them baith?' he was thinking.

'You mean tae tell me ye've been wi' ma wife?'

'That's what this is about isn't it?' the man asked, struggling to open his eyes wide, the cuts from Tom's blows preventing this.

Tom released his grip momentarily. He couldn't take this all in. He looked from side to side in bewilderment. Nellie with this man? What was he saying?

He felt the blow on the side of his head as Jack Brown brought down the empty vodka bottle. It felt like a ton of bricks. He wasn't completely knocked out, but was very dazed. The situation had changed; the man became the tormentor and Tom the prey.

He then jumped on Tom's chest and delivered a few blows to his head.

'Now you bloody fool, see if you can take it. Your wife is nothing but a lousy whore. She's no good either. Your daughter would have been better. Nice young flesh!'

Tom groaned and tried to push up.

'No. No you don't, you big soft shite. It took you some time to catch on. And who do you think fathered her last bairn? Not you.' He laughed menacingly. 'Did you see the hair? It was mine, you stupid bugger. It was mine. Talk about cuckoo in the nest!' he laughed down at Tom. 'You're pathetic man, bloody pathetic.' He laughed again. 'I *nearly* had the young one though, now *there's* something. May as well be first I thought, she'll follow her mother soon'.

Struggling beneath the weight of this man, one of his hands flapped free. He couldn't move the rest of the arm. It was trapped from the elbow up by his assailant's knee.

His hand grasped at something cold lying on the floor under the seat. It felt like a screwdriver. His fingers moved about frantically, as he tried to grasp the object. He finally managed to get hold of it, but could do nothing, as he was still pinned by the upper arm. He would have to wait for his chance, which, to his surprise was only seconds later.

Jack Brown was about to give Tom's face another punch, and as he swung his arm backwards, his knee moved releasing Tom's arm. Tom swiftly brought his hand up and with all the force he could muster, plunged the screwdriver into the man's chest. Repeating this action twice, Jack Brown's limp body fell forward on top of him. Pushing the body to one side, he staggered to his feet.

A moan came from the man on the floor. Tom, looking down, was so overcome with pure hate; he lashed out kicking the body without mercy. He kicked at his head, legs and private parts, and only when he himself felt totally exhausted did he stop, flopping down onto the seat. Blood streaming from his own head wound now ran into his eyes. Taking his handkerchief from his jacket pocket, he wiped his face.

The rage that had burned deep with-in had now subsided, leaving him deflated and worn out. He shivered violently. Looking down at the lifeless body on the floor, he realised what he had done. The feeling of terror now engulfed him. He tried to think, but he could not concentrate. He had not prepared himself for this!

He had to do something to hide his presence here. His prints were all over the caravan; he would have to do something about that. A tin of paraffin stood in the far corner near the stove, Tom saw it and knew what he must do. He went to the other end of the caravan where the pull down bed lay rumpled. The bed had obviously been slept in. He threw the paraffin over the bedclothes making sure it was well soaked. A box of matches lay on the sink top. Taking them, he moved towards the door before striking the match and throwing it onto the bed. The paraffin soaked covers caught alight immediately. Tom jumped from the caravan and standing outside, he watched as the fire roared through the van.

He began to retch. He was sick like he had never been sick before. The vomit came from the pit of his stomach making it burn. He now shook with cold as his teeth began to chatter uncontrollably. Straightening himself up he took a few deep breaths gaining some kind of composure. He couldn't stay around there much longer; so he ran back through the open field vomiting as he ran. Stopping at the other side of the field, he looked back. In the distance he could see the caravan was well alight. Drawing his bloodstained handkerchief from his pocket, he wiped the sweat off his brow. As he attempted to put it back into his pocket he accidentally dropped it.

Reaching the embankment he slipped as he climbed up onto the side of the rail track. He was still running when he reached the lines. Head bent down, he strained in the darkness to see the rails. His head throbbed. He had crossed over the first rail and now made for the shadowed outline of the other. He had only looked one way and was oblivious to the oncoming train ...

Nellie lay on the sofa. She had never shut her eyes all night. In the distance she heard the sound of a fire engine. A cold feeling ran down her spine causing her to shiver.

'Puir sods,' she thought, 'Someboady worse oaf than me.'

The fire engine reached the scene and was followed very shortly by the Police Constable from the local station. When they arrived the caravan was well alight. Someone had seen the flames from the road and had promptly called for help. It took quite some time to get the fire under control but by that time the caravan was totally destroyed. The smell of burnt paint and paraffin mingled in the night air.

When they were sure it was safe, the men entered the burned out shell of the caravan. They were sifting through the ashes when a voice called out.

'Charlie, come over here.' The Fire Officer was looking studiously at the charred ground when the Police Constable joined him. He pointed to a blackened heap lying beneath his gaze.

'Find something?' the Constable asked.

'Aye, what do you make of this?'

The Constable bent over and gave a slight prod with the stick he was holding. 'Poor bugger, it's certainly human remains.' He straightened himself up and placing his hands on both hips he stretched. 'Better call in the cavalry, and I thought I'd be having a quiet night.'

Giving a short laugh, the Fire Officer jokingly remarked, 'Your lives are full of quiet nights!'

'Aye and that'll be right. I should have joined the Fire

Brigade; you lot manage to have the finest dart players in the Lothians,' he replied joking.

They both laughed as the Constable walked off. His car was parked in the lane behind the burned out caravan, as this was the only access for vehicles.

He called from his car radio for the Inspector and dog handler to attend the scene.

The Inspector arrived a short while later. He was an exceptionally big man in his late forties. His hair was completely grey, giving him a much older look.

He walked around the area taking in all the details that lay before him. The Fire Officer went into deep conversation with him and he had studied the charred remains a couple of times before addressing the constable.

'Have you any idea who owns the caravan?'

'Well,' said the constable, 'I know who lived in it up to a few months ago, but whether it changed hands or not, I've no idea. It was an Irish fellow who I've had to visit on occasions. He's no' very well liked about here. Been accused o' paedophilia but it was never proved. If you ask me a shifty bugger he was.' He scratched at his head. 'Aye, it's all of three months since I've seen him around.'

'Whose field is this?'

'The farmer's a man called Eddie Bathgate. His house lies over the other side of the railway line.'

'Go over and get some information on this caravan, and find out what you can about the John Doe.'

They both walked towards the cars and the Inspector continued planning. 'I'll call in the circus.' This was the name they used for the group of men who made up the investigation team. It consisted of the Divisional Officer, C.I.D., Forensic Officer, Pathologist, Procurator Fiscal and the photographic men.

As the Constable was about to drive off the Inspector called to him. 'You said you asked for the dog handler?'

'Yes Sir.'

'Where the hell is he? Call him again. He should have been here by now!' His tone was agitated.

In a very short time the place was alive with men all doing their individual highly skilled jobs. The area around the caravan had been cordoned off and lights installed to enable the team to work through the night.

The dog handler arrived after the team had started their work. He had been delayed as he and his dog had been out doing another job. He was given the details.

'You'd better get to work before this lot has been all over the place,' the Inspector said.

'I'll start over there.' He pointed to the old shed.

'Have any of you been over there?' he called to the men who were now working in small groups.

'Not yet,' they called back.

'Well come on lad,' he spoke to his dog a German shepherd called Lance. 'We'll see what you can come up with.'

The team worked on into the night doing their individual tasks. The forensic team gathered bits and pieces, bagged and labelled them to be taken off for examination. Among the items were the screwdriver remains, as it hadn't been completely destroyed.

The pathologist announced that he was certain the body had been a male, who in fact had died of stab wounds. The fire, he was sure, was created to destroy the evidence.

What had set out to be a simple fire had turned out to be a murder enquiry, as well as arson.

The dog set to work, and had a good sniff at the old sacking that lay in the shed. The handler put him on a long lead as the dog had picked up a scent and was straining to be put to work. He was now taken around the perimeter, about fifty yards from the scene, as it would be easy for the dog to become confused by the different smells from the investigation team.

He was leading the handler enthusiastically as if he had a clear scent. The dog then began to run back and forward as he sniffed the ground in the middle of the field, it was as if he had the scent of two different tracks. He then followed the scent leading towards the embankment when he stopped and barked. The handler saw the handkerchief and radioed to the forensic people. Lance was very anxious to go on. They climbed the embankment and the dog sniffed and barked around a shoe that lay near the top. The handler looked down and shone his flashlight on it. It was covered in blood. He turned his attention once more to Lance as he was now barking furiously.

Looking down the track he saw the gruesome sight and felt sickened. Bits of body were scattered along the rail track.

'For Christ's sake,' he said in a low whisper.

He called the dog back and scrambled back down the embankment. The forensic people had reached the middle of the field where they found the handkerchief. The dog handler approached them and told them of his find. Radioing once more, the Area Inspector was called and given details of the dog's discovery.

The team worked well into the next morning, as they now had to move locations to where the other body was found.

It was now in the hands of the C.I.D. and although it took them no time at all to figure out the situation, there were questions still to be answered. They now knew the body in the caravan was the Irish man's, known as Jack Brown, but they didn't know who the unfortunate man on the railway line was. It was evident that Jack had been murdered and most likely by the unknown man. He had most definitely been at the scene of the crime but until they had an idea of who he was, the case remained unsolved.

Sally rose early to find her mother still dressed and lying awake on the settee. She had slept very little herself, as she lay listening for her father's return. Drifting in and out of sleep, she was only to be tortured by her own lies and the thought of the consequences.

'No news yet ma?'

'No. No' yet. A'll get this fire goin' Sally while you put the kettle oan.' Nellie rose slowly from where she lay on the sofa, her body feeling stiff and sore from lying in the same position all night. She began shovelling the ashes from the grate into a tin pail before laying sticks on top of screwed up paper. She struck a match and holding it to the paper it blazed. As the sticks caught hold they crackled and sparked until she covered them over with pieces of small coals. Soon the fire was glowing radiating its heat through out the room.

The rest of the children rose, and as they were unaware of the events that had taken place, had no idea their father had been out all night.

Sally helped Lucy get dressed for school while Bess and Hugh went through their usual routine of fighting and whingeing.

'Why's she no' goin' to school this morning then?' Bess asked giving Sally dark looks. 'She wasn't there yesterday either.'

'You mind yer ain business Bess!' Nellie clipped her round the ear making her yelp. 'Sally's no' up tae school yet, besides a'm no' that great mysel' this mornin', so less o' it fae you.' She gave her daughter a push that sent her on her way out of the door.

The children all gone, Nellie and Sally sat and finished another pot of tea between them.

'What now ma? What you going to do?'

'A'm goin' tae wait till twelve an' give him time tae come hame,' her answer wasn't very positive.

They both made themselves busy making beds, washing dishes and tidying up, anything to occupy their minds.

The front door opened. Nellie and Sally almost fell over one another as they hurried to open the living room door. Their faces fell with disappointment when they saw it was only Sam.

'What's up with you two? Seen a ghost?' he laughed.

'It's you, we thought it was yer faither,' Nellie said in a matter of fact way as she didn't want to tell Sam what had happened.

'What's taken you tae call in this mornin' onyway?' she asked.

'I've been off with a chest infection. I came to see how you got on yesterday at the hospital.' He looked at Sally whose face had gone bright red.

'Who told you?' Sally snapped.

'Pardon me for asking.' He looked stunned. 'I met Bess and she told me you were going.' He stared hard at his sister.

'I'm sorry Sam.' She felt quite ashamed. 'I'm all right. It's it's...' she was finding it difficult to explain, when Nellie interrupted.

'It's woman's troubles Sam.'

'Oh!' he walked round the sofa and sat down.

'Where's the tea then sis?'

Sally went through the kitchen and filled the kettle.

'There's some carry on up at the railway line this morning,' Sam said.

'Why, what's wrong?' asked Nellie.

'Someone's been murdered at the old caravan site. I met Joe Anderson and he was telling me that they've found two bodies. One of the bodies was seemingly discovered on the railway line. They've cordoned off the whole area. The caravan at the site caught fire too he said.'

'Did he say whay they were?'

'No, he reckons it's a couple of strangers passing through. Where's that tea Sally?'

'It's coming,' Sally was just putting the milk in the cups.

'Did you say you thought I was my da' when I came in?' Sam asked.

'A...aye.' She stammered as her brain searched for a feasible explanation. 'He said he micht come back this mornin'. He's ... he's been up awe nicht wi' his stomach.'

'Well ma, he couldn't get up without it, could he?' Sam laughed at his own joke.

'You! Mr Smart Arse,' she chided.

Sam stayed for an hour and left knowing nothing of the worries Nellie and Sally had. They were both glad to see him go as they were frightened something would slip out in conversation.

He was hardly gone when the door knocked. Sally answered. Flo Begbie stood at the door, looking very pale and drawn. She seemed agitated and distressed.

'Is yer ma in hen?' she enquired. Her head seemed to cower into her shoulders.

'Ma! It's Flo wanting you.' Sally called as she beckoned Flo to go through.

'Weel Flo, how you daein'?' Nellie was surprised to see her, although she had helped at the baby's funeral and had called round once since then.

'Nellie is your Tom here?' she asked wringing her hands in agitation, her eyes darting to the kitchen door.

'No Flo why?' Her blood ran cold causing her to shiver, even though the fire was blazing fiercely in the grate.

'It's just that...' she looked over at Sally who was sitting on the arm of the chair listening with great interest. She then looked towards Nellie and indicated she didn't want to speak in front of the child.

Catching on, Nellie looked over at her daughter. 'Dae ye mind daein the cups Sally ... an' make Flo a brew hen.'

Sally left the room reluctantly.

'Noo Flo, what's this awe aboot?'

'Your Tom, he went tae the caravan last nicht,' Flo said.

'What caravan? What are ye talkin' aboot?' Nellie asked.

'Jack Brown's caravan, the yin they found burned oot this mornin'.'

'*What!*' Nellie's face drained of colour. Weakened legs caused her to topple over and fall into the chair.

'*What's wrong ma?*' Sally rushed out of the kitchen and went to Nellie's side.

'Go through tae the kitchen lass while a have a word wi' yer mother,' Flo said gently.

'*No! No!*' Nellie's voice was adamant. 'She stays! There's enough been hidden. *She stays!*'

'Very well.' Flo's eyes darted from one to another before continuing. 'A met Tom last nicht an' he had found oot where Jack Brown lived. He went efter him Nellie. Tom went efter Jack.'

'Wait a minute Flo, whay telt him?' She waited a few seconds. 'Was it you?'

'No. No.' Flo lied but not very convincingly.

'Dinnae you lie tae me Flo Begbie. You telt him.

Have you only idea what ye've done?' Nellie was now distressed.

'Nellie, a'm sorry. When Tom comes hame fae work, beg him tae go an' clear his name.'

Sally, sitting on the arm of her mother's chair, longed to put her arms around her neck, but just couldn't.

Nellie cradled her bent head in her hands before looking at Flo, despair evident in her eyes she said. 'Flo, Tom didnae come hame last nicht. He walked oot early yesterday an' we've no' seen him since.'

'*Oh my God Nellie*' It was Flo who now shook. 'Do ye think! ... *No*! No it couldnae be!'

Nellie was now panic-stricken. She knew what Flo was about to say. Sam had just told her that there were two bodies found.

Sally too had realised the possibility and now trembled with fear. *She* had caused all of this, not Flo. She had blamed that man of rape, and now he was dead. But she couldn't understand how Flo and her mother knew the man's name. And where was her father? She was terrified.

'A'm no' stayin' here ony longer. A've got tae go doon tae the Police Station. A've got tae ken yin way or an ither.' She was almost hysterical.

'Nellie, a'll call frae the phone box an' get them tae look in oan you. Ye're in nae fit state tae go oot.' Flo rose and hurriedly buttoned up her jacket.

'You watch your mother Sally till a get back.' She let herself out. Flo kept her word and phoned the Police Station, but she didn't return to Nellie's house again, at least, not for a long time.

Hardly an hour had passed before two very burly men from the C.I.D. called. They asked Nellie when she had last seen her husband. Nellie told them the story that led up to Tom's outburst. She also told of Flo Begbie's visit. They asked her if she knew Jack Brown and she had to admit knowing him. It would all come out anyway once Flo was questioned. Nellie, however, said nothing about Jack Brown visiting her at her home, she just admitted she danced with him at the club.

A chill ran through her body when they asked if Tom wore brown brogue shoes. She knew then it was Tom who had been killed on the line.

Sally was not present when Nellie was being questioned. She sat in her bedroom waiting to be called. It hadn't been confirmed yet that it was Tom's body on the line, so she was still hoping her father would show up.

They finished questioning Nellie and eventually called on the very distressed girl. They were very gentle when questioning her. One look at the child told them she was on the verge of breaking up.

Sally confirmed most of Nellie's statement but parts of her story had to be almost forced out of her. They had to suggest the answers rather than be told voluntarily. Clearly Sally was blaming herself.

They produced a photo of the man they called Jack Brown and Sally almost keeled over when she saw the face from the past stare out at her.

Jack Brown had previous convictions, hence the access to the photograph.

Sally, like her mother, identified the photo. She named him as the man who raped her, knowing full well she was telling awful lies. There was nothing she could do. She certainly could not mention the Watson brothers now.

The conclusion was that Tom, finding his daughter's attacker, took the law into his own hands and murdered Jack Brown. He then took his own life knowing he could not face the consequences. At first, accidental death was suggested, because the trains had recently transferred from steam to diesel and it was sometimes difficult to hear them approaching. However, the Procurator Fiscal went along with the theory that Tom Baxter committed murder, arson and then suicide.

They were unable to identify Tom's body as the train had hit him full force and body parts were found scattered up to fifty yards away. His handkerchief and one shoe were all that remained to be identified.

Chapter Eleven

The school year drew to an end but Sally wasn't there to enjoy the fun that usually took place, especially among the students who were leaving. She hadn't been back since her father's death as she had been too traumatised by the event.

She wrestled with her conscience knowing that she had caused it all. Lying to her father had caused his death. Her mother and Flo had told her to keep quiet, and they were right all along. Maybe her mother had been justified all those years ago when she had treated her harshly. Sally's mind raced with thoughts such as these, but she knew one thing for certain, it was her fault.

Nellie too suffered greatly, although she managed to put a face on things for the sake of the family. She felt the guilt as well, wondered over and over again if Tom had found out about her and Jack. If he had, there was no doubt in her mind he knew about young Robert not being his.

She thought about the awful fights she had caused, and the dreadful thoughts that went through her mind when arguing with her husband. Several times she had wished him dead, especially when she couldn't get her own way. She had turned a quiet man into a brutal murderer. His sister was right when she said Tom was too good for her. Tormented with her own thoughts, Nellie found consolation in the bottle. Taking a couple of drinks relaxed her and helped her cope.

Nellie watched young Sally grow more and more withdrawn. She refused to see her friends and had no interest in the rest of the family. Her weight tumbled drastically as she lived on water and crisps. If Nellie lectured her about not eating, she'd fly into a tantrum and retreat to her room, and Bess, she had only to look at Sally to cause a fight. Even young Lucy kept clear, while as usual, Hugh was never around. He didn't seem to be affected at all by his father's death.

The tension Sally was feeling festered inside her until, like a balloon that could take no more air, it burst. It happened on a warm Saturday evening when Bess was watching television, and Lucy, as usual, sat beneath the table cutting out coloured pictures from an old magazine. Nellie was standing outside by the open window, engaged in conversation with a neighbour.

Bess went forward to the television and put the volume up.

Sally appeared in the kitchen doorway and told her to lower the volume.

'What for?' was her reply.

Walking through into the living room, Sally went to the set and lowered the volume herself.

'The window's wide open and you've got this thing blaring,' she said abruptly.

'So what?' was Bess's cheeky reply.

Sally walked back into the kitchen and her defiant sister turned the volume up even louder.

'*Bess*!!' Sally roared.

'You think you can boss me about, well you can't,' came the quick reply from Bess.

Sally walked back over towards the television and lowered the sound once more.

'Now leave it,' she pointed her finger at Bess who had now risen to her feet and faced Sally in a brazened stance.

'*You* think you're *it* our Sally, don't you. You've moped about here since oor da copped it. Well, a heard it's your entire fault. You made him do it, you...'

Sally slapped Bess so hard she toppled back and fell on the floor. She didn't stop at that. Before Bess could recover, Sally jumped on top of her, and, taking her sister's head between her hands, proceeded to bang it on the floor. Bess squealed as Lucy roared in horror.

The commotion was heard by Nellie who ran in quickly and separated them.

'Oh Sally!' Nellie was nearly in tears herself. 'What's makin' you dae this?'

'It's no' Sally's fault ma, it was Bess,' came Lucy's voice from under the table.

'You could've knocked her oot bangin' her heid like that.' Nellie was pulling Sally to her feet when the ear piercing screams that came from her, almost caused Nellie to drop her back onto the floor. The screaming didn't stop despite Nellie shaking her violently. Then, a sudden slap from Nellie stopped the screaming almost immediately but it was followed by the most awful wailing.

Rocking back and forth, she continued making this terrifying sound.

Horrified at the disturbing sight, Lucy screamed in terror followed closely by the sobbing Bess. Nellie had the doctor called immediately.

Sally hugged herself tightly, swaying as if she were in an invisible rocking chair, all the while staring wide – eyed through dead, empty eyes.

Silently, she sat rocking and staring.

Fifteen years of heartache and struggle had now taken its toll. A nervous breakdown was diagnosed, therefore, she was admitted to hospital where she remained for three months, but with help and counselling, she managed to regain strength and struggled back to some kind of normality.

She did a lot of thinking during this period and came to the conclusion that her problem would be easier to deal with if she moved out of the house.

Her friend Anna was a constant visitor, always encouraging her to get well, and, on one of her visits she was accompanied by her aunt Ruby and uncle Jimmy Duncan. They offered Sally a room in their house if she was seriously thinking about leaving home.

Sally discussed it with her mother, and although Nellie didn't like the idea, she was willing to let her try it for a few months as long as she visited regularly.

Ruby busied around all morning preparing for the arrival of her young lodger. Jimmy and Anna were on their way to the hospital as Sally was to be discharged that morning. The Duncan's were excited, as they had always wanted youngsters around the house. This was also a good way to see more of their young niece whom they both adored. Anna would visit them more often now that her friend was staying with them.

The Duncan's lived in Musselburgh, a short distance from Prestonpans. Their house was a beautiful bungalow overlooking the River Forth. Jimmy Duncan was a very keen gardener and since his retirement spent most of his time tending his flowers and shrubs or pottering in the greenhouse.

The rooms of the house were very tastefully decorated. Furniture had been waxed and rubbed until the surfaces gleamed. It wasn't modern furniture but it looked very grand. A writing desk made of all sort of wood inlays stood against one wall. It was a magnificent piece of furniture. There were china ornaments scattered all around, some on the mantle shelf and others on small occasional tables. A cabinet sat in one corner and when the doors were opened, revealed the television set. The house was very grand indeed.

Sally arrived with Anna and feeling a bit uncertain hesitated at the door. Noticing this, Anna and her uncle gave her a few seconds to regain her confidence before ushering her into the house.

On seeing the small party arrive, Ruby shrieked with joy as she welcomed her young guest. 'Come away in, come away in,' she cried steering both young girls towards the sofa. 'I've waited all morning for this,' she said excitedly as she helped Sally off with her coat.

'Auntie Ruby, stop fussing,' Anna said winking at Sally. 'She'll smother you Sally, I'm not joking either.' Both girls laughed as Jimmy pulled a face at Ruby.

They were supposed to be having a light lunch, but the table in the small dining room groaned with cakes, scones, tea-loaves, and sandwiches with all sorts of fillings.

'My goodness,' Jimmy commented entering the room and seeing the food. 'Are you expecting an army?'

'Don't be cheeky my lad,' she bantered with him.

He turned to Sally and grinned impishly. 'Don't think you'll get me sitting through here every day, I like to eat in the back kitchen'.

'Oh you Jimmy, you don't half show me up. You don't know when you're well off,' she chided.

Anna and Sally ate very little although Ruby tried her best to get them to have a piece of everything. 'Try this,' or 'You must have a taste of that,' she went on all through the meal. 'A mouse eats more than the two of you put together,' she said.

'They're both too excited to eat Ruby,' Jimmy scolded her in a gentle sort of way.

'Oh well Anna, you better take Sally through and let her see her room.'

'Oh yes Auntie Ruby.' She looked over the table at Sally. 'Come on Sally.'

Sally was glad to get away from the table and hoped that Mrs Duncan wasn't going to go on like that every

-time they sat down at a meal. She would soon be over weight if she did.

There were four bedrooms, a shower room and a bathroom leading from the hall. The first door was Mr and Mrs Duncan's bedroom. It looked out onto the front lawn while Sally's room lay at the back of the house overlooking the greenhouse.

'Oh what a lovely room. It's absolutely smashing.' She liked what she saw.

'She's all right you know,' Anna half whispered and tilted her head towards the door ignoring what Sally was saying about the room, after all, she had seen it lots of times before. She had taken all the modern luxuries and modern conveniences for granted, forgetting that Sally was lucky to have clean sheets once a month on her bed.

'She's just excited about you coming today. She'll calm down,' Anna went on, 'Jimmy is funny; he's always bantering with her. He never means anything he says to her.'

'Anna, stop worrying, I'm going to like staying here. I know I am.' Sally twirled round again admiring the room once more. It was decorated in pink; the carpet was grey and almost wall-to-wall. A thick deep pink candlewick covered the bed, fitting beautifully with deep frills falling round the sides. Thick velvet curtains in the same rich pink, draped the windows, held firmly back by stiff tiebacks made of the same material.

Once again the room was adorned with china and a full glass vanity set lay on a dark wooden kidney shaped dressing- table. On the floor at the side of the bed was a deep piled furry carpet just ready for sinking her feet into. She had never seen such a beautiful room and it was hers.

Like old times, the two friends sat on the bed chatting. It was a long time since Sally had laughed, and it felt good.

Jimmy Duncan was a very witty man and both girls laughed heartily as they sat in the living room listening to his humorous stories. Ruby sat sewing, feeling very contented with her girls' around her. She knew she'd done the right thing taking Sally in to her home and hoped she would be happy and have a new start in life.

Two months had passed since Sally moved in with the Duncan's. She had settled in very quickly and felt very happy. Although Ruby had stopped forcing her to eat more, she still fussed a lot. Sally, like Jimmy, preferred to sit at the kitchen table. They both retreated there out of Ruby's way whenever they felt she was beginning to fuss, a discreet look between them signalled the time to escape. Sally also shared Jimmy's love for the garden and often joined him when he took refuge in the greenhouse.

She found him very easy to talk to and respected his points of view. One afternoon when they were both sitting in the back kitchen drinking tea, Jimmy asked her about her future. Leaving school early meant she had no qualifications.

'I have been looking in the Evening News these last two nights, but there's nothing that I could do.' Sally confessed.

'Don't underestimate yourself Sally. You're bright, you could pick up almost any job.'

'You mean I can become a brain surgeon?' They both laughed.

'Not quite, not quite. What I mean is you don't have to go for factory or shop work, not if you don't want to. There are office jobs if you would like that. Yes, look for a junior's position and you'll learn as you go,' Jimmy advised her.

Sally did fancy office work, but felt that without her school certificates she didn't stand a chance.

Jimmy looked earnestly into Sally's dark eyes, 'Do you think you're ready for work yet? Do you *really* feel better?'

'Yes Jimmy, I feel all right now, anyway, it's time I earned my keep.' It worried her that she was staying with them, getting the best of everything and not paying for anything.

Jimmy took his pipe from his pocket, and as he prodded the bowl with his penknife, he looked up at her. 'Now listen, and listen good young lady, Ruby and I knew when you came to live with us that it would be a long time before you would be fit enough to work.' He banged the bowl of the pipe into his hand before emptying the contents into a small pedal bin at his side.

'Anyway, Christmas is only a few weeks away, so you can leave things to the beginning of the year. That's if you want to.' He started to take the tobacco from a brown leather pouch and stuff it into his pipe.

'Well, I think you're right Jimmy. After the holidays I'm going to look really hard.'

They sat in silence, Sally sipping her tea while Jimmy lit his pipe. Sucking hard on the stem, the flame of the match disappeared, reappeared then disappeared into the filled bowl of the pipe until the tobacco glowed and blue smoke circled above his head. Closing his eyes momentarily, a look of contentment masked his face as the flavour of his favourite tobacco penetrated his taste buds. Ruby hated the smell of the pipe and chased him out of the living room at the mere sight of it. She tolerated him smoking in the kitchen, but only just, as she chased him from there as well whenever the mood took her. The greenhouse is where he did most of his puffing. He even had a fly cigarette there, something she knew nothing about. That was his domain, until recently; he started to share it with Sally, who found Jimmy's secrets to be highly amusing.

Jimmy studied her face. It was beginning to loose that drawn hollowness and the dark shadows that encircled her eyes had gone completely. Eyes that were dull and lifeless were now sparkling and full of vitality. She was full of energy, energy waiting to be harnessed as she longed to be a part of the outside world. The silence between them was natural as neither one of them felt like they had to make conversation. They felt easy in each other's company.

'Sally, there's an envelope in the top drawer of the wee table in your room. Ruby put it in there this morning. There's money in it to help you buy a few presents for your family.'

Her eyes widened and her expression took on the look of annoyance.

'Jimmy, I don't want you to give me money. You have both been so good already.' She reached over and touched his hand. 'It's kind but...' Jimmy caught her hand as she drew back.

'Now then you listen. You've done a power of good these weeks. I've never seen Ruby so happy, and I must say, I enjoy having an ally,' he smiled and winked. 'You take it, and enjoy spending it. It's given with love.'

Knowing it was useless arguing with him, she shook her head in defeat. 'I'll take it on one condition.'

'And what's that now?' he questioned.

'I'm allowed to pay it back.' Waiting on his reply, she screwed up her eyes and peered at him through narrow slits.

Sucking on his pipe he studied his young friend's determined expression. He could see she was not going to take help easily. 'All right Sal, but you've got to be well on your feet before you give me a penny.'

Smiling back she said, 'It's a deal.'

'Now!' said Jimmy, 'pour me another cup of tea and tell me what Anna's been up to.'

The door opened and Ruby joined them.

'My, you two are a couple of tea Jennies.' Sitting herself down, she pushed a cup over to Sally. 'I'll take one as well before you both drink the lot.'

Waving her hand in the air, she glowered at her husband's pipe without commenting on the smoke.

Nellie saw a lot of Sally as she had kept her word and visited often. Now and again Sally took Lucy back with her to her new home. Mr and Mrs Duncan welcomed the child and grew rather fond of her as she was so enchanting and captured everyone's heart, and as their home was now Sally's, Lucy would be welcome at any time.

Christmas was only a few days away and Sally found herself in a very awkward position. Ruby had been planning the Christmas dinner and was excited at the idea of Sally being with them.

'Just like a *proper* family,' she had commented to Jimmy.

Sally knew within herself that she wouldn't be able to spend Christmas with them as Nellie expected her daughter to be with her and the family, furthermore she knew her mother would need help with the preparation. How was she to tell Ruby she wasn't going to be with them? Wrestling with this problem for days she tried approaching the subject with Ruby but she found it impossible as every time the subject was raised, Ruby would interrupt and carry on planning for the special day.

Jimmy knew there was something worrying the youngster, so, with a nod of his head, the signal was given and they both retreated to the kitchen table, leaving Ruby polishing and fussing around the house.

'Get that kettle on and let's be having you,' Jimmy said in a fatherly way.

Sally did as she was told and made a pot of tea while Jimmy put the necessary items on the table.

'Now then, what's up?' Sitting in his usual seat, he studied Sally's worried expression as she poured the tea.

'Jimmy, I don't know what to say. You see my mother expects me to be with them on Christmas day but every time I try to tell Ruby, she changes the subject or goes on and on about how we're going to spend our day.' Sally sipped her tea while Jimmy, as usual, thought for a minute or two before answering.

'It's only right you go to your family, after all it's the first Christmas without... eh without your father. Your mother will be feeling it.' He shook his head, and continued. 'Ruby doesn't think sometimes'.

'Who doesn't think?' Ruby came into the kitchen and caught the tail end of the conversation.

'Who doesn't think Jimmy? What are you on about now?' Ruby gave her husband's shoulder a gentle push.

'Ruby, there's something we both took for granted,' he said.

'Aye, and what might that be?' she asked.

'It's Sally here, she can't be with us for Christmas. It's only good and proper she spends Christmas with her family. After all, we have her every day now, don't we?' He was trying to be gentle.

Ruby's face couldn't hide the disappointment. She looked as if she was about to cry, but drawing herself up with a deep intake of breath she glanced over at Sally and nodded. 'Quite right Jimmy. She belongs with her family, but she'll be back for tea now surely?' she said with an air of authority

'Oh aye,' Sally blurted out. 'Oh aye, I'll be back here for my tea.'

'Well, we'll have a better tea than dinner.' Ruby marched out, dusting the door handle as she passed. Sally and Jimmy looked at each other and giggled.

Jimmy whispered, 'I'll have to sit through two whopping big meals now, and don't you think you're getting off lightly. You'll eat everything that's thrown at you, so don't fill yourself up at your mother's.'

Groaning, she jokingly mimicked being sick.

She did like her new family very much and knew they were more than fond of her. She also had the freedom to make her own decisions without interference from either of them.

The Christmas incident had taught Sally to speak out without fear. The Duncan's had understood, furthermore she trusted them whole-heartedly.

The bus service on Christmas day was practically non-existent, and as it was wet and windy, Jimmy drove Sally over to her mother's house.

Lucy jumped up and down with excitement as she showed off her presents.

The table was almost ready but for a few last minute items. Sally noticed her mother had gone to a great deal of trouble. The house really looked clean and tidy. Paper chains were strung from the four corners of the room crossing in the centre. A huge multi honeycombed paper ball hung from the nail that held the mirror. Scattered here and there were pieces of tinsel and in the corner of the room stood a rather scrawny silver tree, small fairy lights twinkling from its very sparse branches. For Nellie to have taken the trouble was a feat on it's own.

'I'll finish setting the table ma.' Sally wanted to help, knowing Bess wouldn't unless she was made to do it. Wanting to keep the peace, she decided not to let her lazy sister get under her skin. Hugh was engrossed in the television while Bess sat on the floor in front of the fire reading an annual she had received among her presents.

A large turkey roasted in the oven and the potatoes boiled on top of the cooker. Nellie had made a trifle, as none of the children were fond of Christmas pudding.

Sally's fingers ran across the beautiful white linen tablecloth. She lifted one of the corners and admired the embroidered daisies.

'Ma, what a lovely cloth, where did you get it?'

'You dinnae ken?' Nellie asked carrying the Christmas cake to the table. 'A got that fae your Mrs Duncan,'

'Oh! It's nice. I didn't know what was in the parcels. She had them all made up.'

'Well, it's certainly very posh. A'm only goin' tae use it fer special occasions,' Nellie said with pride.

Sally laughed inwardly as she knew Nellie had never put a tablecloth on the table before. She always used plastic covers. She also recalled times when newspapers were spread over the table making meal times interesting, as reading while eating was the norm.

The Christmas dinner turned out to be a great success. Turkey was served with vegetables, roast and boiled potatoes. They had home made broth before the main meal and finished off with trifle and little mince pies. They all wore the paper hats that came out of the crackers and laughed at the silly jokes that came with the little plastic novelties.

Nellie had done her best and it was much appreciated. Sally felt glad she had decided to spend the day with her family as her mother was now beginning to treat her like an adult and it felt good.

Nellie was also very relieved that Sally chose to spend Christmas with them, as she needed the company of her eldest daughter to help get her through the day. Once the table had been cleared, Hugh and Bess played with their games. They played on top of the table, while Lucy, as usual; played underneath with the doll Mrs Duncan had sent her. The doll came with four dresses and three pairs of small shoes and Lucy dressed and undressed the little doll over and over again. This amused the child for hours.

Shortly after the meal, Sam came to visit his mother and family. He brought sweets for the children, a diary and pen for Sally and he handed Nellie a long thin shaped present, wrapped very smartly in good quality paper, finished off with a small ribbon bow.

'It looks too good to open,' Nellie laughed.

'The woman in the shop wrapped it for me,' Sam confessed slightly embarrassed.

Opening the present, she gasped as she looked at the stunning wristwatch.

'Oh lad, it's absolutely beautiful.' She lifted it out of its velvet box gently, as if it was about to break. 'This must have cost you a fortune. You shouldn't have spent so much on me.'

'I've never seen such a lovely watch ma.' Sally admired the watch that now lay across her mother's wrist.

'Neither have I Sal. No one has ever given me anything like this,' she said as she replaced the watch back in the box ever so carefully.

The watch had an oval shaped face encased in silver and each side of the casing was embedded with marquisettes. A black velvet strap enhanced the watch as it lay in the crimson velvet box.

Nellie looked up into Sam's face, and, gnawing his lip at one side, made Nellie aware that there was something on his mind.

'What's up Sam?' She knew there was something he wanted to say. 'A love ma' present but a feel yer tryin' tae tell me somethin.'

He was now shifting from side to side making it obvious that whatever he was about to say was difficult.

Sam lowered his head before answering. 'I'm going away ma.'

'Goin' away? Where tae?'

'I'm emigrating to Australia with a couple of my mates.'

'Australia!' Her jaw dropped with shock. 'Fer heaven's sake! Australia! '

'Ma, I can't live here any more. I'm embarrassed with what my da did,' his voice trailed away.

'Fer God's sake Sam, dinnae bring that up the day. Let it drop.' She was now showing a great deal of agitation.

'Sorry ma, that's all I'm saying.' He felt bad. He had upset his mother and he didn't mean to.

She looked him full in the face before she finally spoke.

'It's your life Sam, a cannae stoap ye. Ye moved oot years ago, so ye ken what yer doin'. You've aye had a mind o' yer ain. A suppose you take that fae me,' Nellie looked down at the watch. 'So this is a farewell gift?' she said.

'Naw, it's your Christmas present. I hope to see you before I ago ma. Once I've been away a while, I'll save up and come back on holiday.'

'You young yins! You're no' there yet an' yer plannin' tae come back.' Nellie rose, walked to the coal bucket, tilted it up letting the remaining coal slid into the fire.

'When do you go then?' Sally asked.

'Sixth o' January,' he replied, a look of sadness etched his face.

'Weel, ye kept that quiet. Ye must have kent fer sometime,' Nellie remarked as she walked passed him on the way to the kitchen where she washed her hands. 'Weel, as a say, it's your life.'

'You should think of getting away too Sally.' He spoke softly to avoid his mother overhearing. Sally just shook her head and screwed up her nose.

'Well, nineteen sixty-three is goin' tae mark oot a new life fer you Sam,' his mother remarked as she returned to the living room.

'Well I hope it's the start of something new for us all,' came Sam's answer.

'An what daes auntie panty hiv tae say aboot awe this?' Nellie still hated her sister-in-law who returned the complement ten fold.

Sam shrugged, 'She said I should go and make a life for myself as she's no' getting any younger.'

'Well that's that then, the seal o' approval has been given,' she remarked sarcastically.

'Oh come on now,' Sally looked pleadingly at them both. 'It's Christmas day. Talk about this later.

Part Two

Chapter Twelve

'Its come Jimmy, its come.' Sally ran along the hall into the living room clutching the letter she had just received. 'I've got it.' She twirled round and round waving the letter above her head.

'Steady on Sal,' he was laughing at her antics. 'Come on let's be having the news.'

'I've got the job Jimmy. I've got the job.' Breathlessly she jumped with excitement.

'I start next Monday,' she squealed thrusting the crumpled letter and envelope into Jimmy's hand. Jimmy straightened the paper out and read it over.

'Well now, we have an office worker in the family.'

'I didn't think I stood a chance Jimmy.'

'You must have more faith in yourself girl. Now see, you managed to get this job and you didn't think you would, so stop underestimating yourself.'

'Right Sir,' she stood to attention and saluted.

'What are you two up to now?' Ruby entered the room with a duster in her hand as usual.

'Oh, she's only joined the world of office workers,' he winked and nodded to his wife.

'No! Oh well done Sally. I'm really happy for you.' She joined the laughter as Jimmy continued the banter with Sally.

'You and I will be off to Edinburgh on Saturday. You'll need something nice to wear, after all, you're an office girl now,' Ruby fussed as usual.

'Ruby, that's not necessary. I have a good skirt and my red twin set will...' she didn't get to finish her sentence. Ruby was determined to organise the situation.

Sally knew she couldn't win and had to accept gracefully.

They shopped all day Saturday and Sally returned home absolutely worn out, while Ruby was still bursting with her endless flow of energy.

'I'll never be able to pay you both back,' Sally remarked later on over supper.

'We don't want paying back Sally. We only want to see you get on. Now say no more about it and eat up,' Ruby ordered.

The printers occupied the whole of the downstairs floor and an old wooden staircase led up to the bookbinding department. Attached to the wall at the bottom of the stairs, was the clocking-in machine. Passing the bookbinding department upstairs the first office belonged to the Managing Director. An overhead walkway led to an adjoining building where the editorial department was. This is where Sally was to begin her working life. The editorial, as well as the rest of the building was very old and a distinct musty smell of decaying wood mingled in the air. Although there were many windows round the very large room, it was overshadowed by a much taller neighbouring building, preventing the light from filtering in.

Sally had to report first of all to the Managing Director's secretary where she filled in the appropriate forms. The woman facing Sally had a severe appearance and looked as if she was incapable of smiling. She was an unpleasant looking woman who succeeded in frightening the life out of Sally.

'Mr Wilson will see you shortly,' she managed to growl looking Sally over from head to toe. She sniffed disapprovingly.

Sally didn't know whether to sit on the seat nearby, or to stand. She decided to stand.

The adjoining door opened, and Mr Wilson's frame filled the doorway. He seemed gigantic. 'Right, I'll see you now,' he bellowed.

The first things she noticed were his hands. They looked like massive shovels with small beefy fingers stuck on the ends. Apprehensively she moved quickly into his office.

'Sally Baxter is it?'

'Yes sir,' she answered.

'Well Miss Baxter,' he roared, 'I hope you'll be happy here. We all do our bit and things run smoothly. You do as you're told and you'll fit in.' He was sitting at the opposite side of the desk moving from side to side in his black leather swivel chair. A fat cigar dangled from his loose bottom lip. Thick gold linked bracelets dripped from his massive wrist. He wore a navy blue pin striped suit that appeared to be a size too small and the buttons of the waistcoat strained in an effort to hold it shut. A gold fob watch, attached to the waistcoat by yet another thick gold chain, peeped out from his pocket.

As he spoke, saliva ran from both sides of his mouth, making his over- sized lips horribly soggy.

'You will be shown what to do by the supervisor. We print trade directories here, as I explained to you the last time we met. New entries get added yearly and others get taken out due to various reasons, for instance; companies shut down or no longer wish to advertise. You will be involved in something of that nature.'

There was a knock at the door and he roared once more. Sally didn't think the man before her was capable of talking quietly.

'Ah, Mrs Dolan, this is Sally Baxter,' he spoke to the woman who stood at the door. She looked as if she was ready for a quick getaway. Mrs Dolan was extremely thin and appeared to be of a nervous disposition.

'Come this way,' she said meekly, beckoning Sally with a wave of her hand.

Sally followed Mrs Dolan out of the door, through the overhead walkway, and into the editorial section. She was glad to get out of Mr. Wilson's office as he gave her the shivers. If it had been he who interviewed her, she doubted very much whether she would have accepted the job, but her interviewer had been Mrs. Wilson, who took an interest in the business only when she was feeling bored. Most of the time she was off spending her time and her husband's money in the south of France.

Thirteen desks filled the room. The supervisor's desk sat length ways in the middle, separating the desks into groups, six at the top and six at the bottom of the room.

All heads were down as they busied themselves with slips of paper. No one seemed curious enough to look up and observe the new employee. They were either too afraid or conditioned to work without interruptions. Mrs Dolan hadn't uttered a word to Sally either, she just led her towards the back of the room, pointed at the vacant desk, and almost in a whisper said, 'Yours.'

Sally walked round the desk and sat down. Mrs Dolan then went over to a very tiny woman whose feet dangled down from the seat not reaching the floor.

'Annie, will you give Sally some work,' she said.

The small woman who was dressed in a green overall jumped to the floor, walked to the back wall, which was only a partition, and disappeared through the door. She appeared moments later with a tray of what looked like pink cards. Putting the tray in front of Sally she then produced an inkpad and a rubber stamper.

'Sally, is it?' She didn't wait for an answer but continued talking. 'Stamp the cards at the top. See,' she demonstrated a couple of times and then handed the bewildered girl the stamper. The stamp had the word 'Joiner' embossed on the rubber. What she was doing she didn't know but that was how Sally's working life began.

At home, Sally relayed to Ruby and Jimmy what had transpired that day. She mimicked the characters she had met that day and both Ruby and Jimmy laughed until they were sore. She told them about Nettie, who sat in front of Annie, and blew her nose every five minutes, and of Kirstie who walked about with a permanent grin on her face, all the time looking down at her feet. They laughed when she went through the routine in the boss's office, but they never suspected that Sally didn't like the place one bit. In fact, she hated everything about it.

Had Mr Wilson shown her round at the time of the interview, she would never have taken the job. However, she decided to give it a try because she needed the money

She had been with the company four weeks now, and amazingly, was beginning to enjoy her work. She had been given a slightly better job and had become friendly with one of the girls. They didn't sit next to each other, but when they wanted to escape for a few minutes to exchange gossip, they had a signal that said 'toilet'. As they both lived too far away going home for lunch was out of the question so they stayed in the office. Sometimes they went out for lunch depending on their finances, but usually it was a flask of soup and a couple of sandwiches.

From the window nearest Sally's desk she could see over to the bookbinders. She looked over often to where one of the young lads stood. His bench was right at the window and if their eyes met, he gave her a wave. Feeling embarrassed and extremely shy, she never returned it.

One morning when Sally and her friend Avril met in the usual place, one of the women from the bindery joined them. Sally didn't smoke but Avril did, so she was more or less waiting on her friend finishing her cigarette. Nancy, the woman from the bindery, teased Sally, 'Dennis wants a talk with you Sally.'

'With me?' she sounded surprised.

'Aye. I think he's looking to taking you out,'

'Well! You dark horse.' Avril grinned. 'You never said anything to me!'

Sally's face flushed causing her neck and body to feel hot and sticky.

'You're terrible Nancy, he's not interested in me.' She turned away from them hiding her embarrassment. With her head bent over the sink she began washing her hands.

'You've just washed your hands Sal,' Avril teased.

'I'm telling you Sally, Dennis wants to talk to you.' She waited for an answer.

Sally walked towards the drier, and, still without looking at the two women said, 'I don't know. Why hasn't he approached me himself?'

'Because he's as shy as you! You pillock,' she answered impatiently.

'Sally shy!' Avril laughed.

'Well, she's anything but forward,' Nancy snapped.

'When it comes to lads, I don't think Sally knows about such matters. Not like some folk.'

It was at this point Sally shuddered and felt sick. Her mind flashed back to the Watsons. Revulsion is what she now felt. She couldn't bear this conversation any longer.

'I've got too much to do. I don't have the time,' she blurted out. Pushing past them both she hurried back to the editorial. Once at her desk, she was unable to concentrate. She knew what happened that day was no fault of her own, so why did the memory of it make her feel so guilty.

At lunch Avril quizzed Sally until she became quite angry. 'If I want to talk to Dennis I'll do it when I'm ready and if I want to ignore him that's up to me, so will you shut up Avril.'

'Oh my, I've hit a bit of a raw nerve. Sorry Sally.' She dropped the subject and spent the rest of the lunch hour in silence.

Dennis continued to give Sally the occasional wave making her feel more and more embarrassed, although deep down she secretly would like to have spoken to him. They had met down stairs a couple of times when they both had errands at the printers. Although a few words were spoken, she always hurried away. When at a safe distance, she became annoyed at her own foolishness.

'Why can't I stay and chat?' she asked herself. Given another chance, she vowed to encourage conversation.

Anna spent most of her spare time studying as she was determined to do well and get to university. She wanted to become a doctor and knew she had a long hard struggle before her; however, Friday night was set-aside for her friend Sally. Elbows resting on the bed and their hands cradling their heads, they both lay sprawled across the bed. They were both recovering from a fit of laughter as Sally had been doing her weekly impersonation of her work colleagues. Anna liked to hear about the odd people who worked with Sally, especially the one called Beatrice, who told the office her aunt had radio- active teeth and she couldn't turn round quickly as her brain was on a swivel. They had laughed until tears fell from their eyes.

'You want the latest about Beatrice?'

'Yes,' urged Anna. 'What's she been saying this week?'

Sally giggled as she remembered. 'She told Avril that she was pregnant. Avril nearly choked. Seemingly a lad took her for a walk in the park and put his hand up her skirt.'

'You're joking. And she really thought she was pregnant because of that?'

'Aye, that's how utterly stupid she is.'

After the laughter had died down, Sally decided to tell her about Dennis. She longed to talk about him, and after all, Anna was her best friend and that was what best friends did. So she told her. Anna sat open-mouthed in utter amazement.

'You've got an admirer Sally? Well, that's fantastic. What's he like?'

'Now wait, wait Anna, I'm only telling you because we promised to have no secrets. I've not really spoken to him properly yet.'

Anna jumped on the bed with delight.

'Wheesht,' she reprimanded. 'You'll have Ruby popping her head round any minute.'

'You haven't told Jimmy?' Anna asked.

'I was going to, but there's nothing to tell, is there?'

'Do you think you love him?' Anna whispered.

Sally went into fits of laughter.

'You stupid thing, of course I don't. I don't know the first thing about him.'

'Except he's good looking eh!' tormented Anna.

'He's not bad. I've seen worse.' Sally gave her friend's arm a push and promised to keep her informed of any further developments.

Sally sat at her desk and listened to Mrs Dolan's feet clip clopping up and down the office. She stopped at Sally's desk and bending down, spoke in her mousy voice. Her shoulders moving up and down as she did so.

'Will you go through to the bindery Sally and have Dennis trim those sheets on the guillotine? I've written down the size required.'

She handed Sally a stack of paper.

As Sally walked towards the door leading to the walkway, Avril turned round and mouthed, 'speak to him.'

Sally acknowledged with a nod.

'Sally,' she turned round and looked back at Mrs Dolan, 'Wait for the paper and bring it back, I need it urgently.'

'Yes Mrs Dolan,' she looked once more at Avril and winked.

Over in the bindery, Dennis's head was bent over sheets and sheets of paper. His concentration was on his work so he didn't see Sally enter the room.

'Dennis can you cut this paper for Mrs D?' she asked in a matter of fact manner, butterflies fluttering in her stomach.

Raising his head, his eyes lit up when he saw who stood beside him. 'Aye. Are you waiting for them?' Being in his own domain gave him the confidence he usually lacked.

'Yes,' she said, hoping her answer did not sound eager.

'Sit down on the bench then. I'll get them done in a minute.' He looked pleased with himself.

Sally sat down beside him. She felt awkward. She had given him the piece of paper with the required size and he studied it before adjusting the dials on the guillotine. 'You doing anything this weekend?' He was quick and to the point.

Taken aback she practically spat out her answer. 'Yes!' Why oh why did I say that she thought.

'Oh! Where are you off to then?' he was hiding his embarrassment.

'I'm going out with the people I stay with.'

He looked at her with questioning eyes.

'Don't you stay with your folks?'

'No. I stay with relations,' she lied. Then she took the initiative by saying. 'I'm not going anywhere next weekend Dennis.'

He smiled and came straight to the point once more.

'Would you like to go to the pictures a week on Saturday then?' He waited in anticipation, studying her face for an answer.

Sally smiled back and said, 'Yes Dennis, I would.'

'Well,' he said. 'We'll make arrangements next week then.'

Lifting the neatly trimmed sheets of paper, he laid them in Sally's arms. As she stood up his hand touched hers making her wobble slightly at the knees. She wished she had made the date for Saturday coming, as she wasn't going anywhere.

Back at the editorial, Avril bursting with curiosity, looked back at Sally every few minutes. She was waiting for a sign, but as Sally deliberately kept her face expressionless, she reckoned nothing had taken place. Their eyes met, Sally smiled slightly and winked

Unable to contain herself, Avril called out as loud as she could, 'Yes!' The girl sitting beside her almost jumped a mile in the air with fright. Then, both girls took a fit of the giggles. 'Girls please!' Mrs Dolan snapped. Her rules were, 'No Talking – No Laughing and No Breathing in the Editorial.'

It was the Wednesday before she was due to go out with Dennis and he hadn't made any arrangements with her as yet although he waved over several times. She made up her mind to go through and speak to him.

Mrs Dolan called Sally over to her desk and informed her that Mr Wilson wanted to see her.

Sally felt her flesh crawl, as she couldn't stand the man. His saliva coated mouth made her feel sick.

Sally knocked on the secretary's door but there was no answer. Usually you were admitted into Mr Wilson's office by the adjoining door in his secretary's room. A second door from the corridor led directly into his office but only he used that one.

She knocked once more before opening the door. No papers lay on the desk, and the typewriter had a cover over it. It became obvious his secretary wasn't at work as she was always in before anyone else in the morning.

She didn't know what to do. Should she go in and knock on the inner door or knock on the main corridor door? She didn't have to think about it long as the corridor door opened and Mr Wilson's huge fat body blocked the doorway.

'Come in Sally,' he walked backwards into the office and Sally followed.

'I want you to do some filing for me. Do you think you can manage?' he asked.

'Yes Sir.' She knew how to do that all right.

'Well, start with that lot.' He pointed to a mountain of papers that lay on a small table near the filing cabinet.

'After you've done that, can you file those ones in the other cabinet?'

'Yes sir,' she answered once more.

'And can you work the switchboard Sally?' he asked.

'No sir.' She didn't want to either, but the Boss's next sentence gave her no option.

'Well I'll show you. Iron drawers isn't in today, so you can work along here beside me.'

'Oh God,' Sally thought, 'I'll be sick as sure as anything.'

She worked on the papers, putting them into order before filing them away. There came a muted burr from the secretary's office and Mr Wilson led Sally through towards the switchboard.

'Come on,' he said. 'I'll show you how to deal with this.'

The phone call was for the print department and the boss worked with the small silver plugs demonstrating to Sally how it was done. He sat her down on the seat and talked her through the various switches. He had obviously been drinking as Sally caught the distinct smell of whisky from his breath. It was only ten o'clock in the morning and he had already had a good few drinks.

'You can deal with the phones, but in the meantime, tidy my office.' He was uncouth and Sally could not stand him.

She was between his office and the switchboard all morning and at eleven o'clock she went through to the editorial to have her break. When Sally returned, Mr Wilson called her through to his office. He was sitting back in his large leather chair, holding a glass of whisky.

'You want one Sally?' he asked.

Sally was shocked. The girls did say he was an alcoholic but she hadn't seen it for herself. She hadn't seen much of him at all since she started. This was her fourth month with the Company, and apart from passing him on the stair, she saw very little of him.

'I don't drink sir,' she replied.

'Of course not,' he grinned. 'You're only a slip of a lass yet. Not even got a pair of decent titties.' He grinned and looked at her through half shut eyes.

He belched and lifted the glass up to his wet lips and drank the remaining contents.

Sally's face was on fire with embarrassment. She wanted to run from the office, but she remained calm and walked through and sat down at the switchboard.

Mr Wilson took a few incoming calls, and the lines began to get busy around mid-day. She had just put a call through to the print shop and was about to tidy up before lunch, when the big man staggered through. She didn't look up as she chose to ignore him. He walked over towards her and as he drew near her he put his hand out and grabbed her hair. Pulling hard, he forced her head back, and, before she could scream, he bent down quickly, pressing his big wet soggy lips forcefully on Sally's mouth. The smell of whisky was really overpowering and as he kissed her, he grabbed at her breast with his other hand.

Struggling, Sally grabbed at her boss's hair, pulled fiercely on it until he let her go. She jumped to her feet knocking over her chair. Revulsion swelled in her throat making her gag. She felt dizzy with disgust.

'You dirty Bastard,' she yelled, not realising what she was saying. She rubbed her mouth vigorously with the sleeve of her cardigan. 'You make me sick. Do you hear? You're disgusting.' Snatching up her shoulder bag and coat that lay near, she turner and face him. You can keep your bleeding job. I'm off Mister and before I go...' She lifted a large flower vase, threw the long since withered flowers onto the floor before throwing the dirty green smelly water into his face. 'That'll cool you down you...you *pervert.*

Sally marched out of the office and into the street. Without so much as turning back, she caught the bus and went home. She didn't get the opportunity to say goodbye to Avril or exchange addresses. Her date with Dennis hadn't been arranged, so she never saw him again.

Chapter Thirteen

POP! The cork from the champagne flew up and hit the ceiling. Jimmy Duncan stood holding the bottle as the froth spilled over.

'Mind the carpet man,' Ruby reprimanded. 'It's supposed to go into the glasses not on the floor.'

'Hold your tongue woman and give me your glass,' he said to his wife.

Ruby stuck her tongue out, and grabbed it between her fingers while thrusting her glass towards her husband.

Anna and Sally laughed, as Jimmy pulled a face.

'Very funny ... very funny,' he said.

They were gathered together to celebrate a double occasion, Sally's eighteenth birthday and Anna's acceptance into university.

Anna's mother, father, and Sally's new employer and his wife Connie made up the small party.

She had been working for the Mathesons' for almost two years. They ran a small building company and Sally worked with Connie in the office. Connie's husband Ron was simply great to work for making Sally very happy in her job. She had gone to night school and learned to type, and with help from Connie, she managed to run the office smoothly and efficiently.

They filled their glasses and began to toast the girls who sat together by the window watching and listening to the three couples talking over each other.

'What a noise they make. You'd think there were twenty people in here,' Sally remarked.

Anna grinned, 'I know, and they tell us that we're noisy.'

'I heard that,' Jimmy said making his way over beside them.

'You've got big ears Uncle Jimmy,' Anna said.

'I know, and I've also got a big appetite. Fetch some sandwiches through Anna please.' She nodded and left him sitting beside Sally.

'You should have asked her to come Sally,' Jimmy said referring to Sally's mother who shuddered at the very idea. She knew that these people would have welcomed Nellie Baxter despite their different way of life. To console herself, Nellie had turned once more to drink but this time it was much worse. She started with a small one in the morning, tippling at odd times through the day, and by evening she was well out of control.

'No Jimmy, I couldn't take that chance. I was over last night and she's getting worse. I'm really worried about Lucy.'

Jimmy shook his head sadly. 'Did you ask her to get help?'

'She won't listen. She's adamant that she doesn't drink much.'

'Well go over again tomorrow and try to get her to see a doctor, and Sally, bring Lucy over next weekend.'

'Thanks Jimmy, I'll talk to you later about that. Here's Anna with the sandwiches.'

Anna's father, being an accomplished player on the accordion provided the music and in no time at all the party was in full swing. A few drinks later and they were ready to sing.

Glancing at the happy faces, Sally felt warmth from the love and friendship that surrounded her. For the first time in her adult life, she felt relaxed and untroubled.

'This has been a great night. Anna and I would like to thank you Ruby for going to all this trouble.' Sally said as the evening drew to an end.

'Oh shush. We should do this more often.' Ruby was only too happy that the night had gone well. Anna had arranged to stay over night, and after waving her parents and the Mathesons off, she chased Ruby and Jimmy to bed as it was well after mid-night and Ruby looked worn out. She had worked non-stop to ensure the evening's success and gladly left the girls to clear up the glasses.

'You know Sally,' Anna said as they tidied the kitchen, 'You could have been going to University too, after all, you were clever at school.'

'I left at fifteen though,' sighed Sally. 'I never had the chance Anna, my mother and my health saw to that,' she said.

'Do you ever feel bitter Sally? You know, all that's happened. Don't you feel at all bitter?'

Sally thought a minute before answering.

'Yes I do at times. I feel there's still unexplained bits.'

'What do you mean?' Anna sat down on the stool and watched Sally as she slowly wiped the top of the Formica table with a cloth.

'I don't know Anna. It's just that there are things I don't understand – Oh! Listen to me, I am so lucky, I have no right to complain.' Shrugging her shoulders she gave a contented sigh. 'Sometimes I have to pinch myself. No Anna. I have a good job and a really nice home. I wasn't meant to go to University but you were, so you go and stick in. You'll make a fine doctor.'

'Maybe some day Sally but I've got a long way to go.'

'Well you've got all the time in the world, so you just go and do it, but before you do, let's go and get some sleep.'

The following day Sally visited her family. She arrived at four and intended to have a meal with them. She had bought a large steak pie and a cream sponge knowing her mother wouldn't have much in the way of food. She never visited the house empty handed. Sometimes Ruby filled a tin with home baking but Nellie had remarked quite nastily the last time she did so. Charity she had called it, therefore, to prevent a repeat performance, Sally carried no more home baking.

Alcohol had changed Nellie back to the quick tempered, bitter woman she had been in the past, although she showed no sign of violence towards Lucy.

Approaching the house, Lucy excitedly ran to greet her. She had been playing hopscotch on the pavement.

Throwing her thin arms round Sally's waist, she hugged her so tight Sally swayed but quickly regained her balance.

'Watch it Lucy. You nearly knocked me over.'

'Oh Sally. I'm glad to see you.' Lucy squealed.

'It's not that long since I've seen you.' Taking the young girl's hand in hers, swinging their arms, they went up the path and into the house.

Nellie was in the kitchen when they walked in.

'See ma! See! Sally's here,' Lucy announced. She simply adored this older sister who returned the affection tenfold, unlike Bess, who tolerated her only just, scoffing at her childish ideas and fantasies.

Sally stood at the kitchen door and smiling warmly she asked, 'Hi ma, how are you?'

Without looking up, Nellie carried on washing the dishes, answering blandly, 'little dae you care. You prefer tae be wi' others rather than yer ain.'

Sally felt her heart sink as she was hoping to find things different.

'Ma, don't start. Look, I've brought round something for our tea tonight.' Walking into the kitchen she placed the paper bags down on the table.

Looking over towards the table Nellie tossed her head back snapping at her daughter. 'Left -overs?'

'No!' Sally snapped back. She was ready for her mother, as they had this same old quarrel time and time again over the last few months.

'I bought them myself ma as I thought I would stay and have something to eat here.'

'Well noo! Share you can spare the time? Nae party the nicht?' Sarcasm flowed from Nellie's mouth.

'Ma, don't go on. I can't split myself in half.'

Nellie wiped her hands on the towel, and going over to the table looked into the paper bags. Facing Sally, she calmly said. 'If you want chips wi' that pie, you'd better peel the tatties.'

As she spoke, the unmistakable smell of gin reeked from her breath, although there was no visible sign of excessiveness, and, as she was steady and in control of her actions, Sally chose to ignore it.

Silently, Lucy watched the two women. She was well used to her mother's mood swings, and although Nellie never abused her like she did Sally, she was subjected to constant shouting and when her mother drank herself into a state of oblivion, the family were left to fend for themselves. Lucy often made her own meals when her mother was incapable. She also was left to help her mother into bed, where she would strip her and tuck her in. There she would be left to sleep herself into sobriety, or as the case often was, left till she needed another drink.

In looks and in nature, Lucy was very much like her favourite sister, although only nine, she, like Sally, had an independence that was usually apparent in older children. She had the same finely chiselled features and raven hair; although hers was curly, Sally's hair had always been long and straight. There was a difference in the colour of their eyes, Sally's were brown while Lucy's were the palest of blues, but they both were large and saucer like with long lashes that curled back over the lids.

Bess had been working now for almost a year in the Wire Mill but very seldom was she home at weekends. Nellie never objected, as she was glad to see the back of her. She still took little pride in her appearance, although her face was always heavily masked in make-up.

Hugh had joined the army and was now stationed in the Far East. He never bothered to write and spent his leave at the home of his army pals who were all from England.

Sally made the meal while Lucy set the table. Both girls chatted while Nellie chose to stay quiet, answering only when she had to.

The meal was placed on the table and Nellie, Sally and Lucy sat down to eat. The conversation was still very strained but Sally tried hard to make peace with her mother.

"Where has our Bess gone?' Sally asked.

'Staying with some work mate,' Nellie informed her.

'Don't you ask her who?' Sally was curious.

'None o' ma business, she daes as she pleases,' her eyes flashed with irritation.

Feeling her mother was about to use her enquiry of Bess as an excuse to start another argument, she dropped the subject and asked no more of her wayward sister.

The meal over, they watched a bit of television as Lucy did her homework. Nellie had gradually dropped the hostility although she had started to become slightly troubled. Sally had noticed this and knew what was happening. Watching her mother she wondered how much longer she could survive without a drink. She had restrained herself since Sally arrived, but the look on her face suggested she could go on no longer.

'Oh well,' Nellie said lightly, rising and opening the cupboard door. 'I'll have a wee drink tae settle me nerves.'

'Ma,' Sally said, 'you don't need to you know. You're drinking far too much.'

'When you pay fer ma drink Sally, then ye can tell me how an' when a can hiv yin. In the meantime ... shut it!' Nellie defiantly poured out a glassful, went over and sat down. Taking a gulp she looked at her daughter and sighed. 'It's awe a've got Sally. Toms deid; you're gone. Sam's it the ither side o' the world. Bess will be leavin' soon an' Hugh's in the army.' She sounded really sorry for herself.

'There's more to life than that ma, besides, Lucy needs you. She's still here and Bess isn't going anywhere. She's only gone on weekends.'

'Listen Sally,' Nellie looked towards Lucy, 'Lucy go intae the kitchen an' make some tea.'

Lucy protested but did not need to be told twice.

When she was sure her youngest child was out of earshot, she turned her attention on Sally. Looking her straight in the eye, she said without hesitation, 'Bess is pregnant.'

'*What*!' Her jaw dropped as she sucked in air. '*Our* Bess? But she's only sixteen ma!'

'Noo Sally, you think ye ken it awe. A've had mair worry ower them past years than some folk hiv in a lifetime. Noo dae you understand? A canny face things ony mare.'

'But ma, who's she pregnant to? Who's the father?'

'Some lad she works wi. Ye ken oor Bess, ye cannnae believe a word that comes oot her mooth.' She took another drink of gin.

'What's she going to do?' Sally asked.

'Bide wi' the lad as soon as he finds a place.' Nellie glanced towards the kitchen door in case Lucy came through.

'Are you sure she's pregnant?'

Nellie gave a slight laugh as she nodded he head. 'A'm sure.'

The door opened and Lucy came back into the living-room.

The kettle's on,' she voiced. 'You're getting me out of the way because of our Bess.'

'Oh no! What do you mean?' Sally asked the youngster.

'Well,' she said, 'she's going to have a bairn. I heard her and ma arguing. She's going to have a bairn.'

'Bloody leather lugs,' Nellie said. 'Her bloody ears are aye flappin'.'

'I don't know what to say ma. I really don't,' Sally said shaking her head.

'Weel, noo ye ken,' Nellie replied. 'So dinnae begrudge me a drink. It helps tae blot oot ma worries.'

'But you have to face them again when it wears off.' She tried reasoning with her but it was pointless. Nellie had become dependant on alcohol therefore, until she had professional help, there was nothing anyone could do. She had a few more gins before Sally left.

Leaving her mother's place around nine thirty, Sally reached the bus stop with time to spare. Instead of hanging around for ten minutes, she decided to walk on to the next stop. As she rounded the corner, she saw Bess walking on the other side of the road hanging onto a man's arm, the two of them looking into each other's eyes.

Sally stepped into a shop doorway to avoid meeting them. She could still see the pair of them, but they couldn't see her, and as the couple passed in front of the doorway, the light from the street gave Sally a clear view of the man's face. She couldn't believe it. Her mother's old friend Flo had been going out with that man for years. Dempster Simpson. He was old enough to be Bess's grandfather.

'Oh God,' Sally thought. 'The balloon will burst when this gets out.' But she wasn't to know just how loud the bang would be.

She wrestled with this knowledge all night, until she could lie in bed no longer. Rising shortly after four, she sat in the kitchen with a cup of coffee. She heard a door open and Ruby scurrying along the corridor towards the toilet. As she made her way back to bed, Ruby saw the light on in the kitchen and went to investigate.

'Can't sleep?' she whispered.

'No Ruby, I can't'

'A trouble shared....' Ruby said willing to be a confidant.

'Oh Ruby, that sister of mine is in a lot of trouble. I don't care a fig for her but she's adding to my mother's worries.' Despair sounded in her voice.

Ruby sat down at the kitchen table where Jimmy normally sat.

'Bess?' Ruby enquired.

'Yes Ruby. Bess.'

Ruby listened without interrupting as the concerned teenager shared her mother's latest worry. She also told her Bess was keeping company with Dempster Simpson, although she didn't know if he was the father of the child, but the way they were carrying on, it seemed highly likely.

'What should I do Ruby? Do you think I should tell my mother?'

Ruby thought for a while before answering.

'Don't say a word Sally. Your mother will find out soon enough so my advice to you would be to keep out of it. Anyway, maybe he's not the father. Have you thought of that? Just imagine what would happen if you named him and he didn't have a thing to do with it now. No. Let it take it's own course. The truth will out.' Ruby smiled at Sally and shook her lightly by the arm. 'Now go and get some rest or you'll not be fit for work.'

'You're right Ruby, it's not my affair. We'll just have to wait and see.'

Sally didn't have long to wait until the can of worms was opened.

It was a month since Sally saw her sister with Flo's boyfriend, and as nothing was said, she began to think perhaps Ruby's words were right. Maybe she had jumped to conclusions.

It was Saturday night; Sally had gone to her mother's to give her a home perm. Feeling guilty about not going round enough she tried to see Nellie more often. She had noticed Nellie drank less when she had company, so her visits were helping.

She washed her mother's hair and had just started to perm the ends. They had been laughing at Lucy's attempt at baking scones, which turned out more like biscuits, when there came a loud banging on the front door.

'Whay the hell is that noo?' Nellie said. 'Lucy, go an' see who's there before the door gets knocked in.'

The urgency of the knocking alarmed Sally as an inner feeling warned her it was trouble.

'It's Auntie Flo,' Lucy called out, but Flo was in the living room before the announcement of her name.

'Aye, it's Flo. A didnae think a would ever have tae come here because o' your little shit o' a daughter.'

'Wait a minute Flo, what's up? What daughter?' Standing up, Nellie used the towel that lay around her neck, and dabbed at the perm curlers that had been put in her hair.

Sally stood back, pulling Lucy towards her. Expecting a show down, she ushered her young sister into the kitchen. 'Oh no' again,' yelped Lucy. 'I always get shut in here.'

'Shut up Lucy,' Sally scolded quietly. 'Stay in here for now.' Shutting the door on the protesting child, she returned and stood behind her mother.

'That's right hen,' Flo said to Sally. 'What a've got tae say isnae fer her ears.' She now seemed to swell with anger. 'A've been at the club the nicht Nellie, an' a was tae meet Dempster.' She stuck her chest out like a strutting pigeon.

'So!' Nellie snorted. 'What's that got tae dae wi' us? An' what daughter are you oan aboot?'

'A'll tell you Nellie Baxter. Dempster never showed, an' guess why he never showed? He's only been layin' your Bess, that's bloody why.'

'Ma Bess? But... but...' She was stuck for words.

'Aye your Bess. Oh... an' a'll tell you anither thing while 'am at it... you're goin' tae be a granny. Just imagine. If the bloody pair get married yer son-in-law will be aulder than you huh!'

Regaining her composure, Nellie jumped in defence of her daughter, the daughter that brought her nothing but trouble and at one time was the apple of her eye.

'Ye're a liar Flo Begbie. A ken oor Bess is pregnant. Ye'd have tae be blind no' tae notice, but it's tae someboady at the Mill, no' tae a bloody auld man.'

'So a'm a *liar*. You dare call *me* a liar. You! Ye're the biggest liar oot Nellie. Whay was it that lay doon with Jack Broon an' let him faither a bairn? An' whay was it that let her man take the blame? *Bloody you*.' She pointed fiercely at Nellie. 'Ye let Tom Baxter think that he faithered that puir bairn he lies beside. Ye shut up when that lass was raped an awe.' Flo was now pointing towards Sally, who by now had turned very white. 'You call *me* a liar? Well, a've a hell o' a long way tae go tae catch up wi' you.' Flo continued, venomously spitting out every accusation she could think of.

'You get oot o' here, ye loud mouthed bastard.' Nellie was now yelling at the woman who was once her devoted friend.

'We're into the heavy language noo are we?' taunted Flo. 'Weel, a'll tell you somethin' else, shall I? You should ken awe aboot bastards as *ye* had yin an' ye're getting' anither. Best o' luck Nellie, because ye're goin' tae need it. Your Bess has been bad awe her days an' you bloody well ken it. There's the best, the yin beside ye, an' you couldnae see it for jealousy.' With that, Flo left as noisily as she had come in, banging the door shut.

The room was thrown into silence as Nellie slowly sunk into her chair. Leaning back she stared up at the ceiling.

Feeling her feet were glued to the floor, Sally stood rigid behind her.

It was some time before the kitchen door opened and Lucy asked if she could come out now. Putting her into the kitchen was a stupid idea, as she always heard every word.

With trembling legs, Sally walked round and faced her mother. She spoke almost in a whisper. 'Is that true ma? Was wee Robert, Jack Brown's son?'

Nellie's face was now awash with tears. Her eyes were full as they rolled down her cheeks like an overflowing river.

'Yes.' Her answer was almost inaudible. 'But it wisnae as Flo said,' she sobbed. 'You should understand Sally, a was raped by him.'

Sally now remembered seeing him leave the close a week or so before he had near molested her.

'But why was he here ma?'

Nellie told her the story. The true story.

'And you didn't tell dad?' She stood opened mouth before shaking her head in disbelief. 'I could forgive you everything ma, even hiding the fact you knew who assaulted *me*, but I can't forgive you for letting da think Robert was *his*.'

Sally walked to the chair her coat was thrown over. Pulling it on in silence she walked out the door. She had only gone a hundred yards or so when she heard Lucy cry after her. The girl caught up, took Sally by the hand and said adamantly, 'I'm coming too.'

Feeling tired and drained of energy Sally didn't try to dissuade her so taking her young sister's hand she give it a slight squeeze.

Ruby and Jimmy sat relaxing in the lounge when the two girls arrived, Sally looking very haggard, Lucy silently walking beside her. This itself was strange, as Lucy was always noisy and excited when coming to visit.

They knew at once something was wrong. It was Jimmy who spoke first.

'You're back early. We didn't expect you back until ten.' He scanned Sally's face. 'What's wrong?'

'I hope you don't mind Lucy coming to stay for a day or so.' Sally gently moved Lucy towards the couch.

'Of course we don't. Lucy's always welcome, you know that.' Ruby's eyes widened with concern. 'What has happened, is it your mother?'

'Can I tell you both later?' She glanced towards Lucy as she spoke.

The couple caught her meaning and nodded.

Later on that evening when Lucy had gone to bed, Sally told Jimmy and Ruby what had taken place at her mother's house. The knowledge of her father being deceived and cheated by her mother reduced her once more into floods of tears. Red swollen eyes peered over the paper tissue as she blew her nose for the umpteenth time.

'She said she was raped. I just don't believe her. I just don't believe her. She invited him into the house knowing that my father would be out; she even sent us all to the pictures.' She shook her head in disbelief, 'She's such a liar, she's lied all her life.' She sobbed. 'Can you imagine what must have gone through my father's mind when he faced that man? He went after him for me! Did he know about my mother? Oh God, did he tell my dad about Robert?' She looked up at her friends with a look of horror. 'It all fits. It all fits!

'Wheesht lass,' Ruby patted her on the back. 'Don't make yourself ill now. You'll never know, so don't try to relive that night'.

'I'm glad it's out in the open. I'm glad I know,' she sobbed. 'I can't forgive her. I'll never forgive her. She's a liar and a cheat. Now I know why she suddenly ran hand and foot after my da. Her conscience. Now she can't live with herself. That's why she drinks so much'.

'Well maybe,' Jimmy said. 'But she's got to live with it for the rest of her life.'

'And she'll have to live with it by herself, for everyone has left her. I can't see Dempster Simpson staying there with Bess, and Lucy doesn't want to go back. She's had enough. I'll have to find somewhere to stay so I can have her with me.' Sally's breathing became more regulated as her sobbing began to ease.

'You'll do no such thing!' Ruby was quite annoyed.

'This is your home and if Lucy wants to be with you, well that's fine, so be it. There's plenty room here and she's a wee ray of sunshine.'

'Oh Ruby,' Sally began to cry again. This time the two women hugged each other tightly.

Chapter Fourteen

Connie Matheson was a pretty, dark blue-eyed blond, who oozed with personality. Her pale skin looked as if it had never known a spot or a blemish. The corner of her mouth seemed to curl slightly when she smiled. Looking curiously at Sally, her mouth did exactly that as she smiled warmly at her friend and work mate.

'You're nearly twenty-two Sally, and you've never had a boyfriend. It's time you did something about that,' Connie jested while they worked side by side in the office. 'Have you never gone steady?' she asked.

'Nope.' Stopping work for a minute, Sally looked up from the typewriter. 'I have never found anyone I liked. Oh, ... I've gone out on dates, but I find most lads silly and showy.'

'Never mind,' laughed Connie. 'When you find the right one, you'll know.'

'I hope I'm as happy as you are when I do.' Sally started typing once more.

Connie and her husband were ten years older than Sally and were very happy together. They had everything going for them, everything except one thing – a baby. They had put off having a family; everything had gone into the business. Once it was well established, Connie had taken a year off on advice from her doctor, hoping that the rest would relax her and she would fall pregnant. Sally had taken over the running of the office, with the help of a young school leaver called Alexis.

When nothing happened, Connie was referred to the hospital for investigation. During the investigations, they discovered she had a weak valve in her heart and advised against pregnancy. As well as that shattering piece of news, she also learned that due to her fallopian tubes being so narrow, the possibility of her conceiving was rather slim, ... not impossible... rather slim.

'I'll tell you something Connie, Harry Penman has phoned every night for a week. I can't get rid of him.'

Harry was a sales representative for office supplies, and came to see Sally regularly as she was responsible for the buying. He was ruggedly handsome and his dark laughing eyes sparkled with untold mischief. His banter with Sally led them to believe he was more than fond of her. Sally never felt embarrassed when he teased her, instead, she found that she could laugh and joke with him with out any inhibitions

'Well then, what's the matter with you? He's a nice lad,' Connie said. 'He's phoned all week and you're only telling me now.'

'Well I couldn't say anything in front of Alexis. She's all mouth.'

Leaning over, Connie stretched out and clipped Sally's ear. 'Go for it stupid. You can't tell if you like him unless you try him out!'

'I'll see. I'll tell you if I do anything.' Sally promised. 'He's due back soon. I'll make up my mind before he comes back.'

That evening Harry phoned Sally again. He continued to ask her out, but she gave him the same answer.

'I'll think about it.'

'Well now, if you don't want to date me, I'll have to emigrate as your driving me mad.'

Sally laughed and answered. 'If you do, make sure it's Australia, then you can give my brother a call and ask why he's not writing.'

They both laughed. Harry then became silent before speaking earnestly, 'Joking aside Sally, I really do want to take you out. Look, there's a big dance coming up in a fortnight, will you come and be my partner? I can't go on my own now, can I?'

Sally sighed before answering. 'You never give up Harry do you?' Another few seconds of silence before Sally said. 'All right, you win. What I have to do for peace.' She laughed as Harry called out in gratitude at the other end of the phone. 'Mind you,' Sally warned him, 'I'm only partnering you at a dance, so don't get any ideas.'

'Thank you, thank you,' he continued, 'there's only one thing though.'

'And what's that?' asked Sally.

'We'll have to have a trial run. How about this Saturday?'

'Harry you're terrible!'

Her Saturday night out with Harry proved to be an exhilarating experience. Not having entered a theatre in her life, she was secretly overwhelmed. The energy and performance from the artists, stirred Sally's heart, while the magnificent period costumes they wore left her gasping in admiration. They finished the evening having supper in an opulent west end restaurant, a far cry from a night at the local cinema, usually finished off with fish and chips wrapped in newspaper.

Driving home, Harry's humour and infectious laughter had her practically doubled up in pain. Stopping the car in front of the house, he leaned over towards her, gently pulling her to him, unsure of her reaction he kissed her briefly. Waiting on her response he studied her face before taking her into his arms, kissing her softly. Her head reeled as their lips tasted each other tenderly. Suddenly she stiffened and broke free before hurriedly saying goodnight. She was grateful to him for his gentleness, as further advances would have frightened her off completely. Barriers came swiftly down at the least sign of familiarity turning her body rigid, her mind zooming back to the horror that took place nearly ten years ago. She knew she must learn to erase that memory and get on with her life, although she tried ever so hard it was always with her. It was more than the violation of her body that haunted her. That whole episode had led to her father's death; her lies had contributed to that. Everyone had suffered, everyone except the Watson brothers. The thought of the vile pair constantly filled her with so much abhorrence consuming her with rage and revulsion, and try as she might, she couldn't rid herself of the desire for revenge.

Connie drove Sally into town the following Saturday in search of a dress for Sally to wear that evening. The dance, a rather opulent affair, was to be held at 'The Galaxy', a hotel which had a five star rating. Harry's father was an employee with one of the breweries and the dance was being held for staff and their families.

They hunted all morning until they found the right dress. Made from fine black velvet, the flattering halter neck was cut just low enough, revealing the slightest cleavage. The figure hugging skirt reached her calf, the side split showing off a shapely leg. She looked so beautiful. Her raven black hair shone, her huge eyes twinkled as she spun around showing the dress off to Connie.

'Oh Sally,' Connie gasped. 'You're beautiful. That is definitely the dress for you.'

The afternoon was spent at the hairdressers as the two young women relaxed and enjoyed being pampered. Connie had insisted on treating Sally to her hair do.

Back in the car Connie turned her head and looked at Sally briefly. 'You left everything to the last minute Sal. You were lucky to get something in one morning. Usually I take weeks to choose a special dress.' Connie's excitement amused her companion. 'I'll come round and see you off,' she insisted.

'Connie! You don't have to. I'm only going to a dance,' Sally beamed. 'You're more excited than I am.'

Ignoring her friend's remarks and keeping her attention on the traffic, she said obstinately. 'I'll bring round my diamond brooch. It'll look lovely with that dress.'

'Bring a tiara while you're at it,' teased Sally.

'I might do. Aye! I might!' taking her eyes from the road momentarily, jesting, she looked over at Sally and nodded in agreement.

'I give in, but you know, I might change my mind. I'm not there yet.' She watched Connie from the side of her eye.

'You'd never dare Sally Baxter. After spending all that money! And a car coming for you an all.'

'If I don't get a move on when I get home I'll be going the way I am. Here's hoping Ruby doesn't start her twenty questions. I love her to bits but she does go over the score. Honest, she does my head in at times.'

Connie dropped her off at the house and arranged to call round later with the brooch.

Sally was ready and waiting for Harry to call. Connie had brought the brooch round, and fixing it securely to the bottom of the broad strap of Sally's dress, she produced a matching pair of earrings, which she insisted Sally wore. Frightened that she would lose them, Sally tried to resist, but Connie wouldn't hear of it.

'You look like a princess,' gasped Lucy, her eyes wide in disbelief.

'Aye. She looks like a princess right enough,' Ruby repeated, covering Sally's shoulders with her own Italian lace shawl.

'Will you marry him?' Lucy looked all starry- eyed at her big sister.

'Oh shut her up somebody,' Sally scoffed. 'Where does she get her ideas from?'

Six thirty chimed just as Harry arrived at the door to collect Sally. He was shown into the lounge where he introduced himself to Jimmy and Ruby. Sally was still in her bedroom adding the finishing touches to her dress and make-up.

'You know Connie, I'm nervous.'

'Uh huh! Don't tell me you're falling for him,' her friend remarked.

Sally frowned. 'You're as bad as Lucy. You're all *mad.*'

'Come on. Your car awaits you mam!' Connie smiled, as she looked her friend over.

As she made her entrance into the lounge, Harry turned and gave a low whistle. He was stunned at the vision in front of him.

'Oh my, you look gorgeous. I'm going to be the envy of everyone,' he sighed.

Dressed in a black evening suit with a pale blue bow tie and matching cummerbund, white dress shirt that fell into small pleats, he looked extremely handsome. He too had thick raven hair with an unruly strand that persisted in falling over his brow. His impudent eyes flashed under thick bushy eye brows, corners wrinkling adding maturity to his good-looking face.

Sally's heart fluttered. She felt her face flush with embarrassment but being in control of her feelings, hid it well.

'You don't look too bad yourself,' she teased. 'This must be some dance; dinner suit an' all!'

'I don't take my best girl to anything but the best,' he smiled. Offering her his arm Sally held on, giving a slight curtsy as she did so.

The small group followed them along the hall. Outside waited a shiny black rover and as they approached, the driver, who was dressed in a smart grey suit, opened the back door allowing Harry to help his young lady in.

'Now that's the only way to travel,' Jimmy said to Ruby. 'She's going out in style tonight.'

'Aye Jimmy,' repeated Ruby. 'She certainly is.'

Jimmy noticed a worried look come over Connie's face. 'What's up Con?' he whispered.

'I don't know Jimmy. I think there's more to Harry than meets the eye.'

Connie was asking herself what kind of staff dance warrants chauffeur driven cars. The hotel was ten miles away, and hiring transport such as that would have cost an arm and a leg.

Sally was soon to find out.

They arrived at the hotel to find Harry's parents, a handsome couple, waiting for them in the foyer. His mother was dressed very elegantly in royal blue chiffon. A double string of tiny crystal beads hung round her neck, and a pear shaped crystal drop dangled from each ear, reflecting raindrops of coloured dancing lights. Her real mink stole draped loosely round her shoulders; she stood clutching a silver evening bag that was also decorated with the same small crystals.

'Sally, I would like you to meet my parents.' He stretched his hand out towards the couple.

'Mother, Father, this is Sally,' Harry announced proudly.

'How nice,' his mother said smiling sanctimoniously as she looked Sally over slowly from head to toe.

'Pleased to meet you young lady,' the father said, taking her by the hand and giving her a warm handshake.

'Come now, we'll go and get a wee dram before the meal.' Mr Penman ushered them into the nearby lounge. Harry excused himself and headed towards the gents.

Settling down onto the dark leather u-shaped couch, situated under the window, the waitress that hovered over them took their order. Knowing how alcohol had dominated her parents' lives caused Sally to be very wary, so she ordered a sweet sherry.

'Well then Sally, where do you work?' Mrs Penman enquired unenthusiastically giving a forced smile.

'I work for a builder, in the office that is,' she replied nervously.

'What do your folks do?' Studying Sally, she waited for her answer.

Mr. Penman noticed Sally's discomfort, knowing that any interrogation by his wife could be quite daunting, as she had years of practice. Former girl friends of their son had fallen at the first hurdle, as they were not the type she wished for a daughter- in- law. Working class girls were all very well for a bit of fun, but she shuddered at the thought of treating them as an equal. She blamed it on the stupid job he had insisted on taking. He had gone to university and done very well, but determined to fit in, he had chosen a career in sales. 'Experiencing life,' he had called it.

'Libby, leave the lass alone,' snapped her husband.

'Well really,' she snorted indignantly, 'I'm only being polite.' She hated her husband calling her Libby, especially in company. She thought it so common. She was called Elizabeth but he had always called her Libby much to her annoyance.

Sally knew Mrs Penman would not rest until she knew all about her. Like a dog with a bone, once she had her teeth into some-thing, she would not let go.

'It's all right Mr Penman,' Sally smiled. If she were going to enjoy the evening she would have to get this woman off her back.

'My mother and father are both dead. They were killed in a car accident.' Hearing her own words, Sally's blood ran cold. Why had she said that?

'Oh my dear,' Mr Penman was visibly shaken. 'Oh, I'm terribly sorry.'

'That's all right,' Sally lowered her eyes. 'I'm quite used to it. I have been brought up by my aunt.'

Harry came forward as the conversation had ended.

'Right now,' rubbing the palms vigorously together and in his usual cheery manner asked eagerly. 'Getting to know each other?'

They engaged in light conversation finishing the drinks that lay on the small marble table that fitted neatly into the shape of the seating.

Dressed almost as smartly as the guests, a tall slim figure wearing a dinner suit, white gloves and with the sobriety of an undertaker, announced that dinner was about to be served. A couple came forward and greeted

Harry's parents with handshakes and kisses. They spoke very politely and properly. What Sally usually called very 'la- de- da.' A few more came forward and shook hands with the Penmans. Once more the headwaiter appeared.

'Would the directors and their ladies please take their seats? The rest of the company are now waiting to begin.'

Turning her head quickly, Sally stared open mouthed at Harry.

'Directors? You didn't tell me your father was a director,' she felt anger rise.

'Calm down Sally, I didn't tell you as I knew you wouldn't come.'

'You're darn right,' she hissed quietly.

'I'm only a mere salesman. It's my parents who have the wealthy friends. It's not so bad, give it a chance.'

'I've no option now have I?' she snapped.

Harry's father John was in fact the managing director of the Scotia Brewing Company, the parent company of several subsidiaries. It was because of his involvement in this field, he met his wife Elizabeth, whose family at that time owned their own brewery as well as two public houses. John Penman was involved in the take over of his wife's family business with the intentions of closing everything down, thus eliminating the competition. It was during the constant meetings with her father they met. Friends thought them an odd couple; she was so refined while he, though extremely handsome, was rough and down to earth. After the death of her father, Elizabeth became a very wealthy woman and was determined that her only son would marry into a family similar to their own. John, however, thought his son should do his own thing, but that was only a thought, he never dared voice it.

The meal was never ending; Sally hadn't seen anything like it. What she termed a starter was soup before your main meal. The starter here was fish done in some kind of sauce, and then soup followed that. Sally chose chicken cooked in wine for her main course; and the dessert that followed was new to her. Small balls of pastry filled with ice cream and covered with thick chocolate sauce, topped with fresh cream. Cheese and crackers came next, followed by coffee and little chocolate sweets filled with peppermint. She hadn't eaten so much at one sitting in her entire lifetime.

The dance itself was great. Holding her tightly in his arms, Harry led her around the floor oblivious to all who danced near-by. 'You're so beautiful.' Squeezing her he whispered, 'I don't want you dancing with anyone else.'

'Oh, and why not?' She pulled back slightly, smiling. Their lips almost touched.

'Because I'm jealous Miss Baxter.' He stared lovingly into her eyes.

Pulling her closer, she felt the warmth of his body through her clothes. Over come with the sudden rush of blood to her head, she pushed him away.

'Sorry Sally, what's wrong?'

'I... I can't breathe when you hold me so close,' she stammered.

'It's the heat in here. Would you like to go outside for some air?' He suggested.

'Yes, yes I would.' She wanted nothing better than to feel the cool air on her arms and face.

As they passed by their table, Sally retrieved her stole. They walked through the lobby and through the door that led to a sheltered garden.

It was a lovely clear night but the cool air was in stark contrast to the sweltering heat of the ballroom. Pulling her stole over her shoulders, they walked slowly through the garden admiring the brightness of the stars. They tried tracing the well-known constellations, the Plough, Leo, and the Three Sisters, were easy to see. Harry informed her that there were eighty eight constellations in our solar system, and when she showed amazement at his wealth of knowledge, he shrugged saying his information came from the back of cereal packets. Giving him a playful punch, he caught her arm and led her towards a wrought iron seat that stood against the far wall.

Taking her by the hand, he asked with sincerity, 'Sally, will you be my girl?'

His question surprised her so much, she couldn't think straight. She stammered. 'Well...well I don't know. I don't know very much about you except what I've learned tonight. I don't fit in to your way of life. Just look at your folks. They're so posh.'

He squeezed her hand gently. 'I'm not like them. It's I who wishes to court you, not my parents. Oh, I have lots of... "Posh"... as you say; friends, but they mean nothing to me.'

'Court me? You see, even the way you say things. Court me! Only posh folk speak like that.'

'Sally, Oh Sally, you're every bit as good, if not better than them. Give me a chance.'

'No *you* listen to *me*, you know nothing about me. You wouldn't want to know me if you did.'

'Stop it!' Harry snapped. 'I don't care about who or what. I don't care about my folks, and I don't care what you think. You're my girl. Do you hear?' He gritted his teeth with insistence, like a spoiled child who would not give in.

He took her in his arms and kissed her with the slightest force.

She didn't resist. It felt good in his arms. The tingling feeling that ravaged her body was like an electric surge. Her heart raced with anticipation as his tongue searched for hers. Suddenly they broke free and looked into each other's eyes.

'Sally,' he whispered, before kissing her long and passionately.

Her body shook but this time it was not fear but with the greatest of pleasure. She knew within her heart that this wasn't going to last, but decided to take it one day at a time. She was used to doing things that way, after all, hadn't she lived like that all of her life?

Chapter Fifteen

Nellie hadn't seen Sally since the day she walked out. Notes were written by Nellie and given to Lucy, who still visited her mother, but Sally refused to reply, although she did send money round to help financially. Without a word to Bess, Nellie accepted the money.

Bess and her son, now aged three, stayed with Nellie, as Dempster Simpson left Bess a week before the baby was born and went back to his old girlfriend Flo.

'You'll never guess what a heard the day at the clinic?' Bess couldn't wait to tell her mother the news.

'What did ye hear?' Nellie half-heartedly asked from behind her newspaper.

'Oor Sally left in style last Saturday in a big black posh car. She was dressed tae kill an' all, with some fancy fellow hanging onto her.'

Lowering her paper, now full of interest Nellie asked, 'Whay telt ye that?'

'Jean Spencer was visitin' a friend round Sally's way. She said Sally was dripping with sparklers. "Maist likely paste an' gless" a said.' Grinning, she took a great deal of pride in her opinion.

'She's fairly gotten oan,' Nellie remarked with hidden pride.

'Aye. She has. But she's got a short memory.' Bess's voice was full of bitterness. She was unaware of what was said the night Flo called round. All she was told was Flo had named Dempster as the father of her child. The reason for Sally's absence had never been mentioned. 'She's too high an' mighty fer us noo. And a still cannae understand you lettin' Lucy bide wi' her.'

'Shut up Bess. She's done weel. She did it oan her ain as weel. A dinnae begrudge her what she has,' Nellie said curtly.

'No! A've no' had her chances,' Bess whined.

'You had mare chances than she had Bess, but ye never took them. You were far ower lazy, an' whays fault is it ye had a bairn? No' Sally's. No Bess, ye had awe the chances.'

'A hate her,' hissed Bess. 'A bloody hate her.'

Ignoring her daughter's outburst, her thoughts were of Sally wondering who her boyfriend was. She hoped she had found happiness, as she herself had caused her nothing but misery. She hadn't objected to Lucy going off with Sally either, knowing she would be better off with her.

'Mother!' Bess snapped, 'Are you listenin' tae me.'

Looking at her useless daughter through glazed eyes, Nellie's voice was full of remorse. 'Aye am listenin'. That's been ma trouble Bess, a've listened tae you far ower much.'

Unable to grasp her mother's meaning, Bess screwed up her face inquisitively.

Sally had been seeing Harry for three months now and he had become a regular visitor at her home.

Ruby liked him well enough, although Jimmy felt he was a bit too nice at times. Ruby laughed at his theory.

'You should take a leaf out of his book,' she joked. 'You're behaving like a worried father.'

Sally had been taken to Harry's home a few times. She was very impressed. The house, situated in the country, stood in its own grounds and consisted of eight bedrooms, drawing room, study, library and a large dining- room. It also had two lounges; the one sporting a bar was used when entertaining. The other was where they usually sat watching television, simply relaxing. Not that Libby Penman ever relaxed. She was always sitting on some committee or other, or entertaining at home.

Ruby and Jimmy sat in their lounge one evening with Sally and Harry while Lucy was in her bedroom playing records.

Harry had been joking about inheriting the house when his parents 'popped off' as he put it.

'It's only natural that the children should inherit the family home,' Jimmy said. When Ruby and I go this humble dwelling will be Sally's.'

'What!' Sally gasped. 'You mean to say this will be mine?'

'Aye Sally, we've arranged all that,' Ruby informed her. 'Jimmy and I are getting on and ...'

'Stop it Ruby. You'll be here for a long time yet.' She hated people speaking of death. 'Besides I have no claim on this house, it should be Anna's.'

'She gets the money. You get the house and that's that,' Jimmy nodded.

'Well you'll never be without a home, that's for sure,' Ruby commented.

Later on that night when Sally and Harry were alone, Harry asked about Anna. Why did Sally think her cousin should get everything?

'She's not my cousin Harry. Jimmy and Ruby aren't my real aunt and uncle; in fact, we're not related in the slightest. I left home and came to live with them years ago.'

'After your parents died?' he asked.

Sally's face flushed with embarrassment. To avoid Harry's gaze, she diverted her eyes to her hands. Taking great interest in the signet ring she wore, she twirled it around repeatedly as she answered.

'I'm sorry for telling you that Harry. It was a dreadful thing to say but believe me I had my reasons. My father *is* dead, that's true enough, but my mother is still alive. I don't have anything in common with her and chose to forget her.'

Harry sat in silence, studying her anxious mannerisms. Covering her nervous hands with his, he looked puzzled.

'That's a bit hard Sally.'

Drawing her hands from his grasp, she became very upset.

'I thought you said you wouldn't ask questions! I don't want to discuss her, as it's far too hurtful. I told your mother she was dead, as I knew I would've been interrogated.'

Noticing her agitation grow, warned him that he should stop questioning.

'It's all right Sally. It's all right. You must have a good reason, I'm sorry. I'll not ask about her again. Just answer me this though, is Lucy really your sister?'

'Yes, of course she is.'

'Well then,' he said, 'at least you have some kind of family.'

It was Monday morning and it had rained non-stop all night. Sally arrived at the office ready to start another week's work. She had just taken her raincoat off and was about to give her hair a brush, when Connie arrived looking as radiant as ever, only this morning, she seemed to have an added radiance in her smile.

'Good morning Sally, good morning,' she practically sang the greeting as she bounced into the room. Going over to the small tin bucket that stood in the corner of the office, she propped her sodden umbrella in it and hung up her raincoat.

'Well, good morning to you too, although I'd hardly say there was anything good about the weather,' Sally answered.

'I'm not talking about the weather, it's life itself that's good.' Connie teased, not letting her gaze stray from Sally's face.

Sally smiled at Connie's light-heartedness.

'You're very perky for a wet Monday morning. I wish

you would tell me what there is for us to be so cheery about,' Sally said.

Removing her jacket, she stepped over to where Sally sat. She bent over and whispered softly into her ear.

'Whose going to be a mummy then?'

Sally turned round slowly, and with gaping mouth, blinked a couple of times while gazing into Connie's eyes in disbelief. She tried to speak but was dumb struck. Her mouth opened and shut as she performed a perfect impression of a fish taking in air.

Connie laughed, nodding her head endorsing what she had just said.

'Yes Sally! It's been confirmed!' she beamed.

Finding her voice she was overcome with happiness, 'Oh Connie. Oh Connie. I'm so pleased. I've never heard such great news.'

They were both wrapped in each other's arms laughing and crying at the same time when young Alexis came in. She stood stock-still and watched the pair of them as they danced around the office, still in tight embrace. She had witnessed them both often fooling around, but never first thing on a Monday morning. Usually it was a nod and a grunt until mid-morning. Seeing Alexis looking so mesmerised started more hearty laughter.

'Don't tell me,' Alexis held out her hand, as if to stop traffic. 'You've won the pools.' The young girl's eyes widened. 'You've done it, won the big one,' she said excitedly.

'No Alexis, something much better than that,' Connie said happily.

'I don't know what could be better than winning the pools,' Alexis frowned.

'A baby stupid, a beautiful, beautiful, wonderful, adorable, delightful baby!' Connie twirled round like a ballerina on a jewellery box.

As excitement was very high hardly any work had been done all morning. The three work-mates chatted and planned for this baby as if they each had a share in it. Ron popped in around mid-day with some estimates he wanted sent out. Sally hugged him tightly as she congratulated him. Although he said he was thrilled, Sally detected slight restraint in his voice. Realising he was apprehensive triggered a sense of fear into Sally. It was obvious he was worried about Connie's health but she knew there was more to his concern.

Connie herself knew the risks and she was prepared to take them, after all she felt her life wasn't complete without a child. Her craving for a baby became so bad, Ron was willing to adopt, but Connie wanted to wait a little longer.

When she went shopping she watched the young mothers with their babies as they struggled with their bags. She watched and wished it could be her. She studied the mothers as they stood round in small groups, discussing their babies' progress, each one trying to score points as they thought their off-spring more advanced than the others. It was like watching members of a private club that one needed special qualifications to join. She longed to be a member. She wanted to become a mother. Now it was to be.

Ron would make a marvellous father; she had no doubt about that. He used to talk about the son he would have some day. The son he was building his business for. But since Connie returned to work, knowing it could be dangerous for her to give birth, he stopped talking of his son and heir, and now, the doctor had confirmed Connie's pregnancy.

She had broken the news to him that Saturday night. As they both loved to dance, they had a regular booking where they had dinner and danced to fine music provided by the hotel's resident band. The meal that evening was, as usual, first class and the dance band played their kind of music.

It was on the dance floor, as they held each other tight, Connie whispered to her husband that he was about to become a father.

Ron stopped dancing and stood looking down at his wife in amazement.

She confirmed it with a nod of her head.

He then took her in his arms, squeezing her very gently as if she were made of Dresden china. Mistaking the tears in his eyes for joy, Connie kissed him on the cheek, unknown to her, his tears were of concern.

As Connie wanted this baby so badly, he wasn't going to spoil it for her. If she did as the doctors told her, she would be all right. One thing was certain; she would be stopping work immediately. He would make sure she rested, eating the right things at the right time.

Sally left the office at five and hurried towards her car. The rain hadn't let up all day and was coming down as if the heavens had opened up. Her head down, shielding herself with her umbrella, she almost collided with the figure that stood near her car. Lifting her head up to apologise, she was greatly disturbed when she recognised the person as her sister Bess.

'What on earth are you doing standing here in the rain?' Sally looked her over quickly and saw she was soaked through to the skin. 'Jump into the car.'

Opening the passenger's door, Bess hurried inside.

Sally quickly ran to the other side and opened the driver's door. She lowered her brolly, gave it a good shake and slid into the driving seat.

'What's the matter? Is there something wrong?' Sally hadn't spoke to Bess for a few years. She last saw her in the newsagents when she had stopped to buy Jimmy's evening paper.

'You widnae care if there wis!' snapped Bess.

'Now look Bess, I'm in no mood to quarrel with you. I've asked if there is anything wrong. If there isn't, what do you want?' Sally felt no love or affection for the sister who sat facing her.

'A need some money.' It was almost a demand.

Silently Sally studied her sister's face, and thought how hard and debauched she looked. She was a young woman with an old bitter and twisted face. She hadn't changed in nature or appearance. She still looked as if a good wash would do her the world of good. The last time Sally saw Bess she had her baby with her. It didn't surprise Sally in the least to find the child dirty and unkempt. Apart from the sour smell from the baby's clothes, its face was in need of a good wash furthermore its nose looked sore and crusty caused by lack of cleaning.

'Why should I give you money?' Sally asked.

'If you cannae help yer ain,' Bess said sarcastically.

'You're working aren't you. What do you want money from me for anyway?'

'Bills an' things,' shrugged Bess.

'Did mum send you?' Sally questioned. 'I sent money round last week with Lucy.'

'Naw, it's no' for ma. A telt you it's fur me,' Bess was beginning to get irritable. 'You can afford it,' she sniffed a couple of times. 'Awe your fancy clothes an' things,' she looked Sally over.

Clenching her teeth together, Sally struggled to keep control of her temper. Reaching into her bag, she pulled out her purse, unzipped the middle section and pulled out five pounds. Angry at her sister's impudence, she thrust the note into her hand. 'I'll help you this once, but don't ever ask me again, you hear! I don't carry much money around. You're lucky I have that on me. Now get out of the car! And Bess, don't you ever come round here again.'

Hesitating, and with a sneer, Bess said disdainfully, 'It widnae day if your fancy boyfriend was tae ken aboot your family noo, would it?' With an evil leer, she lunged forward, with her nose almost touching Sally's she hissed, 'It's a small price tae pay. A tenner noo an' then! Silence is golden, or so they say.' Laughing, she opened the car-door and slipped out.

Sally closed her eyes, feeling the tears well up from under the lids, her stomach churned nervously. She was once more at the mercy of her family and if she wanted to keep Harry, she would have to pay for Bess's silence. Blackmail!

Watching her sister run along the pavement, she had the overwhelming desire to start the car and mow her down. Bess had always made things difficult for her. Why? There was no other reason than jealousy.

What had started out as a very joyous day had turned out to be as miserable as the weather.

Driving home, Sally found it difficult to concentrate on the road; her thoughts were on the situation Bess had just created. If she did carry out her threat and let Harry know about her father's crime and her pathetic alcoholic mother, he would surely end their relationship. On the other hand, if she herself told Harry first, maybe he would understand, for hadn't he said he didn't care about her family; it was only herself he was interested in. But murder, he would surely change his mind if he heard that! No one in their right mind would want to be involved with the daughter of a murderer. Harry's family certainly wouldn't. The scandal it would cause would be unthinkable. Then there was the other thing!

The steering wheel felt sticky from the sweat that leaked from the pores of her palms. A throbbing headache could be felt across her brow. Pulling over to the side of the road, Sally stopped the car and threw her body onto the steering wheel. With stinging tears running freely down her burning cheeks, she repeatedly thumped her fists on the padded ledge. What had she done to deserve this? Her family had ruined her whole life. She sobbed uncontrollably overcome with hopelessness. After a while, her rapid breathing grew steadier. Regaining control of her emotions, the sobbing subsided then dabbing her eyes, she began to reason with herself. Bess did not know who Harry was. How could she find out? She hadn't the courage to blackmail anyone. She dare not!

She decided against telling Harry, for if Bess's words were just idol threats, she would have nothing to worry about. She thought it best to wait and take everything as it comes.

She hadn't long to wait. Bess was outside the office four days later. Again, Sally gave in to her and handed over ten pounds.

Bess made it very clear she knew who Sally's boyfriend's parents were, and said she wouldn't think twice about paying them a visit.

From that week onward, Sally's happiness seemed to slip away.

Sally wanted so much to tell Harry, but how could she? She knew his family wouldn't accept the daughter of a murderer to be their son's future wife, and Harry, despite his love for her, would have to consider his family's position.

Right from the start of their relationship, Sally knew it couldn't last. She had too many secrets. Their life styles were too far apart.

'How I ever expected to get away with it in the first place,' she thought, but the very idea of loosing him, made her realise just how much she really cared for him. How would she fill the empty gap in her life if she stopped seeing him?

The blackmailing had continued for six months and during that time, Sally had confided in no one. Drained with worry, she made up her mind that it could go on no longer. She became shrouded in a veil of depression.

At home Ruby and Jimmy were beginning to notice the change in Sally's general behaviour. At their regular family discussions, Sally usually did most of the talking, but these days she hardly said a word. Her mind seemed to be elsewhere. Then there was young Lucy, whom Sally adored. Over the past few months, Sally hardly noticed her and when she did, it was only to scold her or find fault in something or other.

Concerned, Jimmy had confronted Sally, only to be put off with hollow reasons. In the past, he had been the first with whom Sally confided. Now, for some reason, she carried her burdens on her own.

He was sure it wasn't anything to do with her relationship with Harry, as they both adored each other, yet something wasn't right. Sally seemed to be on edge when Harry called. He had also noticed that she had developed nervous habits. One of the habits was ever so noticeable; 'Is everything all right?' she would say more than once when Harry called. It was almost as if she expected something to be wrong. She had also begun that irritating habit of wringing her hands. Yes, Jimmy knew there was something troubling her and it was definitely linked to Harry in some way.

Harry too had noticed a change in Sally's nature. At times she became moody and silent, not at all the chirpy, happy and carefree lass he had become to know so well. When he himself had spoken to her about looking downcast and sad, she had laughed and told him he was getting as bad as Jimmy. She assured them both that the only thing worrying her was Connie. Harry believed her, but Jimmy wasn't so sure. He wasn't quite so easily fooled.

As Ruby chopped the vegetables for the stew she was preparing, the telephone in the hall rang. Wiping her hands on her apron, she walked through to answer it.

'All right, all right,' she called, as it seemed to ring with some urgency. 'Hello!' Ruby bawled down the receiver. She had the tendency to roar down the receiver as if the person at the other end was stone deaf. She hated telephones. If anyone else were in the house when it rang, she would pass it. 'No she can't come to the phone, she's in bed with flu. Can I give her a message?' Ruby took the receiver from her ear and held it in front of her. Shaking her head, she stared at the offending piece of plastic.

'Suit yourself madam!' Putting it back on the rest she made her way towards Sally's bedroom door. It was slightly open.

Being well under the covers, her head was barely visible.

Walking over to the bed, Ruby laid her hand gently on the humped up shape that lay so still.

'Sally lass,' she said almost in a whisper.

Sally stirred and looked over the covers at Ruby. Her eyes were red, puffed, and very raw. Blinking, she tried hard to force them open.

'Not feeling any better?' Ruby asked sympathetically.

'No, I'm afraid not Ruby,' moaned Sally. 'I feel as if I have died and no one has told me.'

'Well I'll fetch you another hot drink.' She was about to turn away when she suddenly remembered.

'That was your sister Bess on the phone.' Ruby became alarmed as Sally shot bolt upright in bed.

'Bess! Bess!' gasped Sally.

She hadn't the strength to lift her head a moment ago but the mention of her sister's name made her spring to life with apparent fear.

'What did she want? Did she say anything to you Ruby?' In total panic, she peered through the inflamed slits, waiting for an answer.

Walking back over, Ruby sat down on the edge of the bed.

'Now lass, now lass.' Taking both Sally's hands, she studied her strained white face. 'What's this all about?'

'Ruby, what did she say?' she was almost shouting.

'She said nothing. She wanted to speak to you, and I told her you were too ill. She wouldn't leave a message; in fact she was damn right rude. Sally, what is this all about?'

Slowly, Sally let her body fall back onto the bed.

'It's nothing I can't handle Ruby.' She closed her eyes and lay very still.

Ruby watched the water stream from Sally's eyes. Was it tears, or the usual water caused by having flu? Ruby had no way of knowing.

Five days Sally remained in bed. She didn't receive any more calls from Bess, and Ruby asked no more questions. Harry was away on business and wasn't due back for a few more days.

Sally decided it was time to tell him everything as she couldn't go on the way she was doing. Love was supposed to make you happy, not worried sick. If he really wanted her, he would understand, after all, it was her father who had committed the murder, not her.

'Oh God! How did I let this go on? I've lied and lied all my life. When will I get some peace?' Sally's mind raced over the past months, and thinking how foolish she had been allowing Bess to intimidate her, made up her mind to end her little blackmailing scheme.

'It's a nice night Sally, why don't you get some fresh air? Take a walk over and see Connie. I'm sure she would be pleased to see you up and about.' Ruby fussed as usual.

'Now then Ruby, Sally will go out in her own good time.' Jimmy looked at his wife affectionately as he gently scolded her. 'Don't you heed her Sally, go only if you want to.'

'Well I didn't mean her to go if she didn't feel like it,' Ruby retorted.

'I know woman! Ruby stop faffing around.' Jimmy waved his hands at Ruby as she 'Pooh poohed him.'

Rising from the sofa, Sally smiled at them saying, 'I think I will, it will be nice to see Connie for an hour or so.' She was glad to escape from the pair of them for a while, leaving them to annoy one and other.

Going to her room, she slipped into her coat, and, as she passed Lucy's door, looked in. Her young sister lay on the bed reading.

'I'm going to see Connie. Are you coming?'

'Oh sorry Sal, I want to have a bath and my friend is supposed to be ringing later. Can I give it a miss?'

'Sure,' Sally smiled and closed the door. Lucy's voice called from behind. 'Give Connie my love.'

'I will,' Sally called back.

It was indeed a lovely night. The air was crisp and clear with the slightest touch of frost. The street lighting had just come on, although it was still relatively light. The sky alone was enough to illuminate the town. The moon was full and bright and devoid of clouds allowing the vast sea of stars to twinkle down. Sally enjoyed the walk and felt the better for it.

She hadn't seen Connie for almost two weeks. She stayed away when she felt unwell, and as she developed the dreaded 'flu', she definitely was barred from visiting.

Connie had been confined to bed during most of her pregnancy and was being well cared for by Ron and the district nurse. The doctor at the hospital also made sure she had the best attention available.

The last time Sally had visited, Connie simply glowed with health. Her cheeks were rosy red and her blonde hair had shone like the finest silk. Connie's happiness was about to be complete, and it showed in her face.

Ron had phoned Ruby a few times when Sally was in bed ill. He called to find out the latest on Sally but found himself giving the latest bulletin on Connie's condition. His fears were laid to rest, as his wife had had a smooth untroubled eight months. She was to be admitted into hospital within the next week to enable the Doctors to keep a closer eye on her.

Sally had just turned the corner that brought Connie's house into view when the sight of blue flashing lights sent chills running down her back. The ambulance stood silent, lights flashing furiously; its double doors wide open. Neighbours stood at their gates gazing in at the empty vehicle. She felt her stride turn into a slow run, and, like a motor going through the gears, her speed increased, until she could run no faster. Reaching the gate, she stood motionlessly watching, as the navy blue clad figure appeared holding on to the front of a stretcher.

With pounding heart and violent shaking of her legs, she was gripped with fear. It was greater than the fear of losing Harry. The stretcher was now in full view as the man's companion helped carry Connie out into the night air.

Sally hurried forward to her friend's side, as one of the men was about to order her back.

'It's all right, this is my friend,' Connie said smiling up at the man.

She looked round as she heard Ron call her name.

'Sally. Thank goodness you turned up. You can do me a big favour by driving my car behind the ambulance.' He handed her the keys.

'Oh Ron, what's happened?' she grabbed hold of his arm.

'The baby's decided to come early. Now she's all right Sally,' Ron assured her. 'Watch what you're doing on the road, and don't smash the car up,' Ron teased.

He sounded very cool and calm. Sally watched him as he stepped into the ambulance. The doors closed and it drove off with speed into the night. The neighbours disappeared back into their houses and Sally was left standing alone at the gate holding Ron's keys in her hand. The noise of silence filled her ears as her eyes stung with tears. She didn't know if she felt happy or sad but she would feel a lot better when this was all over.

Sally drove very cautiously as she wasn't quite sure of Ron's car. She stopped at a call box and phoned Ruby with the news and let her know she was on the way to the hospital. She didn't know if Ron intended her to stay. She would have to play it by ear.

Ron was in the corridor pacing, when he saw Sally come through the doors. Walking to meet her, a look of gratitude spread over his face.

'They've taken her to the delivery room.' The calmness Sally had seen in Ron a short while earlier had somehow been replaced with extreme anxiety. 'Oh, I'm glad you have shown up. Will you wait with me?'

'Calm down Ron,' Sally said. 'I can stay if you want me to.'

'I'm glad you came.'

'You've already said that Ron, now come and sit down. I thought you were cool and calm?' She took his arm and led him to the waiting room.

'I was calm when I was beside Connie, but when they wheeled her away, I just went to pieces.'

A nurse appeared and asked if they would like some tea. She had only gone minutes when she returned with a tray containing two cups of steaming black liquid and a plate of rich tea biscuits. She moved some magazines from the small table and placed the tray on top.

'Nurse, could you find out how my wife is doing?' Asked Ron. She nodded and left them to drink the tea. It really was a waste of time bringing tea as neither of them touched it.

Twenty minutes passed and no one came with any news.

'Where is that girl?' Ron muttered as he paced the floor. 'You know Sally, it's times like this I wished I smoked.'

'Ron, sit down, I'll go and find out what's happening.' She slipped out of the waiting room and into the corridor.

'Excuse me!' She spotted a sister hurrying along to what appeared to be the wards. 'Excuse me!' She called again.

The sister stopped and came back along towards Sally. When Sally looked at the woman's face, she was vexed she had called her. Her severe, unsmiling face immediately told her that this woman was an authoritarian. Sally cleared her throat before continuing.

'My friend is very worried about his wife. She was brought in an hour or so ago and no one has come to tell him what's going on. She's having a baby.

The sister clasped her hands beneath her very large breasts, took a sharp intake of breath, causing her bust to inflate to an even larger proportion.

'Young lady,' she snapped. 'Your friend will be informed whenever there is anything to inform him about. Babies don't just pop out you know.' Another intake of breath and up the bust came again. 'Go and wait patiently as the poor mother has to. At least the father can wait in comfort, more than the poor woman can.' She sniffed and hurried back to the wards, leaving Sally quite bemused.

As there was no one else around, Sally made her way back along towards the waiting room. A doctor with his white coat flying open and his stethoscope still hanging around his neck came hurrying towards her. He looked as if he too was making for the waiting room. As they both reached the door simultaneously, he stood to one side, enabling Sally to enter.

Sitting in the far corner of the room, Ron rose instantly, searching the doctor's face for a clue as to what was happening.

'Mr Matheson?' the Doctor asked.

'Yes,' Ron replied anxiously.

'I'm Doctor Stokes.' The two men shook hands briefly. 'Will you come with me please?' He spoke very softly.

Without answering, Ron was out the door following behind the young doctor. He gave Sally a nervous smile as he passed. Left sitting alone, Sally wished she also had been asked to follow, as the waiting- room was a terribly lonely place. Looking down on the plate of tea biscuits, she lifted one and nibbled nervously around the edge.

Sally sat for an hour and a half by herself. At times it seemed that there was no one in the hospital but herself. The scurrying of feet or the clattering of some distant objects occasionally broke the silence.

The soft padding of feet and the chatter of what sounded like nurses broke the silence once more.

The door was open slightly so Sally couldn't help but over hear. 'They say it was her first.'

'I know, what a bloody shame,' came the hurried reply.

'The husband's with Doctor Stokes now, poor soul, he's in a terrible state.'

The nurses had passed the door at this point and the conversation began to drift away.

'Got everything they say. All that...' the rest wasn't clear, but Sally had heard enough. She lent against the wall as the words that she had just heard penetrated her thoughts.

'They say it was her first...bloody shame... the husband's in with Doctor Stokes... pour soul...'

'No, no Connie's lost the baby!' Sally's body went into uncontrollable spasms and she cried aloud, 'Oh God no, please, please don't let this be true! She wanted the baby so very very much.' She didn't hear the nurse come in neither did she feel her arm go around her shoulders. Opening her eyes, and through her tears, she recognised the face of the young nurse who brought the tea so very long ago. She was trying to comfort Sally.

'I'm sorry, I'm so sorry. She was a very special friend of yours.' She looked at Sally displaying sincere sympathy.

'Yes, she's...' Sally looked horrified. 'What do you mean she *was* my friend? What does *was* mean? Oh no, no tell me this isn't happening. Tell me this isn't true. Oh no, not Connie.' Sally pushed passed the young nurse and ran frantically out of the waiting room and into the corridor. She didn't know where she was running to, but she had to find Ron. A door opened and an elderly gent stepped out into the corridor, and, on seeing Sally, he raised his thick bushy eyebrows presuming she was lost.

'This isn't the ward area my dear,' he informed her.

Noticing her great distress, he grabbed her lightly by the arm. 'What's the matter? Can I help? I'm Doctor Tait.' He waited and watched as she gulped in air. Her hand that clutched at her throat trembled.

'I m...ust f...ind Doctor Stokes office sir,' she managed to say.

'You're going in the wrong direction then,' he smiled.

The sound of running feet behind made Sally turn round. The nurse whom she had run from was now directly behind her. 'It's all right doctor, I'll deal with the situation,' she said.

'This young lady is looking for Doctor Stokes office,' the doctor advised the nurse.

'I know but he has someone with him at the moment and as soon as possible, he will...'

Sally interrupted, as she had no intentions of going back to that dreadful room.

'I want to see him *NOW*!' she yelled at them both. 'It's my *friend* who's with the doctor. I have to see him *now*!'

'I suggest you try and get a hold of him nurse,' said the doctor raising his eyebrows.

'Ok ok!' the nurse tried calming her down. 'You

shouldn't have run off like that. I'll take you to the doctor's office, but you may have to wait.'

Sally followed behind the nurse as she turned into another corridor and climbed a flight of stairs. They reached the doctor's office, the white plastic nameplate on the door read 'Dr D Stokes, Senior Obstetrician'.

The nurse knocked on the door and, turning to Sally, told her to stay where she was. Opening the door she went in on her own.

Having waited ten minutes, Sally felt anger rising. Her hand hovered over the handle of the door for a few seconds, trying to find courage to open it. She expected to find the doctor behind the door, but was surprised to find herself in an adjoining room. It was his secretary's office, and she was sitting talking to the nurse that had just escorted Sally along the corridor.

'What are you doing? I told you to wait outside,' the nurse looked apologetically at the secretary.

'I must see Ron. He's with the doctor, why haven't you told him?' Sally screamed once more at the startled nurse.

'Sheesht, sheesht' the nurse put her finger to her lips and looked towards the glass panelled door that led to the doctor's office. A dark silhouette appeared behind the opaque glass, and as it opened, Ron stepped into the doorway, followed by the doctor

Ron looked devastated. Ashen faced, his dark dead eyes sunk back into their sockets. The handsome rugged face that was Ron's earlier was no more. Here before her stood the face and frame of a very old pathetic looking soul. Glancing at Sally he strolled wearily over with outstretched arms.

'It's true then?' Sally sobbed. 'It's Connie.'

'Oh Sally, she's gone, our lovely Connie.'

As Ron's arms enfolded around Sally, they both swayed from side to side, crying sorely on each other's shoulder as if their hearts were about to burst.

They said very little on the way home. Ron took the wheel of the car, insisting he was fit to drive.

His baby daughter was in an incubator but in no immediate danger.

'Would you like me to stay with you tonight Ron?' Sally asked.

'I'll be all right Sally, honest, I need to be alone. I have things to think through.'

'Are you sure you'll be all right on your own?'

He answered quietly, 'I'll have to get used to being on my own.'

Sally's hot, gritty feeling eyes filled once more, but biting her bottom lip, she managed to keep herself under control. Her temples throbbed with pain, caused by overwhelming grief.

'What about the baby? You've not mentioned her yet.' She didn't know if she had a right to ask, but ask she did.

'I haven't seen her yet.'

She detected slight shame. 'Why Ron? She's not to blame,' Sally said.

'Sally, maybe tomorrow. I just couldn't face it tonight.

I know she's all I have now, but I just couldn't face it at the moment.' Nothing else was said until they reached Sally's gate.

'I'll see you tomorrow. Thanks Sally,' he forced a very weak smile.

'Won't you come in for a while?'

'Oh no, I couldn't face Ruby right now. You know what she's like.'

'I understand.'

'I have a few phone calls to get through when I get home. My mother will have to be told tonight, and I will have to get hold of Connie's brother. Get some sleep; I'll need you and Ruby tomorrow, and thanks again Sal.' He waited until she was in the gate, gave a slight wave, and drove off.

Sally drove past the church on the way over to Ron's. The bells peeled loudly and well dressed people flocked to hear the weekly sermon. She had attended regularly herself a few years back, but somehow she had drifted away. Her early years spent in the children's home had laid the foundation for her faith. Had she this faith any more? Yesterday she would have said she had, but this morning, she wasn't so sure. Last night made her realise just how vulnerable people were. She had asked herself over and over again, *why*?

It was obvious to Sally that like her, Ron hadn't slept. She had never seen him unshaven before, and it gave her quite a start. First thing in the morning he was always out smart and clean-shaven, even to do the dirtiest jobs.

He now stood looking through bloodshot eyes, uncombed hair, and in the suit he had been wearing the night before, crumpled and creased.

'Come in Sally. Thanks for coming round,' he said leading her through into the lounge. The room felt strange, it too seemed to miss Connie. Her presence was everywhere. She had decorated the room to her personal taste, and it was exquisite. The furnishings and drapes were in rose coloured velvet, and the fireplace, doors, and panelling on the walls, were carved out in rich brown mahogany. At each side of the fireplace glass units trimmed in the same wood, spanned the full width of the wall. They were both full of lavish crystal. Connie had been an avid collector of crystal, and the display consisted of all kinds of goblets, glasses, vases and bowls. All of it was of the highest quality. On top of the display cabinets, stood an additional collection, this time of Doulton figurines. They were breath taking. The lamps and nick knacks scattered round the lounge were mostly made from crystal. It was indeed a very elegant room, and had Connie's personal stamp.

'My mother will be here sometime this afternoon and my brother-in-law will arrive at the same time. He's travelling up from Sheffield.'

'Have you phoned about the baby yet?' Sally asked.

'Yes. She's fine. I'm going in later. I have some business to do this morning but I won't get it all done this being Sunday, but I shall do as much as I can. Can I ask you to stay here?'

'Of course Ron, anything I can do, just ask.' Sally bit the side of her lip before saying, 'Ron, you'll have to get help with the baby. How are you going to run the business and look after her?'

'I don't know what I'm going to do yet Sal, I want to leave it until after the funeral.' Rubbing his brow, he gave a long deep sigh. 'I just can't take it in, she was so well.'

'Can you talk about it yet, I mean what went wrong?'

Ron took her hands in his, and with his eyes cast downwards, started to talk about Connie's last minutes.

'As things happened so fast, she gave birth to the baby naturally. She wasn't supposed to, but as I said, the baby came too fast. For a first child, things moved exceptionally quickly. Her heart couldn't take it. There wasn't anything they could do. She suffered a slight heart attack during the birth, and a massive one shortly after. They tried resuscitation, but she just wouldn't come back to us,' his voice trembled.

'Don't go on,' Sally said softly.

'It's all right, I'm all right,' he stopped for a few seconds. 'Oh Sally, how am I going to survive without her?' As his head rested on her shoulder, she patted him gently on the back. Raising his head, he apologised, 'I'm sorry, I'm so sorry. I must be embarrassing you,' he wiped his swollen eyes on his handkerchief.

'I'm going to make you some tea and you're going to drink it. 'Walking into the middle of the floor, she stopped, turned round, adding 'and Ron, go and get a shower and change your clothes.'

Taking the kettle to the sink, Sally saw the dirty dishes left over from the previous night. Lifting a cup, she saw

Connie's lipstick imprinted on the brim. She could see the impression of her bottom lip very clearly, as if it had just been put there. Touching it gently, the lipstick transferred onto her finger. Touching her own lips with the finger that bore the lipstick, she murmured, 'Goodbye my dear friend.'

Ruby and Jimmy arrived shortly before Ron left for the hospital. Ron asked Jimmy if he would like to go with him, as he would be glad of some male company. The two men left the women preparing things for Ron's mother and brother-in-law's arrival. A few of the neighbours called in to express their condolences and there were phone calls from Ron's employees and business colleagues. Connie hadn't been dead long, but in a small town, news travelled very fast.

Sally rang Harry's mother to find out if she had a telephone number where he could be contacted. She hadn't of course, and sounded as cutting as ever. She never liked Sally and made it quite clear to her whenever she could, and always when no one else could hear. Sarcastically, she mocked Sally at every opportunity. It bothered Sally at times but she was beginning to get used to her rudeness, besides, she was very seldom at home when Sally called round.

Harry hadn't given Sally a phone number as he usually phoned her every day. He last phoned on Saturday afternoon, and wouldn't be calling again until Sunday evening. She longed to talk with him and let him know about Connie. As he was due back the following day, she hoped that would not stop him from making a call that night.

Jimmy and Ron returned before Ron's mother and brother-in-law arrived and Ruby, in her usual way, persuaded Ron to eat a few sandwiches and drink a cup of tea.

For the first time Ron spoke about the baby, remarking how like Connie she was. Jimmy nodded in agreement. What should have been a jocular discussion was very serious and solemn.

Ruby wanted to stay and serve the meal she prepared to the expected arrivals so after helping with some chores, Sally and Jimmy left.

Harry called on Sunday night as expected. Shocked at the news, and too late to fly home that evening, he promised to catch the morning flight and be with Sally around noon.

Not wanting to have his men lose work, Ron decided to let his foreman run things in the meantime. Sally was asked to open the office as usual to enable others to get on with their work. The business would close down on the day of the funeral.

Monday morning came round and Sally did as Ron asked. She drove to the yard, and, after parking the car she made her way towards the office. The workers stood with their caps in their hands, some had just heard the news. As she walked over to the men, one of them broke the silence.

'Sorry lass, we should 'ave been oan oor way, but we couldnae go till you came in.' Looking down at his feet, he shuffled from one to another. He was a giant of a man, who normally looked formidable, although he was well known for his sense of humour and continuous wit. Tears were in evidence as he spoke. 'She was a lovely lass, an' we are awe very sorry. Can you tell the boss?' he sniffed as he dragged his sleeve over his nose. 'Onything we can dae...just tell him...'

Sally nodded, 'I will Charlie, but he already knows.'

'Aye, weel, we best be oaf.' They moved off slowly and climbed into the workers van.

The office was full of memories. Photos pinned to the wall, silly photos that had been taken just for fun, postcards from distant places, an old lipstick, a very old pair of well worn flat shoes, and Connie's plants. She was always phoning from the house. 'Mind and water my plants,' she would say. One day, just for fun, she had Ron pin a memo on the office notice board *'ANYONE FOUND MISTREATING THE PLANTS OR CAUSING THEM UNNECESSARY SUFFERING WILL BE PROSECUTED.'*

It was going to be very difficult working with the memory of Connie everywhere. Before, the bits and pieces that lay around the office were regarded as being just 'things,' but now they had taken on a completely different meaning.

She would be alone in the office today as young Alexis had been told to take time off which Sally was glad, as she could never have coped with her crying and constant questioning.

The morning was taken up by finishing bits and pieces of work left by Alexis. As Sally had only just returned to work after being off sick, she was catching up with her own mail as well as taking the incoming telephone calls, most of them offering condolences.

Around twelve thirty, Harry popped his head round the door. Instead of welcoming him home, Sally burst into tears. She ran into his arms and he enfolded her in a comforting embrace.

'There now Sally, don't cry, you have to stay strong,' he spoke with tender encouragement. 'Have you had lunch yet?' Lifting her chin up with his index finger, he gave her brow a short tender kiss.

'No, I don't think I could eat anything. I don't feel very hungry,' she sniffed and blew her nose.

'You must eat. I have to go home, so close up here and we'll have a bit to eat over at the house. I have to get out of these clothes anyway.' He was still wearing his business suit.

Keeping control of her emotions Sally went over the events of that awful weekend, while Harry drove the car home.

'But why on earth didn't you phone me right away?' he asked.

'I didn't have your number. I asked your mother and she didn't have it either.'

'She said she didn't have my number?' Harry frowned.

'Yes, that's what she said.'

'Are you sure Sal?'

'Of course I'm sure. Why don't you believe me?' she sounded slightly annoyed.

'It's not that, you know I believe you. It's just that my mother did have the number. I always leave it with them in case of emergencies. As a matter of fact, she phoned me on Friday night.'

'Why does she *do* that Harry?'

'I don't know, but I'm sure as hell going to find out.'

Sally knew his mother didn't think she was good enough for her son. At first things weren't so bad, but this changed when she realised her son was serious about her.

Harry had brought home all kinds of girls in the past, but his mother looked on them as companions.

'Oh drop it, she'll have some excuse, she always does.' Sally knew it would only make matters worse.

They drove through the huge iron gates that led to 'the house' and continued along the private road that was flanked on either side with masses of trees that had long since lost their leaves. Knobble branches stuck out like old men's fingers, while the rotten leaves carpeted the ground. Noisy black rooks could be heard as they gathered in the top branches, and the odd squirrel could be seen scurrying round foraging for food. Just visible through the clearing was the putting green that had recently been installed. The grounds were fitting surrounds for the noble Georgian house that they were fast approaching.

The housekeeper heard the car and promptly opened the great wooden door. Harry ran up the steps while Sally lagged behind. Reaching the top, he turned and waited till she caught up.

The housekeeper, still holding the door spoke. 'Your mother is in the drawing-room sir and wishes to see you when you are ready.' She nodded towards Sally without addressing her. It was evident the housekeeper disapproved of the young master's choice of girl friend.

Harry held out his hand towards Sally and she took it. 'Better go and see what the old battle axe wants,' he said winking while squeezing her hand. 'Thanks Mrs. Thomas,' he said to the housekeeper.

They entered the drawing room hand in hand. Harry's mother was pouring herself tea from a china teapot. She was dressed in pale blue chiffon, her face heavily, although expertly, made up. Her hair, as always, was groomed to perfection. Sally tried to imagine what it would be like if the two mothers ever met. She cringed at the very thought.

'There you are my dears,' her smile as false as the crimson nails that adorned her fingers. 'Sit down. Sit down. I have something to tell you both.' Another smile, this time she looked haughtily. 'Oh, by the way, I'm extremely sorry about your boss's wife. It's tragic, so terribly tragic. Still, that's life. I gather she was told it would be risky.' She held up an empty cup, 'Tea anyone?'

'No thanks mother, we'll get our own. Are you through?' he was angry at his mother's callous attitude.

'Through? Not by a long chalk.' There it was again, that grin.

Sally's stomach felt as if every nerve had been activated. She watched and waited knowing whatever she was about to say would be aimed at her.

Harry's mother continued, 'I had a visitor yesterday, a rather unsavoury individual. She said she was a relative of yours Sally, a sister I believe.'

Sally swayed slightly.

'Lucy?' Harry inquired. 'What are you talking about mother? Lucy is one of the nicest girls...'

His mother interrupted.

'No, no her name wasn't Lucy,' she waved her handkerchief in front of her as if alleviating a bad smell. 'Bess, yes Bess that was this character's name,' she beamed. She was enjoying every moment of this game she was playing. 'And low and behold, Bess has a mother, the same mother that begot Sally. Now tell me, did you not say your mother was dead?'

Sally said nothing, she stared at this woman who had centre stage and was relishing in the leading role.

She began again 'Yes now, this mother is a poor sad alcoholic who is one of nature's low lifers...'

'Mother, that is enough! Stop this right now!' Red faced with rage, Harry sprung to his feet.

With the slightest loss of composure, Elizabeth Penman raised her voice to be heard. 'I haven't finished. I have only just started and you will jolly well hear me out. I knew there was something funny about her from the start, but you wouldn't listen, would you? Oh no. You're just like your father in that respect. You never want to know. This time you have to know, as it affects each and every one of us.'

'No mother, I don't have to listen to this,' he growled.

They both stopped when Sally spoke. 'I have been waiting for this to come out. I want you to sit down and listen to what your mother has to say.'

His mother nodded in agreement. 'I'm glad to see you have some sense my dear, now where was I? Yes, Sally's mother is still alive, but her father is dead. That was true enough. Hit by a train by all accounts.'

Harry looked at Sally who nodded, confirming that it was true.

'Poor man,' he said.

'Poor man my foot; he was hit by a train while running from a murder scene. A murder *he* committed! Burned a poor man to death. The man was carrying on with madam here,' she pointed furiously at Sally.

'Young child of ten or twelve? No matter, young enough to be illegal. And, did she tell you that she spent most of her youth in a children's home? No, I doubt very much that she did. How she managed to hoodwink her way into that charming couple's home, well... I don't know.'

'Mother, I don't want to hear any more of this nonsense.'

'Don't you my son? Well I'm sorry but you have to. So far you have heard of under-age sex, murder and drunkenness. One would think there wasn't much more to add, but not so. This Bess person wants to make a living from it. She has threatened us with blackmail. If we don't pay up your name will be linked to them. Don't you see man what this will do to us. For goodness sake, think!'

'I'm sorry this has happened. Don't give her any money,' Sally spoke in a whisper.

'You're damn right my girl, I wouldn't be giving her a penny as you will not set foot in this house ever again. Nor will my son associate with you in the future.'

'Now wait on mother, I decide who I see, not you.'

'Well carry on my son. We'll see how you get on without your family. If you don't want to think of yourself, think about the family name. Your father has been proposed by the Prime Minister and awaits approval from the Queen to be honoured with a knight-hood for his efforts in British business. Do you want to jeopardise that?'

'I've heard enough.' Harry rose and pulled Sally to her feet. He dragged her outside and practically pushed her into the car. He drove away at speed with out looking at her, nor did he utter a word. Sally too sat in silence. She had nothing to hide now. It was all out. He drove for what seemed ages. The car travelled along the coastal road spinning sharp left into an isolated car park, used frequently in the evening by courting couples. Turning the engine off, Harry sat back in his seat remaining silent. She could stand it no longer, anything, anything but silence.

'I wanted to tell you but I just couldn't.' She spoke with her head bowed low.

'It would have been better had it come from you,' he said.

'I didn't want to lose you Harry.'

'And do you think lies and deceit is the recipe for a good relationship?' His words were harsh.

She never answered.

'Answer me damn you,' he yelled causing her to jump. 'I respected you! I treated you well, and all the time you acted out a lie. I never laid a hand on you, as I wanted to keep you pure! What a laugh! You've been a trollop.'

Sally now grew furious. 'Just for the record, I was never

a trollop. I never went with men! My father murdered the man who went with my mother. Bess is a liar and he never touched me that man... Take me back, take me back to the office now!' her lips quivered but she was not about to shed any tears. The truth about her family was out and she was glad. He wasn't interested in her side of the story, and she wasn't about to grovel.

He never once asked if any of what he had just heard was lies. He was prepared to accept it all as being the truth. Starting up the engine, he reversed back onto the road and maintained his silence once more until they reached Sally's office.

'I was about to ask you to become my fiancée' he sighed deeply.

Sally, still very angry retorted. 'Get lost Harry, you know what you can do with your ring – put it through your nose and let your mother lead you around!' Opening the car door she jumped out ran into the yard and up the flight of wooden stairs that lead to the office.

Standing with her back to the closed door, she looked up to the ceiling as if searching for help, crying, 'Oh lord, why now?' The floodgates opened once more and she cried because of the unfairness of it all. Connie wasn't here to advise or comfort her. How she missed her.

Falling heavily into the seat at her desk and resting her head on her arms, she sobbed herself to sleep. She had slept very little since Connie died and it had finally caught up with her.

Connie's funeral was held on Wednesday. As there was to be a private service in the house, friends and relatives gathered outside. The hearse drew up out side the house, but the coffin was not carried in. The people entered the house and after the service left in their own cars for the cemetery. Sally travelled in the car with Jimmy, Ruby and young Lucy. Ruby searched Sally's face hoping she would give her an answer to the question that was going round in her head. She had noticed Harry wasn't at the service and thought it odd. Sally hadn't said a word about his absence, so Ruby asked no questions.

As the line of cars containing the mourners passed through the cemetery gates, Jimmy spotted Harry in the crowd that had gathered to pay their respects.

'What's he out there for?' he asked Sally.

'Who?' She honestly didn't know what Jimmy meant.

'Harry! He must not have made the house in time,' Jimmy surmised.

She never answered him but Ruby was satisfied with Jimmy's theory. It sounded logical to her.

They gathered round as the minister gave thanks for Connie's life. He ended by saying; 'The baby was her gift to us all and will serve as a constant reminder of the love and life of Connie Matheson.'

The baby was almost a month old before she was allowed out of hospital. It wasn't just her weight that had to be considered, Ron had to be given time to come to terms with the situation before he could deal with the infant. He had gone every night to see her, and as the days passed, he gradually accepted that she had to be loved, and loved, as Connie would have wished. The more he held her, the more he longed for the day she would be taken home.

It was a Saturday morning when Ron drove his mother to the hospital to collect the baby.

She was to be called Hannah, Connie had chosen the name weeks before she was born. Hannah if it was a girl, Joshua if it was a boy. Ron was very tempted to register her Constance, but respecting his late wife's wishes she was named Hannah Constance Matheson.

The nurses had grown very fond of the baby as she had been with them longer than most and the fact she was motherless made her all the more special. Emotions were high as they said their goodbyes. The nursing sister insisted on carrying Hannah to the car and only passed her to Ron's mother once she was seated in the back seat.

She stood until the car was out of sight and before facing the other nurses, wiped the single tear that dropped onto her cheek.

'Poor wee soul, God love her,' she whispered.

When they arrived back at the house Sally and Ruby had everything ready for the new arrival and the table was set for Ron and his mother to have tea.

Although Ron's mother was approaching sixty she could easily have passed as a much younger woman. With her fresh wrinkle free complexion she was a woman who evidently looked after herself very well. Although she was small and on the plump side her good dress sense helped her carry the extra weight with elegance. Her hairstyle hadn't changed for years either. She wore it short with deep waves that were almost embedded into her scalp. The hair itself was white but just barely visible, a lilac rinse shone through.

She resembled Ruby in lots of ways except you couldn't imagine Helen Matheson fussing around with a duster all day. She was more likely to do her housework very early in the morning when there was no one around to see her. Another thing that was so different about Helen for a woman of her years, she always wore very high-heeled shoes. She never ever wore slippers.

Helen had been widowed for some years now and lived alone in a little one bed roomed cottage in a tiny village in the border region. The small cottage was everything to Helen, and her garden, although it was a bit on the large side suited her needs admirably. Ron had built a glass sunroom onto the front of the house and Helen spent lots of her time happily tending the vast variety of plants she had nurtured.

It was this she was going to miss the most, as she had arranged with her son to stay with him from Monday to Friday each week, until Hannah was past the baby stage. She wouldn't give up her home, but she was willing to sacrifice the pleasure of staying in it until other arrangements could be made.

Ruby had volunteered to help, but Ron really needed help through the night and early mornings. Sally too helped out, but she was needed more than ever to help run the business. There was a large job in the pipeline, and if it took off, Sally would be doing more of Ron's work than ever. She now handled the tenders that came in and made important decisions for Ron, leaving him free to be on site with his men.

In view of this, Sally could only help with the baby at weekends, this enabled Ron's mother to return to her home for a few days each week, where she could 'recharge her batteries' as she would say, ready to start once more on Monday.

The third weekend came round and Sally was there as usual to look after baby Hannah.

'Don't mind my asking Sally, but where is Harry these days?' Despite his own problems, Ron had noticed Harry was absent from the scene.

'We've ended our relationship.' Ron, although he had suspected this, felt vexed. He watched her as she changed the baby. Face flushed with frustration, she tried hard to look unconcerned.

'Would you like to tell me about it?' He realised the pain that she must be feeling.

'Not really Ron. We weren't meant for each other, and that's all there was to it.' She made that statement as if to put an end to his questions.

The subject was dropped, Ron knew her too well and decided to wait until she was ready to unburden her heart.

He wasn't the only one who had bombarded her with questions; Ruby, Jim and Lucy all had a go. She did however give them a better reason, but the elderly couple knew it was far from the truth. Ruby suspected Bess to be behind it, but chose to keep her thoughts to herself, for she, like Ron, knew not to pry into her affairs. In spite of Connie's death and the heartache Sally must have suffered, Ruby had noticed the terrible emotional strain she had been under had lessened so she considered the split with Harry to be for the best.

Sally's days were taken up with work and the weekends were all given over to Hannah, so she found it easier to get Harry out of her system. It was easier than she had thought, although now and again in a quiet moment of reflection, his face would enter her mind causing her to sigh and wonder 'what if.' Harry had given up his job with the building supplies company, so at least he spared her the embarrassment of having to do business with him.

In a way she was grateful to Bess, if she hadn't spilled the beans, she would still have been living in a state of constant fear. If she had gone on and married, the press would have had a field day. They would most certainly have pried into the background of the future mistress of Abbey Mount House. If she ever became serious again, the first thing she would have to do would be to tell of her family history. Bess would always be there to make her life miserable if she didn't. Sally was not going to let her spoil things for her ever again.

The phone in the office rang and Alexis answered it. The caller wished to be put through to Mr. Matheson. Sally had her own office now and another young woman, by the name of Winnie Stirling had started in the main office beside Alexis. Ron's office was still down in the yard. Alexis tapped lightly on the glass panel of Sally's door, opened it, and without going in mouthed, 'That was Sir William Bryce-Smith on the phone for Mr. Matheson.'

Sally's eyes widened as if they were about to pop from their sockets, 'How did he sound?' she asked putting her pen down and giving the young girl her undivided attention.

'*OH!* I'd say, as pompous as ever.'

'No hint in his voice then?' Sally asked eagerly.

'None what so ever.'

'We'll have to wait and see then. Lifting her pen once more she resumed writing.

The phone call seemed to last for ages, then, Alexis called out to Sally, 'That's them off now!' she had left Sally's door ajar so that she could keep her informed of what was going on.

Sally knew if it was good news Ron would phone across immediately. The phone did not ring. Twenty agonising minutes passed and still the phone on Sally's desk remained silent. She was about to ring Ron with some petty excuse, as she couldn't stand the suspense any longer, when Winnie called out, 'Here's Ron coming over the yard. It looks like...yes...he's coming up here.'

Winnie could see into the yard clearly from her window, while Sally's window overlooked the street. Ron came up the outside stairs and into the office. Nodding to the girls as he passed, he asked, 'Keeping busy?'

'Oh aye!' replied Alexis, as she stamped a pile of letters with some vigour.

Sally's door was still open and going in, he sat on the edge of her desk. Sally watched him as he rummaged through papers that lay in the wire tray. Without glancing at her, he eventually spoke. 'Have you got last week's time sheets handy?' he asked, his voice sounding dull.

'Yes. They're up on top of the cabinet. See…over there.' She pointed to where the papers lay. Rising from the desk, he walked towards the cabinet. Lifting up the time sheets, he scrutinised the information.

'Big Charlie has done himself out of four hours, or so he thinks.' He took one sheet out, studied it, and nodded his head as if in agreement. He then put the rest of the papers back. 'Sort this out for me Sally,' He said handing her the offending sheet.

Sally's heart sank. The news she was hoping to hear wasn't forthcoming. Another disappointment for him she thought, since Connie died a year ago, he hadn't had a break; he had thrown himself totally into his work. He fiddled about with bits and pieces before leaving Sally's office, then, as he went towards the outside door, he stopped, hesitating for a second or two, he turned and walked back towards Sally's office. She looked up as he approached still with the deadpan expression on his face.

'Oh! By the way,' he said glumly. She knew he hadn't won the contract by his tone and feeling bitter disappointment, waited to be told. A huge grin spread slowly across his face as he said, 'We managed to get that rather wee contract.' His face glowed and a twinkle appeared in his eyes. Sally hadn't seen him look so mischievous in a long time. She lifted the note pad she had been using, and threw it at him.

'You big clown you!' As Ron ducked to avoid contact with the flying missile, she laughed with relief. 'And I was feeling sorry for you!'

Alexis and Winnie joined in the frivolity. 'Well you can start by fishing for tenders. One hundred and ten houses, and that's just the start. And you can get your Lucy over on Saturday night to baby-sit,' pointing his finger at Sally, he spoke positively. 'You and I have some celebrating to do.'

Watching him as he left the office, she thought how much he looked like his old self. The dark rings that had encircled his eyes for so long had gradually disappeared and his skin had once again regained its rugged hue. He hadn't quite regained all the weight he had lost, but as he had been slightly overweight before the loss of Connie, he actually looked better now.

As she thought how handsome he looked, she felt a burning in her veins. The pounding of her heart sent a hot flush through her body. 'Excitement! That's what it is,' she assured herself, after all, she hadn't been out for more than a year. By the time she put Hannah to bed on a Saturday night, drove home, washed and dressed, the night was practically over. Oh she had gone to the pictures with Lucy often, and spent a few nights out with the girls in the office, but she didn't consider those nights to be anything special. This was. This was a night with Ron.

'Well now who's a lucky lady?' teased Winnie, interrupting Sally's thoughts.

'Business Winnie! Just business.' Sally replied.

'It's good to see the boss like his old self again,' Alexis remarked, as if she had read Sally's thoughts.

'Yes it is,' agreed Sally. 'Now we had better get to work or we may see his darker side as well.' Smiling, she crossed the floor of her office and closed the door. Returning to her chair, she sat up and raised her head to the ceiling. Closing her eyes she sighed, saying faintly, 'Thank God. He deserves a bit of a break. Oh! Thank you God!' She sank back in her seat and remained sitting with her eyes closed for quite some time.

Weather wise, Saturday was a dreadful day. It was very cold and the bitter north wind cut through the body like a sharp knife. Sally usually took the baby to the park, weather permitting, but today was a day for the warm comforts of home.

Hannah had learned to walk very quickly. She was off on her own by the time she was ten months old. Now at fourteen months, she was running around and becoming quite a handful. With her petite frame and fine blonde hair she look very elfish. Although she had an extremely healthy appetite, she was as light as a feather. Ron's mother called her, 'my little fairy.' Being a contented child made things easy for all concerned.

Sally was in the kitchen finishing off the ironing while Hannah took her afternoon nap in her pram that was in the far corner. Ron came in carrying an old biscuit lid and on it balanced a pot of paint and the brush he had been using. He was dressed in an old pair of dark brown corded trousers that had all colours of paint dabbed over them, a brown shirt that had seen better days, and the jumper he wore, besides being baggy, was elbowless and ripped beyond repair.

'Any tea?' he asked walking towards the sink. He was about to lay the lid on the spotlessly clean Formica worktop, when Sally gave a yell.

'Don't put that down there without news-paper.' Walking over to a small cupboard, she pulled out some papers. Laying them on top of the work surface she said, 'Now Ron, do you want your ears clipped?' He chuckled as Sally had done the perfect impersonation of his house cleaner, Mrs Kyle, who was employed four days a week and was always 'clipping' somebody's ears.

'Come on Sal make some tea,' he pleaded.

'Well, get rid of all that first.' She pointed to the half empty tin and the dripping paintbrush.

Sally stopped ironing and filled the kettle while Ron cleaned the brush and deposited it into a jam jar containing white spirit. He then put the lot out into the shed. Cleaning his hands, he sat down at the kitchen table that was now set for two. Sitting down beside him, she cut the fruit cake that lay before her into slices.

'Want a piece?' she asked, holding the plate out towards him.

'Who's been busy?'

'Lucy baked it. She's in to baking at the moment. How long it will last remains to be seen.'

Ron poured the tea. They often sat in the kitchen together on a Saturday afternoon, if the weather forced Sally indoors, and occasionally he took a stroll in the park with them. Now and again they spent the day out in the car, taking Lucy along with them.

'Where are you wanting to go tonight? Anywhere special?' He asked.

'No Ron, it's your idea, so you choose.'

'Do you like Italian?'

'Yes, I do; I prefer it to Indian,' she stared in thought. 'I haven't had a meal out since...' She stopped herself from going any further.

Realising what she was about to say, Ron quickly added, 'It's a good job you said yes, for I've already booked a table for us at Deano's...Oh! This cake is good.'

'I'll tell Lucy and she'll bake them until they're coming out your ears.' They both laughed at the thought.

'Talking about Lucy, what time is she coming over?' He asked.

'Seven I think. What time have you booked the table for?'

'Eight o'clock,' he answered, talking with his mouth full of cake. 'I thought we would have some refreshment before we ate. Try and have her come over for six thirty and I'll pick you up around quarter to seven. You can leave here after four. Give yourself time to get ready.'

'Am I that bad looking that I need more than two hours to get dressed and made up?' she bantered..

'Well by the time you apply the sand and cement to your face...Oh...Oh!...only joking.' He held his arm up over his head, as Sally playfully made an attempt to thump him. They were both enjoying the fun, when the baby began to stir.

The restaurant was as always, very busy. If your table wasn't reserved, there was very little chance of dining there at the weekend. Still, there were always a few couples hanging around the reception area, just in case there was a cancellation.

As they were early, Ron and Sally enjoyed a pre-dinner drink in the small lounge bar adjacent to the restaurant.

Chatting idly, they relaxed in the soft gentle light of their surroundings as piped music played softly from speakers concealed in each corner. Little bowls of fresh flowers centred each table, while trellis, part covered in ivy, separated the dining area from the lounge, allowing the tables to be seen from where they both sat.

Looking through, Sally thought how romantic it all looked, for as well as red carnations, each table was lit by a small candle burning merrily in little red glasses, giving off a lovely warm glow. The covers on the tables were made from white Italian lace, each one enhanced by the bright red tablecloths that lay underneath.

Although it was a family restaurant, it was usually couples that patronised it in the evenings, so most of the tables were set for two.

Sally wore a dusty pink fine wool dress that moulded round her shapely figure, its broad matching belt emphasising the narrowness of her waist. Her raven hair tied loosely back, allowing carefully placed strands to fall down the side of her face, shone like silk. Two strands of tiny pearls adorned her neck while a single pear hung from each ear. She looked wonderful and felt how she looked. Great care as always had been taken with her make-up, emphasising her gorgeous eyes.

Ron too looked very smart in his charcoal grey jacket, pink shirt with a grey collar that was now highly fashionable. Sally was quite surprised at Ron keeping up with the times. They looked a handsome couple.

Shortly after seven, the waiter escorted them to their table.

During the meal, they found no shortage of conversation as both their lives revolved around the business, as well as young Hannah. They discussed the job that lay in front of them and agreed that they were in for a very busy time.

'Enough of work now,' he said touching her hand, 'we are out to enjoy this evening. You don't go out nearly enough and it's time you did. Hannah is manageable now and you don't have to devote your weekend to her as much now.'

A slight panic rose within her. 'What are you saying Ron? Don't you want me to see to Hannah any more?'

He shook his head slowly, 'No, no! That's not what I'm saying.' Sally's hand rested on the table, reaching over he squeezed it gently. 'I feel very guilty Sally. You have no social life and I blame myself. I'm very grateful to you, in fact, I don't know how I would have managed at times without you, but I can't expect to take up any more of your leisure time.'

Pulling her hand away from his none too gently, she admonished him whimsically. 'I won't hear any more of this. I do what I do because I choose to, besides, I love to be with Hannah. Weekends are the only time I have to be with her. I can go out any night during the week Ron, so don't think of me as a complete recluse.'

'Sorry, I didn't mean anything by that Sally, It's just that you're a beautiful girl, and you should be...well! I mean; you should have a boy friend and you're not going to get one sitting around the house or running after us.

'I don't want anyone. I'm happy as I am, besides I've had enough of boyfriends.'

Ron was about to ask what had really happened between Harry and her, when the waiter interrupted bringing them their coffee.

'That was a wonderful meal Ron. It was all that I expected. This place certainly does live up to its reputation.'

'Aye, we must do this again sometime,' he said, finishing his coffee.

As he settled the bill, he asked the waiter to call a taxi. Helping Sally on with her jacket, he took her by the hand and led her to the door.

'We're not going home yet you know,' he said mischievously. 'It's early yet, besides we both deserve a good night out. As Lucy is staying all night, we don't have to hurry home.'

'Where are we going?' she asked delightedly.

'We, my girl, are going night clubbing. I'm going to dance this meal off.'

'Can you dance?' she asked, forgetting that Connie often talked about them dancing together.

'Of course I can. Don't let my wooden leg fool you.' Laughing heartily he helped her on with her coat.

The Carriage Club was a private club and although Ron had been a member there for a good many years, this was the first time he had gone there in the evening. He had used their restaurant many times in the afternoons and enjoyed the occasional lunchtime drink, if he happened to be in town without his car. The club was in full swing when they arrived but luckily Ron managed to find a table in the corner. Escorting Sally to her seat, he then called the waiter and ordered a couple of drinks.

Soft, slow music flowed from the small orchestra that occupied the round stage. The saxophonist was on his feet, putting his heart and soul into his music, as if wooing a consenting lover. Several couples held each other close, as they danced lazily, swaying to the gentle rhythm of the music.

'Come on, lets have a go,' he said, taking Sally by surprise. 'I bet you never knew I was taught by Fred Astaire.' Putting his arm around her waist he led her onto the dance floor.

As he held her close, they too began to sway with the music. Sally's heartbeat quickened as she became aware of Ron's warm breath on her neck. He held her so tight; she felt the wonderful warmth of his body as they embraced in dance. Closing her eyes she savoured the wonderful feeling that over powered her. For the first time she saw Ron as a man, not Connie's husband, nor her employer, not even her friend; but a man, a handsome, available man whom she admired and cared for very much.

Back at their table, they sat very close together. Ron watched as she sipped her drink. He too saw Sally in a different light. He always thought she was a good-looking girl, but tonight he was looking at a very beautiful woman. He had never thought of, nor craved for anyone since the death of his wife, but as he watched Sally, he realised how he missed the warmth and tenderness of a woman. He felt an overwhelming desire to enfold her in his arms and draw her close only the fear of rejection hindered him. He thought Sally would probably feel betrayed if he made a pass as she had been a very good friend to Connie and trusted him implicitly.

'Sally,' he cleared his throat before continuing, 'I hope you don't mind my asking, but what went wrong between you and Harry?'

Her smile vanished. She took another slow sip at her drink. She had shared Ron's grief, his happiness and the frustration of business, now it was only right that she should give him an answer to his question.

'Ron, I'll tell you now, you may not like what I'm about to say, but I'll tell you. Please promise you won't let it go any further?'

'Of course I promise. As if I would.' He seemed wounded at her mistrust.

Sally, for the first time told of Bess and her blackmailing stunt. Starting from her years in the children's home, she went on to relate what happened to her father and how it came about, excluding the fact that she had been raped by the Watson brothers, she told of Jack Brown's assault. She also told him of the baby her mother had, and it's tragic end. Ron listened without interrupting.

'Now you know!' A note of sadness infiltrated her voice. 'Maybe you won't want me to work for you, now you know how wicked my family have been.'

Shaking his head sadly, Ron gave a low slow sigh. 'Sally, I've known about your father for years, I can't remember now who told me, but it never mattered to me then, and it certainly doesn't matter to me now. You're you, and you can't go round carrying your family's misdeeds on your shoulders. Now! Regarding Harry, I think you were spared a life of misery. It's all very well being in a relationship, but if you had married into that family, there would always be someone there to tell you when to jump and how high, but I must say I thought Harry had more in him than that. It just proves one thing; the purse strings meant more to him than love. You know Sally, he's very weak and I can tell you this, he'll regret it for the rest of his life because he really did love you. Now, we're missing all that good dance music, so come on get up.'

And dance they did. They were on the floor most of the evening but all too soon they were dancing the last dance. With dimmed lights, the huge glass ball that hung from the centre of the ceiling sent small star shaped lights flashing recklessly across the room.

Holding Sally tenderly in his arms, Ron could no longer ignore the desire that raged within. Their cheeks rubbed gently together, and as he drew his head back slowly, their eyes met. Gazing at each other momentarily, they knew what was about to happen. Their lips touched briefly as if unsure how to kiss. Brushing against each other once more he eventually kissed her passionately, and with meaning. Sally's whole body trembled, as she experienced that wonderful warm feeling she had felt once before. Fire now raged through her veins her heart pounding violently against her ribs, she was sure he would feel it against his body as he held her so very close.

The lights came on as the orchestra played their last few notes. Still holding her in his arms, he released her slowly without saying a single word. It wasn't until they reached the table that he spoke.

'Have you enjoyed the evening Sally?'

Gazing up at him she smiled. 'I've enjoyed myself very much Ron. I really have. Thank you for everything.'

The romance of the evening died suddenly as Ron sat apart from her in the taxi. He made no attempt to hold her despite the signals he gave out minutes earlier. Saying very little on the journey home left Sally very hurt and confused. It was as the taxi drew to a halt outside Sally's home, Ron mentioned the kiss. 'Look Sally, I'm so sorry for, err... you know... back there,' he said apologetically.

Seeing he was deeply embarrassed, Sally treated it with an air of indifference.

They said goodnight, and Sally thanked him once more for the lovely evening. Her true feelings were well and truly hidden. She felt so angry with him, not for the kiss, but for the apology. She also felt anger at herself for being so foolish as to think he felt as she did.

Lying in bed, she relived the moments she had spent in Ron's arms. Mixed emotions pulled at her heartstrings. Had she the right to feel as she did? What had really taken place on the dance floor? She cried as she thought Ron had regretted his actions. Was he just lonely? Was he thinking of Connie? Did he forget who she was?

Sally's head throbbed as her mind swam with doubts, then suddenly she felt sick. How was she going to face him tomorrow?

Alone in the taxi, Ron began to feel anger; anger at his own stupidity. He too was confused. The feelings he had endured were real enough but he couldn't help thinking that his desire for Sally could possibly have been due to his own frustrations. He could not risk loosing Sally's loyalty and undying friendship over a night of passion. Did he long for the warmth of the female body, or was it Sally herself that caused the fire in him to be quenched?

Her beauty would have stirred any heart, but he had to be sure he wanted her for the right reasons. They were both circumstantially vulnerable so treading carefully was of the essence.

Two weeks had passed since they spent that evening together and no difference had been made whatsoever to their relationship at work, nor did it interfere with their friendship. It was if it had never happened. Sally kept her feelings under lock and key and managed to laugh and joke with him, as if she hadn't a care in the world. All the while, she was coping with an ache only Ron could cure. She had never felt like this before. She thought she had loved Harry, and going through the agony when thinking she would lose him, was nothing compared to this. Was there no limit to her torture?

No sooner was she out of one bad situation she seemed to fall into another. In company she was bright and cheerful, but when completely alone, she let her real feelings tear her apart. Sally was now an expert at living a lie. Since her early years she had found that it was necessary to pretend that all was well in order to fit in. It was no different now.

She was about to cover her typewriter when the phone on her desk rang. Ron at the other end of the receiver, asked her to call round later in the evening as he wished to speak to her.

'Yes I can, but what's wrong?' It was unusual for him to be home so early. He was normally last to leave the yard. 'Is your mother o.k.?' She thought that he had, perhaps, gone home to see to Hannah.

'Yes. Oh! You're wondering why I'm at home already. Well I came home at lunch to change my clothes. I had to meet Mr. Gulliver this afternoon.'

'I didn't know you had an appointment with the solicitor to day. It's not in the diary.'

'I didn't tell you, so you were not to know. Will you come round about eight?'

Replacing the receiver back in the cradle, Sally chewed lightly on her bottom lip pulling her face into a puzzled frown.

'What's he up to,' she thought. She had never known him to make an appointment without putting it in the diary. Having a terrible memory, he had to be reminded of everything. Dates and times had to be written down, or he would simply forget. Another thing struck her as odd, the appointment had not been made from his office, as the call would have gone through the switchboard and Alexis would have said something.

'He must have phoned Mr. Gulliver from home.' She couldn't think why, but she was soon to find out.

She arrived at Ron's house shortly after eight. Going to the back door, she let herself in as she normally did.

Helen sat in the kitchen relaxing over a cup of coffee as Sally entered.

'Well you do look nice in that suit,' she said as a welcome to Sally.

'Helen, you've seen this suit plenty of times and you say the same thing every time.' She tugged gently at her jacket.

'Well, you do look nice, no matter how often I see you in it.'

The suit was very plain indeed. A black jacket with medium sized lapels. The collar and the top half of the lapels were made from rich black velvet, as were the three buttons that flanked each side of the jacket. The skirt length was just above the knees, straight, with a small vent at the back. She also wore a simple white open necked blouse underneath. She looked very elegant indeed.

'Do you want a cup of coffee?' Helen asked.

Walking towards the door that led to the stairs, Sally shook her head. 'No thanks Helen; I better let him know I'm here. I had to stop for petrol so I'm a bit late.'

'He's in the study then.' Helen called after her.

Sally reached the study door and as it was Ron's private retreat, knocked and waited.

'Come in,' he called.

As Sally entered he rose smartly going to greet her. As she was about to sit, he stopped her. 'No, we'll go into the lounge, it's much better than here. It's too much like an office and you see enough of them during the day.'

Taking her by the arm he led her into the lounge, and, sitting her down on the sofa, he walked towards the table where two crystal decanters and matching glasses sat on a round silver tray.

'What's it to be?' he asked lifting a glass.

'A sherry if you don't mind Ron. I have the car so make it a small one please.'

He brought her drink over and sat down beside her on the sofa. He held his own glass of whisky out in front of her.

'Well I think it's the custom to clink glasses together when something good happens,' he said.

With taut lips she peered at him suspiciously through narrowing eyes.

'What are you up to now?' she asked studying his rugged face.

Mischievous sparkling eyes met hers. 'I'm not up to anything missy. I just want to drink a toast to my new Director!'

Sally's enquiring eyes widened slowly and now resembled enormous dark pools. 'Oh! Who's coming into the business?' Feeling apprehensive, she watched his grin grow wider. The crease lines round his mouth grew deeper.

'No one's coming in. I've decided to make you a Director. *You* do all the work; in fact it's you who runs the show. It's only fitting you get what's rightly yours. You work hard and make important decisions, so I think you should be wearing the hat that goes with the job you are doing.'

Sally sat in shock. She heard what he had said but was having trouble taking it in.

'Drink your sherry. I think you need it,' he said.

She finally stuttered, 'I think I should've taken something stronger.'

'Do you want something else?' he gazed at her longingly.

'No no! I'm only joking. But Ron, are you sure? I mean... I...I... don't know what to say.'

'Say nothing then. The solicitors are seeing to it. That's why I sneaked off today.' He drank his whisky and laid the glass down on the table. 'And there's something else I've to say. I once told you I was sorry for kissing you, well I'm not. I don't know how you feel about it but I'm not sorry at all.'

Her heart leapt as his last statement sank in. Speechless, she just sat staring at him as he waited for her answer.

'Well, what do you say to that, or have you forgotten how it felt?'

She shook her head and still didn't answer. She was drunk with joy and couldn't move. If it were a dream, she was frightened she would wake up.

He pulled her to him then gazing into her eyes, he murmured.

'Sally, it's up to you. Do you mind if we try again?'

It was Sally who drew close and found his lips. As they kissed they were unaware of Helen entering the lounge. She was about to turn away, but as they broke from their embrace, Ron saw her in the doorway and called to her.

'Mother, come and meet the new Director and the new woman in my life.'

Helen beamed as she made towards Sally.

'I don't know how I kept it to myself, I've known for some time now.' Bending down she kissed her on the cheek. 'Congratulations on your Directorship my dear... and as for hooking my son... I blame that suit. You always look lovely in that suit.'

As they fell into rapturous laughter, Ron slipped his arm round Sally giving her a reassuring squeeze. She felt the happiest woman alive knowing within her heart that this was for real.

Chapter Sixteen

As the tenders for the new houses arrived, Sally sieved though them checking them against one another for price and availability.

One arrived on her desk that aroused her curiosity. It was the name that struck a chord 'Watson Bros'. The Directors names were Jack and Neil Watson. Names that Sally had never forgotten.

They were tendering for supplying and erecting the timber and trestles for the roofs.

She stared at the letterhead that was attached and wondered if it was possible. She had to find out about this company. Their price was good and normally the possible applicants would go into a wire basket for final scrutiny while the others would be filed away. Sally put this one in a blue folder and opening the desk drawer she tucked it away. She knew exactly who to ask. She didn't want to ask Ron at this stage just in case it turned out to be whom she suspected. Charlie was the one to ask. He knew everybody in the building trade.

As the men were picked up early in the mornings and dropped off at night at certain corners near their homes, she would have to wait till Friday and catch him as he came into the yard to collect his wages. The vans brought them to the yard early in the afternoon as they only worked till three o'clock on Fridays.

It had been a very busy week and the office telephone had never stopped ringing. Since word had got around that the job was started, the local men who were seeking work were in pursuit of any available vacancies. Tradesmen as well as labourers chased after the situations vacant appointments.

Sally had to attend various meetings with Ron as he fraternised with architects and site agents. She took notes and made sure he had all the available paper work that was required.

Friday came around and she attached a note to Charlie's pay packet letting him know she wanted to see him. The wages were sent down to Ron's office, as he liked to pay his men personally. Ron would think nothing of the note to Charlie as Sally often had a word with the men about their wages, as it was she who made them up. A private savings scheme was also organised by her, so it wasn't unusual that she requested to see him.

Charlie ascended the outside stairs two at a time, and whistling cheerily he knocked and entered the office.

'Hi there girls, now I've just come up to see which one of you two good lookers wants to come to the watering hole with me tonight?' Rubbing his hands together he looked from one to the other.

'Charlie! When I want to go out with someone as old as you I'll take my grandfather,' Alexis teased.

'Aye and I'm not in need of a white stick just yet,' Winnie said laughing over at Alexis who rummaged in her handbag.

'You're a pair o' cheeky wee monkeys. A suppose I'll have tae take the wife oot the night again.' He spoke in mock disappointment.

'You know Charlie, I don't know how that poor woman puts up with you. I think she keeps you for the laughs' said Alexis. Finding her lipstick at the bottom of her bag, she poised with a hand mirror ready to apply the red gloss.

'Aye maybe, an' a thought it was for ma guid looks.'

Both girls groaned as he ran his fingers through his mop of grey hair.

'Sally's waiting for you, so you had better move.'

' Noo there's a woman a'd dye ma hair for.' he whispered.

'It'll no' be your hair that'll dye if Ron hears you,' Alexis grinned.

He knocked on Sally's door and she called immediately, 'Come on in Charlie.' She was tidying up her desk as he entered.

'You wanted tae see me Sally?' he asked, his head to one side in an enquiring manner. He knew it wasn't anything to do with wages, as he knew exactly what was due to him and if there were as much as a penny out on either side, he would say.

'Charlie, I want you to help me if you can. I wonder if you know anything about this Company?' Opening the desk drawer and moving a few things around, she drew out the blue folder.

'It's not based in Edinburgh it's in West Lothian. I don't know them as we only deal with local companies.' She opened up the file and studied the letter once more before giving Charlie the information.

'Ah now, here we are, Watson Brothers from Bathgate. Joiners, have you heard of them?'

Thinking momentarily, Charlie clicked his tongue, 'Well aye. A wouldn't have kent them if it wasnae for ma wife's nephew like. He's jist been laid off fae there.'

She held her hand out and motioned towards the chair standing in front of her desk. Charlie sat down.

'What do you know of them? I mean the owners.'

He rubbed his chin with his massive big rough hands and went into deep thought.

'They came fae aroond the Port Seton area originally. Noo, the faither had a quarry business. A guid goin' business by awe accounts like. The faither seemingly gambled an' drank enough tae lose his business. He moved tae the west some time ago efter sufferin' a stroke. That's the story a heard like. The sons selt what they could, an' them being joiners started up oan their ain.'

Sally's heart raced as she listened to Charlie's report.

'A don't ken them maself as a said like, but they are supposed tae be a bad lot.'

'Go on Charlie' she wanted to hear more.

'Well, a can only tell ye that their business is in difficulty as men are bein' laid oaf through lack o' work like. Why dae you want tae ken?'

'Oh, I have my reasons. Charlie I would like you to forget about this conversation. Can I ask you that?'

He grinned and nodded, 'What conversation?'

'Thanks Charlie.'

He rose from the chair, and as he reached the door he paused, saying in a very concerned manner, 'A don't ken what you're up tae Sally, but you be careful. They're a couple o' bad eggs them brothers.'

'Don't worry Charlie, I'm only finding out a bit about them as they have forwarded a tender.'

Charlie gave a low grunt as he left. He wasn't convinced Sally was exactly truthful. She was too secretive for his liking. He gave his word to forget about the conversation and that's what he would have to do.

Sitting alone in her office, she stared down at the quotation and the letter attached to it. She bit on the end of her pencil as she planned what she should do. It had to be carefully thought out. She would have to rely on them forgetting they ever knew the name Sally Baxter, that was until she had finished with them. She wanted to bring them to their knees. If she could bankrupt them and leave them without a roof over their heads, she would be satisfied. This is what she had waited for all those years. Revenge, she now had the power to make or break them and this feeling was beyond description.

The building of the housing estate was well on the way and the sub-contractors had been chosen for most of the jobs, all except the joinery work. Sally held back deliberately as that was part of her plan. The Watson brothers were made to sweat it out, as they hadn't been given a yes or no to their offer. They had been on the phone every week for two months now and occasionally

Sally would talk to either one of them and tell them she hadn't made up her mind yet but they were looking good. Most of the time Sally would instruct whoever was on the switchboard to say she was unavailable at the moment.

She played about with them like a cat that had just caught a mouse. They were getting pretty desperate now but Sally had to wait until she was sure their desperation would lead them into being reckless and foolhardy.

Ron had questioned her as to why she was taking so long arranging a sub-contractor for the joinery work. She assured him that there would be no hold ups; in fact she wasn't certain that contracting joiners who supplied their own material was the right thing to do. She said she was thinking of taking on joiners and supplying the material themselves.

She knew herself that time was running out and she would have to make her move soon.

The following day things started to happen. She was hardly in the office when Winnie rang through. 'That's Mr Watson from Watson Bros on the phone again Sally. What shall I say?'

'Put him through Winnie.' She sat drumming her long fingernails on the desk as she waited for the now familiar voice.

'Miss Baxter? Jack Watson here. I have been very patient but I can't wait any longer. Things are so bad that I have to know what's happening' his voice sounded exactly how Sally wanted it to be...desperate.

'I know Mr Watson, I'm terribly sorry but we're ever so busy. We've had so many after the work we're spoilt for choice.' She sounded very sympathetic.

'Well Miss Baxter, I don't think anybody could beat us on price.'

'Exactly what I was saying Mr Watson, but sometimes the work suffers if prices are too low.'

'Miss Baxter, I can assure you that you would be dealing with first class tradesmen who only do first class jobs.' He paused for a few seconds, tension mounting in his voice. 'Miss Baxter, I have to be honest with you, we need this work or we close. That's the hard facts. Things have been dreadful and if we don't start work soon, we have to close the doors. I'm sure you understand how we feel.'

That's what Sally wanted to hear. Jack Watson begging.

'Well to tell you the truth Mr Watson, I was about to ring you today. I have decided to give you the contract, providing you can have the trusses and timber on site in seven days. You see, the work is coming along quicker than we anticipated and now speed is essential.' Her eyes closed and fingers crossed, Sally waited. Would he do it?

'Miss Baxter,' the voice at the other end of the phone had changed completely, it sounded as if new life had been injected into it. 'Don't worry; the material will be on site within seven days. I promise. Thank you very much. Thank you.'

'There's a small problem though,' she changed her voice into a gentle helpless tone.

'Yes Miss Baxter?' he sounded apprehensive.

'I have to leave for France this afternoon and I won't be able to get your contract drawn up until I get back. I'll be gone for eight days not counting the weekend.'

There was silence once more at the other end. Sally prayed and held her breath thinking; he's got to take the chance. He can't do anything else.'

'OK, we'll call it a gentlemen's agreement. I'll go ahead and deliver the material. You arrange for the contract to be drawn up and we'll get together when you get back.'

'That's fine by me,' Sally's tightly clenched fists almost drew blood from her palm as her nails dug into the flesh. The desire to yell with delight had to be restrained for a few minutes longer.

'Thanks very much Miss Baxter, I can assure you once more you will be completely satisfied.'

Sally placed the receiver in its cradle and gave a delighted scream.

'Thank *you* very much Jack, I'm completely satisfied already, you creep! Gentlemen's agreement! You wouldn't know a gentleman if he jumped up and bit you on the nose' she said aloud.

Both Winnie and Alexis had been told what had to be done if either Jack or Neil Watson called. Sally was to be informed but no way were they to be put through to Ron. If they inquired about Sally's where-abouts, they were to be told she wasn't at work and they weren't sure when she would be back.

Both girls assumed she was sick of the Watsons calling and thought nothing odd about their instructions.

Now all Sally had to wait on was a phone call from the

site. She would have to content herself during the next week and hope things went to plan.

The weekend was upon her once more, and she spent it as usual with Ron and Hannah. Ron had invested in a three-berth caravan, which was located on a camp site near Scone, Perthshire. They drove over on the Saturday morning taking Lucy and her friend Doreen with them. Lucy was now seventeen and both Doreen and herself were staying on at school hoping to get grades good enough to secure places at university.

It was early September and the weather was still rather nice. The summer had been exceptionally warm. Out in the country they enjoyed walking and taking in the local beauty spots. They visited the historical areas and spent time exploring Scone Palace.

It was good to get away from everything, even though it was only for a couple of days.

Feeling completely relaxed, Sally sat on the grass beside Ron watching Hannah being chased by the two older girls. She squealed with laughter as Lucy caught her and lifted her high in the air.

Ron put his arm around Sally's shoulder and whispered 'Happy?'

'What do you think?' she said pinching him at the waist.

'I'm sorry we didn't get away somewhere this year, but I'll make it up to you. I promise,' he said.

'Ron, I'm just as happy spending the odd weekend away, honest really I am.'

She really meant what she said. She was happy with

her life. Every minute spent with Ron was savoured. She knew she loved him but as yet she had not declared it. Ron had shown that he loved her, but like herself, had never actually said so.

One thing was sure, if Ron did reject her, it would be of her own doing, as Bess could find nothing to split them up. Ron knew everything about her life, all except her experience with the Watsons, but she was going to tell him all about it when she had taken her revenge on them.

The weekend as always flew past, and once more work faced them.

There had been no contact whatsoever from the Watson Brothers and Sally was beginning to feel a bit nervous. Not at what she was about to do, but nervous in case her plan had fallen through. Then it happened. Thursday afternoon the telephone rang and one of the girls put the call through to Sally. It was the site foreman on the line.

'Sally, this is John Miller.'

'Hi there John, what can I do for you?' her stomach felt as if it were on a roller coaster.

'Sally, do you know anything about these trusses and materials that have arrived on site? They have been sent by Watson Bros of Bathgate. No one has told me about them,' he sounded annoyed.

Sally drew in a deep breath before answering, as she was aware anxiety would almost certainly be heard in her voice.

'John, I know nothing about that, except I've been pestered to death by them. They're never off the phone. They certainly have no contract with us. Maybe they have a job somewhere else and the driver has mistaken the site.'

'No, I thought that as well, but the delivery is definitely for us.'

'Well, I'll get on to them and ask what they are playing at.'

'Sally, be careful, those guys have a reputation. I'm not surprised this has happened. Maybe you had better let Ron deal with them.'

'No John, I'll deal with it, Ron's over at another job. Don't you think I'm capable?'

'I do, but Sally they're crooks. They were behind the burning of Taylor's timber yard. Nothing was ever proven but it was them all right. Stewart Taylor beat them to a contract and was verbally threatened. They probably are about to use strong arm tactics with *us*.'

'Stop worrying. I'll ring you later,' she said.

'What's to happen with this stuff?' he asked.

'Is it off the lorry?'

'Half off.'

'Let them leave it on site for now,' she said.

'What! You can't do that.'

'Well then John, I'll tell you what to do. Tell the driver to contact his office. Let him tell his boss that we don't want the load. I'll wait here as I can bet you anything they will ring me immediately. Now don't worry, I can deal with the Watsons.'

After finishing her call with John Miller, Sally let the girls know she expected a call at any moment from Watson Brothers. 'Put them through,' she instructed.

She sat back and waited. She watched the minute hand move slowly around the big white face of the office wall clock. She couldn't carry on with any other business, as concentration would be impossible at this time. She waited. The only noise she heard was the tapping of the typewriters coming from the main office. She heard the phone ring and the muffled voice of Alexis.

The call was put through to Sally's office. The phone rang and she deliberately let it ring for a good twenty seconds before lifting the receiver.

'That's Neil Watson now Sally,' Alexis informed her.

'Put him through,' she instructed, composing her self.

'Miss Baxter, Neil Watson here. We have just received a call from our driver who is on your site at this very minute. Seemingly your foreman refuses to accept delivery.'

'Yes that is so Mr Watson,' she said coolly.

There was a few seconds silence before he spoke.

'You're aware of this?' he asked.

Beaming with pleasure she answered. 'Of course I'm aware. The foreman phoned here before your driver contacted you.'

'But why, what's the problem?' he asked.

'I don't know why you took it upon yourself to deliver materials when the job was never given to you.'

'Wait a minute,' he growled. 'Jack was told by you to deliver this week. You gave us the contract.'

'I don't remember doing anything of the sort. Your brother has been so desperate for the job he must have picked me up wrong, besides you don't have a written contract do you?'

'No but... but you said you were going to see to it when you arrived from France.'

'France! I've not been in France. Oh no Mr Watson, your brother has heard me wrong. I haven't given the contract to anybody as we're buying our own materials and hiring our own joiners.'

'But you cant!! Do you know what it's cost us for the materials?'

'No Mr Watson but I can't help you. I'm dreadfully sorry if your brother can't listen to what people are saying to him...well...'

'*You listen to me lady!*' his voice was now raised. 'You *can't* do this. We can't give the timbers or trestles back. They must be paid for. Our business is in trouble and this will make us bankrupt. You *did* say we could proceed with this job and you can't go back on that.' His voice shook with anger.

'Now you listen to *me*. I don't *want* your business and you can do what you *want* with the timber and trestles but there's nothing to prove that you had *any* contract whatsoever with us, so you do what you want Mr Watson. I'm sure you've been in business long enough to know you never do anything without a legal contract, or don't you work like that?'

She slammed the phone down and only then did she begin to shake. She knew she hadn't heard the end of it and was prepared for what was to come.

One hour passed and she was surprised there were no further calls.

The door of the office flew open and a stocky, bumptious little man stood in the doorway.

'Miss Baxter?' he shouted. 'Miss Baxter, where will I find her?'

The girls looked at each other, unsure of what they should do. Alexis hesitated for a moment before she gathered her thoughts.

'Who are *you*?'

'*Me?*' Digging his thumb into his own chest he announced, 'I'm Jake Watson, that's who I am. Now where's Miss Baxter?'

'I'll phone and see if she is available.' Alexis said nervously.

'You *do* that Missy!'

Alexis would normally have gone over and knocked on Sally's door, but as she didn't want Jack Watson to know where Sally's office was, she decided to phone her for instructions.

As Alexis lifted the receiver, Sally's door opened. She had heard the commotion and knew what it would be.

'It's all right Alexis.' Nodding in the direction of the frightened girl, Sally gave her a reassuring smile before turning her attention on the irate man. 'I presume you are here to see *me*?' she said haughtily.

'*You're* Miss Baxter?'

'Yes I am. And who are *you*?' she knew who he was all right.

'Jake Watson *that's* who I am.'

'Will you come through,' she stood aside to let him pass into her office.

Alexis and Winnie stared open mouthed at each other before Winnie rose from her seat and headed towards the door.

'Where are you going?' Alexis whispered.

'I'm going down to see if any of the men are back, I don't like this at all.'

'Oh My God Winnie, don't leave us alone. Hurry up, I don't like this either.'

Sally walked calmly to her side of the desk, as Jake Watson stood opposite.

'Take a seat Mr Watson.' Sweeping her hand towards the chair, she looked in complete control.

'*No thanks*. You have a bloody nerve! What are you playin' at madam?'

'Mr Watson, I have already told your brother that we don't want your materials. I never gave you any contract. You have jumped the gun as one would say.'

Purple neck veins ballooned inside his collar as if about to burst. Red and white blotches masked his face. '*Jumped* the *gun. Jumped the bloody gun. You* said we had to deliver the materials within seven days.'

'Now now Mr Watson, don't upset yourself. There's been a misunderstanding here' she said.

'*Misunderstanding*' he roared. 'Do you *realise* we have *thousands* o' *pounds* o' materials that we can't possibly pay for without that contract of yours?'

'I'm sorry Mr Watson, but we are doing the job ourselves. We have the joiners waiting to start work.' She walked back and forward as if in thought, 'but I may be able to help you out.'

'You mean you'll *give* us the job?' He looked at her in hope.

'No, I have just told you, or are you still not listening?'

'What do you intend doing then?'

'I'll buy the materials from you for half the price.'

She felt fear for the first time as he made to pounce forward. He stopped in front of her, his face almost touching hers, his teeth gnashed together. His breath had a terrible smell of garlic and the stench of stale cigars reeked from his clothes.

'*Why* are you *doing* this? If you're out to ruin us you're doing a fine job.'

'*You* should know all about ruining people Jake Watson,' she snapped. 'You did a good job ruining *my* life.'

He sprang back and looked her over as if seeing her for the first time.

'Ruining *your* life? I don't even *know* you! I've never seen you in my life.'

'No I suppose you haven't. You don't usually look at people too closely when trying to restrain them do you!'

'What are you getting at? Are you insane?' he gave a nervous laugh.

'Sally Baxter, *wee* Sally Baxter. Do you know me *now*, or have you raped so many wee girls that my name is insignificant?'

'You, *you're* Sally Baxter?' his mouth gaped open. 'Oh look Sa... Sally,' he stammered as he remembered.

'*Miss* Baxter to you!' It came as a demand.

~374~

'Miss Baxter.' he tried reasoning. 'We were young at the time. You know how it is,' he laughed nervously.

'If it wasn't for you and your brother, my father would still be alive and I wouldn't have had to endure my torment.'

Is *this* what it's all about?' he asked.

'Yes it is Jake Watson, so try explaining that to your legal adviser. As far as I'm concerned, I gave you no contract so either take up my offer or have your homes repossessed as well as losing your business.'

'We both have families and they *too* will suffer if we go bankrupt,' he hissed.

'You didn't think of anybody else's family; so don't expect me to feel sorry for yours. I hate you and your brother and anything connected to you so don't ever look for a soft side in my nature for there is none when it concerns you.'

He walked towards the door, hesitating before pointing his finger violently at her.

'I'll think about your offer, but *you* wait, *you'll* get your day.'

'I've already had that Mr Watson. Indeed I have,' she grinned.

He banged the door behind him causing the glass to shudder.

Charlie had been standing outside Sally's door in case he had to burst in. As their voices were raised in anger, Charlie heard most of what was said. He didn't hear everything, but the pieces were easily put together.

Knocking on the door he opened it without waiting for an answer.

'You awe right?' he asked.

'Yes Charlie. Where did you come from?'

'Winnie was scared so she asked me tae stand by.'

'It's all right Charlie. I knew what I was doing,' Sally smiled. She reached down to the half open drawer of her desk and switched off the small tape that had been recording her conversation with Jake Watson.

'Sally, a over heard you baith. A ken what he did tae ye.' He had to let her know.

She looked hard at Charlie before resting her head in her hands.

Charlie turned making sure the door was shut before sitting down in the chair opposite her. She looked up at Charlie and shrugged her shoulders. 'Well Charlie, you heard that bit so I may as well tell you what I've done to them!'

She told Charlie exactly what she had done.

'What ye 'ave just telt me will go nae further, but ye had better watch oot. A've telt ye before, they arenae nice people, but ye already ken that.'

'Charlie, I intend letting Ron know. I can't hold this back from him.'

'Aye, a think you'd better,' came Charlie's response.

Charlie left the office as Winnie and Alexis were preparing to go home.

'She all right?' Alexis asked nodding her head towards the inner office.

'Aye, she's some wuman,' Charlie replied.

Ron rang Sally at home that evening, as she had gone by the time he arrived back at the yard. He had a word with the site foreman and was told about the delivery that arrived from Watson Bros.

'Can I see you tonight?' she asked.

'Of course you can. Why do you ask?' came his reply.

'Oh, it's just that I have things to tell you and I usually don't see you on Thursday nights.'

'Sally, what's wrong with you? We don't have set nights. If you want to come round, you know you can.'

'Ok' she said, 'but can I meet you for a drink?'

'This sounds rather intriguing,' he said, 'but I'll pick you up, I don't want you in bars by yourself.'

'All right, eight o'clock?'

'See you then. By the way, what was that all about today? Watsons supplying without a contract?'

'I'll tell you all about it tonight.' She hoped he would understand.

Ron arrived at eight o'clock as arranged. They drove to a small pub they frequented now and again. It was a friendly little place that was very quiet during the week. A few couples sat round the small tables while a couple of young men propped up the bar.

Lifting the drinks from the tray, Ron bent over and placed them on the table in front of Sally. As she looked up at him, he planted a quick kiss on her brow.

'I couldn't resist that,' he said giving her a wink.

'I wonder if you'll say that when you hear what I have to say,' was her response.

Sitting down he looked at her in wonder.

'What on earth have you been up to now?' He clicked his tongue and frowned.

'This is serious Ron,' she said biting her bottom lip.

'OK Sally go on, let's hear it.'

Telling him of her experience in the hands of the evil brothers was easier than she thought. As she related her story, the bitterness and anger she had carried round all those years seemed to melt away.

She told him what she had done to the Watson Bros, and her offer to buy the timber from them at half the price. When she was finished, she searched Ron's face waiting for an angry reaction but feeling his hands enfold hers, she gave a sigh of relief

'Oh Sally, you have kept that to yourself all your life. Sally how have you managed to deal with that on your own? God you have gone through the mill,' he gazed into her eyes. 'I don't blame you for taking your revenge out on them, but it could have turned nasty.' He shook his head in disbelief.

'I watched what I was doing. Ron I also taped the conversation. They don't know it but it came out as clear as crystal.'

Ron laughed and bit his lip to suppress his mirth. 'I'm sorry Sally, but you're quite the wheeler and dealer. Take the materials off them at half the price, now that's what I call rubbing their noses in it.'

'Ron it isn't funny.' She looked at him with a very long face. She slowly broke into a large grin that developed into a belly laugh.

Ron insisted that for her own safety, any other dealings with the Watsons would be done through him. As Sally had suggested, a deal with Jack had been made to purchase the timbers and trusses for just over half price.

A month later Watson Brothers went out of business although their houses were not repossessed. It would have vexed Sally if she had caused their families to be homeless, but as things turned out, she did what she wanted to do and closed them both down.

She was now free of all her ghosts.

When the houses were nearing completion, Ron was given another contract for a further fifty. The developer was converting part of his grounds into a private housing estate, and as he was pleased with the job Ron had done, further contracts were imminent.

Alexis and Winnie had gone home at their usual time while Sally stayed on to finish some papers that had to be prepared for the solicitors.

She saw the last of the vans come into the yard and heard the men's cars that were parked in the yard leave.

Sally still left her car in the side lane, as she had to move it from the yard a few times to allow lorries in. She felt it was better in the lane as it wasn't in anyone's way there.

The big gates had been closed and bolted by the lorry driver, so Sally would leave by the side door, dropping the chub as she left.

The phone rang in the main office and Sally moved through to the switchboard to answer it. Alexis had forgotten to switch the phone through to Sally's office before leaving.

'Hi there, when are you finishing?' It was Ron. He had gone straight home.

'I'm finished now. I'm about to get my coat and leave,' she said.

'Do you want me to come over and take you home?'

'What for? Don't be silly, I have my car,' she said.

'I don't like you leaving the yard last. Not in the dark.'

'Ron, I've done that hundreds of times. What's wrong with you?'

'Mmm, just be careful of those stairs.' A few of the wooden steps were well worn and Ron had instructed one of the joiners to replace them. The joiner hadn't yet started the job as he was extremely busy on the site.

Sally laughed as she put the phone down.

She closed the door of the office and walked carefully down the stairs. There was a light shining down on them but the shadows that fell made the light pretty useless.

It was a bitter cold February night. The sky looked heavy while the stillness of the night suggested snow was imminent.

She made her way over to the side door, opening it using the chub. Pulling the door towards her she stepped out onto the pavement. Using her weight she leaned on the door making sure she had closed it properly.

The lane was dark and still. No other car stood there except Sally's. It almost looked abandoned. As she reached her car she fumbled in her pocket for the keys. She was alarmed as she heard a rustle coming from a nearby doorway. She stood and listened. Looking round, no one was to be seen. She shook her head and gave a slight laugh.

'Honestly,' she thought, 'I'm beginning to imagine things.'

Sally had the key in the lock and was about to open the car door when she felt the heavy hand on her shoulder. It swung her round so fast she lost her balance and fell to the ground.

'Oh dear, she's fallen over!' The voice said sarcastically. She recognised the voice immediately. It was Jack Watson.

A terrible fear gripped her as she lay in the gutter. Her ankle was sore, as she had gone over on it. It felt as if it was broken. The pain was awful.

'Look Neil, it's wee Sally Baxter. She doesn't look so wee now,' he sniggered.

'No Jake, she does not,' he answered.

'Touch me and I'll have you,' Sally threatened trying to keep the fear from her voice.

'Do you think you'll be able to prove anything lady?' Jake said. 'Or do you want this in writing?' He kicked her hard on the hip, and followed this by kicking her several more times on the head and body.

She moaned in pure agony.

'Tut tut Jake, you should never kick a lady.'

'It's o.k. then Neil, this is no lady, it's just some old tramp that's lying in the gutter.'

He grabbed her by the collar and pulled her to her feet. He then propped her against the wall and holding her up with one hand, slapped her several times across the face;

one side, then the other. As he tired of slapping, he closed his fist and punched her in the mouth. This sent her head rocking backwards hitting the wall, the terrible thud filling her ears and numbing her senses. Warm blood trickled from her mouth onto her cold swollen lips assuring her she was still alive. She wasn't completely knocked out, but she felt no further pain. She was aware of more kicking but it wasn't until he delivered a blow to her stomach that she drifted into blackness.

Jake had taken a six-inch flick knife from his pocket and was about to cut Sally's face when his brother called out and grabbed the hand that held the knife.

'Jake no!' he shouted. 'Not that for God's sake.'

'For who's sake? Are you going soft in the head?'

'No Jake, but you can't cut her. You said nothing about cutting her up.' He still gripped his brother's wrist.

'And what do you suggest?'

'We've done enough Jake, leave her.'

Jake broke free from Neil's grip and once again made to cut Sally's face. Neil grabbed at him once more causing the knife to slip from Jake's hand. Furious at his brother's interference he let go of Sally. She slid down the wall to the ground.

Jake then took hold of Neil and swung a punch, which connected, with his chin. As the blow hit Neil's chin, pain shot along his knuckles and up his arm. He thought the blow had broken his own hand. Cradling the injured hand into his chest he rocked in agony. Neil saw his chance and threw a punch at Jake who reeled backwards falling to the ground.

He was unaware of people running down the lane as he urged his brother to get up, but Jake lay motionless. Two men who had heard the rumpus and had gone to break up the fight grabbed Neil from behind.

What lay before them was a bloody mess. Jake had fallen on his own knife and it had gone through his back into his heart. Sally lay in an unconscious heap with blood streaming from her mouth and from a gash on the back of her head.

The two men held on to Neil as another passer by ran to call the police.

They hadn't long to wait, as the patrol van was a few streets away checking out other premises. They received the call from headquarters and came immediately.

One of the policemen turned Jake over on his side and found him to be dead. Then, turning Sally over he felt for a pulse.

'She's alive sarge. I can feel a slight pulse,' he said eagerly.

One of the men standing nearby removed his jacket and covered Sally while they waited for the ambulance.

Ron arrived at the lane just in front of the ambulance. He had rung Ruby, and as Sally hadn't arrived home, he rang the office. Getting no reply, he drove over to the yard. Stopping in the street, he saw the blue lights of the police cars flashing. As he was about to walk into the lane, he was stopped by one of the policemen.

'You can't go down there Sir,' he said with authority.

'Look, my girlfriend hasn't arrived home and I'm very worried. She parks her car in this lane and I want to know if it's still there.'

The lane was full of people, police, witnesses and the usual people that are called to a crime.

The ambulance was now attempting to drive down the lane when Ron spotted Sally's car.

'There it is, what's going on down there?' he yelled.

The policeman took his arm. 'I think you had better come with me sir.'

He led him down among the small crowd and as the ambulance men were rolling Sally onto the stretcher the policeman pushed him towards them.

'Is this your girl sir?'

Ron moaned aloud as he looked down upon the still and lifeless body of Sally. Swaying he gripped the young man's arm for support before falling to his knees. 'Sally! Sally! He shook her gently.

'Sorry sir but we must get her into the ambulance,' the medic said sharply. Ron's voice, now low and hostile was directed at the policeman. 'Who did this?

The Policeman shook his head.

He roared again hysterically. 'Who did this for God sake?'

'We haven't established that yet sir, but we would like you to give us a few details about your friend.'

'Not here, I'm going with her. I must go with her.' He attempted going towards the door of the ambulance but he was stopped once again by the police.

'She'll be all right. She's in good hands. We'll take you to her sir. You would only be in the way if you were in there,' he said pointing to the ambulance.

Ron turned and followed the young constable as he made towards the police car. He stopped in his tracks as he saw Neil Watson flanked between two detectives. It wasn't because he recognised the man to be a Watson, as he had only ever spoke to Jake and that was by phone, it was the handcuff that caused him to stop and stare. He then looked down at the dark shape on the pavement nearby. He knew it was a body, but as it was completely covered by a dark blanket, Ron had no idea who it was.

'For goodness sake, what the hell has happened here?' he demanded.

'Is that the bastard that nearly killed my Sally?' He made to rush at Neil but was held back. He struggled with the police until he felt himself being thrown into the back seat of the Panda car.

'Any more from you sir and we'll have to cuff you as well,' the young policeman said.

'I'm sorry, I'm sorry but I have to know what's been going on,' he was in tears.

The ambulance was now out of the lane and speeding towards the hospital.

Ron gave the police Sally's details as they drove him to the hospital.

On the way he was asked a question that gave him all the answers he needed.

'Mr Matheson, do you know Neil and Jack Watson?'

Ron felt the anger rage inside. He made a fist and punched his own hand. Clenching his teeth he breathed in slowly.

'Mr Matheson, do you know...'

'Yes. I bloody well know them and when I get my hands on them they'll wish I didn't.'

'Mr Matheson, that was Jack Watson's body you saw lying under the blanket.

Ron turned his head quickly and stared directly into the face of the policeman. His voice was very much on the defensive.

'Oh No, you're not going to tell me Sally did that.'

'No no,' the policeman gave a slight laugh. 'That was his brother's doing, he confessed to that. Sally was beaten up by Jack but we'll know if that's true once Sally comes to.'

'Do you think she'll be all right?' Ron asked, his voice shaking with emotion.

'I'm sure she'll be all right sir. The doctor is with her in the ambulance so she's in good hands.'

Ron sat in the small sitting room waiting for news of Sally. His thoughts naturally flew back and he relived the last time he had been in a hospital waiting room. The policeman stayed with him reading a magazine in silence. It was obvious to him that Ron didn't want to talk.

It was two years and three months since Connie died and he felt as if he was about to go through it all again with Sally.

He couldn't bear it.

They had taken her to the operating theatre as a small piece of her skull had almost pierced her brain. This had to be removed. One of her kidneys had been damaged due to the terrible kicking she had received and this too was being operated on.

They seemed to be taking forever. Ron sat with his head in his hands. He then looked up towards the ceiling, tears streaming from his eyes.

The policeman dropped the magazine he was scanning back onto the small coffee table, before joining his distraught charge.

'Don't sir, she'll be fine.' Patting Ron's shoulder and nodding once, he repeated his statement. ' She will be fine. She looks a strong woman.'

'I know,' Ron sobbed, 'but there's every chance of more internal injuries, not to mention brain damage.'

He blew his nose as words of comfort still came from his young escort.

'At times like this sir, things often look worse than they really are. It's no good you thinking all negative thoughts, you must think positively.'

Sitting quietly for a few minutes, before looking at the policeman he said sadly, 'You know, I have never told her I loved her. I have just assumed she knew.'

'Well then sir, you can when she comes round.'

'Don't worry I will, I certainly will.'

Every hour that passed Ron went to the telephone and gave Lucy and his mother the same news. 'Nothing to tell so far.' He asked Lucy to stay with Ruby and Jimmy as there wasn't any point of Ruby coming to sit in the hospital. As soon as he had better news, Jimmy would drive her out.

It was almost midnight when a nurse took Ron to the surgeon's office.

On the way, the nurse was only able to tell him that Sally was now in the ward. She knew nothing of the details.

The doctor introduced himself and beckoned Ron to sit. Anxious eyes looked at the doctor.

'Mr Mathison, Miss Baxter is safely back in the ward. We have removed the piece of bone and relieved the pressure on the brain. I can safely say we aren't as worried as we were at first, as no great damage has been done. As for her kidney, it will heal itself in due time. The body has its own way of healing itself. She has severe bruising and will have two beautiful black eyes tomorrow I'm afraid, but she's lucky no further damage was done. If that bone had pierced her brain, the outcome would have been totally different.' He gave his shoulders a shrug.

'Still, as I say, she's been lucky, but she's lost a good deal of blood. As far as we know, there aren't any more internal injuries, but we will have to keep an eye on her. The kicking seemed to have been mostly to the buttocks and legs. They have taken a terrible pounding... Oh yes, her jaw has been fractured, that's the result of a blow or punch.'

Ron chewed on his bottom lip as he rubbed a palm nervously over his knee, listened without interruption.

'Mr Matheson, she's going to be all right. You can go through and sit beside her for a while, although she won't be with us for some time.'

Ron rose and thanked the doctor. He then made for the ward where Sally lay. She had been put into a single room where the young policeman who had earlier sat with

Ron occupied a seat in the corner of the room She was a disturbing sight. Her face, so badly bruised, was barely recognisable. Bruised cheeks and swollen lips that were twice their normal size overshadowed her pale face that was just visible beneath her bandaged head. Both eyes were puffed so much that the lids looked as if they were resting on her cheekbones. She was a terrible sight. Her arm was attached to a tube that in turn led to a bag of blood. An intravenous drip hung above her head. The doctor had said that she had lost a lot of blood, but still Ron wasn't prepared for what he saw. He practically fell into the chair that stood at her bedside.

Taking her slender hand in his, he lifted it up and kissed each lifeless finger. Tears welled-up in his tired eyes as he murmured her name over and over.

The policeman rose and heading towards the door said, 'I'll wait outside. If she comes round...'

The black look that Ron gave him made him rephrase the sentence. 'I mean, *when* she comes round, will you let me know?'

Ron just gave him a nod. He turned his attention back to Sally, kissing her hand ever so gently.

Jimmy and Ruby brought Lucy to the hospital, but the sight of her beloved sister's battered body upset her too much that she had to be taken out.

It was well into the next day before Sally regained consciousness. Ron had nodded off, as sleep had finally overpowered him. He seemed to hear his name being whispered. He smiled to himself as he recognised the voice. He was dreaming of Sally. He was lying in a hospital bed while Sally was leaning over him. She was calling his name but he couldn't wake up. He wanted so much to open his eyes but he just couldn't, he was so warm and comfortable.

The shake that the nurse gave him made him jump. 'Don't you know your young lady's calling you. You're supposed to be watching her,' she laughed.

Ron couldn't believe his eyes. Sally was trying to smile but with terrible difficulty.

'I must look awful,' she whispered.

'Oh no Sally, no. You're absolutely wonderful. You're so... so wonderful. ' Tears rolled freely from his eyes. He kissed her forehead, 'Welcome back. Oh welcome my love.'

'I feel as if I've been hit by a bus. Ron what happened?' she groaned.

'Wheesht. Wheesht Sally. You just get well my love,' he wasn't sure if he should go into details so soon, then he remembered the policeman was standing outside waiting on a statement.

'Sweetheart, don't you remember anything?'

'Yes, I ran into the Watsons. I can't tell you anything more than that.' Her voice was a mere whisper as she struggled to make herself heard.

He took her hand and leaning over kissed her swollen lips gently.

'Water. Can you give me water.'

Filling the glass that sat next to the water jug he held it to her mouth.

'You're not capable of looking after yourself. I'm going to replace you in the office.'

'You're sacking me?' she asked.

'Yes, I'm afraid I have to. You can't possibly do two jobs.'

'Ron what are you talking about? I don't have two jobs.'

'No, but if you marry me you'll have two jobs and I don't want that.'

He couldn't tell what she was thinking as her face remained expressionless.

'Sally, I'm saying I love you.'

She gave a very faint smile.

'That's what I longed to hear,' she whispered. 'I'm finished living with secrets Ron. Now you know all about Sally Baxter,' she said.

'Sally Baxter! Not for long,' Ron said. 'Matheson will suit you even better. Yes. Sally Matheson, I like it.'

THE END

About the author

Born in Scotland in the mining town of Prestonpans, Mary was educated at Preston Lodge High School where she went on to work in the editorial department of Macdonald & Son Printers and Publishers.

She also spent some time working in retail before moving on into the field as sales representative for Bemrose Printers and Publishers. Now retired she lives with husband Jim in the beautiful fishing village of Port-Seton, a mile from where she was born.

may@mayturner.co.uk

Also available by Mary Turner
Three Sons
ISBN 978-1-4259924-2-2